WONDERWALL

A LOVE ME, I'M FAMOUS NOVEL

MICHELLE HERCULES

INFINITE SKY PUBLISHING

Paperback ISBN: 978-1-950991-72-3

PROLOGUE

LIV

"Bottoms up, girls!" Saylor shouts, and everyone at the table raises their glasses.

"To Liv, and to a fantastic time in London!" Kennedy adds.

I toss my head back and let the alcohol slide down my throat, burning everything in its path. I ignore the lime in front of me, choosing to drink tequila how it was intended—straight and without any help. I slam the glass back down almost at the same time my friends do. I'm all warm and tingling inside.

"Patrón gets better and better with each shot," Mandy says as she sways on the spot, and I know she's had enough. I think we've all had enough, but Mandy, being the petite girl she is, can handle even less alcohol than the average person. It's hard to believe she's Irish.

"And the guys keep getting better and better, too," Emma says as she stares appreciatively at two tables down from us, where a group of frat-boy wannabes is parked. They would be in a fraternity for sure if our school had a Greek row.

I wrinkle my nose. "I don't think so."

Now Kennedy is looking their direction, too. She groans.

"Oh, God. I know one of them. He's in my drama class, and he's a pest. Quick, look the other way. Don't make eye contact."

Too late. One of the guys sees us staring and, with a cocky grin on his face, stands up and walks toward our table.

Saylor shakes her head and smiles. "Good luck, girls. I'm about to go on."

"Break a leg, Blue!" Mandy says before she starts to giggle like a little girl. Saylor gets up and looks pointedly at me. I hear her message loud and clear. It's time to take the baby home.

"Hello, ladies." Frat boy turns the chair Saylor has just vacated and sits down, leaning his forearms on the back of it.

With super-tanned skin and shaggy, sun-kissed blond hair, he has the looks of a surfer and kind of reminds me of Owen, my brother-in-law.

"What do you think you're doing, Levi?" Kennedy glares at him.

"What does it look like? I'm bestowing my awesome presence upon you." He tosses his head to the side, trying to get his long bangs out of the way. A second later, they're right back where they were.

"Does your ego have to ride shotgun when you drive?"

"My ego is the one driving, babe." Levi leans back and stretches his arms, making his T-shirt ride up and show us a peek of nice golden abs. Kennedy's gaze travels down and stays there for a long time. Levi smirks when he catches her staring.

"Warning, chicas. That's a classic Levi move." Emma throws my abandoned lime slice at him, hitting him on the chest. He brings his arms down and sticks his tongue out at her.

The background music stops, and a sudden wave of anticipation takes over the crowd. The decibel levels of conversations turn down a notch. Saylor's familiar guitar riff echoes in the room before her voice breaks through the silence.

"Good evening, ladies and gentlemen. Are you having fun yet?"

Her energy is intoxicating, and her stage presence is undeni-able. The crowd cheers and whistles.

"Damn, that girl is hot," Levi says as he stands up. We do the same, because there's no way we can remain seated when Saylor is playing.

She tosses her blue-and-green mermaid hair back and glances over her shoulder at the bass player. It's their 'are you ready' signal. They both nod, and Saylor faces the audience again.

"We are Wreck of the Day."

The first notes of "I Want You to Want Me" by Cheap Trick blare through the speakers, and the crowd goes wild. Mandy grabs my hand and pulls me into the melee, dragging me toward the front of the stage. Shit, Saylor wanted me to take Mandy home, but it'll be impossible now. Oh well, this is my last night out with my girlfriends before I fly across the pond. It's okay to be wild.

Emma, Kennedy, and Levi have followed us, and now we're dancing like there's no tomorrow. I let the music run through my veins, and finally the anxiety of the past week leaves my body. It wasn't only the last-minute preparations for my upcoming trip that have made me tense. It was also the fact that in two days, I'll be in the same city as him. But I can't let the thought ruin my night. I won't. I'm determined to have fun for real, without pretense.

Twenty minutes into our groove, we've lost Kennedy and surfer boy already, and Mandy has almost fallen on her butt twice.

"I really think we should take Mandy home," Emma yells in my ear.

She's right. As much as I would like to stay, I don't want to deal with a pukey Mandy in the nasty bathroom here. Better if she spills her guts in the comfort of our home.

"Where did Kennedy go?" I glance around.

Emma bobs her head up and down in sync with the tempo of the music. "Probably making out with Levi."

"I thought she didn't like him."

Emma rolls her eyes. "She doesn't like him when he opens his mouth. He can't really talk when they're kissing."

I don't like the idea of leaving one of my friends behind with a guy I don't know. "Shouldn't we look for her?"

"Nah, I know Levi from way back. He's harmless. Kennedy is safe with him."

Trusting in Emma's judgment, I take Mandy's hand and begin dragging her away from the stage. She resists my pull. "Aww, Liv. I don't wanna go. I'm fine."

"You're not fine. You're five minutes from embarrassing yourself in front of all these people. You'll thank me tomorrow."

Emma takes Mandy's other arm and we stride across the bar, reaching the exit in less than a minute. The crisp, fresh air of September is a shock against my skin after the heat of inside; it helps make me more alert. There are a few cabs waiting by the curb, and we make our way to them. We dip inside one, and after giving the driver our address, Emma turns to me.

"I had so much fun tonight. I can't believe we won't get to do this for another year."

I can tell she's had fun. There's a sheen of perspiration on her forehead, and her light brown hair is matted and plastered to her head. Her eye makeup is a little smeared, too. I bet mine is in the same condition.

"You can always come to visit me."

Emma's smile falters a fraction. "Ugh, Dad is still set on getting married to bimbo number five during Christmas break. He won't allow me to miss it."

I squeeze her hand. "A year will go by in a flash. And now, with Periscope, I can stream all my adventures live. It'll be like you guys are there with me."

"You're such a geek, Liv. But I love you just the same." She lets go of my hand to give me a side hug.

Once we arrive, Mandy seems weirdly energized for some

reason. As soon as we walk through the door, she kicks off her shoes and makes a beeline for the TV.

It's still early, not even midnight yet, and I don't feel tired in the slightest. We follow Mandy to the living room. Emma plops down on the couch next to her, and I take the love seat.

"Let's binge-watch something on Netflix." Emma takes the remote control from Mandy and starts pressing buttons.

"Oh, I've been dying to watch that new show produced by Tina Fey." Mandy glances in my direction, and I can already guess what's coming. "But we need popcorn."

I throw my hands in the air. "Why must I always make the popcorn in this house?"

Emma smirks at me. "Because you're the best popcorn maker in the world."

With a huff, I get up from my comfy position, knowing my roommates will beg and plead relentlessly before I ultimately give in.

"How are you going to handle a movie night without me? Who's going to make the popcorn then?" I say from the kitchen.

"The microwave," they answer in unison before they start to laugh.

♡ ♡ ♡

Ten minutes later, I go back into the living room with a big bowl of buttery goods. I'm two steps away from the couch when I hear the E! Channel presenter say the name I've been avoiding for the last five years. A cannonball of unwanted memories barrels through me, my heart lurching of its own volition before it lodges itself in my throat. *Traitorous muscle.*

"Can we change the channel, please?" I plead, hating how choked up my voice sounds.

"No way. They're about to replay the interview with Boys Future I missed tonight. I totally forgot to record it," Emma says, almost bouncing with excitement.

Mandy's eyes land on the bowl in my hand. "Popcorn!"

She makes a grab at it, not noticing my stiff posture and deer-caught-in-the-headlights look. Neither of them knows the reason I'm freaking out right now. Only Saylor knows the history because she lived it with me.

My heartbeat is frantic, and I attempt to steady my breathing. *It's been five years, for crying out loud.* I can't hide from my demons forever.

With reluctant steps, I move back to the love seat, but I can't actually sit down. I turn and face the TV instead. When the interview starts and the boy who crushed my soul so long ago appears on the screen, I steel my heart.

I try to pay attention to the questions and what the other band members are saying, but my eyes are glued to Sebastian's face. He's grown into his looks; the once very cute boy is now a roguishly handsome man. His face is more angular, and his shoulders are broader. His hair is short on the sides and longer on top—I can tell it's been styled by a professional—and there's a hint of scruff framing his chiseled jaw.

But one detail, the most important one, remains the same. His eyes. Since we were kids, those volcanic mahogany orbs had the ability to evoke confidence and yearning at the same time. A killer combination. Even through the TV screen, I can feel their combustible power reaching for me.

He's quiet and seems unhappy to be there. When the interviewer addresses him and asks about his relationship status, my hands curl into fists by my side. Sebastian leans back in his chair and strokes his chin, a polished grin unfolding glacially across his face.

"You know I don't like to talk about my private life, but yeah, Gretchen and I are dating."

"There will be a lot of unhappy fans out there."

"Nah, our fans are cool. They know they're our number ones," the blond and lean guy next to Sebastian pipes up.

The presenter nods, barely sparing a glance in blondie's

direction before his attention returns to Sebastian. "Even so, in your line of business, you've had to contend with some overzealous fans. I heard there was one in particular, a girl you knew in high school who wrote emails to you on a regular basis. Is that true?"

My blood freezes in my veins, and I fight to get air in my lungs. *What. The. Hell.* I close my eyes and feel the burn of tears behind my eyelids.

"Yeah, she wrote to me every day for over a year. I still don't know how she got my email address. We were never friends in high school. I had to close that account in the end."

"So, what did she write?" the presenter asks.

"I don't know. I never read any before I deleted them."

I can't take it anymore. I feel the walls closing in, and I know I'm about to lose it in front of my friends. I bolt to my room before any of them can finally notice the state I'm in, then close the door and lock it for good measure. My gaze zeroes in on my bed, and I stride toward it, collapsing on the floor once I reach it. I finally let the sobs rack my body like a devastating tsunami. I hope the TV is loud enough to cover the sound.

How could he? How could Sebastian twist the truth like that for the world to hear?

With shaking hands, I pull the cardboard box out from under my bed. I'm a masochist and I know it. I sniff and then wipe my dripping nose with the back of my hand. My vision is blurry as I lift the lid. Inside, there are hundreds of gossip magazines and clippings from websites, all depicting the same person —Sebastian.

My family believes I avoid any bit of news related to him and his band. And I do. I've never read any of the articles inside that box. My unhealthy obsession only goes as far as collecting them and keeping them out of sight. This is the first time I'm opening my very own Pandora's box just to look at its contents rather than adding to my morbid collection.

I pick up the first thing on the pile, a magazine where Sebastian is front and center on the cover. I trace his face with the tips of my fingers, letting memories flood my brain and overwhelm my heart as I stare at the picture, frozen in time and space while my tears stream down my face like a waterfall. Then I remember his expression during the interview, the slow smile he gave the camera when asked about his girlfriend. There was a hint of a secret in that grin, and I can only imagine what kind of things would elicit such a reaction from him.

I shove the magazine aside and lie on the floor, turning my body into a tiny ball. My tears mingle with the agony that threatens to swallow me whole. I'm tired of being trapped in the past, of feeling broken. When will my heart finally mend?

CHAPTER 1

LIV

There's something to be said about falling in love with someone you already love. It's absolutely wonderful and terrifying. It's cliché, too, but I don't care. I can't explain the fluttery feeling I get in the pit of my stomach every time he's near me or how I want to touch him and run my fingers through his dark hair. My best friend explained that it's just the awakening of my hormones playing havoc with my heart. After all, Sebastian Coleman, at the tender age of sixteen, has turned out to be quite the eye candy. But it's more than pure attraction. It's something deeper that I can't put into words.

"So, are you sure you want to go ahead with this plan of yours?" Saylor asks from my bed, where she's propped up, flipping through a magazine.

"Yes, it's the only way I'll find out if Sebastian feels the same way about me." I stare at my reflection in the mirror, trying to style my hair into a do that will hold.

"You could just tell him how you feel."

I look at her through the mirror's reflection, horror splattered all over my face. "That's the worst idea ever. What if he says he doesn't feel that way about me? Our friendship will never be the same. I can't risk it."

Saylor rolls her eyes. "You and your flair for the dramatic. Maybe you shouldn't read so many romance novels. It's clearly messing with your brain."

"Leave my books out of it. Besides, my plan is foolproof. Sebastian was the one who opened the door when he asked me for my help."

Last month, Sebastian asked me to set him up with a girl in my history class, Anna. The bout of jealousy that hit me then was the final clue that my feelings for him had evolved. It didn't help that she was one of the prettiest freshmen at school with her wavy blonde hair and hourglass figure, like a modern-day version of Marilyn Monroe. I still don't have a clue why he asked for my assistance. Who in their right mind wouldn't want to go out with Sebastian?

To my relief, it didn't work out. They went on a couple of dates, but Sebastian broke things off after that, saying Anna was boring. She was just a pretty face with no substance. Now I have to put my plan in motion before he moves on to the next girl. The line is getting longer by the week.

"But what about Jordan? What if he actually likes you?" Saylor raises an eyebrow at me.

I give up trying to do anything with my long straight hair and turn to face her.

"I don't plan to string him along. I'm not even sure if I'll go on a date with him. I just want Sebastian to 'help' me get Jordan," I say with air quotes.

"So if he gets jealous, you'll know he likes you?"

"Exactly." I walk to my dresser and search for the prettiest top I have. It's a white eyelet snug thing with a sweetheart neckline and cap sleeves. Thanks to my brand-new Wonderbra, it gives the illusion that I'm more endowed than I truly am.

After I get dressed, I spin around. "How do I look?"

Saylor glances at me from head to toe, her scrutinizing gaze making me squirm on the spot. I would never usually ask her for fashion advice, since her taste is completely different than mine —she's all punk rock glamour while I'm a simple, all-American girl—but she knows how to sexy it up.

"Natural-looking makeup, nice tan, hair loose, short denim skirt, ballerina flats, and that cute but sexy top. You look like an innocent little thing trying to hide a wicked streak. Totally Lolita." She gives me her famous Cheshire cat smile, and a slow grin appears on my face as well. That's exactly what I'm aiming for.

With a Cirque du Soleil army of butterflies in my stomach, I make my way to Sebastian's house. He should be back from his hockey practice by now. I ring the bell and wait, anticipation squeezing my heart in a painful vise. A minute passes and nothing, so I ring the bell again before I lose my nerve.

I hear him yell from the second floor. He's coming.

When he opens the door, I have to lock my jaw tight to keep it from dropping to the floor. Sebastian has just gotten out of the shower. His hair is wet, droplets of water glisten on his defined chest, and he's wearing nothing but a towel wrapped around his trim waist. My heart staggers in my chest, trying to break free. My hands begin to sweat, and my cheeks heat up. Thank God my olive skin hides the blush.

"Oh, it's you. Sorry for my attire." He points at the towel. "I thought you were the FedEx guy. I'm expecting a package." He opens the door farther to let me in. Without giving me a second glance, he turns around and takes the stairs two at a time.

My heart plummets. Apparently my new look has zero effect on him.

♡ ♡ ♡

SEBASTIAN

I'm doomed. How am I supposed to maintain my cool around Liv when she's wearing something barely there? I've been trying my best to ignore the fact that my best friend has turned into the girl of my dreams. She's always been pretty, but in the past year, she's bloomed into something else. Now she's fucking gorgeous.

I've never seen her wear a skirt so short, and her tanned, sculpted legs seem to go on for miles. I pretty much had to run to my room to hide my obvious reaction to her. The towel didn't conceal much.

I quickly drop it on the floor and put my boxers and sweatpants on, not bothering with a shirt. My dick is still standing up like a freaking tent pole. *Great.* I jump on my bed and put a pillow on my lap just before her knock comes.

"Bas, are you decent?"

"Yes, come in."

She opens the door and peers inside. Her eyes widen when they drop to my chest. *Is Liv checking me out?* She comes in with hesitant steps, and suddenly there's tension in the air. Or maybe I'm just imagining things. Shit, I have no clue.

"What's up, Liv?"

Her gaze returns to my face, and she takes a deep breath before biting her lower lip. My eyes zero in on her mouth, and I feel the urge—no, the *need* to kiss her.

Get a grip, Sebastian. She's your best friend, for crying out loud, not the flavor of the week.

She walks farther into my room and makes a beeline for my brand-new guitar that's propped up against the wall, under the window. She picks it up and strikes a chord, then looks at me.

"Have you learned to play any songs yet?"

"I've been messing around with those." I point at the music sheets spread out on my desk.

Liv puts the guitar back down before she walks to the desk and grabs a few of the sheets.

"'Lightning Crashes,' 'Hey, Hey,' 'Wonderwall.' Gee, Bas. What's with the whole nineties-angst theme you have going on here?" She smirks at me.

"Hey, don't dis my music choices. They're all awesome songs."

She rolls her eyes and puts the music sheets down. "How about something from this century?"

I shrug. "I'll get to them eventually."

"I guess 'Wonderwall' isn't too bad, though a bit cliché." She sits at the end of my bed, and her itsy-bitsy skirt hikes up farther. She doesn't do anything to fix it. If she were any other girl, I would've taken it as a 'come on' signal, but Liv is just too comfortable with me to be self-conscious about showing too much skin. I don't know if I should be happy about it or not. It definitely makes it hard for me to pretend our friendship remains the same, that the balance hasn't shifted.

"What's wrong with cliché?" I ask.

Her eyebrows shoot up, and I have the impression she stopped breathing for a second. Did I say something wrong? She glances down and begins to play with the hem of her skirt.

"Liv?"

She takes a deep breath, and without looking at me, she says, "Do you remember when you asked me to set you up with Anna?"

"Yes?" I'm instantly wary of the abrupt change of subject.

Is Liv here to convince me to give Anna a second chance? They're friends but not super close like she is with Saylor. That's why I deemed it safe to ask for a little help. I only did it so I could prove to myself that I wasn't falling in love with my best friend.

It didn't work.

"Well, I thought you could return the favor." She peers at me with eyes full of hope and wonder, and uneasiness takes hold of me.

Dread runs down my spine and my stomach clenches. "What do you mean?"

She avoids my gaze once more, looking at the floor this time. "I like your friend Jordan."

I lose the ability to breathe, like I've been sucker punched in the gut. *Jordan? No, she has to be kidding me.* Jordan is a dick and totally unworthy of her. She's too pretty, too smart, too perfect for him.

I can't even begin to process her request when she lifts her face and hits me with an intense stare. There's an odd glint in her eyes. It's like she's paying really close attention to my reaction, and I can't let her see how her request has affected me. *No way, Jose.*

I force a grin to my lips. "Jordan, huh? Can I ask why him?"

She shrugs and breaks eye contact. "He's cute, and I'm sick and tired of being the only freshman who has never gone on a date, or kissed a boy for that matter."

Those facts about Liv are no surprise to me. We tell each other everything. Well, almost everything. But the idea that Jordan might be her first kiss doesn't sit well with me.

"You deserve better than him, Liv," I say before I can stop the words from tumbling out of my mouth.

She gets up and finally adjusts her damn skirt. Her brows are furrowed, and her hazel-green eyes look like a stormy sea. "So, are you saying you're not going to help me?"

I run my fingers through my hair, feeling like crap all of a sudden. "I didn't say that."

She crosses her arms, emphasizing her cleavage even more. Her boobs aren't big, but somehow they're freaking enticing today. *Shit, shit, shit.* Everything is wrong. I should not be having these thoughts about her. Maybe I *should* set her up with Jordan.

"Okay, fine. Stop glaring at me. I'll help you."

I expect to see some satisfaction on her face, but there's a clear flash of disappointment in her eyes.

What the hell?

I'll never understand girls.

CHAPTER 2
LIV

Saylor is still in my room when I get back from Sebastian's, but instead of reading a magazine, she's now engrossed in her homework. She'll never admit it, but she's the biggest nerd in our class.

"So?" She puts the mammoth biology book down and looks expectantly at me.

Without glancing at her, I take the stupid outfit off and throw it in a corner before grabbing my couch-potato clothes—baggy sweatpants and an oversized T-shirt.

"Oh, Liv. He didn't say anything?"

I sit on my bed, curling my legs under me, and finally face Saylor. Her big aquamarine eyes stare at me with fathomless sympathy, and for some reason, it makes my own eyes burn.

"At first he asked me why Jordan?"

"Okaaay, and what did *you* say?"

"I said Jordan was cute and that I wanted to date and have my first kiss already."

Saylor's chin drops before she speaks again. "You did not say that! Are you out of your mind? You don't tell a boy you like that you've never kissed anyone before."

I shake my head. "Sebastian already knows that. I only mentioned it again to see if he would step up to the challenge."

Saylor's lips curl up, and there's a mischievous spark in her eyes. "I'm liking this side of you, Liv. But I guess from your behavior that Sebastian didn't take the bait?"

I raise my hands heavenward. "No! He agreed to help me."

Saylor tilts her head to the side, her eyes narrowing. "Jordan is no Sebastian, but he's cute, although too immature for my taste. Look at things from the bright side. It *is* high time you kiss someone, and it's actually better that your first time is with a boy you don't care much about. What if you suck? I think you should have loads of practice before you kiss Sebastian. Nine times out of ten, it's the kiss that seals the deal. Remember the Cher song— it's in his kiss!" She actually sings the last part. Such a show-off, but she does have a lovely voice.

I bite my lower lip and think about Saylor's words. Maybe she's right. What if I suck? I don't want to slobber all over Sebastian if he does decide to kiss me.

♡ ♡ ♡

The next day at school, I continue with my original plan. Worst-case scenario, I'll get a date with Jordan—not the end of the world. I wear the same denim microskirt from the day before paired with a snug long-sleeve T-shirt. My beloved Uggs hug my feet. As I walk toward my locker, I notice male heads turn my way. I can feel their stare and cringe inwardly with all the attention, but I suck it up and pretend I'm unaffected. Confidence is everything. That's what Saylor has taught me.

I'm at my locker when she catches up with me.

"Girlfriend, you're the talk of the school today. The guys are all asking who the gorgeous brunette is in the hot skirt."

"Guys are stupid. It's just a skirt."

"Is that what it is? For a moment, I thought it was a tube top barely covering your ass."

I close my locker with a bang to give Saylor a piece of my mind, but when I see her grin, I know she's only teasing.

"You're terrib—"

"What in the world are you wearing?" Sebastian cuts in.

He's standing in front of us, and his right hand clutches his backpack strap in a vicious vise. His eyes shoot daggers at me.

Innocently, I look down at my outfit.

"A skirt?" I say.

"Says who?"

Saylor, not missing a beat, turns me around and points at the logo on the back of my skirt. "Abercrombie & Fitch."

"Well, it's extremely inappropriate for school, don't you think?"

I can feel the embarrassment rush to my cheeks, and annoyance crawls beneath my skin. I wanted to stir a reaction in Sebastian, but I'm not enjoying the caveman attitude. "You didn't complain about it yesterday."

Sebastian seems taken aback by my reply and glances down, running his fingers through his hair. "Well, you were with me yesterday, Liv. No harm. I've seen you wearing less. But here at school... doesn't it bother you that guys are practically undressing you with their eyes?"

I roll my eyes. "Please, you're exaggerating. I've seen girls wearing way more provocative outfits to school. Guys are not undressing me with their eyes." They probably are, because most guys are pigs, but I refuse to agree with Sebastian.

He opens his mouth to counter my argument, but Saylor beats him to it. "Lighten up, Bas. Liv is not your girlfriend. So what if she's getting a little bit more attention from the opposite sex? She's gorgeous and should flaunt it. Maybe she won't need you to set her up with Jordan after all. I say she should aim higher, maybe go for that delicious quarterback, Troy. I heard he broke up with his girlfriend last week."

Sebastian's alabaster complexion turns beet red as he narrows his eyes at Saylor. "He's a freaking senior, too old for Liv."

"I think Liv needs an older guy to teach her things," Saylor says before glancing at me. There's a devilish sparkle in her eyes that tells me she's goading Sebastian on purpose.

"Teach her things? What's that supposed to mean?"

Saylor gives him a droll look. "Come on, Bas. You know what I mean." She hooks her arm with mine and drags me with her before he can reply.

We veer toward the nearest restroom. Saylor checks under every stall to make sure we're alone, then turns to me, her eyes dancing with glee.

"Oh my God, Liv. Sebastian is totally into you."

My crazy heart does somersaults inside my chest. He did seem jealous just now. I'm glad Saylor was there to witness it, too; otherwise, I would already be doubting it. But I don't know how to behave from now on. My initial plan only went until this part.

"What should I do?"

Saylor puts her index finger on her lips, frowning as she begins pacing in front of me. The school bell rings, but I don't care. This is way more important than debate class.

Saylor stops midstep and pierces me with her knowing stare.

"Liv, be honest. Do you want Jordan or any other boy to be your first kiss?"

"No. I want Sebastian to be the one."

"I thought so. So here's what you'll do."

She begins to explain exactly what I have to do, and not for the first time today, I'm glad Saylor is my friend. She's indeed the best.

CHAPTER 3

SEBASTIAN

have multiple opportunities to speak to Jordan about Liv but find myself hesitating every single time. I promised her I would, but I quickly discovered that I don't want Jordan or any of the other idiots from school to go out with her. She's too good for all of them. I almost had an aneurism when Saylor mentioned Troy. That man whore. Liv shouldn't touch him with a ten-foot pole.

Liv and I don't have the same lunch, so I usually hang out with my teammates from hockey, and Jordan is one of them. As soon as I take a seat, they all hound me about my best friend.

"Dude, you've been holding out on us. That neighbor of yours is smoking hot," Leroy, our mountain man goalie, says next to me.

I curl my hands into fists and count to ten in my head. I like him. I don't want to punch him in the face.

"Don't talk about Liv like that. She's not one of those girls," I say through clenched teeth.

Leroy raises his hands and backs down. "Sorry, man. I mean no disrespect. Just stating a fact here."

"I can't believe you haven't staked your claim yet, Bas. A girl like Liv won't stay single for much longer," Ansell, the most sensible guy on our team, says.

"Liv is just a friend." My words sound hollow to my ears. I haven't believed in that statement for a long time. But it doesn't matter. Liv is interested in another guy.

"If that's the case, do you mind setting me up with her? I've always thought she was cute, but after she put those phenomenal legs of hers on display...." Jordan whistles, and I want to throttle him.

I glance down and play with my fries, my appetite suddenly gone.

"Earth to Sebastian. Dude, did you hear what I asked? Do you think Liv would go out with me?"

My knee-jerk reaction is to say hell no, but then I remember Liv's request. She likes Jordan; who am I to stand in between them? I stare at him and try to see what Liv sees in him. He's taller than me, muscled but lean. His face is okay. I mean, it's not like I check dudes out, but I know what girls find attractive and not. I suppose Jordan is passable. Too bad his personality leaves much to be desired. I'm about to tell him that yes, Liv would go out with him when I see her name flash on my cell phone screen. I pick it up quickly before the guys notice she texted me.

LIV: Hey, did you ask Jordan yet?

ME: No, I was about to.

LIV: Don't. I need to ask you another favor first.

My fingers freeze over my cell, wondering what kind of favor Liv has in mind now. After a few seconds, I text her back.

ME: Okay, shoot.

LIV: It has to be in person. Can I come by later?

ME: Sure.

I put my phone in my pocket and look at Jordan. He's leaning forward, still waiting for my answer.

"Who was that?" he asks.

"Liv."

An idiotic grin appears on his face, making me despise the sight of him. "What a coincidence. It must be destiny."

"No, sorry, man. I just asked her, and she's not interested."

Jordan's face falls, and I take great pleasure in that, even if my expression betrays nothing. I know I'm being a complete jerk for lying to him, but Liv will thank me one day. Jordan is not the guy for her. Maybe with time I can make her see it as well.

♡ ♡ ♡

can't keep Liv out of my mind for the rest of the school day and even during hockey practice. I wonder what kind of favor she wants to ask me now.

Jack, our coach, can tell my heart isn't in the game. After practice is over, he asks me to wait on the rink. Leroy and Ansell give me a 'good luck' glance before they head to the locker room with the rest of the team. They know what's coming.

Jack is an awesome coach, but he doesn't tolerate bullshit. The tongue lash is hard, and I completely deserve it. Tomorrow we have a big game against Winston High, our rival school. It's on their turf, and we usually don't do well when we play there. More losses than victories for sure. They're counting on me to change that streak. I'm the youngest forward the team has ever had, which shows how good I am, but Jack makes it clear I can be replaced.

At home, I try to distract myself from thoughts of Liv. I take the quickest shower known to man—don't wanna risk her ringing the doorbell while I'm in it again. I pick up my guitar and sit on my chair. After the conversation with Liv, I've decided to learn how to play "Wonderwall" first, since it's the only song she approved from the pile. The first notes aren't that hard, and half an hour later, I think I've got them.

When the doorbell finally rings, I jump off the chair and practically fly down the stairs. My heart is racing as I open the door, and I swallow hard as I stare at Liv. She's back to her usual clothes, simple and understated. The cute sundress isn't supposed to be sexy, but I feel my body react to her just the same. *Liv, whatever you do, don't look at my crotch.*

I let her in, and we go back to my room. Mom doesn't work on Wednesdays, but she's out running errands and won't be back until dinnertime. Even so, Liv feels the need to close the door behind her. My palms are sweating, and there's a weird feeling in the pit of my stomach. It's like I'm getting ill.

I scratch the back of my neck, feeling completely out of my element. I don't know what to say, so I figure I can start with an apology. "Sorry about my outburst earlier."

Liv walks to my dresser and picks up the teddy bear she gave me for Valentine's Day when we were ten. It's not a simple stuffed animal. That bear represents everything good about our relationship. At the time, I gave her nothing in return, because she wasn't my girlfriend and giving Valentine's Day presents to your friends was a girly thing. She almost cried when I shrugged her gift off with a noncommittal response. That happened in front of my parents, and they forced me to apologize to her later with a box of chocolates. It was almost the end of our friendship. But Liv came back the next day with a leather jacket and sunglasses for the bear and said we could call it Terminator. Needless to say, she became my girl that day. I just didn't know what it would mean in the future.

"It's fine, Bas. I'm not mad or anything." She doesn't look my way, and I want to know why. She's never been shy around me before.

"So, about that other favor you wanted to ask me…."

"Right." She puts Terminator back on the dresser and tucks a strand of her hair behind her ear. Her gaze finally meets mine, but only for a second before she looks down again.

"We're burning daylight here, Liv," I joke as I jump on my bed, crossing my hands behind my neck.

Liv takes a deep breath and stares straight into my eyes. "I want you to teach me how to kiss."

My jaw slackens as I gape at Liv while my brain tries to process her words. Did she actually say that? Then I throw my head back and laugh, because honestly, what am I supposed to do? Take her seriously?

"What's so funny?" She puts her hands on her hips.

"Wait? Are you serious?" I don't know if I want her to be or not. The thought of kissing Liv kick-starts my heart, but it also terrifies me.

"Yes, I'm serious. I don't want Jordan to think my kissing sucks. And let's face it, it probably will since I don't know how to do it."

I groan in my head as I picture Liv and Jordan kissing. That's an image I want to ban from my thoughts forever.

"You're not going to suck."

Liv sits on the edge of my bed, her body suddenly too close to mine. She grabs my hand and squeezes it. "Please, Bas. You're my best friend. Teach me."

I search her face, trying to figure out if that's what she really wants. Then my eyes drop to her full lips. I can smell her cherry-flavored lip gloss, and my mouth begins to water. I've never wanted to kiss a girl as badly as I want to kiss Liv right now. But a million doubts cross my mind. What if this lesson ruins our friendship? I'm sure if I kiss her, something will change irrevocably between us. And I can't lose her.

When I don't say anything and just stare at her, she lets go of my hand and stands up, walking away from the bed and giving me her back.

"Fine. I guess I'll have to find someone else to teach me. Maybe one of Owen's friends."

My stomach drops to the floor, dreading the idea. Owen is Liv's oldest sister's boyfriend in college. I have no doubt his friends won't think twice about helping Liv, even if she's jailbait to them.

I stand up and approach her, putting my hands on her shoulders and turning her around to face me.

"Okay, I'll help you."

Her sparkling eyes widen, and a slow, satisfied smile spreads on her face. "Really?"

I take a step back, finding our closeness too enthralling for comfort. Kind of a stupid move on my part, since I just agreed to teach her how to kiss.

"Yeah."

"Now?"

I shrug. "No time like the present." The quicker we get started, the quicker I can put this whole episode behind us—that is, if I survive the experiment.

"What should I do?" She gets closer to me again, all too eager to begin her lesson. Doesn't she find this situation awkward in the least?

I grab her hand and pull her toward my bed. We both sit on it, facing each other. She kicks off her flip-flops and curls her legs under her. Then I notice the tension take hold as a bolt of panic sets in her gaze. I grip Liv's naked arms and rub them up and down, trying to loosen her up. She shivers under my touch. I love the effect I'm having on her.

"First of all, relax. It's me. No judgment here, I promise."

"Okay," she whispers.

"Now, loosen your jaw and close your eyes."

She does as I ask and waits, trusting me completely. I stare at her face, at the tiny freckles on her delicate nose, at her plump and edible lips, and my heart wants to escape the confines of my chest, leap out of my mouth, and take flight.

I capture her face between my hands and lean in, stopping a breath away from her slightly opened lips. I breathe her in, and then my mouth touches hers, sending tingles down my spine. Liv makes a sound that flares up everything male in me. I kiss her then, soft at first, just a brushing of lips. Her lips part as her hands make their way to my biceps, squeezing them like she needs an anchor. When my tongue connects with hers, an explosion of emotions pierces through my body, making my head spin. I prod and explore, finding pleasure when Liv copies my movements, learning from me.

She shouldn't have worried about being a poor kisser. Despite her inexperience, this is the best kiss I've had in my life. Her tongue tastes like the sweetest nectar, and I'll be damned if I'm going to let anyone else experience this.

I'm staking my claim.

CHAPTER 4

LIV

When we finally pull apart, my heart is pounding out of control, and it feels like I've just run a marathon. My lips tingle, and the fire that resides in my core has moved down below, making me feel and want things for the first time. Now I understand why so many people do crazy things in the name of love. It's the best feeling in the universe, and I never want to let it go.

I open my eyes to find Sebastian looking at me with such intensity that my breath catches. I might be inexperienced, but I know that glint in his gaze. It's hunger—and he's hungry for me.

I let go of his arms, not knowing how to proceed from here.

"How did I do?"

Sebastian doesn't answer, just stares at me with his deep, warm eyes. I snap my fingers in front of his face. "Hello? Sebastian. Wake up."

He blinks a couple of times. "What did you say?"

Insecurity rears its ugly head inside my mind. What if my kiss *did* suck? I shake my head and angle my body away from his, ready to stand up.

He grabs my hand. "Where do you think you're going?"

"I thought the lesson was over."

Sebastian laughs softly. "After one kiss? You might be a natural, Liv, but the lesson is far from over. Come here." He tugs my hand, and I don't resist the pull, my body going willingly.

Our mouths collide in a frenzy, and my insecurity is long gone. This doesn't feel like a simple kissing lesson. It's a chaotic and beautiful dance, passionate, urgent, demanding. I want to mold myself to him. My hands circle the back of his neck while his fingers tangle in my hair, bringing us even closer. Somehow, I find myself on my back with Sebastian half on top of me. His left leg is between both of mine, and his free hand traces down my arm until it rests on my hip.

I lose all trace of coherent thought. Time seems to stop around us. All I can think about is Sebastian. How each stroke of his tongue, each touch makes me feel something new, makes me discover hidden secrets of my body.

I don't know how long we stay glued like that, caressing, learning, but eventually the sound of Janet's voice cuts through the world of bliss we created.

Sebastian jumps off me and his bed faster than I can blink. The sudden loss makes me feel abandoned, and coldness envelops me from head to toe. His eyes are as round as saucers, and his breathing is erratic. He looks at me and then at his closed door, swallowing hard.

I sit up and try to fix my wrinkled dress, but I know it's no use. I touch my hair and feel several knots along its length. How in the world did it get so tangled?

Sebastian's hand covers his crotch, and my eyes follow the movement. He's trying to hide how I affected him. My cheeks warm up, and I look away.

He walks around the bed and opens the door to answer his mother. I take the opportunity to check myself in the mirror in his en suite. I stare at my reflection, horror quickly replacing the last vestiges of joy. My lips are red and swollen, my hair resembles a bird's nest, and my skin is flushed. I'm 100 percent sure that the moment Janet takes one good look at me, she'll know I was fooling around with her son, and I really don't want her to think ill of me. I grab Sebastian's hairbrush and start to break the impossible knots.

He appears behind me but maintains his distance. I stare at his reflection and can't help but notice the conflicted emotions churning in his gaze. Does he regret kissing me already?

My hand stops midstroke, and my heart plummets.

"What's wrong?"

I wait one, two, three seconds before he answers. "Your face is all red. I think I took the lesson too far. I'm sorry."

I put the brush down and drop my gaze to the faucet. I can't face him when he tells me we're back to being just friends, that this was a mistake.

"Does that mean I've graduated?" My voice is so thin it evaporates.

"Liv, I—"

"Bas? I thought you were coming down to help me with the groceries."

My gaze snaps back up, and I can see Janet is in the room. She's sporting a serious frown, but her face softens when she sees me. "Oh, hi, Liv. I didn't know you were here."

"Hi, Janet. I just came by to borrow a CD from Bas. I was just leaving."

I rush out of the bathroom and then Sebastian's room like the devil is after me. I keep my face down, trying to hide the reason I was in the house. It's only when I reach the safety of my own room that I realize I have no CD in my hand, which means I just threw my excuse down the drain. Oh well, maybe Janet didn't notice.

My cell phone rings and I dive for it, thinking it's Sebastian. Disappointment floods my heart when I see Saylor's number. I shouldn't be surprised though. She seems to always know when I'm in distress.

"Tell me everything!" she screams.

I take a second to answer because I don't want her to hear the insecurity in my voice. "It was amazing. I never knew a kiss could make me feel so many things." I flop onto my bed and clench my thighs together. There's still a trace of throbbing down below.

"Ohh, are we talking sexy things here, Liv?"

I close my eyes and sigh. "No. Yes. I don't know. I just know I want to do it again, many, many times again."

Saylor laughs. "I'm glad your first kiss wasn't a traumatic experience like mine was. Ugh, Mike Taylor and his mile-long tongue. My face was drenched after he was done. So disgusting."

"The kiss was perfect. Sebastian was perfect."

"And? Are you two dating now?"

I don't answer her, and somehow my silence screams louder than any words.

"Oh no. Don't tell me that idiot didn't ask you to be his girlfriend?"

"He didn't have the chance. His mom came home, and it was a miracle she didn't catch us in the act."

"Bummer. But he was going to, right? I mean, he cannot *possibly* not know by now that you're gaga over him. I swear if he doesn't man up I'm going to kick his ass."

"I hope it doesn't come to that, Saylor. Because if he doesn't love me like I love him, I'm afraid I just lost my best friend."

"Hey! I thought *I* was your best friend."

"You're my other best friend. I can have more than one."

"Fine, but I'm sure everything will be okay, Liv. You'll see. Sebastian would be a fool to let you go, and if he does, then he isn't the right guy for you."

Saylor is trying to cheer me up, but her words make my heart twist further in my chest. Sebastian is the right guy for me, and if he doesn't want to be more than friends, then I don't know what's going to happen to me. My love for him is a deep-rooted feeling that can't be removed without leaving a gaping hole behind. It's bigger than me.

I only have one hour to myself and my thoughts of Sebastian before the house turns into a loud circus. Jeremy gets home from soccer practice, and he doesn't know the meaning of the word silence. Then Kimmy arrives for her weekly dinner with us, dragging her boyfriend, Owen, in tow. Mom and Dad come next, and then my presence is required in the kitchen. It's a rule in the Dawson home that everyone must help prepare dinner, including Owen.

I put makeup on to try to hide the disaster that is my face, but unfortunately, my effort to conceal the obvious is a big fail. The moment I step foot in the kitchen and Kimmy and Owen take a good look at me, they know.

I stop short in my tracks when I notice we have an extra guest. There's a guy by the sink, washing the vegetables, who I've never met before. His hair is light brown, and by the look of his broad shoulders and strong arms, I guess he's into sports. He's wearing a preppy polo shirt and khaki pants, a complete contrast from Owen's casual attire—old jeans, older T-shirt, and a baseball cap flipped backward. I can only assume Owen decided to bring one of his frat buddies with him tonight. *Great. Exactly what I need, more people to witness my humiliation.*

"What happened to your face, sis?" Jeremy asks.

And so it begins. I wonder if he has any clue why the skin around my mouth is so red. He's only twelve, after all.

"Nothing." I look away but still manage to catch Owen's smirk.

His friend turns around, and I come face-to-face with a Calvin Klein model. I don't think he's really a model, but he could be. He's that good-looking. And he's staring at me. More specifically, he's staring at my mouth.

Ugh! Kill me now.

"It looks to me like little Liv has been sitting in a tree," Owen says.

Jeremy tilts his head and frowns at Owen. "That doesn't make any sense."

"Think, Jer, think." Owen crosses his arms and can't hide his amusement. His baby blue eyes are dancing with pleasure as he leans back against the counter behind him.

Kimmy shakes her head, but I see how the corners of her lips tilt up. She's enjoying my humiliation just as much as her idiot boyfriend is. It's probably payback for when I caught her making out with Owen right in front of our house, in his car. Jeremy and I sneaked up on them and practically blinded the lovebirds with our flashlights. The look of fright on their faces was priceless. I guess now it's my turn to be the butt of a joke.

I grab the cutting board and start hacking at the vegetables that are already on the counter. Owen's friend comes up behind me and puts the rest of them on the pile. He leans closer and whispers, "It's not that bad."

I freeze and try to make sense of his statement. I don't even know his name, yet he's coming to my rescue. But before I can say something to him, Jeremy interrupts.

"You've been kissing!" he yells just as Dad enters the room. My cheeks feel as hot as lava.

"Who's been kissing?" Dad asks.

"Liv! She's no longer a mouth virgin."

"Yes, I am!" My face must have turned purple by now, and across the kitchen island, Owen chokes on his water.

"Jer, do you even know what 'mouth virgin' means?" Kimmy pats Owen's back and narrows her eyes at our baby brother. Dad just looks at all of us with a slightly confused frown.

"It means she's kissed a boy with tongue."

"No, it doesn't, you doofus." I throw a piece of pepper at him.

"Oh my God, this is too much." Owen braces against the kitchen island with one hand while the other covers his chest. He's laughing so hard, it's silent and he's shaking. No wonder he choked.

"Shut up, Owen." I glance down again and resume chopping the vegetables like a ninja.

"So what does it mean, then?" Jeremy whines. The one thing he hates the most is to be left out of a joke.

I raise my head again just to see if Owen will dare explain to Jeremy the meaning of that expression in front of my dad. But in true Owen fashion, he doesn't seem one bit intimidated by my father's presence.

"May I tell him, Murphy?"

Dad shakes his head and throws his hands up in the air. "Might as well. But I'm out of here. Don't tell Karen, though. She'll kill me."

Standing now next to Jeremy, Owen leans in and whispers in my brother's ear. Jeremy's eyes widen before he twists his face in an exaggerated scowl. "Eww, that's gross. Why would a girl want to do that?"

"Trust me, Jer. You won't find it disgusting in a couple of years."

Jeremy angles his body to peer at Kimmy. "Do you do that to Owen?"

My sister's fair complexion turns a bright shade of red as she takes a step back, wagging her finger. "Oh no. You don't get to ask me that question, brat."

Jeremy shrugs before he grabs the piece of pepper I threw at him. He shoves the entire thing in his mouth, and midchew, he says, "I guess that answers it."

Owen snorts, which earns him a punch in the arm.

"You and your big mouth, Owen." Kimmy storms out of the kitchen, no doubt going to complain to Mom how incorrigible Jeremy and Owen are.

Owen's friend turns to me. "Are all your family dinners this exciting?"

♡ ♡ ♡

During dinner, there are no more comments or jokes about my red face. Mom only gives me a knowing smile. Later, after Kimmy, Owen, and Derek—that's Owen's roommate's name—are gone and everyone is settled for the night, Mom comes into my room. She sits on the edge of my bed and looks intently at me. I pretend I'm too engrossed in my book to notice her stare.

"So, do you wanna tell me something, honey?"

I keep my gaze glued to *The Iliad*. "Yeah, this is a rare case where the movie was actually better than the book."

"Liv, you know what I'm talking about."

I close the book with a loud thud and replace it with a pillow. I need some kind of protection, because I know Karen Dawson has every intention of talking about the birds and the bees with me tonight. I'm mortified already.

"Not really."

"Oh, come on, Liv. It can't be that horrific to talk to me about your first kiss." There's pure elation in her gaze. Mom is a hopeless romantic.

I look down and trace the swirling pattern on my pillow with the tip of my finger. "You already know. I kissed a boy. Big freaking deal."

"It is a big deal, hon. So tell me, who was the lucky one?"

I don't wanna tell her it was Sebastian, but Mom will keep pestering me until I confess everything. She's relentless when she wants information. So I do confess.

To my surprise, she squeaks in delight. "I knew it!" She reaches over and squeezes my hand. "Is he a good kisser?"

I pull away. "Mom! Come on."

She raises both hands. "Okay, okay. I won't ask for more details. But now that you've crossed this milestone, we need to get serious for a moment."

Oh yeah. Here we go.

"Mom, I know how babies are made already," I grumble and curl my fingers over the pillow.

"Of course you do. But you're young, and it's so easy to get caught in the heat of the moment at your age. That's why the number of teen pregnancies is so high. And we're talking about Sebastian here, the boy who you've had a crush on for years. As much as I would like to believe that you'll be sensible enough to wait a couple of years, as a parent, I can't take that risk. I've already scheduled an appointment with Dr. Zimmerman tomorrow. You're going on the pill."

I don't ask her how she knew I liked Sebastian. Mom is like a hawk; she misses nothing and knows exactly what each of her kids is up to.

I hide my face between my hands. "I don't even know if Sebastian and I are dating."

Mom pulls my hands off my face and forces me to look at her. "I see the way that boy looks at you, and there's nothing platonic about his gaze."

"You really think so?" Hope flares in my chest, unbidden and prevailing.

"I'm positive. Now, do you think you can manage not to get knocked up between tonight and tomorrow?"

"Mom! You're terrible."

She laughs and stands up, planting a kiss on my forehead before she leaves. Despite the embarrassing conversation, she did manage to ease my doubts a little.

CHAPTER 5
SEBASTIAN

I stare at Liv's darkened window for far too long. The entire house is quiet, which doesn't surprise me, since it's already past midnight. I should have called her after she flew out of my house earlier, but I was too confused about her reaction to the kissing lesson and what it meant to our friendship. I'm still confused. I went to bed lying to myself, saying it would be better to sleep on it and talk to her face-to-face tomorrow. But after tossing and turning in bed for nearly three hours, I knew I wouldn't be able to sleep before I saw her again.

There's no doubt in my mind what that weird, swirling emotion inside my heart is. It's almost like an ache. I'm positive I'm in love with my best friend. But does she feel the same way about me? My gut feeling is telling me yes, but there's no way to know for sure until I see her again. And it has to be now.

Gathering my courage, I call her. It rings ten times before it goes to voice mail. Liv's probably muted her cell. *Drat. What am I going to do now?*

I glance at my feet and see some tiny pebbles on the grass. The idea is stupid and totally eighties movies, but what choice do I have? I bend down and pick the smallest stones, hoping I won't end up waking up Liv's parents instead, or worse, breaking her window.

I roll one of the pebbles between my fingers, trying to steady my breathing and slow my pulse. With one big inhale, I let it fly and cringe when it bangs against Liv's window. It wasn't that loud, but in the dead silence of the night, it sounded pretty noisy. I throw a couple more stones before I lose my nerve. I'm about to throw the last one when the light in Liv's room turns on. A few seconds later, the curtain is pulled to the side, and Liv's startled face appears behind the closed window. When her eyes adjust to the gloom, she pulls the glass panel up.

"Sebastian, what are you doing here?" she hisses.

"I have to talk to you. Can you come down?"

"It's the middle of the night."

"I know. Please, Liv. It'll only take a minute."

She bites her lower lip and looks over her shoulder before glancing down again. "Okay, I'll be down in a second."

My stomach begins to clench, and it feels like there's an army of super ants crawling all over my body. I run my fingers through my hair and start to pace in front of the big oak tree that stands between our houses, trying to get rid of the sudden jitters. I hear Liv's front door unlock and freeze midstep. My throat is completely dry, and I don't know what I'm going to say to her. I've always prided myself on being a confident person, but I realize that, when it comes to Liv, I'm not certain of anything.

My heartbeat kicks up a notch when I take in the sight of her. Her pj's are nothing more than a flimsy tank top and tiny shorts. Her hair is secure in a loose braid down her back, but rebel wisps are free and framing her face. She has her arms crossed in front of her chest as she moves toward me, pausing at a safe distance.

"What's going on, Bas?"

I look down like a coward, unable to hold her scrutinizing stare. Words fail me—I don't know where to start. I shuffle my right foot, playing with the pebbles scattered on the grass like a moron. To my surprise, Liv moves closer and touches my arm. My head snaps back up, and I see all my worries and doubts mirrored in her eyes.

"It's about the lesson, isn't it? I've ruined everything." She lets go of my arm and takes a step back. Her voice is heavy with hurt and melancholy.

On an impulse, I take her hand and lace our fingers together. She stares at our entwined hands, then at me.

"No, you didn't ruin anything. That was the best idea you could ever have."

"Why?" Her whisper is so soft, it feels like the wind.

"Because it made me realize how stupid I've been."

"What do you mean?" She moves closer to me. We're only a few inches apart now. With my free hand, I caress her cheek, and she closes her eyes for a second, leaning against my touch. A soft sigh escapes her lips.

"I should have never fought my feelings for you."

Her eyes fly open, and her breath catches. "You have feelings for me?"

"You have no idea." I don't recognize my own voice, so filled with need.

"What are you trying to say, Bas?"

I take a deep breath. *Here goes nothing.* "Liv, will you be my girlfriend?"

She gasps and I think I've said the wrong thing for sure. But then I see her lips curl into a shy grin.

"Yes!" She jumps in my arms, catching me off guard. I take a few steps back, trying to keep my balance, but my foot slips on the moist grass and down we go with a muffled thud. I'm mortified, but Liv's intoxicating laughter makes me laugh, too.

"You're crazy." I capture her face between my hands and tug her to me.

Her kiss is just as sweet and powerful as before. It makes my entire body tingle; it makes me want to drown in her essence. She's an invader, conquering all of me. Everything is Liv. I could stay like that, lying on the grass with her in my arms, all night long. But too soon she pulls away, bracing her arms next to my shoulders.

"I better get back inside."

"Why?" I touch her lips with the tip of my thumb, and she shivers.

"Because we have school tomorrow, and also, the longer we stay here, the greater the chances my parents or yours will catch us."

She pushes herself off me and stands up. I rest my elbows on the cool grass and let my gaze wander the entire length of her body. Blood rushes to my crotch as a desire I have never known courses through my veins. Liv offers me her hand, helping me get up, too. I don't let go of her once I'm standing. Instead, I pull Liv to me again, my mouth crashing against hers like I'm a parched land and she's rain. I know she's right, but I can't bring myself to let her go back inside. In such a short period of time, I've become addicted to Liv's touch.

My hands land on her hips and squeeze them, bringing us even closer. I know she can feel how much I'm burning for her. She moans and kisses me back with just as much ferocity. My entire body is on fire, and her heat emanates through the thin layers of her clothes, scorching me further. When she breaks the kiss and pushes me away, I'm adrift.

"I really have to go, Bas."

"You know, it's hard to believe you when you keep looking at me like that."

"Like what?"

"With those bedroom eyes."

She shakes her head and looks down. Then she peers at me from under her thick, long lashes. "Good night, Sebastian."

She turns on her heels and runs back inside before I can do anything to stop it. She knows me too well. If it were up to me, I would never let her go.

CHAPTER 6
SEBASTIAN

I take two deep, steadying breaths before I ring the doorbell. I've stood in front of this red door countless times before, but I've never been this nervous. The tie Mom insisted I wear feels like a cord around my neck, cutting off my air supply, and my hands are clammy.

The door opens, but instead of Liv on the threshold, her dad, Murphy, greets me. I tighten the hold I have on the rose bouquet in my hand and swallow hard. Murphy's usually friendly face is closed off, and his eyebrows are squished together, forming a deep V on his forehead.

That can't be good.

"Sebastian."

"Hello, Mr. Dawson." I don't think I should call him Murphy now.

He narrows his eyes at me before he opens the door all the way to let me in. I enter the foyer and look left and right, searching for Liv. *Where the hell is she?*

"She's not ready yet. Why don't you follow me, Sebastian?"

The way he says my name makes me think I'm about to be flayed.

He leads me to the living room, where Liv's entire family is congregated. Even Kimmy's boyfriend is there. Everyone is staring at me like I've committed the biggest sin. Do they know about my midnight visit two days ago?

"Take a seat, Sebastian." Mr. Dawson points at the La-Z-Boy chair, *his* chair, and it feels like I'm sitting on needles instead of the plush seat.

Kimmy and Owen are sitting together on the love seat, and Karen and Jeremy are on the couch. Mr. Dawson sits down between them, rests his elbows on his knees, and leans forward. His lips are nothing but a white slash.

My mouth is dryer than when I was stupid enough to eat a teaspoon of cinnamon powder on a dare. I want to say something to break the tension, but Mr. Dawson speaks before I can.

"There's no sense beating around the bush here, so I'll get straight to the point. What are your intentions with my daughter?"

My mouth drops open and the blood drains from my face. All my thoughts vanish from my head. I feel like I'm stuck in a *Twilight Zone* episode where I wake up and everyone is different except me.

"I, sir…."

"You can understand my concern. You've been frequenting this house quite often under the guise of friendship, and now I've learned that you've been coming here to kiss my daughter behind my back. I won't stand for that."

Seriously, this is a nightmare. No way I'm having this conversation with Liv's dad. No way. I look at Owen with a plea for help in my eyes, but the bastard just stares at me like I'm a fucking perv. His lips are curled into a sneer. *What the hell?* He's way worse than me, making out with Kimmy out in the open for anyone to see. I've never heard Mr. Dawson give him any grief, *ever*.

My gaze returns to Liv's dad. "Sir, I swear I never meant to take advantage of Liv's friendship. I was caught completely off guard when things between us changed. I have the utmost respect for your daughter and—"

"Are you prepared to make a commitment to her right now? I won't let you continue your liaison with her if you don't."

My heart rate spikes, and all I can hear is the sound of my pulse in my ears. Mr. Dawson can't be serious. He wants me to do what, get engaged with Liv?

I'm still trying to come up with an answer when I hear a giggle behind me. Then the entire room erupts in laughter.

"Oh my God. That was priceless," Owen howls.

Mr. Dawson is laughing so hard, he actually doubles over on his seat. I'm too shocked to react. Liv walks by me and goes straight to the mantelpiece on the wall behind the big couch. She picks up a video camera that was hidden in plain sight. It was focused on me the whole time.

"No you didn't," I finally say.

"I sure did." She glides over to me, and I stand up. "You should've seen your face. Oh, wait. You can." She's still recording it.

"Liv, let me upload that to YouTube. Pleeease," Jeremy says.

I point at him. "Don't even think about it. You do it and you're dead meat."

Jeremy looks at Mr. Dawson with wide eyes. "Dad, did you hear that? He just threatened me. You can't let him date, Liv. That's just wrong."

Mr. Dawson ruffles Jeremy's hair before he walks my way. He has a big grin on his face now. "I hope you won't hold a grudge against us, Bas."

I rake my hand through my hair. "I really thought you were serious."

Mr. Dawson turns to Liv's mom. "Did you hear that, Karen? I haven't lost my touch."

I raise my eyebrow at Liv. She smiles and shakes her head. "A million years ago, Dad wanted to be an actor." She turns off the camera and puts it away.

I finally remember the flowers that are now completely mangled after I put them through the wringer and hold them out to her.

"Sorry, they don't look so good right now."

She takes the destroyed bouquet from me and brings it up to her nose. "They still smell good. Thanks, Bas." She leans in and kisses me on the cheek. Heat surges through my body, melting what was left of my tension away.

I finally notice what she's wearing and my heart begins to race again. Her dress is not provocative by any means. It reminds me of dresses from the fifties. The upper part is tight and sleeveless, no plunging neckline, and the skirt is flowy, hitting her above the knees. So why does it feel like there's a mad drummer inside my chest? Will I ever learn to control how my body reacts to her? She's like the tide, coming and going, leaving me, the shore, at its mercy. Wet when she rises, dry when she recedes.

"Bas, I want you to know that we're very happy about this development."

Mr. Dawson's voice brings me back to the here and now. But I don't break my hypnotized stare from Liv's face, and I can't hide my feelings either when I say, "Me, too."

"Where are you taking my baby sis? It'd better not be a dive, Coleman," Kimmy asks from across the room.

I lace my fingers with Liv's and turn around.

"The Cove?" I hate how my answer sounds like a question.

"Ohh, fancy." Kimmy hits Owen on his chest with the back of her hand. "See, this is how you do it."

"Hey, I've taken you to better places than The Cove."

"The annual frat gala doesn't count, Owen."

Kimmy and Owen begin their usual banter, but it's easy enough to block them out. I glance at Liv, dying to lean down and kiss her on the lips. I resist the urge; I don't want to piss off Mr. Dawson for real now.

"Are you ready?" I ask.

"I've been ready for the longest time."

CHAPTER 7

LIV

The Cove is one of those fancy restaurants where people only go to celebrate special occasions unless they're filthy rich, considering you basically have to pay to breathe.

"Bas, this is really unnecessary. We could've gone to McDonald's and I wouldn't care. This will cost a fortune." I glance at the menu and balk at the ridiculous prices. I'll have to work at Dairy Queen for a month to pay for a full meal. I see a salad in my future.

Sebastian shrugs like it's no big deal. "I got a gift card from Uncle Paul for my birthday."

"A gift card I'm sure he intended for you to buy something nice with."

"Well, I want to take my girl out to dinner. As long as I'm happy, he's happy."

"You know you don't need to impress me with fancy dinners, right?"

Sebastian stares at me intensely with a wolfish grin on his face. "Yeah, I know."

In the end, he convinces me to order whatever I want, not only the salad. It's pointless to argue with him, so I decide to enjoy the moment. And to be honest, this *is* a special occasion. It's monumental. Our very first date. I can hardly believe it.

After dinner, instead of going back home, we go for a stroll in Littleton's downtown. It's Friday night, and the streets are buzzing with people, the restaurants lining the main street packed with lines at the doors. Our town is famous for its quaint atmosphere, and it attracts visitors from neighboring cities, including LA. It's not shocking to bump into celebrities now and then, since Littleton has some of the best restaurants in California and there's way less paparazzi here.

The weather is pleasant for early November. We walk by Lake Cassidy, which the downtown area was built around. The many trees along the pathway are decorated with twinkling lights, and there's a joyous feeling in the air, making me even happier than I already am.

We didn't order dessert at The Cove—there was nothing on the menu that appealed to us—so when we pass by the still-open ice cream shop across the street, I pull Sebastian in its direction.

"My treat," I say as we enter the store. The smell of chocolate, caramel, and everything delicious hits my nose, and my mouth begins to water.

"Nuh-uh. We're on a date. You'll hurt my male pride."

I roll my eyes at him. "Don't be silly, I've paid for you many times before."

Sebastian tugs me to him and, using his free hand, tucks a loose strand of hair behind my ear. "That was before we became more."

"All right. Just this once. I know how hard you work at Kinkos to pay for your hockey gear. I won't have you spoiling me."

"Baby, it's my job to spoil you now. Get used to it."

We get our ice creams and resume our walk, making our way to the illuminated fountain on the town square and taking a seat on a bench facing it. As I lick my delicious treat, I feel Sebastian's gaze on my face, his stare intense and hot. I stop eating, and heat rises to my cheeks when my gaze connects with his. He robs me of air.

"God, I want to kiss you," he says in a hushed tone that's loaded with meaning.

I scooch closer to him. "What are you waiting for, then?"

He breaches the small distance that remains between us and his lips touch mine. His tongue sweeps into my mouth, cold and chocolate flavored. Every single cell in my body begins to tingle, and I forget everything around me. Sebastian's tongue dancing with mine is all I care about. Then I feel something cold and slimy drop onto my lap.

I break the kiss and look down.

"Oh, shoot. My dress!" Sebastian laughs, and I smack him on the arm. "Look at what you've done."

"Me? I just said I wanted to kiss you. You were the one who almost jumped me."

I glare at him for a brief second before I grab his hand, the one holding the ice cream cone, and aim it at his chest. That wipes the smirk right off his face.

"Ah, Liv. Come on! Dad will kill me. This was one of his favorite ties." Sebastian tries to clean the smear off, but all he does is make a bigger mess. The silk tie is ruined.

A bout of guilt sneaks in. It wasn't my intention to get him in trouble with his father. I'll have to replace the tie, but it was totally worth it.

I stand up and make my way to the fountain, knowing if I don't get rid of the stain on my dress, then *my* mother will have a fit. When I reach it, I look over my shoulder. "That will teach you not to laugh at me."

I sit on the fountain's ledge and gather some water with my hand, pouring it over the stain and letting the fabric soak. I'm glad the dress is black. The water is freezing, and goose bumps take over my arms.

I should've never given my back to Sebastian. I know better.

Suddenly, a splash of ice-cold water hits my face. I let out a girly scream, and Sebastian just guffaws away.

He wants war, he'll get war. I go after him, trying to think of a way to make him pay, but he's faster than me and maintains his distance. He's expecting retaliation, and retaliation he'll get, but not in the manner he thinks.

I just had a brilliant idea.

I go back to the ice cream shop, knowing Sebastian will trail after me. I pretend to ignore him, but I'm acutely aware of his presence, that he's watching my every move. I get another cone while he waits outside, then join him, still pretending he's not there. Instead, I devote all my attention to the pistachio and vanilla ice cream in my hand, licking and sucking it, moaning with pleasure like it's the best thing I've ever tasted in my life. All the while, Sebastian watches me with his mouth half open and eyes bulging out.

"You're evil," he finally says.

"I know."

CHAPTER 8
LIV

A MONTH AND A HALF LATER

stare at my stupid front door and can't believe I was dumb enough to get myself locked out of the house wearing nothing more than flannel shorts and a threadbare T-shirt. The cold December air seeps through my inappropriate clothes, and if I don't start moving, I'll turn into a human Popsicle.

It's only three in the afternoon. Mom and Dad won't be home until past eight o'clock.

Grumbling, I make my way to Sebastian's house, hoping he hasn't gone to hockey practice yet. His car is still parked in front of the house, but that means nothing; he could've gotten a ride with Ansell, which happens more often than not. I ring the doorbell and start to jump up and down in a vain attempt to warm myself up. I hear the sound of hurried footsteps on the stairs inside and breathe out a relieved sigh.

Sebastian opens the door. He eyes me up and down, and his eyebrows shoot up to the heavens.

"Liv, what are you wearing? It's freezing outside."

"Thanks for pointing out the obvious, Captain." I push my

way inside. "I got myself locked out of the house when I went to check the mailbox."

Sebastian shakes his head and chuckles. "Only you. Come here." He pulls me to him and begins to slide his warm hands up and down my frigid arms, the friction making my limbs thaw out.

"Mom and Dad won't be home for hours, and Jer is at Ian's house. I have to finish reading *The Taming of the Shrew* and write a stupid report on it, but it'll never happen now. I'm screwed, Bas."

"Don't despair, my dear damsel in distress. Super Bas is here to save the day." He takes my hand, and I follow him to his dad's office. "I'm pretty sure there's a copy of *The Taming of the Shrew* here."

We both stare at the floor-to-ceiling bookcase, filled to the brink with books of all sizes and shapes. After a minute scanning the shelves, Sebastian pulls out an old leather-bound book and gives it to me.

I see the faint golden lettering on the cover, and worry releases its grip on my heart. I need to ace this report; otherwise, there will be hell to pay.

"Oh thank God." I clutch the book to my chest and get on the tip of my toes to place a soft kiss on Sebastian's lips.

"That's it? All I get is a measly peck on the lips?"

The doorbell rings and cuts off the comeback that was on the tip of my tongue.

"Your ride?" I ask.

"Yeah, Ansell is running late." We go back to the foyer, and Sebastian grabs his jacket from the rack by the door. He puts it on, and I can't resist teasing him a little bit.

"I guess I should be thanking him as well."

Sebastian frowns and sucks his lips in.

"I don't think so." He hoists the duffel bag sitting by the door onto his shoulder and steps closer to me again. "I'll be back around five thirty. I think Mom and Dad have a dinner thing tonight, so they won't be home until very late. There's food in the fridge if you're hungry."

"I'll be okay, Bas. Shakespeare will keep me company." I wave the tiny book in my hand.

Sebastian leans in and kisses me, probing my lips open with his tongue. It's warm and tastes like mint. I kind of wish he would stay. My arms encircle his trim waist, bringing us closer. He groans before pulling back.

"I'll never be able to leave if you keep kissing me like that."

I take a couple of steps back, giving him my most smoldering look. "I'll see you later, Bas."

♡ ♡ ♡

SEBASTIAN

The house is quiet and dark when I return from hockey practice. I call out to Liv but don't get a response. She must be really into the book. I head to the kitchen.

My head was not in the game again during hockey practice, but at least this time I managed to fake my distraction. All I could think about was that Liv was in my house and that both our parents would be gone for part of the evening, leaving us truly alone for the first time since we started dating. They're happy Liv and I are together, but at the same time, there's an obvious concern when they look at us. At least, I know what *my* parents are thinking when they stare at with me with rapt attention every time Liv is around.

I know my parents are concerned about how fast my relationship with Liv has progressed and how attached we are. Dad even had the talk with me about responsibility and such before I picked her up for our first date. It wasn't a sex talk, per se. *That* happened when I was thirteen.

I shake my head as I open the fridge. I don't want to think about my folks when I have Liv all to myself for at least a couple of hours. Every time I'm near her, it feels like I'm going to combust on the spot, and when I touch her? Forget it. It's fire meets gasoline. It's a miracle I don't explode every time we make out. Anticipation makes my stomach clench as I wonder how far we'll take things today. Liv and I have only been dating for a month and a half, but it's like our relationship started on the twentieth date. I have known her for most of my life, after all, so the intimacy we share is unique.

I make a couple of sandwiches, knowing Liv most likely didn't eat anything. I also grab a couple of sodas and some chips before I head upstairs. When I enter my room, I find Liv sleeping on my bed with *The Taming of the Shrew* lying open across her chest. She looks so peaceful, and I take a moment to drink her in. My gaze wanders slowly up her toned legs, reaching her itsy-bitsy shorts that are now my second-favorite article of clothing Liv possesses. The denim skirt is the first.

Her snug T-shirt has rolled up to reveal her flat stomach, and I want to glide my tongue over it, dying to taste her smooth skin. My body reacts of its own accord, desire runs free through me, through my veins, invading everything. I finally move from the spot by the door and walk in. When the door closes, I wince as it clicks shut, but Liv doesn't even stir. I put the food on my desk and tiptoe toward the bed, then try to move the book out of the way as gently as possible so as not to wake her up. I want my lips to do the job like she's a fairy-tale princess and I'm the prince. But she purrs like a kitten—a very sexy kitten—and I don't mind that she's awake before I could kiss her.

"Bas," she whispers softly.

I lie on the bed next to her and place soft kisses on her collarbone, then up her neck, her cheek, the corner of her mouth. She hums and I discover my new obsession—I'm going to collect every sound she makes, record them, preserve them, so I can listen to them later when I'm alone and relive our sweetest moments.

She stretches, bringing her body flush against mine. "You're home."

"Yeah, baby." I trail my hand down her arm, loving how her skin feels so soft and warm under my calloused touch.

Liv rolls to her side, and without opening her eyes, her lips find mine. Our tongues mingle, probe, tease, and with each stroke, my body temperature rises further. I move on top of her, and when her legs open to accommodate me better, I think I'm going to die. My hips grind against hers, and a new kind of ache emerges. This is torture, sweet, sweet torture.

Liv's hands trace the side of my rib cage, going lower until her fingers curl around my T-shirt. I lean back and let her remove the piece of clothing, then stare at her with hooded eyes, silently begging her to allow the next step. I won't do anything she's not ready for; I'll ask every time even if we've already done it before. But I don't need to say it out loud with words. We've developed our own set of signs, and we can read each other's mind. It's our very own superpower.

Her eyes urge me to go on.

I lean down and let my tongue glide over her collarbone before going lower, toward the V of her shirt. Her hands are in my hair as she arches her back, sighing, making everything feel that much warmer. I want to touch her everywhere.

My hand sneaks under her T-shirt, crawling up inch by inch until it reaches the edge of her bra. I stop and wait for her to hold my wrist, tell me I've gone too far. But she doesn't, and I keep going, and now my hand covers her breast completely. Our kissing becomes more frantic, our teeth colliding, nipping at each other's lips. I play with her, tease her, but all it's doing is making me needier.

"You're killing me, Bas." She can barely get the words out with our mouths fused together like that.

I laugh. *No, she's the one killing me.* I want to taste her smooth skin, to mold myself to her until we become one. I pull back and send her my silent plea again. I can read it in her face, in her gaze, that she's okay with it, but she feels the need to reassure me with a quick nod. I slide her gauze-thin T-shirt over her head. She's wearing a simple white cotton bra underneath, but it's sexier than anything Victoria's Secret can produce. I start to bring my body down again when Liv puts her hand on my chest.

"No, wait." She sits up and, without taking her eyes off mine, unhooks her bra. Painfully slow, she pushes one strap down, then the other. My breath catches at the sight of her breasts, and my mouth goes dry. I want to taste them more than anything in my life.

Liv pushes me off her and stands up. Confused, I follow her movements like she has a magnetic field surrounding her. She takes a deep breath, and I can't read her anymore. She's put up a shield, and I don't understand why she's shutting me out now. Her thumbs hook on the elastic band of her shorts, and she slides them down her legs. No, not only the shorts, her underwear, too.

That's it. I have died and gone to heaven.

I swallow hard and clutch the bedcover beneath me. It takes all my willpower to remain immobile, to just watch her and not reach out to her. She's more beautiful than I could have possibly imagined. I let my gaze travel down her body, wanting to memorize every single detail, every curve, every angle. When my eyes finally connect with hers again, there's a mix of emotions in them, but the one that speaks the loudest is love.

"You're beautiful." My voice is hoarse, like I've been screaming all day.

I've been dreaming about this moment since Liv came into my room and asked for those kissing lessons. No, if I'm honest with myself, I began fantasizing about her the day she showed up at my house wearing that miniskirt. But unlike kissing, I have no idea what to do when it comes to sex.

"Liv, are you sure?" I don't try to hide my feelings. I'm so afraid. Afraid she'll change her mind and bolt out of my room. Afraid she won't.

"More than anything," she whispers.

She grabs my hand and pulls me up. I go willingly, but somehow I'm still unable to move on my own. She doesn't break our locked gazes as she unzips my jeans, sliding them halfway down my thighs before letting gravity do the rest. Breaking free from my momentary paralysis, I kick the jeans off, and with trembling hands, I get rid of my boxer shorts, too.

Time seems to stand still as we stare at each other. We're both breathing hard, and there's an electric charge in the air. I raise my hand and caress Liv's cheek with the tips of my fingers. She trembles at my touch and closes her eyes. I hold her face between my hands and kiss her softly at first, but then she steps closer, invading my personal space and taking over every-thing. Her chest is flush against mine, her heat scorching my skin, and my hunger for her comes back with a renewed force. I increase the tempo of our kiss, letting the fire consuming me take the lead. I suck her bottom lip when her hand moves down.

"Liv, I'm about to burst already."

She giggles, then squeezes me for a brief second before letting go.

I walk backward, dragging her with me, and then let myself fall on the bed with her on top. She opens her legs to straddle me, and my last shred of sanity evaporates. I never knew sex could feel like this, all-consuming, overpowering. And this is only foreplay. I can't think straight, too focused on enjoying all the pleasure our flesh rubbing together is giving me. She's moving her hips now, and I know I'll come in the next minute if she doesn't stop.

I roll us over so I'm on top of her, then reach for my night-stand and retrieve a condom from the drawer. I try to tear the foil packet with my teeth, but my inexperience hinders me. I'm also too fucking nervous. Liv laughs and takes the packet from me, tearing the thing easily with her nimble fingers.

"Do you want me to...?"

I take the condom from her hand. "If you touch me again, I'm afraid there will be no use for this."

I lean back and attempt to put the condom on. I've practiced this a thousand times, but nerves and Liv's stare make it seem like I'm trying to build a rocket ship. After what feels like forever, the condom is finally in place. I move forward and brace my arms next to her shoulders, my knees astride her thighs. I pause and search her gaze again. Despite my burning desire for her, if I find a trace of uncertainty or fear in her eyes, I'll back down, no questions asked.

I feel her tremble under me.

"We don't have to do this, you know. I'm fine with waiting," I say.

"I want this to happen, Bas. I really do." I see it in her eyes, the certainty, and also a yearning that matches my own.

I bring my body to hers. Our skins clash, hot and smooth, as we kiss with the conviction that there's no return. We're committed to it. We let ourselves go, embrace the inevitable. I grasp and stroke every inch of her skin I can find, and she does the same to me. My hand gets between our bodies, gliding down her stomach until it finds her center. Her breathing becomes more and more erratic as I touch her.

This is all new to me, so I'm going on instinct now. I've read somewhere that it'll make her first time less painful if I make Liv come first. I increase the tempo of my hand to match her labored breaths. Her muscles clench around it, and I believe she's close. A second later, she arches her back as she cries out my name, a shudder going through her entire body. It's the most beautiful thing I've ever seen.

I wait until her body relaxes completely under mine. Her lips unfurl in a slow grin before she flutters her eyes open. Her hand glides from my back to my hips until she's touching me again, guiding me to where I want so desperately to be. My body begins to tremble, out of nervousness or need, I don't know.

"I'm ready, Bas."

I love those words. They've just become my favorite words in the world.

I kiss her, sliding forward inch by inch, letting her get used to me. She's so tight, I don't think I'll last long. I close my eyes and bite my lips, fighting the release that's around the corner. She moves under me and brings her hips up, making me lose my restraint.

I slide all the way in and enter heaven.

CHAPTER 9
SEBASTIAN

I trace Liv's face, from her hairline down to her cheeks and then to her swollen lips. She closes her eyes, and I feel her body shiver next to mine. We're entwined in a perfect lover's embrace, our skin still warm and sweaty from lovemaking.

I could get used to this.

"How are you feeling?" I ask.

She opens her startling eyes again and gives me a smile that I know is only for me. No one else will ever experience it. It's an 'I love you, Sebastian' smile, and I'll treasure it for the rest of my life.

"Amazing. You?"

I chuckle. "Do you have to ask?" I kiss her gently, savoring the softness of her lips, their amazing taste, then pull back. "But I'm serious. Are you sore? Did I hurt you?"

"I'm okay, Bas. It didn't hurt as much as I thought it would, and the pain only lasted a few seconds."

I feel a tiny pressure on my chest give way. I'd never hurt Liv on purpose, and I'm glad our first time wasn't a traumatizing experience for her; I've heard awful stories from my friends, and

I dreaded that happening with Liv. I trail my hands down her naked body, still not believing she's here in my bed, that she's mine.

"Are you hungry? I brought sandwiches and sodas."

At that precise moment, Liv's stomach grumbles. We both laugh. "I guess I am. Who would've thought sex would increase one's appetite?"

I jump out of bed and put my boxers back on. Liv sits up and pulls the sheet with her, covering her breasts. The sight of her like that, in my bed, makes my heart overflow with a feeling that's hard to describe. It's happiness, euphoria, and also an irrational fear that what we have won't last. *No, I won't let my thoughts stray that way.* I smile at her, hoping she can't read what's on my mind, and give a sandwich to her.

"I promise something fancier next time. Chocolate-covered strawberries and champagne."

She shakes her head before she takes a bite of her snack.

"This is perfect," she says after she swallows.

I sit next to her and kiss her exposed shoulder. "You deserve the best the world has to offer. I promise to give you that."

She grabs my hand and kisses my open palm. "All I want is you, Bas."

I drink her in, unable to hide my feelings from her. I love this girl with my entire being. I don't care that I'm only sixteen and that most people will dismiss my feelings as young love, a crush. I know what I feel. The emotion inside me isn't fleeting, and it isn't a phase. My love for Liv is the kind immortalized by literature and movies. It's epic, and it'll transcend more than a lifetime. I can live a thousand lives and my soul will always search for hers. I'm bound to Liv for all eternity. I know it in my bones.

I'm not even a sappy romantic and look at what kind of thoughts erupt in my mind when I look at her. I have it bad.

"What are you staring at?" She drops her gaze.

"You."

"Why? Do I have food on my face?"

I put my index finger under her chin and bring her gaze back up again. "I'm staring at you because I like what I see. That's all."

She leans forward and stops a breath away from my lips. "I like what I see, too." She breaches the gap between us and kisses me.

I cup the back of her head, and she lets go of the sheet covering her torso. Her warmth radiates through me and stirs something down below again. My hand skims the underside of her breast as our kiss becomes something more, something vital.

"Bas, my parents are probably home by now. I gotta go," she says against my lips.

"Hmm?" I pretend I didn't hear her, moving my lips from her mouth to her chin, down her neck. Her breathing becomes shallow, but she pulls away, resting her hands on my chest to keep me from following her.

"Bas, I'm serious."

"Okay, okay." I rub my face, trying to dispel the lust fog clouding my brain. I shouldn't even attempt a second round with her now anyway. She says she's not sore, but I'm pretty sure she will be in a couple of hours. I should let her recover.

Liv gets out of bed and searches for her clothes scattered on the floor. I lean back on my elbows and watch unapologetically.

"Stop staring, Bas." The corners of her lips twitch up.

"I can't help myself when you're parading that hot bod of yours in front of me."

She hits me with her T-shirt before putting it back on.

"So, what do you want for your birthday?" I ask.

"Bas, you don't need to give me anything."

I roll my eyes. "You're going to make it difficult, aren't you?"

"Of course." She smirks.

Fully dressed now, she comes to me and places her hands behind my neck. My arms encircle her waist, and I pull her closer.

"Thank you," I say.

Her eyebrows furrow, marring her lovely face. "For what?"

"For letting me be your first. Your first everything."

Her face relaxes, and she traces my hairline all the way down to my jaw. "I wouldn't have wanted anyone else but you. Thank you for making my first everythings the most treasured experiences of my life."

"There are more firsts in your future, Liv. And I want to be there for all of them."

♡ ♡ ♡

After she leaves, I can't think of anything else besides our first time. I keep replaying it, like a movie in my mind. My chemistry book lies open on my desk, and that's the only attempt I made at studying. Mom will flay me alive if my grades dip below a C, but my concentration has yet to make an appearance.

I decide to brainstorm ideas for Liv's gift. Her sixteenth birthday is two days before Christmas, which means I need to find two perfect gifts in a week. Don't ask me why I waited so long to start searching. I'm a guy—procrastination is in my DNA.

After an hour searching online, I believe I found at least one gift for my geek girlfriend. She's a fan of romance and fantasy novels, and I know she'll love a signed first edition book by her favorite author. The only drawback is that the shop is in downtown LA., and they won't mail it to me. I convince the shop owner to keep the book reserved for a couple of days until I can persuade my parents to drive me there. I'm not allowed to drive outside of Littleton yet—Mom has trust issues in regard to my driving skills.

The moment they arrive home, I make my way downstairs. They're outside, chilling on the patio. There's an open bottle of wine on the table already. When I slide the door open, Mom and Dad turn to look at me.

"Hi, honey. How was your day?" Mom asks.

I shrug. "The usual."

"Did you see Liv today?" She narrows her eyes at me. I think she can either hear my thoughts or mothers have an uncanny ability to detect when their sons have had sex.

"Yeah, for a little bit." My face heats up, and I look at my shoes.

"Hmm."

I don't like when Mom makes that sound; it means she's connecting the dots. I need to change the direction of her thoughts.

"Uh, that's what I wanted to talk to you about. You know that Liv's birthday is coming up, right? I think I found the perfect gift."

"That's great, Bas. What did you get her?" Dad asks.

"A signed first edition book by her favorite author."

"I'm sure she'll love it." He takes a sip of his wine, and just like that, the topic is out of his head.

"I know she will, but here's the problem. I found it at a store in downtown LA., and they won't mail it. I'll have to pick it up."

"You're not driving to LA. You've just gotten your driver's license, and you barely passed your street exam," Mom says, and don't I know it? She reminds me every day.

"Yeah, I figured as much. Would you be able to pick it up for me?"

"Bas, you know how hard your dad and I work. The last thing we need is to venture in that jungle for an old book."

"Come on, Mom. Please. It's for Liv. You like Liv, right?"

She rolls her eyes. "Of course I like Liv, but couldn't you have picked up something at the Littleton Mall?"

"Honey, give the kid a break. You should be proud that you've raised a hopeless romantic. He wants to do something nice for his girl." I can't believe Dad is coming to my rescue, but I won't question his motives.

"I'll tell you what," he continues. "I'll take you out to dinner tomorrow after we pick up Liv's gift."

I can see the change in Mom's face. Dad knows how to mollify her like no other. No wonder they've been happily married for twenty years already. I can learn a lot from him.

CHAPTER 10

LIV

Saylor bangs her notebook loudly against the table. "Okay, spill! What's up with those annoying secretive smiles that keep popping up on your lips every ten seconds?"

I bite the inside of my cheek to keep the grin off my face. "What smiles?"

Saylor narrows her eyes at me. "Don't pretend you don't know what I'm talking about, Liv."

I've been dying to tell Saylor the reason I'm on cloud nine since I saw her this morning, but I knew she would make a big fuss about it, and I didn't want the whole school to hear the news, too. Now, sitting at her kitchen table trying to study, I'm just holding my tongue until she figures out why I can't stop smiling like a fool.

"Can't I just be happy for no reason?" I chew on the end of my pencil.

Her eyes widen, and her mouth makes a perfect O. "Holy shit! You had sex!"

The corners of my lips twitch up. "It took you long enough to figure it out."

She hits my arm. "Bitch! I can't believe you didn't tell me. When did it happen? And how was it? Tell me everything."

"Ouch! Don't need to get violent." I rub the sore spot.

Saylor stands up and begins pacing in front of me. "I can't fucking believe it. Olivia Marie Dawson traded her V-card in before me. It must be the end of times."

"You *did?*"

Saylor and I turn at the same time to find Mandy, Saylor's next-door neighbor, standing by the kitchen door with eyes as round as saucers. She's a year younger than us, but she's so petite, she looks twelve. Her bright red hair and freckled face don't help make her look older either.

"Oh, hi, Mandy. I didn't know you were coming by today," Saylor says.

Mandy looks down, tightening the hold she has on her backpack straps. "Grams had to run an errand, and Connor is at work. I hope it's okay if I study in the living room."

She turns to leave, but Saylor reaches her in two steps and stops her. "Why don't you sit down with us? There's plenty of room here."

Mandy glances at me, unsure, and nibbles her lower lip. I've hung out with her a couple of times before. She's a sweet girl, but she's abnormally shy. I know it's her personality, but the fact that she's been homeschooled her entire life doesn't help either.

She sits next to me and begins taking stuff out of her backpack without making eye contact with either Saylor or me. Suddenly, she says, "I'm sorry for blurting out that question like that. I didn't mean to eavesdrop or pry."

"That's okay, Mandy. I didn't mind."

"And speaking about prying. I want details, Liv. *Pronto.*" Saylor plops into the chair opposite mine and leans forward, resting her elbows on the table.

I sense Mandy's open curiosity as well.

"Well, what do you want to know?" I ask.

"Duh! Everything. Let's begin with when." Saylor is literally at the edge of her seat; she can barely contain her excitement.

"Yesterday afternoon."

"Where?"

"In his bedroom."

"Classic," Saylor says and then turns to Mandy. "When you find a boy who is crazy about you and you're crazy about him, a bedroom is always the best location for the first time. You can get adventurous later."

I shake my head. "Since when are you the expert on first times?"

She rolls her eyes. "Since always. Now, when did you know that the moment had arrived, that you were going for it?"

I want to be honest with Saylor, but then I look at Mandy. I don't want her to get the wrong impression. Saylor has mentioned that Mandy's grandmother is superprotective of her, and she's so sheltered. I don't even know if she's allowed to watch TV.

"You can say in front of Mandy. She's not breakable," Saylor says.

"Okay, okay." I take a deep breath. "I knew the moment had arrived when I stripped for him."

Saylor's eyebrows shoot to the heavens, and for the first time since I've known her, she's robbed of words.

"You stripped for your boyfriend? Weren't you embarrassed?" Mandy asks.

"Not really. I guess when you're really close to someone, being naked in front of them isn't a big deal."

"Are you in love with him?" She's looking at me with such hope in her eyes that it makes me wonder what kind of life she has. She seems starved for love.

Saylor snorts. "Liv is in so deep, she doesn't know which way is up anymore."

♡ ♡ ♡

SEBASTIAN

I haven't been alone with Liv since Wednesday afternoon, and I'm already having withdrawals. I stole a few kisses here and there at school, but it wasn't enough to extinguish the fire she ignited.

My schedule on Friday is insane, and I don't get home from work before ten o'clock. I park my car and notice the TV is still on in Liv's living room. I know it's late, but I can't resist. My parents went to pick up Liv's birthday present in LA today, and like Dad had promised, he took Mom out to dinner. My house is empty, so there will be no distractions for me there.

I call her cell phone as I jog across the front yard. I don't want to press the doorbell and run the risk of her dad answering the door.

Liv picks up on the second ring. "Hey, are you home?" she asks.

"Yeah. I'm actually standing in front of your door."

"Come to the back. I'll let you in through the kitchen."

"Okay."

Putting my phone back in my pocket, I hurry to the back of the house and open the gate to the patio gently, trying to minimize the noise. Once I'm inside, I tiptoe toward the kitchen door. I kind of like sneaking around like this.

Out of nowhere, a shadow jumps on me, and I let out a yelp.

Liv giggles and puts her index finger on my lips. "Shhh. You'll wake my dad up."

I grab her finger and pull her closer to me. "Then stop scaring the bejesus out of me."

I press my lips to hers, and she melts against me. I don't know how it happens, but in two seconds flat, I've pushed her against the fence and am kissing her like I've combined all our past and future kisses into one. One thing I know for sure, though: she's wearing way too many clothes. God, I never thought I'd say this, but I miss summer already—more specifically, summer clothes.

I move from her mouth to her neck, pushing the fabric of her sweater out of the way so I can taste her skin.

"Bas, someone might see us. Mom and Jer are still up."

"I don't care." I trail my tongue over her collarbone, making Liv moan and tremble in my arms. "Let's go back to my place. My parents are still out."

"I can't. Mom wi—"

A throat clears behind us. I jump back, and my heartbeat kicks up a notch. I turn around slowly to see Liv's dad glaring at me from the open kitchen door.

"It's late, Sebastian. Either you come inside to wait for your parents or go home."

Heat crawls up my neck, and I glance down, nervously raking my fingers through my hair.

"Sorry, Mr. Dawson. I guess I'll go home now." I look at Liv apologetically.

"Are you sure you don't wanna come in? We can watch a movie," she says.

I would love to spend more time with her, but I'm too embarrassed. Also, I don't want to deal with a pissed-off Mr. Dawson.

"I'm kind of tired. I just came by to say hello anyway." I move toward Liv and lean down to place a kiss on her lips. Then I remember Mr. Dawson is still watching us like a hawk, so I settle for a peck on her cheek. "Night, Liv. I'll see you tomorrow."

CHAPTER 11
LIV

We get the call in the middle of the night. I don't hear the phone ring, but when Dad shakes me awake and I take a good look at his grim expression, I know something terrible has happened. My first thought is Kimmy.

I sit up. "Dad, what's wrong?"

"Liv, there's been an accident." Dad pauses and glances down. "Sebastian's parents. They're gone."

The blood drains from my face, and breathing becomes impossible. "What do you mean, they're gone?"

"They died in a car crash, honey."

I cover my mouth with my hands and try to process Dad's words. *No, they can't possibly be gone.* My body is shaking, and it feels like my heart is being crushed by the weight of the entire world. I shove the covers aside and jump out of bed. I don't even attempt to find my shoes and put on a jacket. I have to see Sebastian.

Dad reaches for me and stops me from bursting out of my room.

"Dad, let me go. I need to see him." My voice is frantic, and it matches the desperation in my heart.

"Your mom is with him now. Get dressed and we'll go together."

$\heartsuit\ \heartsuit\ \heartsuit$

There's a police cruiser parked in front of Sebastian's house, and when we get inside, I see two cops. One is talking to Mom in a corner of the living room, and the other is sitting next to Sebastian on the couch. I get tunnel vision, my eyes focusing on him. I think the cop is saying something to Sebastian, but he just stares straight ahead, seeing nothing.

I want to run to him, but my feet seem glued to the floor. I force them to move, one step in front of the other, and slowly I make my way to Sebastian. The cop looks up with eyes full of pity, and I hate him for it. Sebastian always loathed pitying looks. The cop stands up, and I take his place. Sebastian doesn't acknowledge my presence, so I grab his hands. They're so cold.

"Bas, I'm so sorry," I say through the huge lump in my throat.

I want to be strong for him, but my emotions are too powerful and they take over, dragging me under a sea of pain. The tears begin falling, and I can't do anything to stop them.

I let go of his hand to drape my arm around his shoulder and pull him to me. His body is stiff next to mine. It feels like I'm hugging a statue. Suddenly, he jumps off the couch and runs out of the room. It takes me a second to catch on and follow him.

The front door is open, and farther ahead I see Sebastian. He stops short of the sidewalk and collapses on the cold ground. The anguished scream he lets out comes from the pit of his stomach, and it's so filled with hurt that it pierces my soul, freezing it, making me wish I had the power to absorb his pain somehow. Loud sobs rack his body, and I'm unable to keep my distance. I stride toward him and kneel by his side. I put my hand on his arm gently, almost afraid to hurt him further, like he's a wounded animal. In a way, he is.

"Don't touch me! Stay away from me!" He raises his hand, pushing me away.

I fall on my butt and can't help feeling a sadness that has nothing to do with this tragedy. His harsh words are like a slap to my face. I know he's hurting and that he doesn't mean them, but the emotion lingers. I'm devastated by the loss of his parents, too. I just want to be there for him.

I feel a hand on my shoulder and look up to find Mom next to me. "Come inside, honey. He needs time to process the news."

I don't want to go. I glance at Sebastian one more time, at his closed-off body language, and I know there's nothing I can do for him right now. He's shutting me out. He's shutting the whole world out.

I wipe away the tears and let Mom drag me up. My eyes land on Sebastian's car.

"I hid his keys. It was the first thing I did when I got here. He's not going anywhere."

I let her take me back to the house, but I can't help looking over my shoulder. My heart folds in on itself as I take in Sebastian's broken and lost image. I can't begin to imagine what's going through his head.

Once inside, I see Dad having a hushed conversation with the cops.

"We've contacted Sebastian's immediate family. His uncle will be here tomorrow. Since the Colemans listed you as a contact in case of emergency, I believe it'll be all right if the kid spends the night with your family," the taller cop says.

"I still can't believe John and Janet are gone. What a tragedy." Dad puts his head in his hand as though his thoughts are too heavy and he needs the support.

"Truck driver fell asleep and crossed the median. The collision was frontal. They didn't stand a chance," the second cop says, and I don't want to hear anymore.

I go to the window and pull the drapes apart. Sebastian is

still down on the ground, in the same position I left him. His head is hidden between his hunched shoulders, and he's shaking. I can hear his sobs through the closed window. Mom goes back outside and puts a blanket over him. He doesn't flinch, doesn't acknowledge the gesture. My heart shatters for him once more. The certainty that what I'm feeling right now is not even a tenth of what Sebastian is feeling makes me hollow inside. The burning in my eyes returns, and I begin to cry anew. The tears are hot and unmerciful.

Eventually the cops leave, and somehow Dad manages to drag Sebastian back to our house. He's no longer crying. His eyes are not only dry now but devoid of any hint of emotion. I don't try to approach him again, afraid of another rebuff. My heart can't take it.

If only I could capture his gaze, see for myself that somehow Sebastian will emerge from the darkness unscathed. But that's wishful thinking. No one can come back from such a tragedy without scars.

♡ ♡ ♡

The following weeks pass in a daze. There's no school to distract me; Christmas and New Year's Eve come and go like they never happened. I do things, say things, and they all have no meaning. Sebastian hasn't talked to me since the accident, and my worry for him surpasses everything. It's all I can think about. He's trapped in a fortress of misery, and I feel like a failure for being unable to breach the wall he's built around himself. His armor is thick and impenetrable, and sometimes, when I catch him glancing my way, his stare is so cold it stops my heart.

The funeral is the only vivid memory I have of the past days, and I wish I could banish it from my thoughts. But when I close my eyes, all I can see is the closed caskets and Sebastian in his dark suit with a blank stare. Beautiful words were spoken about John and Janet, but they didn't seem to have any impact on Sebastian. He didn't cry once during the service.

That was when I realized the boy I loved would never be the same again.

CHAPTER 12
SEBASTIAN

My parents are dead. Vanished. Gone. Turned into nothing more than a pile of annihilated flesh. And it's all my fault. If I hadn't begged them to pick up that stupid gift for Liv downtown, they would still be here with me. Dad with his absentminded, funny ways, and Mom with her sharp and keen eyes. Complete opposites but so perfect for each other. The crater in my chest seems like a void, a black hole that has expanded and swallowed my entire essence.

I dreamed about them last night. They were sitting on the patio outside, sipping wine and chatting happily. In the dream, I didn't join them, just watched from afar, trying to capture their spirit, to understand what made them so happy still after twenty years of marriage. I wanted that for Liv and me. When I woke up, it took me a while to realize that I would never hear the sound of their laughter again, that I would never witness their captivating banter.

Misery hits me like a bulldozer, destroying everything good in my life. Even my love for Liv is tainted now. I can't stand to look at her. What once brought me the most euphoric feeling in the world now only makes my guilt expand tenfold. It isn't her fault—the blame for what happened lies solely on my shoulders

—but she was the catalyst. And my brain can't seem to forget that.

A few days after the funeral, my uncle came to talk to me. He explained what would be my fate. When he told me I would have to move to London to live with him, I didn't even blink. He'd been braced for a fight, expecting me to beg to stay in Littleton. That's the last thing I want. I need to break all ties with this place. I don't think I'll be able to survive if I stay and have to be constantly reminded of the part I played in my parents' death. I asked him when we could leave, but things aren't that simple. Even though he was appointed my guardian per my parents' will, the court still needs to sanction it.

I begin counting the days, and it's the only thing I'm capable of. I don't know what'll happen when I cross the ocean. I don't know if it'll make things easier. I know nothing, only that staying is impossible.

Liv comes to the house every day, talks to my uncle or aunt, and leaves a few minutes later when I refuse to see her. I watch her go back to her house, her shoulders slumped forward, her steps halted. Defeated. She stops halfway between our houses and glances back at my window. I don't hide, but I also don't show any indication that I care that she came to see me. I just stare back at her, willing my heart to kick-start again, but the useless muscle is mangled beyond repair. If I'm capable of any feelings toward her, it goes unnoticed. Missing her is an ache that's easy to forget.

CHAPTER 13
LIV

How many dreams die in a day, in a minute, in an hour with so few words? A short little note, and then there's nothing. I didn't even get the note. I got a vacuum, a blank space, an emptiness so absolute that it numbed my being, my soul. Sebastian is gone, out of my life so suddenly that it takes hours for me to comprehend what happened.

And when I do, I shatter in a million pieces.

CHAPTER 14
SEBASTIAN

pinch the bridge of my nose and throw my head back, waiting for the magic to happen. It doesn't take long, and boom, I'm more alert than a hunting dog on a mission. I lean back on the couch and take in the circus surrounding me. The house is filled with people, all drunk and high out of their minds. Loud music blares in the background, some new pop song that makes the girls scream and dance like there's a pole in the middle of the room.

I feel warm lips on my neck, followed by something wet. It should turn me on, but I'm kind of disgusted. I'm two seconds away from standing up when the owner of that sloppy mouth decides to sit on my lap. No sooner is she on top of me than she begins to grind her hips against mine. I ignore the fact that I'm not really into her and let her do her thing.

I twist her dark hair around my hand and pull her head back. Her eyes are closed, and for a moment, I think she's Liv. But when she opens her eyes again and her dark gaze connects with mine, the spell is broken. Brown eyes stare back at me, not hazel-green. I get angry at myself for allowing the delusion to take hold, then angry at her for not being the one I want. I push her off my lap not too gently and stand up. She yells at me, but I'm already moving.

That's the reason I never hook up with brunettes.

I weave through the party, looking for Oliver. The unwanted memories of Liv have killed my buzz; I can use some of his self-deprecating humor. I find him in the game room, killing at a game of pool, as usual. Several girls from school surround the table, all vying for his attention. He doesn't give a rat's ass about them. Oliver is like me, always looking for something new, something fleeting, to take his mind off the darkness I know surrounds him, too. He never stays with the same girl for more than a couple of days. What's the point?

He slams the eight ball into the hole with an awesome and almost impossible shot, and his groupies scream in appreciation. *Gag me.* Why are girls so stupid? They make it so easy, and then they have the gall to call us bastards.

Oliver grabs the one closest to him, a mousy girl wearing too much makeup and dressed like a whore, and kisses her. After he's done, the girl stares at him with heavy-lidded eyes. She'll soon fancy herself in love with him and try everything in her power to get his attention again. She doesn't know that he's already moved on.

Oliver lets her go when he notices me.

"Bas, where have you been?"

I ignore his question. "What's the plan? I'm kind of sick of this party already."

Oliver puts a hand over his chest, twisting his face in an exaggerated hurt expression. "You wound me. My parties are legendary."

"Whatever. I wanna go out. Are you coming?"

Oliver's gaze travels around the room, and then he looks at me again. He's taking my statement as a challenge. I can see it in the excited glint in his eyes. "Let's go to that new karaoke bar in Peckham."

"What about all these people?"

He goes back to the now-trashed living room where the majority of his guests are. There are empty bottles and glasses scattered everywhere. A couple is making out on the couch, and someone is passing a joint around. The smoke lingers in the air, mixing with the smell of expensive cologne, alcohol, and vomit.

Oliver stands on top of the dining room table and hollers, "Party's over, folks. Let's get moving."

There are a few grumbles and complaints, but quickly enough, the herd begins to evacuate Oliver's Kensington home. In reality, there aren't that many people here, maybe twenty, tops. He never invites a big crowd. He may seem carefree and relaxed, but he likes to know what everyone is doing in his house at all times. You may break things, trash things, and he doesn't care. He just needs to be *aware* that you're doing all of that.

Oliver isn't a popular rich kid—he's an institution at the International School of London. He comes from old money, and here in the UK, it means his parents go to parties at Buckingham Palace. To this day I don't know why he decided to befriend me. I was a jerk to him when we met two years ago. I was a jerk to everyone. But he did, and now he's my best friend—the only friend I have in this dreadful town.

♡ ♡ ♡

We hop into a cab and head to The Singing Olive, the wackiest karaoke bar I've ever seen. It takes almost forty-five minutes to get there, but I think it'll be worth it. The left side of the brick building has a massive sculpture of a pair of tits protruding from the wall, and from one of the nipples, an almost neon green liquid spouts into the open mouth of a hobo statue on the sidewalk. There's a group of people taking pictures in front of it. I'm not inside the bar yet and I can already feel the unique and vibrant wave of the place humming above my skin.

A girl named Chelsea and her friend have joined us. Both blondes, thank God. It's Saturday night and The Singing Olive is packed, but then all bars and independent clubs in Peckham are jammed on the weekends. Peckham used to be a shithole a couple of decades ago, but it's undergone a renaissance and is currently the hottest place to live and party in South East London. There's a line outside of the bar, but we don't have to wait. Oliver knows the secret code of all bouncers—money.

It's dark and loud inside. There are paintings of flying pigs carrying little harps on the walls, and blue neon lights highlight the design details that are meant to be highlighted, like the bar, for instance. The waitresses' uniforms consist of tight shorts and tops that barely cover their boobs. None of them are flat chested. They have glow-in-the-dark necklaces and are all wearing their hair in pigtails. My gaze follows one of them as she passes in front of me. She notices my stare and winks but doesn't stop. I know I could have her number, maybe even hook up with her tonight, but I don't feel like putting in the minimum effort that would require. Besides, there's Chelsea's friend. She's not as pretty as Chelsea, but she'll do in a pinch.

I follow Oliver as he walks farther into the bar, searching for a place to sit. We snag the last available table, all the way at the back of the open room, next to the wall. It doesn't give us the best view of the stage, but it doesn't matter. We're not here for the show—at least *I'm* not. I just want to escape my demons for a little while.

The party at Oliver's place wasn't cutting it for me. I need to immerse myself in other people's happiness. That's how I've been living my life for the past two years, either drowning my sorrows in booze and drugs or living vicariously through strangers. There was no happiness to be found in Oliver's house. Everyone there was just as pitiful as me.

We order a round of shots and beer. Before the drinks even

make it to the table, Oliver is sucking face with Chelsea. That leaves me with the friend. She told me her name back in the cab, but I can't remember anymore. Not that it matters. I peer at her and she glances down, pretending she's shy. I know she's not because her hand is squeezing my thigh. That irritates me, so I don't do what's she's expecting me to, turning my attention to the stage instead. I also remove her hand from my leg. She's pissed and makes a disgruntled sound that tells me how much, but I couldn't care less.

Oliver kisses Chelsea for another minute before he decides to enjoy the show.

"Good Lord, that guy is awful," he says.

That's how the next thirty minutes go: Oliver kissing Chelsea, drinking, and poking fun at some unfortunate soul who's brave enough to face the crowd. I don't kiss Chelsea's friend. I don't even attempt to make conversation. I just drink and laugh at the expense of the bozo of the hour.

Chelsea has moved onto Oliver's lap, and I think they should get a room, not because they're making me uncomfortable but because I want to lose her friend, and I know Oliver won't dump Chelsea before he bangs her.

He looks over her shoulder. "Bas, let's show those losers what real talent is."

I can sing without disgracing myself and so can Oliver. But I know the crowd doesn't care about that. If they smell fear, they'll eat you alive and spit out the bones.

Chelsea has now returned to her own chair, trying to adjust the skimpy dress that barely covers her ass. I feel her friend staring daggers at my face. I bet she wants me to go up on that stage and make a fool of myself. She doesn't know that I'd much rather risk public humiliation than sit next to her for another minute.

"Why not?" I shrug.

"Hey, let's sing something by Abba," Chelsea says, almost bouncing off her chair.

Oliver shakes his head. "Ain't happening, luv. Why don't you just sit tight and watch the pros?"

She pouts and crosses her arms, but in true Oliver fashion, he doesn't even notice. I see everything, because like I said before, I live vicariously through strangers. The situation is not happy now, but it's entertaining at least.

Oliver flags a waitress and puts our names on the list. Fifteen minutes later, we're on stage, and I have no fucking clue what we're going to sing. We literally spent those fifteen minutes debating back and forth which song we should pick without reaching an agreement. Then the intro to "Africa" by Toto starts and I want to throttle Oliver. That was his first suggestion, the one I vetoed on the spot. It used to be one of my parents' favorite songs. It brings back too many unwanted memories, too many unwanted feelings. But I don't want to be a dick and leave Oliver to fend off the wolves alone. He had no way of knowing what a sensitive bastard I am. At least it's not bloody Abba.

The alcohol helps, and soon I find myself belting the lyrics out with Oliver. I pretend I'm having the time of my life, that the jagged fissure in my heart didn't just rip wide open again. I keep on pretending as the song goes on so I won't bawl my eyes out forever. Before I know it, the song is over and the tough crowd is screaming, whistling, cheering us on. I'm hit by a wave of euphoria, a high I've never experienced before. It's amazing and I want to do it again. But there are other people waiting to take the stage.

Oliver and I bow like a couple of dorks before we leave the spotlight. As he passes the trio that's about to go on, he says, "Try following that."

We make our way back to the table and cross paths with Chelsea and her friend. I guess Chelsea took Oliver's rebuff of her Abba suggestion as a challenge, as she's now sporting the same ugly scowl as her companion.

The trio that followed us isn't bad. They don't get booed, but they also don't get the same standing ovation we got. Chelsea and her sidekick are next. They do sing Abba. I don't know the name of the song, just that Mom used to like it. I tune them out and order another drink, scotch neat this time.

"Man, they suck! I don't think we should be seen with them after that," Oliver says.

They must be really bad if Oliver is willing to ditch Chelsea before he sleeps with her. I no longer care. I'm still riding my high.

Someone pulls out the chair next to mine, and I glance in their direction. I raise my eyebrow, waiting for an explanation from the short man sitting next to me. I know Oliver is one second away from telling him to get lost; he doesn't handle intrusions well, and this guy is invading our space.

"Good evening, gentlemen."

"Hey, that seat is taken, pal," Oliver says.

"Don't worry, I won't take up much of your time." The man licks his lips and folds his hands on top of the table. "My name is Hans Armstrong, and I work for Schutz Productions. You must have heard of us."

I have no bloody clue what this dude is talking about, but Oliver perks up on his seat. "You work for Michael Schutz? The music producer?

"The very same." He hands us his business card. "I spot talent for Mr. Schutz, and I gotta say, your performance blew my socks off."

"You're shitting me." Oliver gapes at Hans.

"Mr. Schutz is putting together a new band, and I think you should audition for him."

Oliver and I stare at each other, unable to hide our emotions. I can see Oliver is impressed and in awe, but I'm leery and kind of skeptical. Shit like this doesn't happen in my world.

"Think about it. This is a once-in-a-lifetime opportunity. Call me if you're interested. Mr. Schutz will be in London until the day after tomorrow, so think fast." He stands up and leaves

Oliver and me sitting there like two stupid kids who have forgotten how to speak.

I turn to Oliver. "Did that just happen?"

"I don't know. Pinch me."

I do, kind of hard, and Oliver punches my arm. "Wanker!"

I pick up the card and inspect it. "You know, this could be an elaborate joke."

"Nah, I think he was telling the truth. What do you say? Shall we go for it?"

I can't deny that I loved singing on that stage, but the thought of doing it for real has me apprehensive. What will happen if this Schutz guy likes us? What if we get famous? I laugh at myself. What are the odds we'll get picked? I'm being ridiculous. But it would be fun to audition. A new experience, a different kind of high.

"Yeah, why not? But what about your dad? He'll flip if he finds out."

Oliver smiles like the imp he is. "Exactly. One more reason to try."

CHAPTER 15

LIV

sit by myself at the white-lined table and play with the corsage on my wrist. The dress Mom picked pinches my skin, and I can't wait to get out of it and back into my comfortable clothes.

After months of nagging, Jordan finally convinced me to attend prom with him. It's the last place I want to be, but Saylor and my family ganged up against me, so here I am, having the time of my life. *Not.*

Jordan is next to the refreshment table with his friends. I can feel him glance in my direction from time to time. I know he's telling his sidekicks how he plans to take my virginity tonight. He's that transparent. We've been dating for almost a year now and I still haven't slept with him. No wonder he assumes I haven't traded in my V-card yet.

The first year after Sebastian left, I became a recluse. I went through the motions, going to school, coming home, eating, and sleeping like a robot. I was just numb. The only time I let my emotions take over was when I poured my heart out in the daily emails I sent him. He never replied to any of my messages, but I still held on to the hope that my words would penetrate the barrier he'd put between us.

Then one day my email bounced back. The account I was trying to reach was nonexistent. My heart shattered into a million pieces all over again that day. He had severed the last link I had to him.

Jordan began hounding me soon after that. He asked me out relentlessly for over a month. I didn't want him or any other boy at school, but I was sick and tired of the looks of pity my parents and Kimmy kept giving me. And Saylor was also on my case, saying I was too young to throw in the towel like that. So I gave in, and Jordan and I became an item.

I stare at Jordan and think that maybe I should sleep with him already. Get that out of the way. Finally rinse Sebastian's taste out of my mouth. In another lifetime, I could have been attracted to Jordan. I can't deny that he's super cute. His light blond hair is a nice contrast to his forever-tanned skin, and his body is ripped thanks to hockey. So why can't I feel an ounce of desire when he kisses me?

He comes back to the table and sits next to me, leaning closer to whisper in my ear. "Do you wanna get out of here?"

I look at him and take a deep breath. I've made my decision. "Yeah, sure."

Predictably enough, Jordan has a room booked at the same hotel where prom is being held. I don't say a word as he goes to reception to pick up his card key, we enter the elevator and take it upstairs, and then walk side by side in the hallway toward our room. But when Jordan opens the door and expects me to follow him inside, I freeze. He looks over his shoulder, then turns around when I don't move.

"Liv, are you coming?"

I can see the bed from where I stand, and out of nowhere, a burning sensation erupts behind my eyes. My gaze shifts to him again, and the panic in my eyes is too obvious. His expression crumbles.

"I'm sorry, Jordan. I can't do this."

"Liv, come on. Don't be like that. Just come in so we can talk." He takes a step toward me and raises his arm.

I shake my head and shuffle back, the first tears spilling down my face. "I tried, Jordan. I really did."

Then I bolt.

"Liv, come back!"

I hit the elevator button and the door opens immediately. Thank God it's still on our floor. I don't know if Jordan followed me or not, but I don't care. All I want to do is get out of here. I think about calling Saylor, but the thought of ruining her prom makes me feel even worse than I already do. I did enough damage already ruining Jordan's.

I hail a cab and give the driver Kimmy's address. She and Owen just moved in together, and their house isn't far from Littleton's downtown. I call her on the way over to warn her of my imminent arrival, but it rings and rings before going to voice mail. When the taxi stops in front of her cute one-story home, I understand why. There are several cars parked on the street, and I can hear music coming from inside her house. The last thing I need is to break down in front of a bunch of strangers, but I don't have enough money with me to pay for a ride back home.

I pay for the fare and make my way to Kimmy's door. It's unlocked and I open it slowly, trying to walk in without anyone noticing my arrival. But fate has other plans. Derek, Owen's former roommate, walks out of the half bath near the foyer the moment I step foot inside.

His eyebrows shoot up. "Liv? What are you doing here? Wasn't prom tonight?"

I don't have time to school my emotions, and he notices right away that I'm about to crumble. He breaks the distance between us and touches my arms.

"What happened?" His voice becomes harder, and his cool, steely gray eyes narrow on me.

"Nothing." I stare at his chest.

He increases the pressure on my arms and I feel something. A zing, a spark.

"Are you sure?" he asks.

I look up, right into his eyes. I know he won't let the issue go until I tell him something. "I broke up with my boyfriend."

Derek drops his hands from my arms and takes a step back. Conflicting emotions swirl in his gaze, and that intrigues me.

"You probably wanna talk to Kimmy, huh?"

"Yeah."

His eyes dart around the room, and he scratches the back of his head. I can't help but notice how the sleeve of his polo shirt strains against his bicep. I feel another spark, right in the pit of my stomach. My strange reaction to Derek's proximity is making my head spin. I've hung out with him in the past and felt nothing.

"She stepped out with Owen to get more ice. She should be back soon," he says.

"Oh, that's okay. I'll just hang out in her room until she comes back."

I don't move. Instead, I stare unabashedly at Derek. I haven't seen him in a year, and he's even better-looking than I remember. I don't know why I'm feeling what I'm feeling, but I don't want to overanalyze it. It seems my body is finally waking up from a thousand-year sleep. I want to see where this leads.

Derek's eyes drop to my lips and he swallows hard. I think he wants to kiss me, and I'm caught by surprise when I realize I want him to.

"Why don't you come outside on the patio? Everyone is there." He turns his head toward the back of the house.

"I don't know...."

He runs his hand through his light brown hair, and my fingers are itching to do the same.

"I'm such an ass. You probably don't want any company right now," he says.

Kimmy's home has an open floor plan, and from the foyer I can see the kitchen counter and the bottle of tequila on top of it.

Derek follows my gaze. "Do you want a shot?"

I'm already moving toward it, and before Derek can stop me, I pick up the bottle and take a huge swig from it. The liquid burns my throat, but I gulp it down without even choking.

Derek rips the bottle away from me a second later.

"Easy there, girl. Owen will kill me if I get his baby sister drunk." He's frowning, and the warring emotions are back in his eyes.

"Owen is not my brother." I glare at him.

"That's a technicality." He puts the tequila bottle down and positions himself between me and the counter. It's like he's shielding the booze from me with his own body.

I don't know if it's the alcohol already coursing through my veins, but I let myself be snared by Derek's stare, and a slow fire erupts in my belly before moving south. I haven't felt anything like it in so long that I almost don't recognize it. Desire.

Then I do something completely out of character. I kiss Derek. No, not kiss. I attack his mouth. He resists for only two seconds before giving in to my assault. And boy, does he know how to kiss. The slow fire has turned into a churning volcano, consuming everything in its path.

Derek pulls back and I want to follow him, but he puts his hands on my shoulders so I can't. His touch burns my skin, and I begin to imagine all the things he can do to my body with those hands.

He peers into my eyes, breathing like getting air into his lungs is an impossible task. "Not that I'm complaining, but what are you doing?"

"I'm cleansing my palate," I say.

His eyebrows scrunch together, and his look of confusion is so freaking adorable that I melt on the spot. "I can't be your rebound guy, Liv."

"Why? Because I'm Kimmy's little sister? I'm eighteen, Derek."

He brings his forehead down to mine, his hot breath caressing my skin, and I close my eyes. Sebastian's image appears for a fleeting moment, and before it can douse the fire I had forgotten for so long, I banish it to the darkest corner of my mind. I bring my hands up to Derek's chest and feel his heart beating at an increased pace just like mine is.

"Don't say that." His voice is strained as his fingers dig into my skin.

"Why not?" I whisper.

"Because now I don't have any excuse to push you away."

"I don't want you to push me away."

I do what I wanted to five minutes earlier and run my fingers through his soft hair. Derek closes his eyes and locks his jaw tight. I know he's fighting the attraction between us. I'm beginning to think he's been fighting it for a long time.

"What do you want from me, Liv?" He lets go of my shoulders and drops his hands to my waist, then my hips. He's giving up the fight.

"I want you."

CHAPTER 16
SEBASTIAN

can't believe Oliver and I made it to the final round of auditions. We called Hans Armstrong the following day after the karaoke bar, and he put us on the list. We only found out later that the other guys had to wait in line for hours, months before, to guarantee a spot, and many hopefuls had been sent away.

The first round was awful. Not only did I have to sing in front of a bunch of strangers but they had also expected me to dance. They split us into groups and taught us a quick choreographed routine. I don't dance. Never could. I almost walked off the stage. If it weren't for Oliver, I would have. I couldn't memorize the steps, and my performance resembled a drunken hippo walking on stilts. Needless to say, no one was impressed. I actually couldn't believe it when they told me I had moved on to the following round.

"Do you have any idea what we're expected to do now?" Oliver asks next to me as we wait for the audition's coordinator to call us.

I shrug. "Probably more singing. I hope they don't make me dance again."

Oliver chuckles. "Remind me to ask for a copy of that tape."

"Sebastian Coleman?" the coordinator calls out.

I take a deep breath and stand up, jitters taking over my body. I thought auditioning would be more fun than this. I guess I never believed I would advance this far in the process. Now that I'm so close, I want to be selected.

"Break a leg," Oliver says as I walk toward the unknown.

I enter the empty, semi-dark theater, the only source of illumination coming from the fully lit stage. I glance at the few seats taken. Hans is there, looking bored out of his mind. For a guy whose job is to spot talent, he doesn't look like he actually enjoys the gig. There's a lady with a mass of curly blonde hair sitting next to him; I recognize her as the choreographer who thought I could memorize a dance routine on the fly. And lastly, there's the head honcho, the guy who has the final say on who gets picked and who doesn't—Michael Schutz.

I get on the stage and move to where the mic is under the spotlight, uncertain of what I should do. On a hunch, I brought my guitar with me this time. I figured if I had to sing again, I could pick one of my favorite songs. Also, the guitar is a great shield.

"All right. Sebastian Coleman, is it?" Michael Schutz addresses me.

"Yes, sir."

"I see you brought reinforcements. Are you trying to compensate for your lack of bare minimum body coordination?"

Heat rushes to my cheeks, and I curl my hands into fists. "No offense, sir, but I have plenty of body coordination. I just don't dance."

Blonde lady snorts, and Hans rolls his eyes. To my surprise, Michael actually grins.

"No shit, you don't dance. I've seen elephants with more grace," he says.

I don't know what to say to that, so I keep my mouth shut and shuffle on my feet. *Is he going to ask me to sing or what?* The anticipation is killing me. I want this stupid audition to be over already so I can go back to my miserable life.

Michael glances down at his stack of papers, then at me again. "Tell me, Sebastian. Why should I pick you to join this band over the other twenty remaining candidates who can sing as well as you and *can* dance?"

I don't even let myself process his words, just say the first thing that comes into my head. "I can't tell you why you should pick me. I can't read your mind or pretend that I understand how this business works. All I can say is that I've been spending the last two years of my life seeking the most exhilarating experiences, the most mind-blowing highs, and nothing, absolutely nothing, compared to the feeling I got when I was singing in that karaoke bar where Hans found me. I can't dance for shit, that's true. But I was a hockey player once, and a pretty damn good one. If I can play that game, I can learn jumps and pirouettes."

Michael narrows his eyes at me. I can tell he's appraising me, mulling my words over.

"Fair enough," he finally says. "Whatcha gonna sing for us today?"

Without missing a beat, I say, "'Lightning Crashes' by Live."

I strum my guitar and let the first notes of the song take over, permeate through my skin, carry me to a place I don't usually allow myself to go. This song is powerful, painful and liberating at the same time. It represents everything in my life I want to remember and everything I want to forget. I give it my all and forget there are other people in the theater with me, that there's probably a cameraman recording my performance.

When the final chords dissipate in the air, I close my eyes and take a moment to let the emotions wash over me. My heartbeat is erratic, and I'm breathing hard.

My eyes snap open when I hear clapping. Michael is standing up. He's the one making the noise, a shit-eating grin on his face. I glance at Hans, who's smirking smugly. Dance Lady is dabbing the corners of her eyes with a tissue.

"Brilliant. Fucking brilliant." Michaels walks to the front of the theater.

"Thank you," I say in a daze.

He hops onto the stage and shakes my hand. "I'm glad Hans convinced me to give you a second chance. Who cares that you can't dance? You're going to take the world by storm."

"Are you saying I'm in?"

Michael gives me a toothy smile. I can practically see the dollar signs in his eyes. "Welcome to showbiz."

CHAPTER 17
SEBASTIAN

"Holy fucking shit. Look at this crowd, Bas!" Oliver screams in my ear as we wait to go on *The Today Show*'s stage at Rockefeller Center.

There must be over ten thousand screaming fans out there, and I won't deny it, I'm as flabbergasted by this reception as Oliver. We became an instant hit back in the UK when we released our first single, "Popular." It reached number one on the UK Singles Chart within a couple weeks of its release. We were all the media could talk about, the five unknown guys who had shot to fame overnight. The only thing is, it didn't quite happen overnight.

A week after my final audition, I signed the contract with Schutz Productions, and then I met the other band members—identical twins Kyle and Travis O'Malley, equally loud and obnoxious blokes from Ireland; Anthony Bowman, a no-nonsense kind of guy from Liverpool who had perfected the art of sarcasm; and my best mate, Oliver. I already knew Oliver had gotten a spot. It was all he could talk about. I guess Michael couldn't resist the allure of having a member from the crème de la crème of London's society join the ranks. And Oliver had an awesome personality that would do well in front of an audience.

People can say anything about Michael, but one thing can't be denied—the guy has the Midas touch when it comes to launching musical careers. Like I said, our success didn't happen out of the blue. There was an entire team of producers, PR agents, and marketers working behind the scenes, paving the way for our debut. Articles were issued and rumors were created, all with the intent to create a buzz about Michael Schutz's brand-new project, Boys Future.

To capitalize on our success in the UK, Michael sent us to the US to embark on a radio promotion spree, as well as our first North American concert tour as an opening act for Mod Attraction. Singing on *The Today Show* will be our first US television appearance. I was expecting a couple thousand fans, not this massive crowd. I had no idea we were this big here.

My heart is beating so loud and so fast that I'm afraid it'll leap out of my chest. I'm so freaking nervous, I feel sick. It doesn't help that I'm wearing clothes that are too tight for my taste, and there must be five different kinds of products in my hair. I don't dare touch it.

I wonder if Liv knows I'm in New York City, if she'll be watching the show. But I can't dwell on those thoughts; otherwise, I'll go insane. What's done is done. Too much time has passed for me to have any hope that she's still waiting for me. Not after I cut the last link we had by closing my email account. She must've moved on by now, and it's for the best.

Fuck, I'm lying to myself. It's so not for the best.

This is the first time I've been back on American soil since I moved to England, and I have to admit, it's doing things to me. As soon as we landed at JFK Airport, I was hit by a melancholy so grand, I almost cried like a baby in front of my bandmates. I can't imagine what will happen to me when we fly to LA for the tour's final concert.

CHAPTER 18

LIV

I hop on one foot as I try to put my shoe on while standing. Derek will be here any minute, and I'm not freaking ready yet. I glance at the postapocalyptic state of my room, searching for my clutch. It looks like a Jack Russell on speed has been set loose in here.

I hear the intercom buzz and I panic.

"Saylor! Can you get that?" I scream.

I hear her mumble some kind of complaint. I'm glad Saylor and I got to be roommates during our first year at DuBose College, but boy, can she get grouchy sometimes.

Derek is taking me to a sold-out performance of *Swan Lake*, and we can't be late. They don't allow people in after the curtains open. The only reason I agreed to go is because Derek promised to make it worth my while, which is code for mind-blowing sex.

I finally spot my black-and-white purse under a pile of discarded clothes. I pick it up, and now I'm faced with the impossible task of cramming everything I need inside. I've just managed to organize all my items into the tiny container when I hear his voice behind me.

"Liv, are you ready?"

I turn around and my chin drops at the sight of Derek standing by my bedroom door. He looks good in anything, but in a suit? I almost don't want to go to a fancy ballet anymore. His hair is styled back with a bit of gel, turning it darker and making his eyes pop. He's clean-shaven for the occasion, and I want to lick his chiseled jaw.

With a small shake of my head, I take my mind out of the gutter and find my words. "Yeah. I'm ready."

He gives me an elevator look, his hot gaze making it difficult to stay upright without assistance. My legs are liquefying beneath me.

"You look stunning, as usual," he says.

"You don't look too shabby yourself."

I try to walk around him, but he grabs my forearm and spins me so I'm facing him. He leans down, bringing his lips to mine. It's just a brief and sweet kiss, but I'm already panting like a horny dog. He pulls back and my eyes flutter open.

"Get a room, you two," Saylor says from the open kitchen.

Derek turns to her. "No time. We're already late."

He laces his fingers with mine and tugs my hand. "Come on."

When we reach the parking lot, I see a limo parked in the loading-zone-only space. I stop in my tracks and look at Derek.

"What's this?"

He shrugs and a small smile plays with the corners of his lips. "I thought it would be nice to arrive in style. Like prom night."

"Derek...." I don't know what to say.

The gesture is thoughtful, wonderful, and romantic, but it's so not *us*. Since we hooked up after my prom night last year, I made it clear that I wasn't looking for a serious relationship. I couldn't do serious relationships. Derek seemed to want the same thing; he was so busy with med school that he didn't have time for commitment. What we have now is an exclusive, sex-only kind of deal.

"Come on, Liv. Don't frown like that." He twirls me around, then pulls me to him, hiding his face in the crook of my neck. He kisses my sensitive spot there and then whispers in my ear. "I've never done it inside a limo before."

I laugh and the sudden tension leaves my body. The limo isn't the grand gesture I thought it was; it's just another adventure with Derek. I kiss him long and hard. He trails his hands down my body and clutches my hips, bringing us flush together. I can feel Derek's desire, and for the second time today, I don't want to go see Odette have her heart broken by the prince.

Derek leans back and smiles at me, then releases the fierce hold he has on my hips and puts some distance between us. "Liv, you're such a temptress, but I'm afraid we really must go."

I let him lead me to the waiting limo with the promise of a very interesting ride on the way back home.

♡ ♡ ♡

SEBASTIAN

The rest of the crew of Boys Future is out celebrating the end of a successful tour with Mod Attraction. I'm not. Instead, I drove to Littleton and am now parked in front of my old house. I've been sitting here for over an hour, just staring at the place I used to call home. Uncle Paul sold the house soon after my parents' death and added the money from the sale to my trust fund. A trust fund I'll probably never need now.

If I'm honest with myself, I'm also here hoping to see Liv. I know I shouldn't, but I can't help it. Being back in California created havoc in my mind. I couldn't come this close to her and not try to catch a glimpse.

I laugh at myself. I'm being delusional. No way I'll be satisfied with only a glimpse. If I see her, I'll want to talk to her, touch her, kiss her. Joining Boys Future was the best thing that happened in my life, and not because of fame and money. It put me on the road to recovery. I've finally found something I'm excited about, something that fires up my veins. It woke me from my numb state. The pain over the loss of my parents will always be there, but now it's doable; it doesn't drown me in sorrow anymore.

But a new ache has surfaced with a vengeance. I can feel my love for Liv again, and with that comes the anguish of missing her. Sometimes it's hard to concentrate on anything else. She's all I can think about, day and night.

I thought I had my crazy obsession under control. I had convinced myself that Liv was out of my life for good. The fact that I'm sitting here stalking her parents' home shows otherwise.

A car pulls over and parks in front of their house. My pulse increases, and I hold the steering wheel in a merciless vise. *Is that her?* A tall guy exits the vehicle and hoists a backpack onto his shoulder. The spark of excitement leaves my body in a big whoosh, and I sag in my seat. The guy looks in my direction, and that's when I recognize Jeremy, Liv's younger brother. He's only fifteen and is already taller than me. That's what I call a growth spurt.

He squints and then strides toward my car. I could just turn on the engine and bail before he can reach me, but on a split-second decision, I open the door and get out. I walk around the vehicle, and it's only when we're a foot apart that I see recognition in his eyes.

"Sebastian?"

"Hi, Jer. Long time."

Jeremy just stares at me with his mouth slightly open. He probably thinks he's seeing a ghost.

"Are you here to see Liv?" he finally asks.

I should say no, come up with an excuse, but I can't.

"Yes," I reply.

Jeremy nods like my answer makes perfect sense. "She doesn't live here anymore."

My heart plummets to the ground, and I'm not fast enough to

hide my disappointment. What did I expect? She's nineteen. Of course she doesn't live with her folks anymore.

"Do you want her address?" Jeremy asks, and hope surges through me.

"Yes," I say again. It seems I'm only capable of monosyllabic answers right now.

I retrieve my phone from my pocket and type down her address. She's attending DuBose College and shares an apartment with Saylor on campus. It's just outside of LA.

Before I can thank Jeremy, he says, "This is your chance to repair the damage you inflicted, Sebastian. Break her heart again and I'll break your fucking face."

He turns on his heels and walks to the house, not sparing me another glance.

♡ ♡ ♡

I arrive at Liv's apartment complex, and the first thing I notice is the limo parked out front. I take the empty spot across from it in the parking lot and wait. I spent the entire drive here trying to psych myself up for this long-due reunion. I'm a bundle of nerves, and I have no bloody clue what I'm going to say to her. She must hate me.

I glance at my reflection in the rearview mirror and wince. Shit, I don't look my best right now. The tour was intense, and sleeping wasn't one of the things I got to do a lot. Too much partying and schmoozing with celebrities has taken its toll on me. I also could've shaved. Well, too late now.

I take a deep breath before reaching for the door handle.

My attention is drawn to the couple approaching the limo. The sun hasn't set yet, and I recognize her instantly—Liv. I freeze as my lungs gasp for air. She's more beautiful than I remember. Her hair is longer and dances with the soft breeze, her skin glowing under the late-afternoon light. I will her to glance in my direction, but she only has eyes for her companion. I'm paralyzed, unable to do anything besides watch them. The guy twirls her around before bringing her close to him. She laughs and then kisses him.

Bitter realization completely annihilates me. She's moved on. She's in love with another man. My heart rips in two. My soul shatters in pieces.

They get into the limo, and soon after, it drives away. I don't move from my spot until much later.

Eventually I meet with my bandmates at some swanky club in downtown LA. After that, everything is a blur.

It's the night I push the envelope and test the limits.

It's the night I almost die.

♡ ♡ ♡

LIV

His hand travels up my thigh as his tongue darts in between my breasts. I throw my head back and moan his name out loud, maybe too loud. I hope the window separating us from the limo driver is soundproof. Derek's fingers skim the edge of my panties, sending electric pulses to my core. I squirm on his lap, trying to coach his hand to where I so desperately need it.

Derek's free hand tangles with my hair, bringing my mouth to his. I grind my hips against his, making him groan. I love that sound, and it makes me even crazier with need.

He pulls back slightly. "Liv, you'll be the death of me."

"That's the intention." I suck his bottom lip, then kiss his jaw.

"Hey, I was thinking...," he starts.

"You were thinking." I continue my path down his neck. The tie he was wearing is MIA, and the first three buttons of his shirt are already open.

"That it would be fun if you came to my sister's wedding."

I stop kissing him and freeze. Derek notices the sudden stiffness of my body, and in contrast, his own slumps in the seat. The hand that was on my hip is now gone. I push myself off his lap and sit flush against the car door, creating an unmistakable gap between us. It feels like a chasm has been opened, dividing us.

Derek doesn't look at me, rubbing a hand over his face as I fix the skirt of my dress. A long minute passes without us saying anything, and the uncomfortable silence is like a bad weather of emotions. He finally glances in my direction. "What is it, Liv? What did I say that was so wrong?"

"A wedding, Derek? You want me to attend your sister's wedding as your date? That's not what we do, remember?"

His gray eyes are sparkling with fury now. "And what exactly do we do? Fuck? That's it? Our relationship consists solely of sex, nothing more?"

Now I'm pissed, too. "We don't have a relationship."

He shakes his head and lets out a derisive laugh. "No? Let me correct you there, Liv. A relationship is a connection, an association, an involvement between two people. What we have *is* a relationship, whether you like it or not."

"Don't twist my words. You know exactly what I meant. We don't do commitment. That was the agreement. And meeting your entire family—at your sister's wedding, no less—screams commitment to me."

"And what's the problem with that?"

Derek's words are a knife through my heart. He cannot possibly be implying that he wants more from me. Can't he see I'm damaged beyond repair, that I'm incapable of loving again? I like him, and truth be told, I care for him, but I don't think I can ever love him.

My anger turns to sadness like a light has been switched off. Tears pool in my eyes, and I look away.

"I can't do this, Derek."

He scooches closer to me and grabs my hand. "Why, Liv? Why can't you give us a chance?"

I turn my face to him as the first tears roll down my cheeks.

"Why can't things stay as they are now? Why do you want to go ahead and complicate everything?"

He lets go of my hand to capture my face. "Because I'm in love with you."

I shake my head and push him away. "Don't say that."

He's silent for a moment. His jaw is locked tight, and his eyes are narrowed to slits. "Is this about him?"

I suck in a breath and curl my fingers on my lap.

"You're still hung up on Sebastian Coleman, aren't you?" Derek continues.

I don't say anything. I can't, because he's 100 percent right.

The limo stops, and through the tinted window, I can see we've arrived at my place. My eyes dry up and I open the car door, then pause for a moment. Not in a million years would I have thought I'd turn out to be the villain of the story, the heartless bitch. But that's exactly what I am.

I turn to him once more, my face cold, made of stone. His heart is shattering before my eyes, and I can't offer words of comfort, soften the blow.

All I manage to say is "Goodbye, Derek."

CHAPTER 19
SEBASTIAN

"This is unacceptable!" Hans hits his desk hard with his open palms, rattling the knickknacks he has on it, including the picture frame of his trophy wife. "Did you forget who your target age group is? Teenagers, Sebastian. Fucking *teenagers*. I cannot have the star of Boys Future get caught drinking or high off his ass every single week. You're making the tabloid magazines' owners richer and giving *me* an aneurism. Michael is fucking pissed. He wants your balls fried and dipped in hot sauce."

I wince at Han's words, not because they have any effect on me but because he's hollering and I have a splitting headache. I partied with Oliver last night and, as usual, went overboard.

This is so bloody unfair. Oliver was in worse shape than me, so why isn't he here receiving a tongue lashing from our manager, too?

"Take a chill pill, will you? You know the tabloids always exaggerate." I massage my temple.

"So you're saying you didn't demolish that hotel suite in Sweden last weekend?"

"Well, no, but that wasn't my fault. DJ Fat Thin was the one who showed up with an entourage."

Hans leans back in this chair and pinches the bridge of his nose. "I really thought you dating Gretchen would put a stop to your reckless behavior, but I see you haven't changed one bit."

"Gretchen and I aren't official or anything. We're just hanging out."

"Well, make it official. Maybe it'll help improve your image."

"Stay out of my personal life, Hans," I say through clenched teeth. "If I make it official, it'll be on my terms, not yours."

Hans's gaze becomes hard as he stares at me over his crooked nose. "You signed away any right to a personal life when you joined Boys Future. Michael made you, and he can destroy you just as easily. If you don't clean up your act and stay out of trouble before the world tour starts, you're out of the band."

A big knot forms in my stomach and bile pools in my mouth. He can't be serious. "You're bluffing. Boys Future is Michael's golden goose, and you know if I leave, the band is done."

"Cocky, aren't you? Well, Michael is willing to take the risk. The others might not have your talent, but the band has legions of fans already. Boys Future will survive without you."

I should just tell him to fuck off and then march the hell out of his office, but the idea of not being part of the band, of not being able to sing in front of millions anymore, isn't appealing. It's fucking terrifying. I've barely been holding things together as they were. If I lose the only spark left in my life, what will happen to me?

"Fine! I'll confirm the rumors about Gretchen and me at the E! interview tomorrow. Happy?"

"Not quite, but it'll do for now. And you better behave on this US trip."

♡ ♡ ♡

The meeting with Hans has left me reeling, and by the time I get to my apartment in Camden, I'm ready to explode. The first thing I notice when I open the door is that Oliver has moved from the small couch in the living room to my suspended bedroom. I can see his huge feet sticking out of my bed, though his loud snoring is a dead giveaway. I close the door with a bang and make a beeline to the laptop on my desk, turning that sucker on and Spotifying the shit out of Oliver. Iron Maiden blasts from the wireless speakers mounted on the walls. Oliver jumps off the bed like he's been electrocuted and almost falls over the railing.

"What the fuck, Bas!" he screams and throws a pillow at me.

I ignore him and go make some breakfast. Bacon on bacon sounds good about now. I only had time for a quick coffee before I had to meet with Hans; now it seems the walls of my stomach have glued together. I'm so hungry, I could eat through the entire McDonald's breakfast menu twice.

Oliver comes down the narrow stairs still wearing the same clothes from yesterday. They're wrinkled beyond repair and reek of smoke and whiskey. His blond hair is sticking out at odd angles, and his electric blue eyes are bloodshot. Hell, he looks worse than me.

He takes a seat at the kitchen table and leans his elbows on it, hiding his face between his hands. "Fuck! Kill me now."

"Morning, sunshine," I say.

"Mate, what the hell did I drink last night?"

Everything and then some. It's hard to remember after the fifth shot. He probably did more than drink, though. And I would've done the same a couple of months ago. But since I started seeing Gretchen, the need to drink myself into oblivion has disappeared. I still get drunk, especially when partying with Oliver, but hardcore drugs are off the menu. There's something about Gretchen that makes me want to get my shit together. *Am I falling in love with her?* I want to believe so, but then I remember what it's really like to be in so deep that the feeling overwhelms all of your senses and the person you love becomes everything. And there are days when Liv is still my everything.

CHAPTER 20
LIV

I curse Mom and Kimmy as I push my overloaded luggage cart through the arrivals hall at Heathrow Airport. It's their fault that I have three huge suitcases instead of two. It was a miracle customs didn't stop me.

As soon as the sliding doors open, I stretch my neck, searching for the sign with my name. Hollingsworth Hotel has sent a car to pick me up, which was very nice of them. I don't know many employers that would bother to do that for their interns.

The area in front of the arrivals hall is packed with people, most with the same eager and happy expressions on their faces. I avoid making eye contact with them as I look for my ride. I've always felt awkward when I couldn't spot Mom or Dad right away at airport arrivals. It made me feel like I was on display or something with all those people staring at me.

I finally see my name in a myriad of signs and exhale in relief. This is my first time traveling abroad on my own, and even though this is England and everyone speaks English here, I can't help feeling apprehensive.

The driver seems bored, and when he notices my approach, his demeanor doesn't change.

"Miss Olivia Dawson?" he asks.

"Yes, that's me."

He folds the sign into a tiny, perfect square before placing it in his jacket pocket. "My name is Mr. Abbot. I'll take it from here."

I step back and let him handle the cart. "Thank you."

With long strides, he weaves in and out of the trafficked airport hallway like a pro. I trail after him with difficulty, getting too distracted by my surroundings. I know it's only the freaking airport, but it's the freaking airport in London! I can't believe I'm here.

I feel pressure on my bladder and remember that I need to pee badly.

"Mr. Abbot," I say as I increase my pace to keep up with him.

He slows down and looks over his shoulder. "Yes, miss?"

"I need to use the restroom."

He nods once and resumes walking at a rapid pace.

What's up with this guy? He's like the roadrunner.

He stops abruptly a minute later, and I can see the restroom sign ahead. I walk past him and go take care of business. I'm washing my hands, looking at my bedraggled reflection in the mirror, when I catch a glimpse of a cover magazine with Sebastian on it. My stomach ties in knots. There are two girls next to me and they have the magazine open, poring over it with eagerness.

"I'm so fucking jealous. I want Gretchen's life," one of them says.

"Screw Gretchen's life. All I want is Sebastian Coleman. He's so freaking gorgeous. Look at those bedroom eyes. I bet he's wicked in bed."

I shuffle back suddenly and end up knocking my bag over, spilling half of its contents on the floor. The two girls glance my way for less than a second before going back to their stupid magazine. They don't offer to help me. It's okay. I don't want their help anyway.

I drop to my knees and hastily put everything back before I get up and run out of that restroom as fast as I can, startling some ladies who were about to go in.

I feel so stupid. I can't let stuff like that affect me anymore. What happened on the evening of my farewell party was bad enough; I won't be able to function if I don't get my head straight.

I'm in Sebastian's domain now. Boys Future might be popular in the US, but here in the UK, they're king.

♡ ♡ ♡

Mr. Abbot stops in front of the famous Hollingsworth Hotel, and I stare out the window with my mouth agape. It's more amazing than in the pictures. It's a limestone brick-faced building inspired by Italian Renaissance architecture. Huge arches flanked by Greek columns are the first details guests see. Only the crème de la crème of society can afford to stay here.

I'm surprised the driver has actually parked in front of the hotel, like I'm a guest, not a lowly employee. A bellman opens the door for me, and I exit the vehicle in a complete stay of awe.

I notice he's unloading my luggage from the cab and putting all my stuff onto a trolley. "I'm not sure if you should be doing that. I'm not really a guest. I'm an intern."

He pauses and finally takes the time to look at me. A slow grin unfurls on his face. "Fresh meat. Excellent. I'm Yoann." He offers me his hand, and I shake it. "I'm also an intern," he continues. "Welcome to the Hollingsworth."

"Nice to meet you, Yoann. I'm Liv. How long have you been working here?"

"Six months next week." Yoann looks over my shoulder and quickly resumes his task. I turn around and see a sour-faced, half-pint man glowering in our direction.

"Are you gonna get in trouble for helping me?"

"What? No, it's my job to help with the luggage, and he doesn't know you aren't a guest." He winks at me. "Where are you from?"

"California. You?"

"California? Nice. I've always wanted to visit. I'm from Lille." He begins pushing the trolley toward the hotel's sliding doors, and I follow him.

The inside of the Hollingsworth is just as grandiose as the outside. The lobby resembles the great hall of a sixteenth-century palace, with embellished walls, high arches, and gilded details everywhere.

"That's in France, right?" I continue the conversation.

"Yeah, sorry. I forget that most non-Europeans don't have a bloody clue where Lille is."

"Well, your accent gave you away."

He smiles at me again, and I realize he's one of those rare people whose smile illuminates their entire face, lighting up their eyes.

"Touché," he says.

Yoann takes me in the opposite direction of the reception area and stops next to a couple of plush sofas.

"Do you know where you need to go?" he asks.

"I have no idea. The instruction email I received said I was supposed to contact Mrs. Helen Becket from HR." I retrieve the printout of the email from my purse.

"Oh, yeah. The Queen of Human Remains."

I raise an eyebrow at him. "Human Remains?"

Yoann chuckles. "Inside joke. We have a few. I'm sure by the end of the week you'll know them all."

"So, where I can find her?"

"Follow that corridor all the way to the end and turn right. The HR office will be the third door on your left."

"Okay, thanks."

* * *

My meeting with Mrs. Becket is short and to the point. I don't think she's happy she had to come to the office on a Sunday because of me. She gives me a list of all the important information regarding my internship and accommodations, then talks about the dos and don'ts all employees must abide by. I have the feeling she's sick and tired of repeating that speech day in, day out, based on the robotic manner with which she delivers her spiel. I fill out boring paperwork, and at the end, she gives me my room keys.

When I return to the main lobby, Yoann is gone. An older bellman stands in his place. He notices my approach and asks, "Are you Liv?"

"Yes. Where's Yoann?" I glance around but can't see him anywhere.

"There was a big group coming in, big tippers, and I didn't want him to miss his place in the queue."

I frown at him. "Miss his place? I don't understand."

"We take turns. You help a guest, you go back in the queue. Sometimes you're lucky and get someone who tips nicely. Other times, not so much."

"Oh, I didn't know that. It was nice of you to volunteer to help me, but what about your spot in line?"

"My shift is almost over, and I've just helped a customer. I'm okay." He pauses and stares at the keys in my hand. "Are you ready to check out your accommodations?"

"Yes, please."

We take the same elevators the guests do, and I wonder if there are any for employees' usage only. During the ride up to the fifth floor, I learn that my new bellman's name is Angelo and he's a transplant from Greece. He moved to London when he was fifteen and has worked at the Hollingsworth for almost twenty years.

We exit the elevator, and now I'm just following Angelo, as Mrs. Becket didn't give me any verbal directions when she handed me my room keys. I'm sure there must be a map somewhere inside my employee package, but it's just easier to let my new friend guide me. He seems happy to do so.

We go through double doors that have a clear sign saying "Employees Only," and once we cross the threshold, the change is distinct. Instead of the plush carpet with a deep gold-and-burgundy pattern, a worn and smelly gray carpet covers the hallway. The walls are painted an ugly beige color, and smudges can be seen everywhere.

"Quite a shocker, huh?" Angelo says.

"Yeah, a bit. I mean, I didn't expect it to be Buckingham Palace, but maybe they could've used happier colors?"

"It's better than some of the students' houses in town. At least here you won't have to fight roaches and bedbugs."

"Gross!"

"Here you are—room twenty-four."

I insert the key and only manage to get the door unlocked after jiggling the handle a couple of times. And oh my God, the room is tiny. I don't think two people can maneuver inside without getting in each other's way. It's a rectangle box with a small window. There is a single bed to the right and a wardrobe and sink to the left. No bathroom. An ancient TV stands on a small table by the foot of the bed.

I glance over my shoulder. "No fridge?"

"Nah, you're lucky they gave you a TV. If you want a fridge, you'll have to buy one."

Angelo puts my three suitcases on the little space between the bed and the wardrobe. It isn't wide enough to qualify as a passageway. I have no idea where I'm going to store those monstrosities once I unpack them.

"Well, let the fun begin," I say.

I fish a ten-pound bill from my pocket and offer it to Angelo. He raises his hands and shakes his head. "No, no. There's no need."

"But you helped me and you didn't have to."

"You can buy me a pint later." He shrugs.

"All right, then. Well, thank you so much."

"See you later, Liv." He walks away, and I close the door.

The room is even more claustrophobic now, but I like my privacy. I get my laptop and sit on my bed, leaning against the wall. I look for the piece of paper containing the wireless password, and five minutes later, I'm connected to the world again. I call my parents first, and they want to know everything—how was my flight, did I sit next to an obnoxious person on the plane, how far was the airport from the city, what do I think about my room, and so on. It's hard to keep the conversation brief, but as I talk to them, I keep eyeing my suitcases. I won't be able to relax until my little room is sorted. I say goodbye after ten minutes and begin putting everything away. An hour later, all of my belongings are where they should be, and I've even managed to stuff the stupid suitcases under my bed.

My stomach grumbles and I realize I haven't eaten anything since the meager breakfast they served on the plane. I get my purse and decide it's time for some exploration when someone knocks on my door. I open it without bothering to use the peephole and find Yoann standing there.

"Hi, Yoann."

He peers over my shoulder. "Are you all settled?"

I turn back to glance over my room as well. "Pretty much."

He barges in without asking, and I have to take a step back so he won't stomp on my feet.

"They gave you a TV? Cool. Can I check something?"

I shrug. "Be my guest."

He picks up the remote control next to the television and begins pushing buttons. A screen for the hotel's paid movie channel pops up. He puts in a code, then turns to me. "Voila!"

"What did you do?"

"I just gave you free movies."

"Really? That's awesome. Thank you!"

He grins at me and then makes a grand gesture with his

arms, like he's presenting a masterpiece, not my bento-box room. "So, what do you think?"

"Cozy?"

He laughs. "That's one way to put it." He looks down at my purse. "Are you going somewhere?"

"Yeah, I'm starved. I was gonna grab something to eat. Do you want to come?"

"I actually came by to ask if you wanted to come to the pub. There's one just around the corner, and a bunch of us will be there. They have food."

He doesn't need to ask twice. "Lead the way, monsieur."

CHAPTER 21
LIV

Yoann wasn't lying—the pub is literally around the corner. We head inside and go straight to a table at the far back of the bar. Most of the seats are taken by people with unfamiliar faces.

"Hello, folks. Meet Liv, Hollingsworth's newest intern," Yoann says, commanding everyone's attention.

"Welcome," most say in unison, while others simply nod and raise their glasses.

I take a seat next to a guy wearing a Minions T-shirt under his trim jacket. His dark hair is styled to perfection, and he's wearing more perfume than me.

He offers me his hand. "Hi, I'm Lloyd. In which department are you interning?"

"Events."

Lloyd lets go of my hand to cover his chest. "No shit. *I* work in the events department. Mellie is going to be so jealous that I got to meet you first."

"Hey, Liv!" Yoann hollers from the opposite end of the long table. "It's tradition for fresh meat to buy everyone a round of drinks."

Even with the distance and poor illumination, I can see the corners of Yoann's dark eyes crinkle. I have the feeling he likes to prank people. I turn to Lloyd and whisper, "Is that true? I won't mind if it is."

"Nah, he's totally lying." Lloyd faces Yoann. "Don't even try to scheme Liv, Yoann. She's my intern and therefore under my protection."

"*Your* intern? I thought she was Patsy's intern," a girl with pixie blond hair across from me says.

"Piss off, Femke." Lloyd throws a paper coaster at her.

Femke gives me an appreciative look, like she's checking me out. "Where are you from, Liv?"

"California. And you?"

"The Hague."

"That's awesome. A trip to the Netherlands is definitely on my agenda."

"Fuck. You actually know where The Hague is. Most Americans would just stare at me with a blank expression."

I narrow my eyes at her. I don't like to judge people right away, but her personality is beginning to get on my nerves.

"Ignore Femke. Her Dutch bluntness is more acute today than ever. It must be her time of the month."

Femke flips Lloyd off and turns her attention to the girl next to her. I pick up the menu on the table and scan through the offerings. I have no idea what's good here, but I don't think I can go wrong with fish and chips.

"So, how do you like your accommodations?" Lloyd peers at me over the brim of his beer mug.

"Why does everyone keeping me asking that? It's not that bad."

Lloyd raises both eyebrows. "If you say so."

"Ryan is here!" the girl with curly hair next to Lloyd says, almost bouncing off her seat. "Ryan, over here!" She raises her arm and waves at someone.

My gaze follows hers and I see a blond god approach our table. He must be over six feet tall with broad shoulders and perfect hair. He could be a lost Hemsworth brother.

He glances at Lloyd briefly before his light blue eyes land on my face. I'm staring at him like a fool, and if the smirk on his lips is any indication, he's noticed. He steals a chair from a neighboring table and places it next to mine.

"Hi there. I don't think we've met," he says after he sits down.

Lloyd rolls his eyes. "Hands to yourself, Ryan. This is Liv, and she's my protégé."

"What, I can't say hi?"

Lloyd scowls at Ryan before he finishes his beer in one big gulp. "I need another drink."

A waiter comes by and Lloyd flags him. I take the opportunity to order dinner.

"What are you drinking, Liv?" Ryan asks.

"I guess I'll have beer as well."

"Oh, we should do some shots. Would you do a shot with me, Ryan?" the curly haired girl says.

She leans forward, making sure her boobs squish together. I want to laugh at her obviousness, but then I take a look at Lloyd's face and he's fuming. I'm not sure if the reason is that the girl is almost sitting on his lap or the fact that Ryan is checking out her cleavage.

Ryan glances at me. "Sure, I'll do a tequila shot if Liv does one, too."

I shake my head. "Sorry, I'll pass. I don't want to start my first day at work with a hangover."

In the end, Lloyd orders four tequila shots and drinks two. Ryan asks me a bunch of questions and ignores every attempt Curly makes to engage him in conversation. Lloyd seems to relax when he realizes I'm not there to compete for Ryan's attention. I don't have the slightest intention to start any type of romantic relationship until I get my head straight. I have to get over Sebastian on my own, not use another guy to do it. It didn't work out the last time I tried, and I have no reason to believe it will now. I'm still remorseful over how I handled the situation with Derek last year. He didn't deserve what I did to him.

"I'm going to the loo," Lloyd announces suddenly and gets up.

As soon as he vacates the chair, Curly takes his spot. "Ryan, did you like those brownies I baked for you?"

"Yes, Renata. They were very good. Thank you."

My food arrives and I almost weep with joy. It smells sensational, or I'm just really that hungry. I dip a fry in the tartar sauce and stuff the entire thing in my mouth. I close my eyes for a second and moan.

"Enjoying yourself?" Ryan asks with a grin.

"It's so good. I would offer you some, but I don't want to," I say before I take a bite of the fish.

Ryan shakes his head and laughs. "That's okay. I already ate. I think I'm going to use the restroom as well."

He stands up, and all the girls in the vicinity turn their heads to stare at him. I can't say I didn't peek, too. His ass looks damn fine in those jeans.

"Ryan seems to like you," Renata says next to me.

I shrug and keep on eating. It's not like I can add anything to her comment.

"Do you fancy him?" she continues.

I put the fork down and glance at her. "I just met him."

"So? I wanted to snog him the moment I saw him. He's freaking gorgeous."

Renata sounds so out of her depth that I feel sorry for her. I don't think I can compare her lustful feelings toward Ryan to my own problems of the heart, but I know what it feels like to have no control over your emotions. It sucks.

"Don't worry. Ryan is all yours."

She sighs and rests her elbows on the table. "I wish. He's so out of my league. But one can dream, right?"

"Absolutely."

♡ ♡ ♡

Five minutes later, I realize I have to pee as well. As I walk through the busy pub, I search for Lloyd. Neither he nor Ryan has returned to the table yet, and I wonder where they are. I quickly find out that the restrooms are on the second floor. I had planned to call Saylor earlier, but with the unpacking and the need to nourish myself, I ended up forgetting. She must be freaking out right now. I decide to check my messages as I head up the stairs. There's a new one from Saylor asking when we can Skype. I type back a quick reply, then put my phone away.

I think I will forever blame the jetlag for this, but in my distraction, I end up entering the wrong restroom. It wouldn't be a big deal if not for the scene I witness.

Lloyd and Ryan. Kissing.

They both turn my way when they hear the sound of the door opening.

"Uh, sorry. Wrong room."

I shuffle back as fast as I can and close the door. A second later, a flustered Ryan grabs my arm, spinning me around.

"Liv, wait."

He looks desperate, and I don't know what to think of the situation, especially when Lloyd emerges from the restroom looking miserable. Lloyd stuffs his hands in his pockets and stares at the floor.

"It's okay, Ryan. You're with Lloyd. It's no big deal."

"Shhh. I'm not with Lloyd. Can you please forget you ever saw that?"

Lloyd whips around to face Ryan, and I think he's about to cry. He stomps past us and down the stairs.

Should I follow him? God, what kind of drama did I get myself into?

I pull my arm from Ryan's grasp. "You don't have to worry about me."

By the time I get back to our table, Lloyd is gone.

CHAPTER 22
LIV

wish I'd had the chance to exchange digits with Lloyd last night. I wanted to ask if he was okay before facing him at the office. But the butterflies in my stomach have nothing to do with that. This is my first official job in an events department, and at one of the most prestigious hotels in the world to boot. It's a dream come true.

When I helped plan Kimmy and Owen's wedding last year, I found my calling. I want to work as a wedding planner after graduation, and maybe one day open my own company. The experience I hope to acquire here at Hollingsworth will be invaluable.

I'm early and there's no one in the office yet. The decoration is modern with white sleek furniture, glass desks, and walls painted a vibrant aqua blue. But what I like the most about the office are the huge windows that go up to the ceiling, bringing plenty of light into the room. There are four desks in total in the open floor space facing those windows. To my left is a room separated by a glass wall, and I assume it's Patsy's office. I walk in farther and round a corner, finding a big meeting table and file cabinets flanked against the walls. There's a small efficient kitchen at the far end with one of those cool vintage fridges in bright pink. I also spot a state-of-the-art espresso machine on the counter. As far as offices go, I think I hit the jackpot.

I walk toward the desks and find the one belonging to Lloyd immediately. There are several picture frames with him and a bunch of people taken on different occasions—at a pub, at the beach, at a costume party. Apparently he's a social butterfly. There are also *Game of Thrones* figurines scattered all over the clear desk and a stuffed Minion next to the monitor. I smile. If we can get past the awkwardness created last night, I think we'll get along fine.

The desk next to his right is also taken. There's one single picture frame of a woman with auburn hair and freckled skin next to a ridiculously good-looking man. He gives Denzel Washington a run for his money.

I reach the following desk and see my name printed on a note. There's also a black folder with the Hollingsworth logo on it. I sit down and look inside, finding several pages of literature about the events department, important telephone numbers, codes for the computer and printers, and also a list of upcoming events that I'm expected to dive into headfirst.

Ten minutes later, Lloyd comes in the office looking worse for wear. His clothes and hair are immaculate, but his eyes are bloodshot, and dark scruff frames his jaw.

"Good morning," I say.

He mumbles a response and flops onto his chair, resting his elbows on the desk and hiding his face between his hands. A minute later, he raises his head again and looks at me. "I hate Mondays."

I grin and shake my head. "Rough night?"

"Yeah." He pauses and licks his lips. "Listen, Liv. About last night—"

"Lloyd. It's okay. You don't have to explain anything to me. And don't worry. I won't tell a soul."

His face crumbles. "Ryan got to you, didn't he?" Lloyd looks away and runs his fingers through his hair. "Fuck, I hate this. I swore to myself I would never get involved with a closeted man. And look at me. I'm a mess."

"So, how long have you been dating Ryan?"

Lloyd snorts. "*Dating?* We're not dating, Liv. I'm Ryan's dirty little secret. We've been hooking up since April."

"I'm sorry."

"Don't be. My suffering is self-inflicted. I'm the fool who fell in love with a guy who doesn't have the guts to be true to himself."

"Morning, darlings!" a super-excited female voice greets us from the door.

Lloyd and I glance in her direction, and I see my other coworker for the first time, the auburn-haired girl with the gorgeous boyfriend. She strides toward her desk carrying at least three bags of different sizes with her.

"Are you moving in, Mellie?" Lloyd asks.

"Fuck no. I have to lose at least two stone before Christmas, so I'm hitting the gym during lunch hour. Hence I look like a mental pack mule. Ugh! Being healthy is so hard."

Mellie finally notices me and her eyes light up. "Oh, I apologize for my rant. You must be Olivia. Welcome."

"Thank you. You can call me Liv."

Lloyd swivels his chair my way. "I hope you don't get offended easily. We all curse like sailors here."

"It's okay. I can handle it."

♡ ♡ ♡

My boss doesn't get in until an hour later. Patsy Saunders is a tall, willowy woman with peroxide-blonde hair and intelligent eyes. After a minute in her presence, I discover she can't utter a single sentence without cursing at least once. Lloyd wasn't kidding. They all have foul mouths.

"All right, Liv, here's the gist. To survive in this department, you must be able to work well under pressure, be willing to offer your firstborn child to the Devil to please a client, and be able to think outside the box. There's not a bloody day in this office when we don't have to deal with a fucking crisis."

I nod as excitement slowly builds inside, creeping in and taking over everything. That's what I love the most about events —the craziness, the problems, and challenges I have to face on a daily basis.

Patsy continues. "There are just a few lines you can never cross. You must never, ever get involved with a client. When I say go over and above to keep them happy, I don't mean spreading your legs for them. If someone propositions you, let me know. Hollingsworth has a reputation to preserve."

I nod and sink lower in my chair. This is definitely the most unusual conversation I've ever had with a supervisor.

"You'll have about a week to learn the ropes before things get really shit crazy around here. My suggestion is to become best friends with Mellie and Lloyd."

I'm dismissed after that, and I scramble out of Patsy's office as fast as I can. She's more intimidating in person than over the phone for sure.

CHAPTER 23
SEBASTIAN

All I want to do when I get home is collapse in my bed. The trip to the US was a short one but intense. Interviews after interviews, performances on TV shows, magazine photoshoots. I'm destroyed. But Gretchen wants to meet for lunch because she's flying to São Paulo tonight.

I take a quick shower, shave, and am out the door in less than thirty minutes. We're meeting at a cool little Italian restaurant in Soho. The cab I called is already waiting for me when I hit the street. I never bothered getting my own car here; every time I go out, I usually get hammered, so what's the point of driving?

The ride doesn't take long for a Saturday afternoon, and thirty minutes later, I'm at Tre Gatti. I pay for the fare and exit the vehicle quickly. I'm really not in the mood to deal with fans right now, so I lower my head and hope no one on the sidewalk will recognize me. I should've worn my baseball cap, but Gretchen hates it.

I enter the restaurant and spot her right away sitting at a booth at the far end. The hostess recognizes me and blushes like a little girl, though she must be in her forties. I tell her I've already located my companion and walk toward Gretchen. The hostess is probably crushed that she didn't get to escort me to my seat, but I really don't care.

Gretchen is wearing a cream cashmere sweater paired with her trademark pearl necklace. Her blonde hair is pulled back in a bun at the base of her neck, and loose strands frame her lovely face. Her gaze is down, glued to her phone, and she doesn't see me until I slide into the booth opposite her.

Her eyes widen when she glances up. "Bas!"

"Hello, luv. Miss me?" I fake a British accent.

She smiles from her cheeks. "Yes. Did you miss me, too?"

I make a serious face and look down at the menu. "No."

She swats my hand. "Jerk!"

I peer at her again, grinning this time. "Of course I've missed you, silly."

I'm not lying to her. I did miss her, but I think I've missed Liv more—a girl who hasn't been in my life for almost five years. How fucked up in the head am I? Here I sit opposite one of the prettiest girls I've ever known, yet I'm still hung up on my ex.

"How was your trip? I tried to watch some of your interviews, but I've been so busy this week preparing for my trip to Brazil."

I shrug and flag a waiter. "Same boring shit. I'm exhausted."

"Too exhausted for some one-on-one time after lunch?" Gretchen gives me a smoldering look as her foot slides up my leg. My cock jerks in response.

"I'm never too tired for that."

The waiter comes over, and I order a glass of red wine and a mini cheese pizza. Gretchen only orders a salad.

"I can't believe you always get the mini pizza when you come here. They have other stuff on their menu, you know."

"And I can't believe you only order the salad." I give her a meaningful look.

She glances down at her hands. "I'll be on the runway this week, Bas. Walking side by side with supermodels. I have to keep my curves under control."

I reach out and grab one of her hands, squeezing it. "But I love your curves."

She gives me a less enthusiastic smile this time. "I know you do."

The waiter comes back with my wine and I let go of Gretchen's hand. We don't do public displays of affection. Gretchen has been under media scrutiny for a long time, and she hates the tabloids as much as I do. Her mother used to be a famous model in the eighties who married an equally notorious tycoon. Her lineage alone would be enough to put her under the media's radar, but it wasn't until she started blogging that she became famous. Now she's an It Girl with several fashion designer collaborations under her belt and invitations to participate in photoshoots and runway shows. She was in one of our music videos, and that's how we met.

"What are your plans for tonight?" she asks. "I know Ollie must be jonesing to hit the clubs."

"No plans yet, but you know Ollie. He'll come up with something to do."

CHAPTER 24
LIV

My first week of work goes by faster than I expected. It's always hard to learn the ins and outs of a new job, but Lloyd and Mellie are super helpful. I couldn't have asked for better coworkers; they really took me under their wings. Mellie has already invited me for dinner at her house the following week, and Lloyd is taking me shopping on Oxford Street today.

He picks me up at the hotel and we ride the tube together. We haven't talked about the Ryan incident since Monday, but I have a feeling it'll come up eventually since Yoann invited me to go out with the crew later. I'm sure Ryan will be there, too.

"So, are you going out with the gang tonight?" Lloyd asks five minutes into our ride.

"Yes. Are you coming?"

He scrunches his nose. "No. I'm going to hang out with my friends from uni tonight. I think I've made myself too available for Ryan, you know? I'm always out with the interns in the hopes that he'll fancy a quick shag later. I've decided that if he wants me, he'll have to make an effort now."

"How about finding another guy? One who isn't ashamed to be seen with you in public?"

Look who's talking. I haven't managed to forget my first boyfriend, yet here I am, doling out relationship advice.

Lloyd's shoulders slump forward. "I know. Don't you think I haven't tried? I'm in so deep, I don't know which way is up anymore."

"Oh my God! That's exactly what my best friend Saylor once said about me."

"Oh yeah? And what happened to that relationship? You didn't mention a boyfriend."

I look at my shoes. "It didn't work out. He broke my heart into smithereens. Five years later and I'm still not over him."

I can't believe I admitted that to Lloyd. Maybe it was the fact that he used the same words Saylor once had that made me feel like I could confide in him, at least partially. I have no intention of ever telling anyone at work that I used to know Sebastian Coleman from Boys Future, much less that we used to date.

"Five years? Oh God! I don't want to be hung up on Ryan for that long."

"I'm sure you'll be fine. My case is extreme. Before I ever dated my ex, he used to be my best friend. I'd known him my whole life. I guess that's why it's so hard to move on."

Lloyd narrows his eyes at me, and I don't like the spark in them. He's planning something. "I know the perfect guy for you, Liv!"

I groan. "Oh no. Don't even think about setting me up with one of your friends."

"Oh, come on. It doesn't have to be serious. You're in London! Loosen up and be adventurous. It's okay to have a relationship only for the benefits."

"Been there, done that. It didn't work. I think I'm gonna take my time abroad to rediscover myself, alone, without any man or drama."

Lloyd frowns and pouts. "You're no fun."

♡ ♡ ♡

When I get back from the shopping trip around four in the afternoon, it feels like I've run a marathon. We must have walked the entire length of Oxford Street twice. Lloyd is a freaking maniac when it comes to shopping.

I collapse into bed and only get up hours later when I hear the sound of an incoming Skype call. I see Saylor's picture flashing on the laptop screen and scramble to click on the green button. I've been trying to get a hold of her the entire week, but our schedules have been completely opposite and our free times never coincided. I've spoken with all my roommates already, but there are some things I can only say to Saylor.

"Finally!" she says when her image appears on the screen. "It feels like I haven't seen you in years."

"Not quite. How is everything? Are the girls behaving?"

"Emma and Mandy are fine, but Kennedy's acting weird. I think it has something to do with her blast from the past."

"Blast from past? What do you mean? An ex-boyfriend?"

"No, more like an ex-friend turned enemy."

"Is she okay? She seemed fine when I talked to her two days ago."

Saylor shrugs. "She'll be okay. You know how over the top drama majors can be. Who in the real world has enemies, anyway? Life is not a soap opera."

I hug the pillow on my lap. "My life feels like a soap opera sometimes."

Saylor tilts her head to the side. "What do you mean? What happened now?"

I tell her about Lloyd and Ryan's story, not leaving any detail out. Once I'm done, she laughs and says, "I can't wait to meet Lloyd. I think we'll get along perfectly. And this Ryan guy sounds like a first-grade douchebag. Ugh, I want to punch him in the face already."

"Trust me, I feel the same way. And I'll probably see him

tonight. I don't know how I should behave around him. No one knows what happened, and if I give him the cold shoulder, people will think I'm a bitch."

"Act normal. You said in your email that a group of people is going out, right? You won't need to hang out with him. Now, speaking of going out, what are you going to wear, girlfriend?"

"I don't know. I was thinking of jeans and the new top I bought today."

Saylor gives me a facepalm and shakes her head. "Come on, Liv. That's too safe. You're going clubbing in London. It's time to flaunt your amazing legs. Wear your denim miniskirt."

"I didn't bring any miniskirt."

The only denim miniskirt I've ever purchased was the one I used to make Sebastian jealous back when we were teenagers. After what happened between us, I shoved that garment back in a drawer and never wore it again. I should've donated it to Goodwill a long time ago, but I couldn't let go of it. It's a part of my history, even if it doesn't bring me any good memories anymore.

"Are you sure? Check the inside pocket of your backpack."

"Saylor, you didn't." I do as she says, and there it is, that tiny piece of material.

"I sure did. You need to exorcise your demons. You haven't been with anyone since Derek."

Guilt sneaks in. It happens every time someone mentions Derek. I really hate myself for what I did to him. Not only did I crush his heart, but I also managed to ruin his friendship with Owen. I drop my head into my hands and fight the tears that are threatening to fall. I'm not sure what's upsetting me the most right now, thoughts of Derek or that stupid skirt.

"Liv, what's wrong?" Saylor asks.

I shake my head and glance at the screen again, forcing a smile to my lips. It's absolutely pitiful. "Nothing. I just had a weak moment for a second. I'm fine now."

Saylor narrows her eyes at me. She knows I'm bullshitting

her, so before she can call me on it, I continue in a cheerier tone. "You're right. It's only a skirt. I need to make some new memories with it."

"That's my girl. Now, go get ready, and don't forget to send me a picture of the complete look. I need to approve it."

I roll my eyes. "Saylor, are you sure you want to be a rock star? Maybe you should give styling for celebrities a shot."

Saylor makes a gagging sound. "God no!"

♡ ♡ ♡

Most of the crew going out tonight won't get off work until later. It's Saturday, and many of them have shifts in the three restaurants Hollingsworth has. There are also some poor interns who got the shorter stick and have to work at the reception desk or valet until past midnight. Only Renata, Yoann, Gavin—one of the guys I met at the pub last Sunday—are ready.

We head to Soho, and I'm surprised when the cab drops us in front of yet another hotel—Hotel Soho. Not a very original name, but the hotel itself is very unique. Boutique hotels are usually known for their peculiar and stylish decoration, and a lot of them are on the smaller size. This one isn't an exception. All the furniture I see in the narrow lobby is lacquered black, and the walls are covered with wallpaper in a rich deep burgundy pattern. The carpet is dark purple, almost obsidian. The elevator that takes us to the bar on the rooftop is minuscule; it barely holds the four of us.

"I'm going to suffocate," Gavin says.

The small metal box makes a horrendous sound as it lurches upward. "Oh God. I hope it doesn't break down." Renata makes a worried face, clutching her purse in a vise hold.

"You bloody wimps. The lift is fine. I'll show you." Yoann begins to jump up and down.

"Stop!" we scream in unison, and the crazy fool laughs.

"Let's take a picture to immortalize this moment, in case the cables snap and we plummet to our deaths." Gavin takes his cell phone out, and we all huddle even closer for a group selfie.

The elevator finally stops, and when the door slides open, twinkling lights greet us. The small terrace is crowded, and lounge music seeps through the hidden speakers. There are a few wrought iron tables spread throughout the space, but they're all taken.

Yoann said on the way here that this is one of the hottest spots in London, and it shows. Everyone is dressed like a million bucks, making my denim skirt feel out of place. I'm glad Saylor convinced me to wear my spiked strappy sandals tonight.

We manage to carve a path to the edge of the covered area where the bar is, but we soon realize only one of us will be able to actually reach the counter to order drinks. It's just too busy in here.

Yoann turns to us. "All right. What's your poison?"

"Strawberry caipirinha for sure," Renata says and then glances my way. "Liv, you should try it. It's delicious."

"I might if you tell me what it is."

"It's a Brazilian cocktail. It's a mix of cachaça, which is like the Brazilian equivalent of vodka, sugar, ice, and strawberry."

"That does sound good. I'll have one, too."

Yoann ventures inside, and we snag a high table that was just vacated. I look around and let the incredible atmosphere surrounding me soak into my pores. A spark of euphoria unfurls in the pit of my stomach. Renata sways to the music to my right, and Gavin is blatantly checking out girls, regardless of whether they're accompanied by a guy or not.

We stay at the Hotel Soho for a couple of hours, and by the time we're ready to meet with the rest of the group, I can already feel the effect of the two caipirinhas I drank. Renata was right, they were delicious.

Before we leave, Gavin receives a text from Ryan.

"No bloody way!" he says.

"What is it?" Yoann angles his body, trying to read the text on Gavin's phone.

Gavin glances at us with a bewildered expression on his face. "You're not going to believe who was at Ocean Grill tonight and Ryan got to wait on."

"Who?" we all ask in unison.

"Fucking Onno."

"Wait, from The Titans?" I say.

Gavin gives me a droll look. "Do you know any other famous Onno?"

"That's awesome." I ignore his jab. Meeting Onno is pretty amazing. He's the lead singer of one of the most iconic rock bands of all times. The guy is a legend.

"And there's more. Onno invited Ryan and his friends to hang out with him at his brand-new club, Dijng."

"Are you serious?" Yoann's eyes bug out.

"Like a heart attack."

♡ ♡ ♡

We meet Ryan outside the club. Our gazes lock briefly, but he breaks the connection first. I think he's still embarrassed that I caught him with Lloyd. What he did last week was a douche move, and I'm still annoyed with him. But I shouldn't judge him too harshly. You never know what kind of personal demons people are battling on a daily basis.

There's a huge line in front of Onno's club that goes around the block. This place is definitely happening. The spark of euphoria from before has multiplied tenfold. Saylor will flip if I manage to meet Onno in person.

"Where's everyone else?" Yoann asks Ryan.

"I got them in already. Come on, let's go."

I follow him toward the main entrance. The bouncer nods to Ryan and lets us through the corded area. He walks in like he owns the place, passing the cashier's desk and going straight to the coat check counter.

"We don't have to pay?" I shout over the noise.

He glances at me with an eyebrow raised, like he's surprised I'm speaking to him. "We're on the VIP list."

"That's so cool," Renata gushes as she gets up close and personal with Ryan, touching his arm.

He stiffens at the proximity and clenches his jaw. He's not even trying to pretend he's into girls this time. Or maybe I'm noticing his reaction because I know his secret.

As soon as our coats are checked, he turns his entire frame to me, giving Renata his back.

"Come on, let's get something to drink. I'm parched." He grabs my hand and tugs me along without giving me a choice. I don't have time to process what he's up to.

We reach what seems to be the main bar of the club, and from where I stand, I can't see the counter. There are too many people standing in front of it already, trying to get the attention of the busy bartenders.

Ryan turns to me. "What are you drinking?"

I pull my hand from his grasp and fold my arms in front of my chest. "What's going on, Ryan?"

He rakes his fingers through his hair as he glances down. "I just can't deal with Renata tonight. I'm a mess."

I narrow my eyes at him. "Does it have anything to do with you and Lloyd?"

His head snaps back up. If he tells me to shush, I'm going to tell him to take a hike. But all he does is exhale loudly and slump his shoulders forward.

"Liv, now that you know about me, can I be candid with you?"

"Sure."

"I have no idea what I'm doing with Lloyd. I've always had girlfriends in the past. I was never attracted to guys before. But it all changed when I met him."

Hearing the conflict in Ryan's voice makes the ill feelings I had toward him dissipate somewhat. "Ryan, I can't begin to imagine what you're going through, but you can't keep treating Lloyd like a dirty secret. You have to get your shit together."

"I know, I know."

"Where the fuck is Onno?" Gavin shouts behind us.

"To be honest, I don't know," Ryan says, the vulnerable, tortured look gone from his chiseled face.

Gavin's expression falls, but faster than lightning, the up-to-no-good smile is back. "Well, let's get some bloody drinks, then."

I see Renata and Yoann just behind Gavin. Ryan offers to buy the first round of drinks, and I order water this time. The potent Brazilian cocktail is still muddling my brain. I move to stand closer to Renata, but one look at her glacial expression and I change my mind. She's glaring at me openly, and I mentally curse Ryan for entangling me in his shenanigans.

When Ryan returns with our drinks, I sense Renata won't go down without a fight. She squares her shoulders and prepares for the attack. I'm all for girl power and fighting for what you want, but I also believe there's a big difference between being fierce and being utterly pathetic. Throwing yourself at a guy who is clearly not interested in you is the latter.

"Wanna dance?" Ryan asks out of the blue.

He doesn't give me a chance to reply, just drags me to the dance floor. It's the second time in the span of a few minutes that I've been pulled against my will somewhere, and I'm pissed. I'm not an idiot. I know he's using me as a shield against Renata's advances.

I stop abruptly and refuse to take another step. Ryan turns around when he senses my resistance.

"What do you think you're doing?" I say.

"Liv, please. Can you just play along this once? You have no idea how relentless that girl can be."

I open my mouth to reply when a wiry guy with spiked blue

hair taps Ryan on the shoulder. "Ryan, my man. You've made it."

Ryan smiles from ear to ear. "Hey, Beau. I sure did. Thank Onno for me, will ya?"

"You can thank him yourself. He's upstairs in the VIP lounge. I'm headed that way. Come."

Ryan glances at me with an eyebrow raised. I throw my hands up in the air. "Fine! Just this once, and only because I want to meet Onno."

We follow Onno's friend until he stops in front of a flight of stairs that has been corded off. He says something to the bouncer stationed there, and the man nods and lets us through. We go up, and with each step I sense the difference in the atmosphere. When we reach the landing, we're greeted by a dark and much cooler room. The music playing in the background is not techno crazy and not nearly as loud as in the club downstairs. We've definitely crossed into a different world.

Beau takes us to a big table where my eyes immediately zero in on the famous man. He's like a king holding court. His long hair falls to his shoulders, and his face is partially hidden by a thick beard. He has his trademark blue-tinted glasses on despite the darkness in the room. I'm not sure how he can see properly, though obviously he can see just fine, as he notices our arrival before we even make it to his table and gives Ryan a genuine smile. When Ryan introduces me to the rock legend, it feels like I'm stuck in a dream. It's such a surreal moment. My heart is pounding as I say a shy hello to him. There are other people sitting at the table, but I barely register their faces, too busy thinking of ways to ask Onno for a picture without sounding like a complete moron.

Then I feel a weird prickling sensation on the back of my neck, like someone is watching me. My eyes dart around the room and find nothing. I must be imagining things.

We sit down, and Beau introduces us to the four other guys there. The first thing I notice is their overelaborate hairdos and trendy clothes. Beau watches me closely as he says their names, as if he's expecting a certain reaction from me. Two of the guys are identical twins, and the third is a ginger. It's only when I look twice at the blond guy sitting closest to me that a spark of recognition fires up in my brain, but I can't place him. The dimness of the lounge doesn't help either.

After a minute, Beau says, "Unbelievable. We've got nothing. I think you're becoming a fad already, lads."

"Sod off, Beau," one of the twins says.

"Okay, this is going to drive me insane. Am I supposed to know who you guys are?" I ask.

"Really, you don't recognize them?" Ryan asks.

"Nope."

Beau throws his head back and laughs. "Oh, that's precious. I can't wait to see Bas's face when she doesn't recognize *him*."

Bas? A foreboding feeling takes hold of my heart, twisting it in a merciless grip. *No, it can't be.*

Someone approaches our table and stands behind Blondie. I look up and lock gazes with the last person I ever expected to see here. The last person I expected to see ever.

Sebastian.

The blood drains from my face, and I find it impossible to get air into my lungs. My mouth becomes as dry as sawdust. Sebastian's dark gaze is like a laser beam, drilling a hole through my face. The world around me ceases to exist; sounds become muffled. It's like there's only Sebastian and me in the room. When Ryan touches my arm, I snap back to the moment and notice everyone is staring at me.

"Liv, are you okay?" Ryan asks.

"Yes, I'm fine. I-I… need to use the restroom."

I don't know how I manage to get up and walk away from the table without tripping. Mercifully, the restroom is empty. I rest my hands on the cold dark granite counter and try to control my breathing. I'm on the verge of a panic attack.

Sebastian is here. Sebastian is here. The chant in my head doesn't stop. I can't process it, can't believe it. Seeing him face-to-face is a million times worse than watching him on television. I'm back at that cold January afternoon when I found out Sebastian had left for London without saying goodbye. The hurt is overwhelming, and it annihilates me all over again.

I splash cold water on my cheeks and forehead, careful to avoid ruining my eye makeup. I stare at my reflection and focus on my breathing. Saylor would chew my ass off if she knew how crazy I'm behaving right now.

"Get your shit together, Liv! You're no longer the innocent fifteen-year-old girl madly in love with your best friend." I listen to the Saylor in my mind, knowing she's right. I *am* a strong, independent woman who doesn't take crap from anyone—most of the time, anyway. I can't let Sebastian's presence ruin my night. He's done enough damage already.

My heartbeat returns to normal, and I exhale in relief. I'm back in control. I can go out there and pretend I have no idea who Sebastian is either.

I put another coat of lipstick on. A minute later, I exit the restroom with new confidence in my step. I barely take two steps before I feel a hand on my arm.

"Liv."

My name on Sebastian's lips is like a caress all over my body, and my traitorous heart reacts to it of its own accord.

CHAPTER 25
SEBASTIAN

can't believe my eyes when I catch a glimpse of Liv gliding across Dijng's VIP lounge. I'm sure my mind is playing tricks on me, or I must have drunk more than I remember. I follow her with my eyes, staying glued to the spot. Liv and her companion stop at Onno's table—*my* table. Seeing her in the flesh after all these years is akin to being sucker punched in the gut. My heart feels like it's being squeezed by a boa constrictor.

I clench my jaw and will my body to move, to get the hell out of this club before Liv sees me, but I'm a masochist. She glances over her shoulder, looking in my direction like she can sense I'm watching her. I take a step back, farther into the shadows. Her gaze passes me and continues searching. Her friend touches her arm, bringing her attention back to him. They take a seat. That's just fucking great.

Why is she here?

Now I'm pissed. How dare she show up like this on my turf and play havoc with my head? On a subconscious level, I know my thought process is ridiculous. I'm the one who fucked things up, but I hold on to my anger just the same. It's the only thing that'll prevent me from begging her for forgiveness. I stride to the bar and order a few shots of whiskey, drinking them in succession without stopping to breathe. My throat is nice and scorched, and I can feel the amber liquid burning my veins. The shots aren't enough to dull the pain, but they give me the courage to face the girl I can't seem to forget.

I make my way to the table and stop right behind Oliver, my best friend. I catch the end of the conversation, hear my name, but I can't be bothered to contribute to it. I'm too busy drinking in the sight of Liv. God, I've missed her so much.

She glances up and her eyes connect with mine. Even in the gloominess of the room, I see them widen in surprise. Her stare seems to last an eternity, and I find myself drowning in her gaze. The guy she's with asks her a question, and the spell is broken. She stands up suddenly and walks away as fast as she can. I watch her leave, and my mouth goes dry when I recognize the skirt she's wearing. It's the same skirt that tied her to me forever and damned my soul.

"Bas, where have you been? We've just met a bloody unicorn," Oliver says, breaking my trance.

"What?" I ask.

"That girl who was just here. She didn't recognize any of us. Either she's been living under a rock or she's a fucking unicorn."

"I don't follow."

"Unicorn? Rare mythical creature?"

"I gotta pee," I say and begin moving. I'm a bloodhound trained on Liv's scent.

I wait for her outside the restroom without a clue about what I intend to do.

The door in front of me opens, and I get tunnel vision. Liv becomes everything again. My heart lurches in my chest, and the longing there explodes with a vengeance, taking over my emotions like a ruthless army. Liv doesn't see me at first, and before I can stop it, I'm reaching out to her and saying her name like I want to make love to her right here, right now.

She freezes midstep. Her eyes are bright and unblinking. The air around us becomes charged with combustible energy. I move closer, my body is unable to fight her pull.

"I can't believe you're here." I raise my arm to touch her silky hair, but Liv takes a step back.

"Long time no see, Sebastian. How have you been?" Her voice is hard, full of contempt. It's a bucket of icy water on my face. I wake up from stupidity land, and anger rears its ugly head again.

"Terrific. You?" I answer.

"Couldn't have been better."

"Did you know I was going to be here?" The question rolls off my tongue before I can think through what I'm doing.

Her jaw drops. "Excuse me?"

"Oh, come on, Liv. What are the odds that you would come to the same place as me?"

"Un-fucking-real," she mutters.

I've mastered the art of douchery, so I keep digging my grave. My lips curl into a sneer. "Two years in this bloody business and I've learned to spot potential stalkers."

Liv's eyes narrow to slits, and her hands turn into fists by her side. "No, Sebastian. Two years in this business have turned you into an egomaniacal, delusional liar."

"Are you saying it's by chance that you're wearing the same damn skirt you used to seduce me five years ago?"

Anger flashes in Liv's eyes, and I half expect her to slap me. Perversely enough, I want her to do it. I'm out of my mind. Why am I saying all these horrible things to her when all I want is to bury my face in the crook of her neck, hug her tight, and never let her go again?

She doesn't hit me. Instead, the corners of her lips twitch upward. "What, this little thing here? Who said I'm wearing it for your benefit?"

She walks around me and sashays back to her boyfriend.

I want to punch a fucking wall.

♡ ♡ ♡

LIV

My body is shaking as I make my way back to Ryan. In all the times I imagined seeing Sebastian again, I never foresaw the conversation going as horribly wrong as it did just now. The man I just saw is a stranger; there isn't a shred left of my Sebastian in him.

They say grief can change a person in many ways, sometimes for the better and other times for the worse. Sebastian is clearly the second case. The loving and kind boy I fell in love with five years ago died with his parents, and a cold and twisted monster has taken his place.

Hanging out with Onno has lost its appeal; all I want to do is get away from here and hopefully never see Sebastian again.

Ryan sees me coming and stands up, noticing something is up the moment I reach him. He puts his hands on my naked arms and searches my face.

"What's the matter? You're as white as a ghost."

"I have a killer migraine. I gotta go home."

"I'll take you."

"No, Ryan. You don't have to. I'll be fine on my own."

"Nonsense. You look like you're about to pass out."

Ryan says goodbye to Onno and ushers me out of the VIP lounge. He puts a protective hand on my lower back, and the gesture makes me want to cry, but I rein in the tears. I don't want to explain the reason behind them.

We get our coats, and before I can blink, we're inside a cab and heading back to the Hollingsworth. Glancing at Ryan as he stares out the window, I squeeze his hand.

"Thank you for coming with me. I'm sorry I ruined your evening."

He turns to me with eyebrows furrowed. "You didn't ruin

my evening. Onno is cool, but those guys from Boys Future are assholes. I was happy to leave."

Ryan's actions tonight might have been all over the place, but what he just did for me is what stands out. "Listen, if you ever want to talk about… you know, I'm here."

A small smile appears on his face, a smile that doesn't reach his eyes. "You don't know what you're getting yourself into. Drama seems to follow me."

"Well, I'm an honorary member of the same club."

CHAPTER 26

LIV

arrive at the office bright and early on Monday morning. After spending the entire Sunday holed up in my room, I can't wait to interact with people. My reclusion yesterday was self-imposed. Thanks to the awful encounter with Sebastian, I didn't feel like facing anyone. Today, I'm Scarlett O'Hara, ready for battle.

It's seven thirty, and I'm surprised to see Mellie and Lloyd are already behind their desks, working like busy bees. It seems they've been in the office a while.

"Oh, thank the Lord you're here, Liv," Lloyd says.

"What's the matter, guys? Why are you here so early?"

"Well, Patsy called, asking us to be at the office 7:00 a.m. sharp. I can't believe she didn't contact you, too."

I sit at my desk and turned my computer on. "Why?"

"Well, she received a call last night. A very important prospect is coming to check out the premises on Wednesday, and Patsy wants to make sure everything is perfect. This is a big deal," Mellie says.

"Who's the prospect?"

"Gretchen Smith," Lloyd squeaks.

My hands freeze over the keyboard. *No, it can't be the same*

Gretchen. When I don't say anything, Lloyd continues, "Media darling, Sebastian Coleman's girlfriend."

I feel light-headed all of a sudden, and I'm glad my face is hidden behind the computer screen.

"Any idea what kind of event Gretchen is planning?" I manage to say through the lump in my throat.

"A surprise birthday party for Sebastian," Mellie almost shouts in excitement. "Fingers crossed she picks the Hollingsworth."

No, no, no. This cannot be happening. Did I throw stones at the cross in my previous life? Why am I being punished now? Seeing Sebastian once was bad enough. I can't possibly help plan his freaking birthday party. I just can't.

Patsy comes into the office like a hurricane, carrying an over-sized bag and a Starbucks coffee in one hand. She has a news-paper under her arm and a cigarette between her lips. "Team, my office. *Now.*"

Mellie and Lloyd scramble to their feet, but I remain glued to my desk.

"What are you waiting for? Move, girl," Lloyd says as he walks by me.

I snap out of my shock, then grab a pen and my notebook to follow them into Patsy's office. She begins talking before I can sit down.

"I can't stress enough how securing Gretchen's business is of the utmost importance for this department. So here's the plan. Lloyd, I need at least five design ideas for the décor. Use the Venetian room as your canvas. I want to see a mood board and final drafts of the designs by tomorrow."

Lloyd doesn't even look up as he writes on his notepad.

Patsy continues, "Mellie, you'll coordinate with Chef François and begin brainstorming ideas for the sampler he'll prepare on Wednesday. It needs to fit the themes Lloyd comes up with."

Patsy's eyes land on me. "Liv, your job is to pore over the

internet and print out any article you can find on Gretchen and Sebastian. I mean *everything*. I want to know every single detail about their relationship, how they met, etc. I know you can't believe what the tabloids say, but there's usually some truth behind those stories. Also, I want a full report on Gretchen: what are her likes and dislikes, how was her life before she became Britain's darling, and so on. Have the report ready on my desk by the end of the day, though Lloyd and Mellie might need it sooner to help with their tasks."

I leave Patsy's office in a daze. She couldn't possibly have given me a worse assignment. Finding out more about Sebastian's girlfriend and their relationship will be akin to stabbing my chest with a dull knife. I take a deep breath and channel my inner Scarlett O'Hara again. *I can do this.*

But when I type Sebastian's and Gretchen's names into Google, I begin to doubt. Not because it's going to be excruciating learning more about them as a couple but because there are thousands of search results. Now I wish I'd brought my morbid collection of gossip magazines with me.

"Oh, darn it! I'll have to cancel dinner at my house, Liv. I'm so sorry. I hope you don't mind. I know I'll be working late this week."

"It's okay, Mellie. We have a lot to do in such a short period of time." I turn to the computer screen again. Ugh, I don't know where to start. I put my head in my hands, pull my hair, and groan. "This is impossible. How can we finish our tasks by the deadline?"

"Welcome to the world of events coordination, luv," Lloyd says from his desk.

"Oh, I have a brilliant idea." Mellie glances my way. "My youngest cousin is completely obsessed with Boys Future. She has a stack of gossip mags about them, organized in chronological order. I'll make a call and have them delivered here within the hour."

"Won't your cousin mind?"

"She doesn't need to know. She's away at uni. My aunt will help." Mellie winks at me.

"Focus on Gretchen for now. But forget Google. You'll be better off reading her blog. It's VelvetandChocolates.com," Lloyd says.

And that's what I do for the next couple of hours. The most recent post shows pictures of Gretchen backstage at a fashion show, her hair in curlers. She must be getting ready to walk on the runway. She's so pretty it hurts my eyes. I click on the archive link and begin reading her entries in the order they were posted, from oldest to newest.

At first, I hate her with a passion. But as I begin to follow her journey, her adventures suck me in, and I have to concede that she seems to be a very cool girl. Her writing is engaging, and, despite her privileged background, I never get the sense that she's a snob.

When I finally reach the part where she met Sebastian, my heart rips open again. She was in one of Boys Future's music videos. The masochist in me can't help but watch the damn thing.

By the time I'm done, I'm back to hating Gretchen Smith.

CHAPTER 27

LIV

knew without a doubt that Gretchen would choose the Hollingsworth for Sebastian's party. I'm that lucky. *Murphy's Law, you suck.*

Mellie and Lloyd are on cloud nine that we won Gretchen's account, and it's all they can talk about. I'm sick of hearing them gushing over her and their comments about what a perfect couple Sebastian and Gretchen make. At least I'm not completely involved with the planning and preparations for his stupid party. Our department still has plenty of other events that require our attention, and since I'm the newbie and Gretchen's account is being considered a top project, I wasn't assigned any tasks related to it. *Yet.* But since I'm buddies with Murphy now, I know his stupid law will change things in no time.

Six days before the party, I come into the office after my lunch break and find Mellie pacing in front of my desk.

"Bloody hell. Where have you been?" Her usually immaculate hair is the worse for wear with loose wisps here and there.

"Across the street getting food."

"I called you a thousand times. We have an emergency."

I retrieve my phone from my bag, and sure enough, I see ten missed calls from Mellie. *Crap!*

"Sorry, I must've put it on mute by accident. What happened?"

"A disaster is what happened. Patsy was supposed to run an important errand for Gretchen's party this afternoon, but she fell earlier when leaving her house and broke her arm. She's at the hospital right now."

"Oh no! That's awful."

"I know! I can't leave the bloody office because I have a gazillion things to do here, and Lloyd is already all across town picking up the special décor we ordered for the party. That means you'll have to take care of Patsy's errand."

"What is it?" My stomach is already in knots. I'm afraid to know.

"Gretchen commissioned a gift for Sebastian, and Patsy was supposed to pick it up today. But the place is in Arundel. It's about two hours from London. You'll have to drive there."

"Drive? I don't own a car. Can't I take the train?" The thought of driving on the wrong side of the road terrifies me. I was never one prone to panic attacks, but I think I'm about to have one right now.

"No, you can't take public transportation. The gift is a piece of art, and it's big. Patsy said you can borrow her Land Rover. It's parked in the hotel's garage."

I wonder for a second why Patsy's car is here at the Hollingsworth, but it's a moot point trying to understand her weird habits. "You're joking, right?" I say.

"Does it look like I'm joking? Here's the address." Mellie gives me a piece of paper and I just stare at it, trying to come up with another solution that doesn't involve me driving Patsy's car. I'm gonna crash it, I know I will.

"You better go right now. You're bound to encounter major traffic thanks to the shitty weather outside."

Frigging fantastic. Not only do I have to drive my boss's very expensive car, but it also has to be on the day that it's raining cats and dogs. The fact that I have to collect a special gift Sebastian's girlfriend commissioned for him is not even fazing me right now.

"Ask one of the valet guys to get the car for you." Mellie leaves the office without a second glance in my direction.

Resigned, I put my coat on, grab my purse, and make my way to the Hollingsworth's main entrance. As I wait for the car, I try to calm my nerves. A million years ago, I learned how to drive a stick, but I've never actually owned a manual car. This is a recipe for disaster. I'm sweating already, though the temperature must be below fifty. I should just take a cab, but the round trip will cost my entire salary. It's better than dying, though.

The valet comes back with Patsy's Rover and hands me the keys. I stand paralyzed next to the car, fear crippling me.

"Liv?"

I close my eyes for a second and my hands curl into fists. *No. I must be hearing things.* Slowly, I turn around, and sure enough, Sebastian is standing a couple of feet away from me.

"What are you doing here?" he asks.

Without thinking, I answer him. "I work here."

His eyes widen and his jaw drops. "As a valet girl?"

His condescending tone aggravates me. "None of your business. Now if you excuse me, I have someplace to be." I make a move to get into the car, but Sebastian's hand on my arm stops me.

"Where are you going?"

"Sebastian, I don't have time for this. I have to get to Arundel and back before the day is over and hope not to die in the process."

He leans closer to me to peer inside the car. I get a good whiff of his expensive cologne, and hell and damn if it doesn't make my legs turn into jelly.

"Whose car is this?" he asks.

"My boss's."

He turns to me, and I'm acutely aware how dangerously

close his mouth is to mine. "Do you even know how to drive a manual shift?"

I take a step back and cross my arms. "Yes I do. Owen taught me."

"So he's still in the picture, huh?"

Sebastian's curiosity about my life is making my head spin. Why does he care after all these years? Is this the same guy who accused me of stalking him a few weeks ago? I should just tell him to get lost and continue on my suicide mission, but for some reason, I want to answer all of his questions.

"Yes, very much so. He's my brother-in-law now."

Sebastian looks at the rain, then back at the car. Before I can stop him, he gets behind the steering wheel and glances at me. "Get in. I'll drive you to Arundel."

"You can't be serious."

He pierces me with his killer stare, a stare that tells me I don't have a choice. I sense the people around have taken notice of us —more precisely, they've taken notice of the very famous singer sitting inside the car. The last thing I want is to cause a commotion, so before any fan can approach him, I get in the SUV, knowing my heart probably won't survive the journey.

SEBASTIAN

I don't know if I should laugh or curse the gods. I went to the Hollingsworth with every intention to look for Liv but never imagined that fate would make it so easy for me.

I haven't been able to get her out of my mind since our encounter at Dijng. Finding out where she worked was easy enough. Staying away from the place for all these weeks, not so much.

Today, I lost the fight, and now I'm stuck inside a car with her for at least a few hours. My heart hasn't stopped beating like it wants to find a way out, and I have fucking butterflies in my stomach. *What am I? Twelve?*

Liv hasn't uttered a single word since giving me the address of an art studio in Arundel. She's looking out the window with her arms crossed. I peer at her several times, trying to guess what's going on in her head, but I can't. I used to be able to read her like a book, and the realization that I've lost my special power crushes me.

I put on the radio to fill in the silence, and Kelly Clarkson's voice barrels through the speakers. *Dear God.* I switch stations on the spot, but Liv puts it back on Kelly.

"I like this song," she says.

I grind my jaw. "Since You've Been Gone" is playing, and no one can accuse me of being self-centered for thinking Liv is sending me a message. I hear it loud and clear. She's moved on.

So what the hell am I doing here?

"What's in Arundel?"

She sighs. "A piece of art one of our clients commissioned for a party we're organizing."

"So you're not a valet girl."

Of course I know she isn't, but irritating her is the only way I can get her to talk to me.

"No, Sebastian. I'm not a valet girl. I work in the events department. Happy?" I sense her glare, and her annoyance fires up something in me. I can still push her buttons. Maybe not all is lost.

"How did that happen? I mean, I don't remember you ever showing interest in that kind of stuff."

I peer at Liv and find her staring at me through slits. "Lots of things can change in five years."

They sure can. While other things have remained the same, no matter how much I want them to be different. Like my feelings for her. I wish I could be free of them since I can no longer have her love, but it seems I'll be bound to Liv for all eternity. That's my punishment, to never stop loving the woman I left behind.

A minute passes before she speaks again.

"Why are you helping me, Sebastian?"

I can't tell her the truth. I can't tell Liv that being near her after all these years is as vital to me as air. She'll think I've lost my mind. And she'll be right.

"Who says I'm helping you? This is a public service. I don't want you causing an accident."

"Unbelievable. Are you only doing this to aggravate me? What's your damage?"

"I'm kidding. Gee, relax. I thought it would be nice to catch up. And I've always wanted to visit Arundel. I heard it's a very co—"

"Wait a second. You came to the Hollingsworth looking for me?"

I suck my lips in. I'm tempted to come up with a convoluted story, but fuck it, I'm tired of lying.

"Yes."

"Are you for real?"

"What?" I take my eyes off the road again only to be blasted by her furious glare. It makes me want to do things to her I have no business thinking about. Not when she's clearly with someone else and I have a girlfriend.

Gretchen. She doesn't deserve this. I guess I didn't leave the bastard from my anger phase behind after all. He's still alive and kicking.

Liv breaks our staring contest first. I turn my attention to the road, but I'm still reeling inside. The guilt I feel about Gretchen is smothered to death by the need to be near Liv, the need to hear her voice, even if she's telling me to go to hell. But she's not talking now. Her silence is heavy, a mountain between us. It doesn't deter me, though. The desire to know all I've missed in her life since I left Littleton surpasses everything, even my pride.

"So, how's your family?" I ask.

"They're fine," she answers without missing a beat, and I'm surprised. Happily surprised.

"When did Kimmy and Owen get hitched?"

"Last year." There's a pause, and I glance at her once more. A tiny smile appears on her lips. "They're pregnant. My niece or nephew will be here in December."

"Really? That's awesome. I hope it's a girl."

"Why?"

I grin at her. "Because Owen deserves the pain. I want to see him suffer when his daughter starts to date."

Liv's smile broadens and warmth floods my heart, knowing I put it there.

♡ ♡ ♡

never thought I would be thankful for bad weather and traffic, but I am. It takes us over two hours to reach Arundel, and in that time, I'm able to collect little pieces of Liv. Is it enough to satiate my hunger? Not by far. It only makes me want more. But there are things I'm not ready to know, will never be ready to know. Like who the limo guy was and how long it took for her to forget me, to forget *us*.

It's still pouring when we get to the art studio. Liv turns to me. "You can stay in the car."

"Nah, I'm curious."

There's a flash of apprehension in her eyes. "No, really. Stay. I'll be in and out in a flash."

I realize Liv isn't trying to be nice. She doesn't want me to go in for some reason. Is it the artwork she doesn't want me to see? That just piques my curiosity more.

I get out of the car and run for cover. A second later, Liv does the same. I wait for her just outside of the studio, under a tree. It doesn't do much to protect me from the rain. She pauses when she reaches me, her gaze connecting with mine. And I want to kiss her. Badly. I'm about to give in to the impulse when she walks around me and disappears inside.

I follow her in and am blasted with a mix of strong smells—

fresh paint and old, musty furniture. My nose itches and I fight the urge to sneeze. It's definitely not what I expected from an art studio. It looks more like a secondhand art supply shop with its narrow and overflowing rows of things I suspect an aspiring artist would need. To my left, the entire wall is dedicated to displaying different types of frames.

Liv walks toward the counter at the far end, and a few seconds later, an older man appears through a side door. "Can I help you?"

"Hi, my name is Olivia Dawson. I'm here on behalf of Miss Gretchen Smith to pick up the painting."

I freeze and grapple with what I just heard. *What. The. Fuck. Why is Liv running an errand for Gretchen?*

The man's gaze settles on me, and I see a glint of recognition in his eyes, but he can't possibly know who I am. He doesn't strike me as the type of guy who follows gossip magazines or listens to pop music.

"Very well. Follow me," he says and disappears again through the side door.

We do as he says and reach an open space that clearly serves as a storage room for his art. There are paintings spread out everywhere, most of them depicting classical portraits.

"I haven't had the chance to pack it up yet," the old man mumbles.

Liv stops in her tracks and turns to me. "Maybe you should stay here."

"Why?"

She bites her lower lip and looks down. "You aren't supposed to see this."

Oh, fuck. Now I have to see it. I walk around her and reach the art studio's owner in a few strides. He's standing next to a painting almost three feet high. For a split second, I wonder how in the world we'll fit that monstrosity in the car, but then I finally *see* the painting. I'm staring at a picture of Gretchen and me, dressed like we've just sprung from a

Jane Austen novel. It's the most atrocious thing I've ever seen.

Liv makes a strangled sound, and I look over my shoulder. She's covering her mouth with her hand, trying to suppress her laughter.

"I have no words," I say.

She finally lets go and her loud laugh echoes in the room. Liv's amusement is contagious, and soon I find myself laughing, too. What was in Gretchen's mind? And where did she think I would hang that thing?

The artist frowns at us, and that only makes us laugh harder.

"I'll go get the packing supplies," he grumbles.

After the giggles die down, I manage to ask her what the heck is going on.

"Gretchen hired our department to throw you a surprise birthday party at the Hollingsworth. And I'm assuming *that* is one of your gifts," she answers.

♡ ♡ ♡

LIV

"This will never fit. I say we leave it behind. I don't want it anyway," Sebastian whines.

"Shut up and help me." I wiggle the painting as I push it inside the trunk. I can see there's still plenty of room for it, but somehow it's sticking out of the car and won't move forward. One of the corners must've gotten stuck to something. I'm soaked to the bone trying to load Sebastian's stupid gift, and all he's doing is complaining.

Begrudgingly, he moves to the back seat of the Rover and begins to pull the painting toward him. I feel the mysterious resistance give way, and the piece of art finally slides all the way in. I remove my coat before I get into the car, as it's not doing anything besides freezing me to the core. The knit dress I'm wearing underneath is damp, but it's not like I can ride back into town wearing nothing more than my underwear.

I wriggle my hair and big droplets of water fall to the floor. I must look like a drowned rat now. Thank God I'm not wearing mascara today. Sebastian takes the driver seat and turns the heat up to the max. The jacket he was wearing before is gone, and the long-sleeved shirt he has on makes me want to straddle him and find out if his kiss is still as incendiary as before.

I look away. I have no business feeling this way. Just because we can still get along perfectly as if time hasn't gone by doesn't mean I can forget all the hurt he inflicted.

We drive in silence for about thirty minutes, and in that time, I think about all the strong female heroines I admire. I can feel myself being sucked into the vortex that is Sebastian, and I can't allow that to happen. I want to kill the butterflies going nuts in my belly. I imagine what Scarlett O'Hara or Faith from *Buffy* would do. Neither of them would sit quietly next to the boy who destroyed their hearts without an explanation.

"Why did you leave?" My voice is weak, almost a whisper. *So much for being strong.*

"Excuse me?"

I take a deep breath and try again, with more conviction this time. "Why did you leave me without a word? Did I mean so little to you?"

Sebastian doesn't answer right away, and I peer at this profile. His jaw is clenched, and if I could look into his eyes, I bet I would see a storm brewing there. His reaction fires up my veins. He has no right to be upset at my question. My eyes begin to burn and I look out the window, fighting the angry tears.

"Your silence says it all," I say.

"Don't talk about things you don't understand."

I whip around to face him again. "I would if you explained them to me."

"It doesn't matter right now, does it? You've moved on, I've moved on. Let's leave the past in the past."

"When did you become such a coward?"

My phone rings before he can reply. I pick it up and see Ryan's name flashing on the screen. Perfect timing.

"Hi, Ryan." I force a smile to my lips even though all I want to do is cry. But hell if I'm going to do that in front of Sebastian.

"Lunch tomorrow sounds perfect. I can't wait to see you." I put an extra layer of sugar in my voice.

I can feel Sebastian glaring at me. A real smile unfurls this time, an ugly one that has nothing to do with being happy. Without glancing his way, I say, "Better watch the road, Sebastian."

CHAPTER 28
LIV

Sebastian didn't say a word to me after Ryan's call. We made the two-hour trip back wrapped in a smothering silence. As soon as we stopped in front of the Hollingsworth, he scrambled out of the car and disappeared inside a cab that had just dropped off some guests. He didn't say goodbye this time either.

Watching him leave like that left me feeling small, insignificant, crushed. I cried myself to sleep last night. I'm not the heroine of the story, just the dumb blonde who gets killed in the first scene of a slasher movie. I can't tell Saylor or anyone else about this last encounter. I'm too ashamed that I let Sebastian trample all over my heart again.

Ryan is supposed to pick me up for lunch at noon, and now I regret agreeing to the idea. I haven't had the chance to tell Lloyd yet. I don't want him to get the wrong impression.

I'm finishing up compiling a list of flower suppliers when Mellie comes into the office and collapses into her chair.

"I'm beat. I need a cig and a drink."

"Already? It's only Tuesday," I tease, knowing how hard she's been working these past few weeks.

"I know. I'll look like a zombie on Saturday. Oh, you're helping by the way. No need to thank me."

I glance at her and she's grinning.

"What?" I squeak.

"You'll be stationed at the greeting table, making sure only people on the list get in. You'll meet a ton of celebrities. We usually hire models for such occasions, but Patsy didn't think Gretchen would like that idea, so I suggested you and Lloyd. He's over the moon, of course."

My jaw drops and my brain can't come up with anything to say.

Mellie doesn't notice my panicked expression. "Oh, are you free for dinner tomorrow at my house? I know I've postponed that a million times, but I think we deserve a break. Simon, the darling he is, offered to cook. Lloyd is coming, too."

At that precise moment, Ryan arrives. Mellie's eyes follow him as he strides to my desk. Even wearing simple faded jeans and a sweater, he looks scrumptious.

"Hi, Liv. Are you ready?"

"Yeah, just give me a second."

"Hello there. I don't think we've met." Mellie stands up and walks toward him.

"Oh, Mellie, this is Ryan. He works at Ocean Grill. He's also an intern."

They shake hands, and then Mellie turns to me with a gleam in her eyes. She mouths, "Hot," and I have to fight the urge to giggle. She's nuts.

She turns to him again, "Say, Ryan, are you free tomorrow night? I'm throwing a small dinner party and invited Liv. You're more than welcome to join."

I freeze as my gaze darts between Ryan and Mellie. *Say no, Ryan. Say no.*

"Yeah, I'm free. I would love to come."

I'm face-palming in my head. *Disaster.* Maybe he'll change his mind when I tell him that Lloyd will be there, too.

"Shall we?" I say.

♡ ♡ ♡

Ryan doesn't seem to care that Lloyd will be at the dinner party. I actually see a spark of excitement in his eyes when I tell him. So in the end, he does come, and we arrive together. It looks like he's my date, and that's exactly what Mellie's friends think.

Lloyd knows what's going on. I cornered him earlier at the office and explained the whole thing. He didn't seem to mind that Mellie assumes Ryan is my boyfriend. He was more focused on the fact that he would see Ryan, since they haven't hung out since the pub incident. Once again, I'm sucked into their love drama.

Mellie and her boyfriend, Simon, share a two-bedroom apartment in Kensal Rise. Lloyd was quick to point out that it's one of the coolest neighborhoods in London and that the likes of Daniel Craig, Lily Allen, and Sienna Miller live there. When I teasingly asked if Daniel Craig was Mellie's neighbor, Lloyd gave me a droll look.

Mellie answers the door, and before we even cross the threshold, she hands us a glass of prosecco. A most exquisite smell hits my nose, and my mouth begins to water. It's an open floor apartment, and I can see Simon in the kitchen from where I stand, cooking something obviously delicious by the aroma alone.

I take in my surroundings. Mellie's living room has rich, dark floors that contrast nicely with the white walls and offer the perfect canvas for the colorful furniture in bright turquoise and hot pink. The couch is a conversation piece, as the fabric depicts the British flag. The built-in shelving has a lime green backsplash and the chandelier is also hot pink, adding more pop to the living room. I love it. It's so Mellie.

She introduces us to the couple sitting on the couch, her neighbors Marcia and Harold. *Darn, no Daniel Craig.* Marcia stares openly at Ryan, and when he shakes her hand, she blushes like a little girl. *Good Lord, is anyone immune to his charms?*

The doorbell rings again, and a second later, Lloyd bursts through the door, not waiting for Mellie to open it.

"Good evening, ladies and gentlemen," he greets us all with an overly enthusiastic tone.

Ryan's entire demeanor changes, and now that I know about his feelings toward Lloyd, I can see the signs clearly. He likes Lloyd, *a lot,* more than he wants to admit to himself. I notice Lloyd has brought someone with him, a guy with curly brown hair and striking light green eyes. He's shorter than Lloyd and stocky but attractive in a rugged way. He holds no candle to Ryan, but it doesn't really matter. Ryan is looking at Lloyd's date like he wants to throttle him.

Go, Lloyd.

Lloyd eyes the prosecco glasses and takes two. He gives one to his date. "Here, honey."

Lloyd's date glares at him, and alarm bells sound in my head. *What's he up to?*

"Aren't you going to introduce your friend?" Ryan says.

"Oh, of course. Where are my manners? This is Maurice. We went to uni together."

Marcia and Harold say hello, and I do the same. I don't like when Maurice looks me up and down, like he's checking me out. Suspicion begins to nag at me. Before Lloyd can say anything else, I lace my arm with his and say, "Lloyd, I need to ask you something about our VIP project."

I drag him to a corner of the living room and whisper in his ear. "Want to explain what's going on?"

"I don't follow."

"Bullshit. Is Maurice really your date?"

"Fine," he grumbles. "He's not, okay? He's one of my mates from school. He agreed to pretend to be my date so he could meet you."

I pinch the bridge of my nose and close my eyes for a split second. "What did you promise him, Lloyd?"

Lloyd sucks his lips in and guilt flashes in his eyes.

"Did you say I would go out with him?" I continue.

"Maybe."

"Lloyd, I'm gonna kill you," I say through clenched teeth.

"Hey, what are you two gossiping about?" Mellie approaches us.

"Nothing. I was just asking Liv what she's going to wear for Gretchen's party," Lloyd says.

"Oh, Liv. Tell me you don't have a dress. I want an excuse to buy a new one. We could go shopping together."

"Hey, if you're going shopping, I'm coming, too," Lloyd says. "I could use a new suit."

Simon appears out of nowhere and embraces Mellie from behind, resting his chin on her shoulder. "Hey, no work talk during dinner. You promised."

Mellie melts into his arms, and I'm hit with a pang of jealousy. I want that in my life. A stupid voice in my head tells me I could've had it with Derek, but I stomp on it until it dies.

"We're not talking shop. We're talking shop*ping*," Mellie says.

"Even worse." Simon glances my way. "Hi, you must be Liv."

"Nice to meet you, Simon. I've heard so much about you. Your food smells divine."

"I hope it tastes good, too," he replies.

Mellie rolls her eyes. "He's being modest. Simon's cooking is out of this world. You'll see."

We make our way back to the living room, where Marcia and Harold seem to be doing their best to entertain Ryan and Maurice. They're sitting opposite each other, and by their body postures, they're ready for a duel.

"Dinner is served," Simon announces.

Ryan sits next to me and opposite Lloyd, which means Maurice is in front of me. He's not even pretending he's gay. Several times I catch him staring at my cleavage. If Ryan wasn't so busy trying not to look at Lloyd, he would've noticed that Maurice is a fraud.

There's no way in hell I'm going out with him.

I take a bite of the shrimp and almost have a foodgasm. I actually moan out loud.

Mellie smirks at me. "What did I tell you?"

"Oh my God. This is the best thing I've ever eaten in my life, and I'm not even a Thai food fan."

"I'm glad you like it." Simon chuckles.

The dinner goes smoothly, and an hour later, Marcia and Harold bid us goodbye. Simon yawns, and I take that as my cue to leave as well. But Lloyd and Mellie have other ideas.

"I'm not ready to go to bed yet. Let's go the pub across the street," Mellie says.

"Sorry, hon, I'm exhausted," Simon tells her. "I have an important meeting first thing in the morning."

Mellie pouts. "You're no fun. But I love you just the same." She leans in and places a soft kiss on Simon's lips.

I would much rather go home, but Ryan is game for the pub and so is Lloyd. I promise myself that I'll stay for only an hour. If Ryan wants to stay after that, then he's on his own.

It's past 9:00 p.m., and the pub is mostly empty. We grab a round booth, and somehow I get sandwiched between Mellie and Maurice. Lloyd and Ryan sit respectively at the ends of the bench. We order a pitcher of beer, and the conversation veers mostly toward work. I kinda feel bad for Maurice, since he has no clue what we're talking about.

That is until he puts his hand on my leg.

I freeze for a second before I remove his offensive appendage from my thigh. I try to scooch closer to Mellie, but there isn't much room.

"So, Liv, how do you like London so far?" Maurice asks, unfazed by what just happened. How Lloyd is friends with him is beyond me. He's a first-class douche.

"I love it." I don't make eye contact and take a sip of my drink.

He leans closer and whispers in my ear. "Fuck, you're hotter than I expected. I can't wait to nail you."

I choke on my beer, and all eyes on the table are now on me. After I recover, I turn to Maurice. "Excuse me?"

He pulls back from my personal space and then glares at Lloyd. I do the same.

"What's the matter?" Mellie asks.

"I gotta go." My tone is urgent and leaves no room for arguments.

Ryan and Mellie get up so I can do the same. I practically march out of the pub, but the cool evening air does little to calm my irritation.

A minute later, Lloyd comes after me.

"Liv, I'm sorry."

I whirl on him. "You should be. Your friend is an asshole. How could you set me up like that, Lloyd?"

"I wasn't thinking."

I cross my arms in front of my chest and clench my jaw. Lloyd is giving me the lost puppy look, and it's freaking working. My anger begins to dissipate. I know what it's like to be in love like that. Craziness is part of the deal.

Ryan comes outside to check on me. "What just happened in there?"

I throw my hands up in the air. "You know what? I'm sick of you guys dragging me into your messed-up relationship. Ryan, stop giving people the impression that you're into me. Lloyd, stop setting me up with your friends. And lastly, fucking kiss and make up already! The sexual tension at dinner was giving me hot flashes, and I'm way too young for that."

Ryan and Lloyd stare at me like I've lost my mind.

Maybe I have.

CHAPTER 29
LIV

I ignore Lloyd the next day at the office. I'm back to being mad at him. Just thinking that Lloyd told his friend I would sleep with him makes my blood boil. Lloyd keeps sending me instant messages that I promptly close without reading. I'm glad my don't-mess-with-me body language is enough to ward off any attempt at actual conversation.

Mellie is working off-site today, so I don't have to answer her questions. I'm not sure I can be honest with her without revealing Lloyd and Ryan's secret.

When I get back from my lunch break, I find a box of chocolates on my desk with a simple note saying "Sorry" in Lloyd's handwriting. He doesn't come back to the office that afternoon, so I guess he's also out running an errand for Saturday's party. If Lloyd thinks a box of chocolates will be enough for me to forgive him, he's probably right. *Stupid boy and his shenanigans.*

At 6:00 p.m., I shut down my computer and make my way back to my room, carrying Lloyd's chocolates with me. I'm not in the mood to hit the grocery store or eat out, so chocolates for dinner it'll be. I search for the key inside my giant hobo bag as I exit the elevator, and like always, I can't find it. Every time this happens, I swear I'll switch my stuff to a smaller bag, but I never do.

I'm still moving shit around inside the giant black hole, looking for the damn key, as I round the corner toward my room. The box of chocolates is under my arm now, hindering my movements. I'm not paying attention to where I'm going, but it's not like I run the risk of bumping into someone.

I finally find the little sucker, and when I look up again, Sebastian is in front of me. I stop dead in my tracks. His hands are shoved inside his jeans pockets, and he's looking at me like there are a million things he wants to say.

I'm speechless for a moment, getting lost inside his warm gaze. Just as easily as five years ago, he's reeling me in, and I hate how weak he makes me. I summon the irritation I've felt all day and aim it at him.

"What are you doing here?"

"Hi, Liv."

I narrow my eyes before I stride toward my door. I have it down to a routine—insert, turn, hip bump, and the door unlocks. I ignore Sebastian and how close his body is to mine. His heady cologne is all I can smell. It gives me goose bumps and makes my heart pound away. I don't look at him, even though I'm dying to. *Stay strong, Liv. You can do it.*

"Is it a bad time?" Sebastian asks.

I turn around with every intention of closing the door in his face, but he's already inside.

"What do you think you're doing?" I shuffle back, not trusting myself if we get too close again.

"Paying you a visit." He shrugs, then looks around. "Boy, this room is a broom closet."

"How did you know where I lived?"

He faces me with a mysterious grin on his lips. "I have my ways."

I drop my bag and the chocolates on my bed. "Listen, Sebastian. I've had a long day, and I'm exhausted. I'm not really in the mood to… I don't even know what this is."

"Have you eaten already?"

"What?"

"Food. Are you hungry?"

"No." My stomach decides to rumble just then, giving me away. *Why does my body always betray me?*

Sebastian smiles. "Have dinner with me."

I stare at him, trying to figure out what kind of game he's playing. "Is this a joke?"

"I'm hungry, you're hungry. What's the big deal?"

"What's the big deal?" My voice rises to a shrill shout, and Sebastian winces. "You have some nerve! I gave you the chance to explain why you acted like the biggest asshole on the face of the earth, but did you take it? Noooo. That's fine, though. I was willing to forget everything you've done to me because I didn't want to be one of those girls who holds a grudge forever. But you're seriously asking for it. Let's start from the beginning, shall we? First, you abandoned me five years ago without so much as a goodbye."

Sebastian opens his mouth to interrupt me, but I continue. "I know the circumstances were awful and you were in a very dark place, but I didn't deserve that. Second, you cut all ties you had with me, never answered any of my emails, never called. You could've been dead and I wouldn't have known. And finally, let's not forget the lie you told millions of people about a girl from high school who was cyber-stalking you. That was really the cherry on top of the cake."

Sebastian stares at me with eyebrows raised and mouth open. After my spiel, I'm out of breath.

"I guess it's a no to dinner, then," he finally says.

"It's a hell no."

He raises his hands. "Okay, okay. I'm leaving."

On the way out, he stops and turns to me again. "Before I

forget, I don't want you calling the authorities when you bump into me again at the hotel. I'm not stalking you. I'm staying at the Hollingsworth. *Indefinitely.*"

CHAPTER 30
SEBASTIAN

"Come on, guys. Let's try this again from the top. Five, six, seven, eight," Zawe, our choreographer, commands, and our newest song, "Feel This Night," blasts through the speakers.

I've gotten better at dancing, but do not expect me to perform any complicated routine while I sing. And this particular set of steps is making me dizzy already. I turn the wrong away for the thousandth time and smash into Anthony. The music stops, and everyone in the room, besides Oliver, is glaring at me.

"For fuck's sake, Coleman. Stop messing this shit around. I don't wanna be here the entire night," Kyle says, and I flip him off.

"Wanker," he spits back.

"All right, all right. Let's try this tomorrow. We're not getting anywhere here. Sebastian, you'll stay. I'll run the routine with you again."

Fuuuck. I so do not want to be here right now. I grind my jaw and look at Zawe, knowing very well that my glare won't intimidate her. She's the toughest lady in the business and can bust anyone's balls, including mine. I should be thanking her that she's willing to work later than usual to help me, but it's not only my lack of coordination that's the problem here. I can't stop thinking about Liv. All I want to do is go back to the Hollingsworth and stalk her some more.

After our trip to Arundel, clarity came over me. I want Liv back in my life, not only as a friend but as everything she used to be. The fact that so far, the only thing I've accomplished is to make her hate me more is driving me insane. She wants an explanation I can't give her. If I tell her that I partially blamed her for what happened to my parents, I'll lose her forever.

Oliver slaps my shoulder. "Good luck, mate. Call me when you're done. We'll do something."

After everyone leaves the dance studio, Zawe pierces me with a knowing gaze. I don't like how she's scrutinizing me.

"Are we doing this or what?" I say, letting the irritation seep into my tone.

"Are you familiar with Einstein's definition of insanity?"

"Yeah…."

"Well, do I look insane to you?"

I clench my jaw, bracing myself for a chiding. I've seen Zawe go off on Kyle, Travis, and even Hans before. Not pretty.

"I know everyone has problems, Sebastian. But to let them interfere with your professional life is disrespectful to your colleagues and unacceptable. You need to get your head straight."

I begin pacing as frustration runs freely through my veins. "Don't you think I want that? But I can't sleep. I can't eat. I can't concentrate on anything else besides her."

"You mean Gretchen?"

I turn to face Zawe. She has an eyebrow raised. She knows I'm not talking about my girlfriend. "No."

Before I can stop myself, I'm spilling my guts to Zawe. I tell her everything, not leaving any gruesome detail out. She doesn't interrupt me once, and her facial expression doesn't morph into a disgusted, or worse, pitying look.

I feel ten times lighter after I'm done but not in the least bit better. I still don't know what to do.

"You know what you need, Sebastian? To grow a fucking vagina."

"What?"

"I'm quoting Betty White here. Wise lady. Stop acting like a coward. Be honest with the girl you love. The way I see it, you can't lose."

"Didn't you hear what I just said? She'll never forgive me if tell her the truth."

Zawe raises an eyebrow and puts her hands on her hips. "Do you have her now?"

I stare dumbfounded at my choreographer. She's fucking right. I don't have Liv, so there isn't anything to lose.

"Now, let's run this routine one more time, and then I'm calling it a day," Zawe says.

We practice for another hour, and by the end of it, I manage to finish the routine without messing up. When I leave the rehearsal studio, I don't call Oliver. I don't even go back to the Hollingsworth. I go home instead. I'm still thinking about Zawe's advice, but I need to take care of something first before I even attempt to contact Liv again.

At home, I make a beeline for my stash of drugs. I haven't done anything stronger than smoking pot and drinking since I started going out with Gretchen, but I wasn't able to throw my supply away. Darkness still threatens to take hold of me now and then, and getting high is the only weapon I have. But no more. I take them with me to the bathroom, lift the toilet lid, and flip the box over, dumping its contents into the bowl. There's no hesitation when I push the lever down and watch a junkie's amusement park being flushed down the drain. It's easy, so very easy. And I know why.

The next step will be harder. I'll hurt someone I care about, but it has to be done. I can't string Gretchen along when I'll never be able to give my heart to her. Life was easier when I could just use girls and discard them without a shred of guilt, but I'm not that person anymore. I was never that person. I'd been taken over by a monster.

I only have to pretend for one more night. I can't break up with Gretchen when she put so much work into preparing a surprise birthday party for me. It would be unnecessarily cruel to humiliate her like that.

But once I'm free, Liv better prepare herself, because I'm coming at her with the entire arsenal I have. I'm winning her back, no matter what.

CHAPTER 31
LIV

Mellie, Lloyd, and I manage to find time to go shopping on Friday after work, and we head straight to Selfridges. I'm on a budget, so I search the sale rack first. I find an awesome vintage dress a la Marilyn Monroe with a plunging neckline and bare back. The fabric is fluid and has metallic thread interwoven in it, making it shimmer as I move. It's gorgeous. I try it on, and Mellie and Lloyd say the dress was made for me. It fits like a glove.

After they find their outfits, we stop by the store's champagne and oyster bar to unwind. Mellie finally broaches my freak-out at the pub from two nights ago.

"You better ask Lloyd what happened." I nod in his direction.

Lloyd glances at the table and plays with his flute of champagne. "Maurice wasn't my date."

Mellie looks from Lloyd to me, her eyebrows furrowed in confusion. "I don't understand."

"I kind of told him that if he pretended to be my date for the evening, I would set him up with Liv."

"Why?"

"Oh gosh, Lloyd. Spill it already," I say.

"Because I wanted to make Ryan jealous."

Mellie's jaw drops and her eyes widen. "Ryan? Oh, Lloyd. But he's straight."

She sees the expression on my face and continues. "He's straight, right?"

"Not anymore," I answer.

"Holy fuck! I cannot believe it. My gaydar has never failed before." She turns to Lloyd. "Are you hooking up with him?"

"A few times, but I'm not sure if I will anymore. He's completely closeted."

Mellie reaches over and squeezes Lloyd's hand. "Oh, honey. I'm sorry. But what did Maurice do to you, Liv? You were pissed when you left the pub."

"Ugh. He thought it was okay to cop a feel, and then he said he couldn't wait to nail me."

"What an asshole!" Mellie says.

I pierce Lloyd with my laser stare. "Which makes me think Lloyd might have given Maurice a very wrong idea. What exactly did you tell him, Lloyd?"

"I can't tell you. You'll hate me."

I roll my eyes. "Stop with the drama. I'm not going to hate you, unless you told him he could have me as his sex slave."

"I may have told him that you were an exchange student looking to have some fun in Europe."

"Oh, for fuck's sake, Lloyd! That's totally code for saying she wants to sleep around. You're the asshole." Mellie glares at him.

I rest my head in my hands. That explains a lot.

We don't linger at the bar since we have a big day ahead of us tomorrow. I take the tube back to the Hollingsworth and try my best not to let nerves get the best of me. I haven't seen Sebastian since he paid me a visit, but I couldn't stop thinking about his parting comment. For two days straight, I've kept looking over my shoulder, dreading and also hoping to see him. It's been exhausting. But tomorrow there's no doubt that I'll see him again in the arms of his gorgeous girlfriend. I wish I could find a way to dress my heart in armor to protect it from being mangled further. It's going to happen, and it'll be a bloodbath.

I don't sleep well that night, tossing and turning, replaying every single encounter I've had with Sebastian since he crashed back into my life. I can't begin to imagine what's going on in his head. Maybe if I knew, I could prepare my defenses better.

Morning comes whether I've slept or not, and I feel ragged. I volunteered to help set up for the party as a way to get it into my thick head that my world and Sebastian's will never mesh again.

When I arrive at the Venetian ballroom, Mellie and Lloyd are already there. They're huddled together, peering at something on one of the tables by the door. When I get closer, I see it's Lloyd's final design of the décor.

It's an ice rink.

And so it begins, the slow decimation of my heart.

♡ ♡ ♡

The first thing I see as I enter the transformed ballroom is the massive ice sculpture of a hockey player. It bears a vague resemblance to Sebastian. What's with this girl and her obsession with capturing him in different art mediums?

Because I knew what to expect, the pain isn't as acute anymore. It was the right move to help set up for the party.

I walk across the room and find Pasty speaking with the head of the waitstaff. She turns her attention to me.

"Liv, darling. I'm sure Mellie has already told you that you'll be stationed at the entrance, where you'll make sure only guests on the list are granted access to the party. Lloyd will help you, and security will be there as well. This is a very coveted event, and make no mistake, there will be plenty of people trying to sneak in."

She gives me an earpiece and shows me how to use it before she dismisses me. I make my way to the reception table and find

Lloyd standing next to it. He glances my way when he realizes I'm there, then grabs my arm and squeezes it.

"Oh my God, Liv. Isn't this exciting? Do you know how many celebrities we'll get to see tonight?"

"I can't imagine."

"Tons, that's how many. Too bad we aren't allowed to take pictures. My Instagram account would blow up if I could post pics of tonight. Oh well, I guess I'll have to rely on my memory alone."

Guests start to arrive in small groups at first, but when the clock hits eleven, that's when the flood comes. Patsy was right, we have to turn away several people who aren't on the list of invitees. The stories some of them come up with are so convoluted that it's hard to keep a straight face.

When we catch a break, Lloyd leans closer to me and whispers in my ear. "Do you know how hard it is to keep laughter bottled up? I swear I'm getting a workout."

I smile. "I know, right? I'll end up with abs of steel by the end of the night."

"Oh, posh alert. That couple is definitely on the list. The guy is the son of a wealthy banker."

"What about her?"

Lloyd shrugs. "Probably a high-class hooker."

I have to swallow my shocked gasp and plaster a smile on my face as the aforementioned couple hits our table. Wallace Kirkpatrick the Third is definitely on the list. I tap next to his name on the tablet, and they're off.

I decide to see how many people we can still expect. The room is already busy, and the music is blending in with the cacophony of voices. My gaze is down when I hear Lloyd slip a "Holy shit" under his breath. I look up and recognize the tall blond with the wicked blue eyes I met at Dijng— Oliver, Sebastian's bandmate. His eyes light up when he recognizes me.

"I can't believe it. It's Unicorn!"

From my periphery, I see Lloyd glance my way. He's probably confused as hell. I never told him that I met the guys from Boys Future and Onno when I went out with Ryan. I didn't want to give him another reason to be jealous.

Blondie is flanked by the twins, Kyle and Travis. I know all of their names now thanks to the report I had to write on Sebastian, Gretchen, and Boys Future. Such useless information taking up space in my brain.

"What are your names, gentlemen?" I ask, not disguising that I know who they are and I'm totally faking ignorance on purpose.

One of the twins turns to Anthony, the fifth member of Boys Future. "This is bollocks. She knows who we are."

"Don't mind Liv. She's just being extra careful. You know how Americans can be. Enjoy the party," Lloyd says, probably thinking I've lost my mind.

Oliver chuckles as he passes me. "See you later, Liv."

Once they're out of earshot, Lloyd is in my face. "What was that all about? Have you met them before?"

"Yeah. Remember that night I went to Dijng with Ryan, Yoann, Gavin, and Renata? Well, Ryan and I met Onno and those guys there."

Lloyd is staring at me with eyes as round as saucers, speechless for a change. When he finally remembers he has vocal cords, he whisper-screams, "Biotch! I can't believe you never told me that story. Did you meet Sebastian, too?"

I feel guilty that I never told him about the VIP room and even guiltier about the secret I vowed not to tell anyone here. But I have the feeling that the truth is about to explode in my face. I'd rather Lloyd find out from me. He'll hate me if I don't tell him that Sebastian and I used to be next-door neighbors, though I'm not sure yet if I want to disclose the rest.

But I know now it's not the time. We're working, and there are way too many people around who can overhear our conversation.

"Yes, he was there."

"Is he as good-looking in person as he is on TV?"

"No."

Lloyd deflates like a balloon. "*No?*"

"He's something else in person. You'll see."

Lloyd smirks at me. "I knew you weren't immune to some fangirling. Sebastian Coleman, huh? He's the one who rocks your boat?"

I face forward so Lloyd can't read the truth in my eyes. He has no idea.

I hear Mellie's voice through the earpiece. She needs me at the main bar. I tell Lloyd and ask if he'll be okay.

"I can manage," he says.

When I reach Mellie, she's talking in urgent tones with one of the waiters.

"What's the matter, Mellie?" I ask.

"Liv, do you have any experience waitressing?"

"Uh, no. Why?"

"Bollocks." She chews on her lower lip and drops her gaze to the ground. After a few seconds, her eyes connect with mine again. "Can you hold a tray without spilling stuff all over?"

"I guess so."

"Okay, please don't hate me, but I need you serve drinks to the guests. There was a situation a few minutes ago, and we had to fire three of our waiters. We're short staffed now."

"What happened?"

"I can't explain now. I need you to cover for at least half an hour until I can get some waitstaff from the restaurants."

"Sure, no problem."

Mellie gives me a tray full of shot glasses with purple liquid inside. "Cover the right side of the room, smile, be pleasant, but don't engage in any lengthy conversations. Come back when your tray is empty."

"Okay."

I should be freaking out right now, but oddly I'm not. Serving drinks isn't that bad, and it gives me something to occupy my mind. I just have to avoid Sebastian, his girlfriend, and his stupid bandmates. Easy-peasy.

I turn around and almost collide with a waiter who's trying to get behind the bar. The tray in my hand wobbles perilously, and I have to hold it with both hands to avoid a disaster. *Shit*. I glance at Mellie and she's shaking her head.

"Don't worry. I've got this."

Maybe.

CHAPTER 32
SEBASTIAN

haven't had a drink in twenty-four hours, and my body has noticed. Giving up hard-core drugs was easy for me, but alcohol? That's a different story.

I'm not in a good mood, and if it weren't for the possibility that I might see Liv tonight, I wouldn't have come. I'm inside a limo with Gretchen sitting across from me, looking like a Botticelli painting. Her white Grecian-style dress hugs her in all the right places, and her hair is braided into an elaborate do. She's sipping a glass of champagne and her posture is rigid. The few times I managed to catch her eyes, she averted her gaze. She's noticed the change in me, the change between us. Since Liv came blasting into my life again, I've been distant and hanging out with Oliver way too much. Which means a lot of partying and boozing.

I'm itching to pour myself a generous dose of whiskey, but I don't want to get hammered tonight. If Liv is there and I lose control, I won't be able to keep my hands to myself. I might kidnap her, keep her captive until she agrees to give me another chance.

Actually, that doesn't sound like a bad idea.

Gretchen's ploy to get me to the Hollingsworth is a private

dinner prepared by the renowned Ocean Grill chef. The limo stops in front of the luxurious hotel, and not a second later, the door is opened by a valet. There are a few paparazzi waiting for us, and by the low number of them, I know those were the selected few Hans handpicked. He'll dictate which shots will make it to the tabloids.

We turn heads as we enter the hotel's grand foyer. Out of the corner of my eye, I see some people take out their phones to snap pictures of us.

When the elevator's doors open on our floor, Gretchen laces her arm with mine and gives me a tight smile that doesn't reach her eyes. Can she sense that this will be our last public appearance together?

The door to the ballroom is closed. I push it open and prepare to make a surprised face. A hundred faceless people shout, "Happy birthday," as Gretchen and I come into the space. I'm soon swarmed by well-wishers, their voices blending together. My eyes dart around the room, looking for Liv, but it's too dark and crowded to see beyond a few feet.

I feel a tug on my sleeve and glance sideways. I forgot about Gretchen. She's smiling like she means it this time.

"Happy birthday, Bas." She gets onto the tips of her toes to kiss me. I'm surprised when her tongue darts into my mouth, even if briefly. I pull back, not comfortable with the situation at all. I don't want Liv to see this if she's here.

A waiter comes by carrying a tray with shots. It's not whiskey, but hell, I'm not about to be picky now. I grab two glasses and gulp them down like they're water. It's a disgusting fruity thing disguised as alcohol, but it helps.

"Bas, easy now. You don't want to get pissed tonight, right?"

I give her a droll look. "I thought this was a birthday party. *My* birthday party."

"I know, but there are important people here, friends of my parents. I don't want to be embarrassed."

I don't know where this is coming from. Gretchen was never

one to police me about my drinking in public like that. She was more about the subtle hints. Clearly not tonight. Her comment only makes me more irritated.

"I didn't ask you to invite them. Now, if you'll excuse me, I gotta mingle. I'm the man of the hour, after all."

♡ ♡ ♡

LIV

My heart is squeezed so tight, it's almost impossible to breathe. That kiss between them… I wish I could banish it from my mind, but I know it's branded there forever. I have a job to do, though, so I put on my fake smile and pretend I'm not dying inside.

I cover my side of the room, not paying attention to my surroundings. I'm so focused on keeping my happy façade up that I don't notice I'm headed straight to Travis and Kyle. They see me before I can change course. If I turn around now, it'll show I'm bothered by their presence. I don't want to give those idiots that kind of power, so I square my shoulders and cross the remaining distance between us.

"Drinks, gentlemen?"

They look me up and down, undressing me with their eyes. I bite the inside of my cheek to control my temper.

"It seems Unicorn has many talents. I wonder what else she can do," one of them says. I can't tell them apart.

"Shut up, Kyle." Oliver comes out of nowhere and stops by my side. "Don't pay any attention to their juvenile remarks. Their mental development got stuck in prepubescence. It's a condition I'm afraid there's no cure for."

"What a tragedy. For society, I mean."

Blondie smiles at me. "I'm Oliver, by the way, but you can call me Ollie."

"Nice to meet you. So, drinks?" I need to get out of here.

Oliver looks at the tray with suspicion, then at me. "I don't know. What is it?"

"I haven't the faintest idea. I'm just assisting with the drinks until extra help arrives. We're short staffed."

"I'm not sure you were supposed to tell us that." He laughs.

"I guess not."

"Well, there's no harm in trying. What doesn't kill you makes you stronger, right?"

"Hey, I think Unicorn should take a shot with us," Kyle says as he puts his arm around my shoulders. I tense up immediately.

"Take your paws off her, Kyle. *Now,*" Sebastian says from behind us.

Kyle takes a step back. "I was just being nice to a fan."

Sebastian steps between Kyle and me, using his body as a shield.

"Bas, have a drink with us," Oliver says, trying to diffuse the tension. At least, I think that's what he's doing.

Sebastian finally glances my way. His eyes seem to be on fire, and they ignite a spark in the pit of my stomach.

"Only if Liv drinks with us," he says.

"I can't. I'm working."

"Bullshit. It's my birthday, and I'll take it as a personal offense if you refuse."

I glare at him.

"Oh, you better do what he says, Unicorn," Oliver says. "Bas always gets what he wants."

I'm beyond furious at him for putting me in this awkward situation. I don't want to get in trouble.

I glance over my shoulder and don't see either Patsy or Mellie. Oliver's right, Sebastian always gets what he wants. Drat. At this point, I need a drink.

"Fine," I say.

Sebastian takes the tray from my hand and places it on the high table next to him. He picks up two shot glasses and offers me one. When my fingers brush his, the little spark in my stomach turns into a bright flame. I hold my breath and peer into his eyes. He feels it, too.

"All right. To Sebastian!" Oliver raises his glass and throws his head back, downing the shot in a single gulp.

I bring the glass to my lips and do the same without taking my eyes off Sebastian's. It's a terrible idea, but I can't look away. The shot is some kind of grape-flavored vodka. It's not the best thing I've drunk in my life, but it's enough to get rid of my uneasiness.

Sebastian and I are still locked in a battle of heated staring when his girlfriend materializes by his side.

"Hello, darling. Having a good time?"

He blinks and looks at Gretchen. "Yeah, sure."

She turns to me, her eyes doing a quick scan as her smile tightens. "Hi there. I don't think we've met. I'm Gretchen, and you are...."

"She's Unicorn," Kyle is happy to supply.

"Excuse me?" Gretchen frowns.

"Never mind Kyle. He's drunk." Sebastian's irritation is clear in his voice, and Gretchen twists her face into an angry scowl.

Okay, it's time to leave.

I take a step forward to retrieve the tray and resume my rounds.

"You work here?" Gretchen's tone becomes icy as she shoots daggers at me with her eyes.

"Yes."

"I was told there would be no mingling between my guests and staff. This is unacceptable."

I don't know what to say. She's right. She can get me fired if she wants to.

"Will you chill out, Gretchen? She wasn't mingling with anybody. I practically forced her to take a shot with us," Sebastian says.

She narrows her eyes at him. "Why?"

"Why not?" Sebastian spits back, and the tension around us

becomes unbearable. I don't want to witness their lovers' quarrel.

I take that opportunity to grab my tray and leave before Gretchen decides to complain about me.

When I make it back to the bar, Mellie tells me reinforcements have arrived. Good, because I was about to give her an excuse not to go back there. I'm ready to return to the security of my room, where I don't have to shield my eyes from hurtful sights.

She pulls me aside and hands me a glass of champagne.

"Aren't we going to get in trouble for drinking during the job?" I ask.

"Hell no. Besides, you don't need to help at the greeting table anymore. All the guests have arrived, so you're off duty. Enjoy the party."

Patsy joins us and I freeze for a second. She eyes the champagne flute in my hand and grabs one for herself.

"This party is a total hit, don't you think?" She practically inhales the champagne and then puts the empty glass back on the bar counter. "Gotta go mingle, see if I can get more business for the hotel. Later, girls."

And just like that she's gone.

"Does she ever stop to breathe?" I ask.

"No, never. I seriously don't know how she does it. You know she has four kids under the age of six, right?"

"No, I didn't know that."

"Yeah, and she's a terrific mom. Completely dedicated. I seriously don't think she sleeps. *Ever.*"

Mellie leaves me alone with my thoughts and my drink. I move out of the way to a dark corner near the bar, planning to finish the champagne and get out of here.

"Hey, Liv. I didn't know you'd be working tonight."

My gaze snaps up, and I see Ryan in front of me.

"Ryan, hi. Same here. I thought you were working at Ocean Grill."

"I was, but they had to pull me over here." He glances at the party. "I'm glad, though. This is a cool party. I've never been around so many famous people before. I'm kind of starstruck."

"They're just people, Ryan."

He smiles at me. "I know, but what can I say? I'm only a farm boy from Australia. I'm entitled to be in awe." He looked around, the grinned. "Gotta run. These people drink really fast."

I finish the champagne and veer toward the exit, skirting around the room where it's easier to maneuver and there's less chance of me running into someone I shouldn't. Suddenly, I'm grabbed by the arm and pulled behind a big ornamental piece. I yelp, but the sound is muffled by the loud music.

"Shh, Liv. It's me."

"Sebastian! What the hell! You almost gave me a heart attack."

"Sorry." He laughs, and I realize he's less than stable on his feet. How much did he drink already?

"What do you want? I'm working," I say through clenched teeth.

"I wanna talk to you."

I pull from his grasp and cross my arms in front of my chest. "About what?"

"Has anyone told you how beautiful you look tonight?" He stares at me with glazed eyes, and I want to punch his face. I move to leave, but he grabs my hand. "Liv, please stop."

"Don't you have someplace to be, like by your girlfriend's side?"

"I want to talk to you. Is that a crime?"

"We have nothing to talk about."

"You didn't wish me happy birthday, yet."

"Oh, God. Are you a child? Happy birthday, Sebastian. Happy now? Can I go?"

"No, I'm not happy and you can't go."

He drags me with him, and to avoid causing a scene, I let him. We exit the busy ballroom via a side door and find ourselves in an empty hallway. But Sebastian doesn't stop there.

He pulls me into a family restroom and locks the door behind us.

Before I can say anything, I'm against the wall and Sebastian's lips find mine. I try to fight him off, tasting the alcohol on his tongue, but it's a useless battle. I can't win. All of the feelings I've suppressed in the last five years come back like a tsunami, powerful and devastating. I kiss him back with the same fury, with the same hunger.

His hands roam down my naked arms, giving me goose bumps. I tangle my fingers in his hair, bringing us closer. Sebastian grunts as he begins to grind his pelvis against mine.

"Liv, I've missed you so much," he says against my mouth.

Hearing him say those words snaps me out of my temporary insanity, dousing the fire and bringing clarity. *What am I doing? Am I that stupid?* I shove him off me with all the strength I have. He takes a couple of wobbly steps back.

"This can't happen."

Breathing hard, Sebastian looks at me with hooded eyes. "Why not?"

"*Why not?* What the hell is wrong with you? You have a girlfriend, Sebastian. She's across the hallway."

"Liv, let me explain." He moves closer again, but I sidestep him.

"Explain what, Sebastian? Never mind. I don't wanna hear it." I unlock the door.

"Please don't leave." The desperation in his voice almost unravels me. It matches the despair in my heart.

I close my eyes to keep the tears from falling. "You left first, remember? Now it's my turn."

I burst out of there before he can change my mind. I don't look back.

♡ ♡ ♡

SEBASTIAN

I go back to the party seeing nothing, talking to no one in my path as I make a beeline to the bar, going behind it and retrieving a full bottle of whiskey. I break the seal and start gulping it down on the spot, witnesses be damned, resolution to stay clean be damned. Without Liv, I have no reason to remain sober.

Oliver finds me and pulls the bottle from my grasp.

"Are you fucking mental?"

"Give that back!" I try to reach for it, but my movements are sluggish.

"I'm not gonna watch you try to kill yourself again. One time was enough."

He's referring to the day I saw Liv together with the limo guy. It wasn't the drinking that almost killed me but the heroin OD that put me in the hospital for a week. If Oliver hadn't found me in time that night, I wouldn't be here.

"Fine, I'll find something else." I walk around Oliver, but he grabs my arm.

"You're not going anywhere but home."

"Let go of me! You're not my fucking mother!" I push him hard but end up losing my balance and falling on my ass.

People are staring, but I don't give a fuck. Out of the corner of my eye, I see Hans and Michael. I can't focus on their faces, but I'll bet they're not laughing. Fuck them, too.

Gretchen appears out of nowhere and squats by my side. "Sebastian, are you okay?"

When she tries to help me, I pull my arm away. "Fuck off, Gretchen."

She sucks in a breath and I see the hurt in her eyes, even in my inebriated state. Without another word, she gets up and walks out of the room.

Oliver and Anthony drag me up against my will. Once I'm standing, I take a few steps back, putting some distance between us. Then I see the blond guy Liv was with at Dijng. Not pausing to think, I reach him in two strides and punch him in the face. The tray he was carrying flies out of his hand as he falls down, glasses shattering everywhere.

"Bloody hell!" Oliver shouts.

The music stops, and all I can hear are shocked whispers mingled with the sound of my pulse in my ears. Liv's boyfriend touches his bloody lips as he stares at me wide-eyed. A skinny guy in a dark suit kneels next to him. Oliver and Anthony each grab me by an arm and take me away from the scene before I can do more damage.

This time, I don't fight them.

CHAPTER 33
SEBASTIAN

I wake up in my own apartment alone. I glance at the big clock on the wall and see it's almost noon. My head is pounding, and the sun streaming through the windows is only making it ache worse. I'm lying on my couch wearing yesterday's clothes. At least I was able to somehow remove my suit jacket. I see my phone on the coffee table and reach for it. There are a dozen missed calls from Hans but none from Gretchen. Maybe she'll dump me after last night's spectacle, saving me the trouble.

I get up and go in search of an Advil. I hear another ping from my phone and glance at the screen. It's a text message from Oliver saying I made the news. *Just fucking great.* I thought paparazzi weren't allowed into private parties.

I know I'll have to deal with Hans at some point today; might as well find out how royally I've fucked up. I open the URL link Oliver sent me. That's when I notice my swollen knuckles. Memories begin to slowly trickle in, and the picture they paint isn't pretty.

I think I assaulted Liv's boyfriend.

The browser finally opens, and the online article fills in the blanks for me. I'm in deep shit. I call Hans without listening to his voice messages. He answers on the first ring.

"About fucking time!" he shouts over the phone.

"Hans—"

"Shut up and listen, you little prick. Michael is done with you. He wants you out."

"No, let me explain."

"I said shut up. Besides being the stupidest motherfucker on the planet, are you deaf, too? I convinced him to give you another chance, your *last* chance."

I exhale in relief. "Thank you, Hans."

"Don't fucking thank me yet. Michael will be watching you closely. One wrong move on your part and you're history."

"Do you know what happened to that guy I punched? Is he pressing charges?"

"I haven't heard anything about it. You better pray he doesn't, because that will be your last strike. Now go call Gretchen and beg for forgiveness. God knows you need some good press now."

I don't contradict Hans and say I'm about to break up with her. He'll chew my head off. I have no choice but to continue with the charade, because I'm not ready to leave the band yet. And after last night, I have no hopes of getting Liv back.

LIV

When I receive a text from Lloyd at eight in the morning, I'm already up. Well, truth be told, I never went to sleep. I keep replaying that kiss in my head over and over again. A part of me is proud that I was able to fight my feelings for Sebastian and walk away. The other part, the stupid one, is regretting it. One thing I know for sure now—his kiss is still as combustible as before, still has the power to take over my whole being, making me want to drown in him.

I read the text and am taken aback. Lloyd is asking me to come to Ryan's room. *What the heck is he doing there?*

Five minutes later, I'm knocking on Ryan's door. Lloyd opens it wearing his boxer shorts and a sweatshirt that's too big for him. He has bed hair, and a shadow frames his jaw. But it's the dark circles under his eyes that make me apprehensive.

"Oh thank God you're here." He moves out of the way to let me in.

Ryan's room is the same size as mine, but somehow it looks smaller. Ryan is sitting on his bed, leaning against the propped-up pillow and sporting a shiner.

"What happened to you?"

He grimaces. "One of those Boys Future lunatics punched me."

A trickle of dread runs down my spine. *Please don't let it be Sebastian.*

"Who?" I ask.

"Coleman," Lloyd answers.

I rest my head in my hand and sit down on the only chair in the room. *Shit, shit, shit.* What's gotten into Sebastian? He's indeed a completely different person.

Even knowing it's crazy, guilt makes my heart smaller. Somehow I'm responsible for this mess.

"I'm fucking pressing charges. The guy is a menace."

My head snaps up, the guilt morphing into panic.

"Ryan, that's a terrible idea. Why would you wanna get dragged into the spotlight like that?" Lloyd says.

"Because people like him need to know they're not above the law." Ryan turns to me. "Liv, help me out here."

I shake my head, an automatic act on my part. Even after everything Sebastian put me through, the need to protect him prevails.

"Ryan, please don't do this."

He narrows his eyes at me. "I can't believe you're taking Lloyd's side. God, Liv. I never pegged you to be one of those crazy fans. I'm not changing my mind."

I can see in his eyes that he'll go through with it. The only way to convince him otherwise is to tell him the truth.

"You don't understand. I'm the reason Sebastian attacked you."

"What?" Ryan and Lloyd say in unison.

"I know him."

Lloyd squats in front of me. "What do you mean, you know him?"

I take a deep breath. "He's my ex-boyfriend. *The* ex-boyfriend."

Lloyd is so shocked that he falls on his butt. His eyebrows almost meet his hairline. "You mean the one from the story you told me?"

"Yeah."

"What story?" Ryan asks.

Lloyd lets out a humorless laugh and runs a hand through his messy hair. "That's shit."

I scoff. "You don't say."

Ryan waves at us. "Hello? Clueless guy here with a busted lip. Can someone fill me in?"

I face Ryan and tell him everything, from the very beginning when Sebastian and I became best friends until the day he left without saying goodbye. But I don't mention the stolen kiss in the restroom. I never want to tell anyone that.

When I'm done, both Ryan and Lloyd are speechless.

"Now do you understand why I think I'm the reason he punched you?" I ask.

"He thinks Ryan is your boyfriend." Lloyd smacks Ryan's chest. "See, this is your fault."

"How is it my fault that Sebastian can't control his temper? He's the one who fucked up."

I can see by their light banter that they've made up. At least there was one positive outcome from this whole mess.

"Guys, focus here. That's why I'm asking you not to press charges, Ryan. I don't know what's going on with Sebastian, but I can tell he's still fighting his demons."

Ryan stares at the ceiling and groans. "Ugh! Fine, I won't go after him. But if he harasses me again, I promise you that his face won't be so pretty anymore."

"How macho of you," Lloyd says and then turns to me. "Liv, it's obvious that Sebastian wants you back. What are you going to do about it?"

"Nothing. Absolutely nothing."

"Do you still love him?"

I avoid his gaze and look down at my lap. "I never stopped."

CHAPTER 34
SEBASTIAN

don't go back to my room at the Hollingsworth, but for some perverse reason, I don't check out of it either. There's no logic behind it. I could just as easily get another suite, but letting go of the one I have now would be admitting defeat. It would mean I'm giving up fighting for Liv for good. I can't do that, even knowing with absolute certainty that she'll never want to speak to me again.

I called Gretchen after my talk with Hans, and after a lot of groveling, she finally agreed to come to my place in Camden for dinner. I hate this situation, but I got myself into it. I need to get Hans off my back. Postponing the inevitable a couple more weeks won't be so bad.

Right, keep lying to yourself, Sebastian.

I'm preparing the only dish Mom ever taught me, ham and cheese lasagna. I also made sure to buy salad, knowing Gretchen probably won't even touch the high-calorie dinner. Liv never had any qualms about her food, and this dish in particular was her favorite. Is that the reason I'm cooking it now even knowing my girlfriend won't eat it? Fuck, I *am* a basket case and a masochist.

The doorbell rings and I press the intercom button to

unlock the door downstairs. I hear Gretchen's light steps on the stairs, and a few seconds later, she opens the door to my living room. She's wearing a black classic coat that hits her knees, and when she removes it, I have to lock my jaw tight to keep it from hitting the floor. Gretchen has on a snug black sleeveless dress that puts her best assets on display. My body stirs awake, even if my thoughts have been taken over by Liv's image.

I clean my hands on the apron I'm wearing and go to her. I lean down to place a kiss on her lips, but she turns her head, giving me her cheek instead.

Yeah, she's still mad at me.

She walks to the bar and ignores the bottle of champagne chilling in the ice bucket. Instead, she pours a shot of tequila. In the few months we've been dating, I've never seen her drink anything besides champagne and wine. The fact that she doesn't even wince when she drinks the shot in one gulp proves she's been holding out on me. It makes me wonder what else she's been hiding.

Five minutes later, we're sitting at the dining room table facing each other, eating in silence. Well, I'm eating. Gretchen is just playing with her food.

"Not hungry?" I ask.

She looks up at my question, and her green eyes are so sad, it makes me feel even shittier than I already am. What right do I have to keep lying to her? I don't love her, and even the affection I used to have has now faded. Is staying in the band worth smearing my soul further? Have I not done enough damage to it to last me several lifetimes?

"Aren't you even going to say you're sorry?" she says.

I put my fork down and wipe my mouth with a napkin. "I thought I did that already over the phone."

Gretchen sighs and looks at her plate. "You didn't even open the special gift I got for you."

Oh, fuckery fuck. The damn painting. I had completely forgotten about it. I force a smile to my lips. "You got me a gift on top of that awesome surprise party?"

She scrunches her eyebrows together. "Are you being sarcastic?"

"Me? No. I really did like the party."

I'm not lying. I loved the party because I got to be near Liv again, even if only for a brief, catastrophic moment.

"What about that poor waiter you attacked? What did he do to you?"

I grind my jaw. I was really hoping she wouldn't bring that up. I can still feel the remains of jealousy in my veins.

Gretchen is watching me expectantly, so I have to give her something.

"I heard him talk smack about the band. I guess I just couldn't control my temper." I'm disgusted by how easily the lie rolls off my tongue.

Gretchen seems to be mulling my answers over. It's almost like she desperately wants to believe my lies, even if she knows I'm bullshitting her.

She stands up and comes to me. I scooch my chair back with the intention to get up as well, but Gretchen puts her hands on my shoulders to keep me in place and then straddles me. Her slender fingers trace my jaw, then go up to my hairline before disappearing inside my hair. I grab her hips and pull her even closer to me. She bends down and kisses me, not softly like she usually does but with a fiery passion. It catches me by surprise, and I respond in kind.

Everything happens in a blur then. We're all about limbs, tongues, and teeth. I stand up with Gretchen latched on to me, her legs wrapped around my waist. I move to the couch and drop her there, wearing nothing but her lacy panties. I remove the rest of my clothes and reach for my wallet on the side table, pulling a condom from it. I put it on and see Gretchen has gotten rid of her underwear already. I take a step toward her, but her face morphs into Liv's. I freeze and stop breathing. *What the fuck is going on here?* I shake my head and blink a couple of times. Liv is gone, and so is my erection.

Gretchen's face falls as she sits up, covering her breasts. "What is it?"

"I'm sorry. I think I'm still hungover."

She avoids my gaze and gets up from the couch, collecting her clothes quickly before making a beeline to the bathroom. A minute later, she emerges fully dressed while all I've done is put my boxer shorts back on and sit down.

"I have news," she says as if nothing happened.

"Oh yeah?" I don't even try to fake interest. I'm still reeling from my hallucination.

"I'm going to Africa on a charity trip during Christmas break."

"Okay." I don't know what else to say.

"Maybe you could join me?"

Oh hell no. I don't plan for us to be together until then.

"I can't. I'll be on tour, remember?"

She purses her lips and plays with the pearl necklace she always wears. "You don't have concerts scheduled that week. I checked with Hans. We would be back in time for the New Year's Eve concert."

Of course. I should've known. This has Hans's fingerprints all over it. He was probably the one who suggested it.

"Uncle Paul will kill me if I miss Christmas. It's a big deal in my family."

Another lie. Since I moved out of my uncle's place, I haven't spent any holidays with them, especially Christmas. I hate it with a passion. It's the saddest time of the year for me, and I usually end up getting trashed with Oliver in some exotic location. It's a well-known fact about me that I'm sure Gretchen is aware of.

"Oh, okay. Of course. I didn't think about that," she says with a hint of disappointment in her voice. "Well, I'd better get going. I have an early flight to catch tomorrow."

"Where are you going?" I perk up in my seat. I didn't even try to hide the excitement in my voice, knowing she'll be out of town again. I'm despicable.

"Gosh, Sebastian. I've told you countless times. I'm going to Thailand for a photo shoot, and then I'm meeting my parents in New Zealand. I won't be back until mid-November, and by then, you'll be on your tour already."

I honestly have no recollection of her telling me any of that. But again, my mind has been preoccupied with something else. *Obsessed* with someone else is more accurate.

"Sorry, preparations for the tour are all I can think about."

Gretchen laughs without humor. "Actually, this is perfect. I think we could use sometime apart from each other. You know what they say: absence makes the heart grow fonder."

They also say "out of sight, out of mind," but I don't bring that up.

I stand up and cross the distance between us to hug her. Her sweet perfume invades my nose, but it does nothing to stir my heart awake. Only the scent of one person can do that.

CHAPTER 35

LIV

"Hey, Liv, are you alone?" I look over the computer screen to see Ryan's head poking in the partially open office door.

"Yes. Mellie and Lloyd are running errands, and Patsy is with a client."

"Good." Ryan opens the door all the way and strides in, exuding his usual cocky confidence. He sits on the edge of my desk, and I swivel my chair to face him.

After Ryan agreed to not press charges against Sebastian, my reservations toward him faded away completely. And since he and Lloyd decided to make up, we became closer by default. They're still keeping their relationship on the down low, so I'm the only one who's aware they're a couple. Ryan isn't ready to come out yet. I understand his predicament, even if I think it isn't fair to Lloyd. But if Lloyd is willing to put up with it, who am I to say anything?

"To what do I owe the pleasure of your visit?"

"Do you wanna go costume shopping with me after work?"

"Aren't you working tonight?"

"I had the lunch shift today, and I've requested Saturday off. You know, for the party."

We're all going to the Halloween party at the pub next to the Hollingsworth. I'm sure there are way more exciting parties in town, but since Halloween falls on a Saturday and a lot of the interns have to work that day, the group decided to go somewhere nearby.

I haven't really gotten close to any of them. I still have casual conversations with Yoann and Gavin when I bump into them, but those encounters are usually brief. It's easier to bond when you work together. Also, I missed going to the pub with the crew on several occasions, either too tired or simply not in the mood to be social.

"How did you manage to pull it off?" I ask.

He grins. "I can be very persuasive."

Yeah, it helps that his manager is a woman with a major crush on him. "What about Lloyd? He'll kill us if we go costume shopping without him."

Ryan rolls his eyes. "He's being a complete diva and refuses to tell me what he's wearing for Halloween. He says it's a surprise."

"Hmm, I sense a competitive streak here." I try to suppress a smile and fail miserably.

"So, what time can you leave?" he continues.

"I should be done by five."

"Great, I'll be back by then. The store closes at eight." Ryan stands up.

"Wait, do you *want* Lloyd to know we're going without him?"

Ryan peers at me as a wicked smile unfurls on his lips. His blue eyes light up with mischief. "You betcha."

"You're mean! Remind me to always be on your good side."

♡ ♡ ♡

SEBASTIAN

"You're out of your mind. We're gonna get caught," Oliver whines as he fidgets with his Zorro costume.

"Stop being a pussy. No one will recognize us. Just make sure you don't remove your mask and you'll be fine," I say.

"This bloody fake moustache itches. Tell me again how I let you convince me to do this. We had invites to the best Halloween parties in London, yet you want to crash a provincial Hollingsworth employee party?"

I put my helmet on and ignore his comment. He knows very well why I want to crash this particular party. He's my best friend, so of course he knows about Liv and how out of my mind I've been since our paths have crossed again. He knows why I got trashed at my birthday party and punched her boyfriend. He's the one keeping Hans off my case, and he even stopped partying so much so I wouldn't be tempted to join him. Our friendship is based on a mutual understanding that sometimes it's impossible to stop dragging our dead horses around. He has his and I have mine. We don't talk about it, but we know what it takes to keep our heads above water.

I returned to my suite at the Hollingsworth last week. It was a Herculean effort to stay away from Liv for that long, but I had to get my head straight. Plus, I know Hans is watching my every move. I can't let him find out about Liv. He'll ruin everything.

"I need a shot," Oliver declares as he strides toward the fully stocked bar. He pours a couple of double shots and hands me a glass.

I gulp the amber liquid down, letting it burn my throat. One shot, even if it's a double, won't affect me that much; it's just enough to take the edge off. I'm fucking nervous. My gut feels like it has been twisted into impossible knots. I cannot screw up tonight. Somehow, I need to get Liv alone so I can finally come clean about everything. I've decided to confess it all—the reason why I abandoned her, what kind of monster I turned into after that. Liv already hates me. I have nothing to lose, so I might as well place all my chips on one bet.

I didn't want to get Liv into trouble, so I didn't look for her at work. I bided my time, collected information, knowing I needed to approach her in a place outside of the hotel. On my first day back, I chatted with the bellman helping me. Angelo is an older chap from Greece, and he loved to talk. He didn't know who I was at first, which I found refreshing. And when he did, it didn't change his attitude toward me.

He's the one who told me about the party tonight, without me having to resort to bribery. I asked him if he had plans for the evening while we rode the elevator together this morning. He said he was too old for Halloween parties, but that the younger kids—that's how he referred to the interns—were all going to the pub next door.

Oliver and I leave my suite a few minutes later, he in his Zorro costume and me wearing my old hockey uniform, including the helmet. I have no intention of being recognized and mobbed tonight. Sure, it says Coleman on the back, but I doubt people will make the association with Sebastian Coleman from Boys Future. At least I'm praying they won't. The only person I want to recognize me is Liv.

The party is at the pub around the corner from the Hollingsworth. The place is open to the public, so technically we aren't crashing. We could've been partying it up with A-listers at the coolest places in town, but there's nowhere I'd rather be tonight.

Man, Oliver would give me so much shit if he could listen to my thoughts.

The place is already bursting at the seams, and as soon as we enter, Oliver carves a path for us to the bar. I hear him curse as he fights for space—he's not used to situations where people don't make way for him. Sometimes I forget where he comes from, that he's posh, a word I quickly learned at the International School of London.

The crowd begins to get on my nerves as well, so halfway to the bar, I stop and turn around. I'm not from a wealthy background, but I don't like to be pushed and shoved either. Oliver knows what I like to drink anyway.

I decide to circulate, see if I can spot Liv. I didn't realize how hard it would be to find her with all the costumes and shit. I hope she's not wearing a wig or a mask. That'll make things difficult, and the helmet already limits my vision. At least the pub isn't big.

Oliver finds me ten minutes later, and I can see his sourpuss expression beneath his disguise. He shoves a pint into my hands.

I frown at the glass, then back at him. "What the hell is this?"

"It's a fucking beer."

"You don't say. Since when do we drink beer?"

"We're blending in. Stop being a dick and drink it already."

Blending in, my ass. Oliver is afraid I'll get hammered again and lose control. He's babysitting me, and it pisses me off. I should never have asked him to tag along with me.

Thirty minutes and two pints later, there's still no sign of Liv, and my irritation has escalated.

"This party blows. Come on. Let's get out of here," Oliver says.

It took him long enough.

Then out of nowhere, a good-looking brunette wearing a slutty nurse outfit bumps into him, spilling her drink all over Oliver's five-hundred-pound rental. He looks down at his now-soaked costume and then up at her. If he were a cartoon character, I'd see steam blowing out of his ears. He's ready to lash out at her, but once he realizes she's a hot chick with a nice rack, his frown turns into a sly grin.

"Watch where you're going, darling."

"Sorry," she says, clearly irritated. She doesn't look at him twice and begins to walk away.

Undeterred, Oliver raises his arm and blocks her path.

"That's all I get? A measly sorry? How about you buy me a drink?"

Her face contorts into a grimace. "Shouldn't you be buying *me* a drink? If you hadn't been standing in the way, I would still have mine."

"All right, I'll buy you a drink, but only if you blow me."

Her gaze turns nasty before she shoves him and storms away, saying a string of words in another language.

I do the only thing I can in this situation.

I laugh. Hard.

"Shut up, jackass."

"I can't. This is too much. When was the last time a girl said no to you?"

"Never, thank you very much. What a bitch!" Oliver brings his cape to his nose. "Ugh! Rum and Coke. Gag me."

"It must be the fake mustache, then."

"Obviously." Oliver's gaze wanders around the room before his eyes land on me again. "Mate, I love you, but I'm out of here. Stay out of trouble, and no punching anyone. I'll be at Legacy. Call me if you change your mind."

He takes off and I ponder what I should do next. I'm getting antsier by the second, and my body is calling for something stronger than warm beer. I'm two seconds away from caving in when I finally see Liv by the pub's entrance.

Her hair is curled and shorter, reaching her chin, and she has a beret on. Her makeup is a ghoulish combination of white, black, and red. That's all I can see of her costume.

The pressure on my chest increases when I see the boyfriend next to her. He's wearing a pinstriped suit and fedora. I get it now. They're dressed as Bonnie and Clyde zombies. *Fuck, they're already picking matching costumes?*

He leans down to whisper something in her ear, and she smiles at him. I want to rip his head off. He looks over at the jam-packed pub and puffs out his chest, like he's preparing for battle. *What a moron.* Liv shakes her head and laughs. He leaves her alone and ventures in, probably going toward the bar.

The music is loud, some kind of pop song I don't recognize. Liv seems to like it, as she begins to bob her head up and down, in sync with the rhythm. She looks happy, and I wonder if I have the right to ruin her evening.

The thought is fleeting and soon forgotten. It's too late now.

As I get near her, the crowd begins to thin, and soon I have a vision of her entire outfit. I was right, she's dressed as Bonnie; the short-sleeved sweater and high-waist pencil skirt are a trademark of the look. There are smears of fake blood on her torso and arms. Desire erupts low in my guts. She's the hottest-looking zombie I've ever seen.

"You can eat my brains if you want," I say near her ear.

She jumps and puts a hand over her chest as she looks at me. Then her eyes narrow.

"What the hell are you doing here, Sebastian?"

"You know very well."

She crosses her arms and stiffens her back. The irritation in her eyes only makes me want her more. "Actually I don't. Now if you'll excuse me, I'm here with someone."

She pushes past me, going farther into the pub. I follow her like a freaking lost puppy.

When we reach the bar, we come upon a quite interesting scene. Liv's boyfriend is wrapped up in another chick's arms. Liv stops dead in her tracks. The blond idiot finally notices her presence and looks at her like a deer caught in headlights. The girl embracing him turns to us and smiles.

"What's going on here, Ryan?" Liv's voice is hard, not hurt as I expected it to be.

"Liv, I…," he starts but doesn't finish. I can practically see his brain trying to come up with an excuse. Douche.

"Do you work with Ryan?" the girl embracing him asks.

"No, not really. I'm sorry, who are you?"

The petite Asian beauty glances up at Ryan with adoration in her eyes, then turns to Liv again. "I'm Penelope, Ryan's fiancée. I just flew in from Sydney to surprise him."

Man, I have no words. If I weren't enjoying this situation so much, I might've said something. But Ryan's just made my life so much easier. I look at Liv, her posture rigid and her eyes nothing but slits. I think she's on the verge of punching the guy.

"Oh, how nice of you. I'm Liv, Ryan's friend." She extends her hand to the girl, and they shake. "I can't wait for you to meet Lloyd. I'm sure he'll be *ecstatic* to get to know Ryan's fiancée."

I notice a sudden change in Ryan's face, and his entire body seems to freeze.

Wait. Am I missing something here? I think I actually catch a plea in his eyes.

Liv turns on her heel and walks back the way we came. I trail after her, and once we're outside the pub, I grab her by the elbow. "Liv, wait."

She jerks her arm from my grasp. "Let go of me, Sebastian."

"Are you mad at me? I'm not the one two-timing you with his fiancée."

"What?" she says before she throws her head back and laughs.

I wasn't expecting that. I'm as confused as a Kardashian shopping at Walmart.

"Oh, that's rich. You must have selective amnesia. Wasn't it you who kissed me a few weeks ago when your girlfriend was in the other room?"

Well hell. She has me there.

Liv strides away in the Hollingsworth's direction, but I can't let her go before I have the chance to explain.

"That was completely different. For fuck's sake, Liv, talk to me."

She pivots and advances toward me. When we're a breath away from each other, she pokes my chest with her index finger. "There's nothing to talk about, Sebastian. You were a jerk five years ago, and you're a jerk now."

"I'm sorry," I say, and I mean it.

"You're *sorry?* For which part? For when you fucked me and then left the country without so much as a goodbye? Or are you sorry for lying to the world, saying I was your stalker? No, maybe you're sorry for sexually harassing me at your birthday party." She screams the last part, and now people on the street are beginning to pay attention.

The last thing I need is for an idiot with a phone to recognize me and post a video of this fight on YouTube. The scandal would seal my fate.

I touch Liv's arm tentatively. "You have no idea how truly sorry I am for all of that. I'm begging you to let me explain."

"Well, Sebastian, it's too late for explanations. You had your chance. Now leave me the fuck alone!"

I let her walk away this time, knowing it's futile to try to convince her to hear me out while she's fuming. I don't move from my spot as I watch her leave, taking in a couple of deep breaths and letting the cool air fill my lungs. I need to get my nerves under control. Liv thinks she had the last word, but she's mistaken if she believes I'm going to back down. She'll hear me out, willingly or not.

I go back to the hotel after a couple of minutes. As I'm striding toward the elevator, I see something at the gift shop that catches my eye—a teddy bear similar to the one Liv gave me. Terminator.

I change course and head to the shop, buying the toy on a whim. I don't remove my helmet, not caring about the weird look the clerk gives me. Then I go back to my suite, change out of my hockey uniform, and order room service. Twenty minutes later, I'm on my way to Liv's room.

CHAPTER 36
LIV

The first thing I do when I get to my room is throw the stupid beret into a corner and unpin my hair. The bobby pins are digging into my skull and giving me a headache. I also remove the Halloween makeup; I don't want to wake up in the middle of the night and get scared from catching my own reflection in the mirror.

I hear a ping from my phone and see it's a message from Lloyd asking me where I am. *Shit.* The exchange with Sebastian has derailed my thoughts, and I completely forgot to warn Lloyd about Ryan's fiancée. I might've gotten closer to Ryan these past few weeks, but my loyalty still belongs to Lloyd.

God, I can't believe Ryan kept such a secret from us. It's one thing to not be ready to come out, quite another to carry out a secret affair with Lloyd when he has a fiancée back home. There's no excuse for that. Lloyd will be a mess when he finds out.

I stare at my phone, not knowing what to do. I can't possibly tell Lloyd what I saw over the phone. I have to go back to the party and find him before he finds Ryan. Ugh, I hope the idiot had enough brains to take his fiancée somewhere else.

I text Lloyd back to say I'm on my way and then put my coat

on again. I open the door and almost scream when I see Sebastian standing in front of me, poised to knock.

"Oh hell no!" I try to shut the door, but he's faster than me and stops my attempt by positioning his body between the door and its frame. I know it'll be pointless to keep him out, so I decide to let him in and get this conversation over with.

I move to the window, putting as much distance between us as I can. Sebastian closes the door behind him with his foot without taking his eyes off me. I don't like how his intense gaze is turning my insides into mush and carving giant holes in the walls protecting my heart.

"Don't you ever give up?" I say.

"When it comes to you? No."

"That's a load of crap. You gave up on me, on *us*, five years ago when you left with your uncle without a glance back."

I'm glad my anger is alive and kicking, so when I feel the sting behind my eyes, it's easy to keep the tears at bay. I can't let Sebastian know how much he still affects me.

He moves my way, his untameable mahogany eyes fixed on my face. I want to break free of his combustible stare, but he has me completely ensnared. If he tries to kiss me again, I don't think I'll have enough strength to run away this time. My breathing becomes shallow, and my heart can't decide if it wants to stop beating or run a marathon.

"I made a mistake five years ago. I was stupid and young. I had just lost all I had ever known. My family, my life as I knew, it was over. I was grieving, Liv. You can't fault me for that." His hushed answer has an intensity that nearly breaks me.

"I know all that. That's why I kept on writing to you. *Every day*. I was grieving, too, Bas. I wanted you to know that you weren't alone in your pain. I loved your parents just as much as I love my own." My voice falters at the end, and a rogue tear escapes my eye. I wipe it off quickly. "What I don't understand is why you never contacted me again. You seemed fine moving on with your life. I deserved at least a Dear John letter."

"I did come back for you."

"What?" My heart is pounding away now.

Sebastian puts whatever he has in his hands by the foot of my bed and rubs his face, looking everywhere but at me. "It took me three fucking years to get my shit together and realize what a dick I'd been. After Boys Future's first American tour, I came by your parents' house, and Jeremy gave me your address on campus. But I was obviously too late." Sebastian raises his gaze to mine again. "I saw you with somebody else."

My mouth is dry and my chest is caving in. I remember like it was yesterday when Boys Future came to the US for the first time. They sang live at freaking Rockefeller Center. Which means Sebastian could have only seen me with one person.

I can't get enough air in my lungs. Sebastian was there, mere feet away from me on the day I broke Derek's heart. How could fate be so cruel like that? If he'd shown up a few hours later... I can't even finish that thought.

Sebastian breaches the final distance between us and I dare to look into his eyes, trying to find the answers I so desperately need. But I can't begin to decipher what his gaze is telling me. I've lost the ability to read Sebastian's mind with a simple glance. We've lost our connection.

That's the only explanation I can give myself for getting caught by surprise when Sebastian brings his lips to mine. The warm, feathery touch sends an incendiary wave through my entire body, waking up a primal desire within my soul.

Like a house of cards, my barriers come tumbling down. I give in to that kiss, unable to resist Sebastian's pull. Suddenly, the last five years have never happened and we're right back to where we left off. Reason takes flight, leaving my emotions free to seize control. We yank at each other's clothes in a frenzy, barely taking the time to breathe. I feel the cool air hit my skin, but Sebastian's body heat soon envelopes me. He pushes me against the wall and kisses my neck as his hands cover my chest. A soft moan escapes my lips, and I feel him smiling against my skin. His lips trail down, scorching everywhere they touch. He tugs the fabric of my bra, freeing my breasts, before his warm tongue circles one of my nipples while his hand plays with the other. I want to die right here, right now. I grab his arms and use them as an anchor, because my legs can no longer support me.

Sebastian sucks and plays for what feels like an eternity; it's impossible to tell time when my whole body is humming and my brain is fuzzy as hell. He abandons my breasts to continue his path downward, kissing my belly and then stopping when he reaches my skirt's waistband. I look down at him as he looks up. Our gazes collide, and then, like magic, I can read him again. We've recovered our superpowers. He's asking me if he can go on. I nod, unable to form words.

He pulls the side zipper down, never once breaking our heated connection. The feelings I've tried so hard to repel break free from their prison and overwhelm me. *Sebastian is here in my room. This is really happening.* He tugs my skirt down excruciatingly slowly, and when it pools around my ankles, I step out of it. When he hooks his fingers into each side of my panties, an involuntary gasp escapes my lips. He gives me a crooked smile before gliding his tongue over the sensitive skin where my thigh meets my pelvis, dangerously close to the throbbing between my legs that won't quit.

"Sebastian," I whisper before I rest my head against the wall and close my eyes.

"I've been dying to taste you since that afternoon five years ago."

He slides my panties down, and my body begins to shake in anticipation.

"God, you're breathtaking." He kisses me then, right there on my core.

His tongue is eager and lethal. The throbbing becomes incessant as the heat intensifies, spreading through my limbs like a fire jet. I bury my fingers in his hair, tugging roughly, urging him to keep going, to never stop. With each stroke, I climb higher and higher, dying to reach the top but wanting to prolong the journey at the same time. I can't fight the force propelling me upward, though, pushing me toward the edge. I take another step, and the ground disappears beneath my feet, but I don't fall. Instead I fly, rocketing through the sky as I scream Sebastian's name.

He bites the inside of my thigh lightly and groans. My legs are boneless; Sebastian's arms wrapped around them are the only thing keeping me upright. After a moment, he stands up and we lock gazes. His warm eyes are dark with need, and his hunger makes something uncoil in my belly. He isn't done with me, and I'm sure as hell not done with him.

He picks me up and gently lays me down on the single bed, then pauses for a moment, his eyes roaming over my body. My breathing becomes shallow again as I drink him in. His sweater and T-shirt are long gone, and his low-rise jeans emphasize the famous V that makes sensible women weak in the knees. His abs and chest are more defined than when he was just a teenager. They look like sculpted marble, and I want to lick every ridge.

Sebastian unbuttons his jeans and pushes them down his legs together with his boxer shorts. My eyes fixate on his erection, and the urge to touch him is almost unbearable. I raise my arm, offering him my hand. He laces our fingers together before coming to bed, lying half on top of me. He kisses me again, the sweetest of kisses, like he's worshipping my mouth. But the sweetness doesn't last. We've been deprived of each other for far too long. The tempo of our tongues mingling together increases as he rolls on top of me. I part my legs and feel him at my entrance. I squirm beneath him, trying to bring us even closer. Sebastian is shaking on top of me, and I know he's about to lose his restraint.

"Condom," I manage to say.

He leans sideways to reach for something on the floor. A second later he has a foil packet between his fingers, and like our first time, his hands are unsteady. His nervousness makes my heart tighten. I take the packet from him and tear it with ease, knowing our first time is on the forefront of his mind as well. I give him the condom, and he sits on his haunches to put it on. He stops for a moment, waiting again for my signal. This time, I do manage to find my words.

"I'm ready, Bas."

He releases a shaky breath before he collapses on top of me, and with a powerful push, he's inside. And here is where the similarities end. During our first time, he was careful to the point of being cruel. He's not holding back now, and I'm glad he isn't. We're making love, but it's not gentle; it's raw, demanding, desperate. I raise my knees and hook my feet behind his back as his tongue invades my mouth. The sound of flesh pounding against flesh mixes with our moans of pleasure in a delicious symphony of complete surrender.

It doesn't take long for the fire to spread from my core to my whole body again. I cry out when another powerful wave of pleasure hits me, and a second later, Sebastian does the same. He shudders in my arms, enjoying the last tendrils of his orgasm, before his body stills and he hides his face in the crook of my neck.

Our breathing is ragged, and his heart is beating as fast as mine. We stay glued like that, in a perfect lovers' embrace, for a few minutes with Sebastian's fullness still filling me. Slowly but surely, the lust fog dissipates and reason returns, killing my bliss. The hard part must continue. Knowing about Sebastian's visit of two years ago is just the tip of the iceberg. I need more explanations, need to know what happens to us from here onward.

Sebastian rolls off me and then off the bed.

"Ouch."

I laugh and turn on my side, leaning on my elbow. "Are you okay?"

"God, your bed is tiny. I would fall to the floor every night if had to sleep in it."

"I'm used to it."

He removes the condom and gets up. His gaze darts left and right before he looks at me. "Where's your bathroom?"

"Outside." I try to suppress a grin, but it's impossible.

"You have to use a communal bathroom?" He sounds appalled, making me laugh again.

"Uh, yes."

"God, how barbaric."

"You sound like an over-entitled ass. It's not that much different than the dorm rooms on campus."

Sebastian frowns, and a flash of something indescribable appears in his eyes.

"Well, I never went to college. Where's your trash can?"

The mood has definitely shifted in the room, and I feel the tension bearing down on me. I get up as well and find an empty plastic bag. "Here, you can use this."

I put on the fleece robe that was folded over my chair and turn to him, taking the trash bag from his hand. "I'm going to clean up. I'll be right back."

Sebastian isn't frowning anymore when he says, "I'm not going anywhere."

It's the fastest trip I've ever made to the bathroom. Even though he said he's not going anywhere, I can't take the risk of him disappearing on me again. I need answers.

When I return, I find Sebastian semi-dressed, lying on my bed with his hands crossed behind his head. And when I say semi-dressed, I mean he put his boxer shorts back on and that's it. Suddenly, I don't know what to do or how to react. I close the door behind me and lean against it, terrified of taking a step closer to him.

I notice the bottle of champagne and the open box of chocolate-covered strawberries on my desk a second later. Next to it is teddy bear that has an uncanny resemblance to Terminator.

"I told you next time there would be champagne and strawberries. Sorry it took so long for me to deliver my promise."

Something explodes in my chest, and my eyes become a

waterfall. The hurt, the humiliation, the despair all come back at once, squeezing my heart like they want to pulverize it. Hot, angry tears roll freely down my cheeks, and I slide down to the floor, covering my face with my hands. I'm sobbing so hard, my entire body is shaking.

I hear Sebastian stand up and kneel in front of me, but I can't face him. He removes my hands from my face before pulling me onto his lap. He cradles my body like I'm the most precious thing in the world, and I let myself fall into that embrace. It's the only thing I'm capable of doing right now. Sebastian is my salvation and my destruction.

"Why did you leave me? Why?" I say between sobs.

"Liv, I'm so, so sorry. You have no idea. I was a fucking idiot."

"I loved you so much. You destroyed me."

Sebastian releases his tight hold on me and leans back. I glance up at his face.

"*Loved* me? As in you don't love me anymore?" There's pain in his tone. And doubt.

I don't answer him. I can't. I'm so freaking afraid to confess the truth, afraid he'll trample all over my heart again.

"Liv, I never stopped loving you."

My heart stops for a second and then starts beating again at a rapid pace. I want to believe his words so desperately, but can I?

Unable to withstand his intense stare, I look down at his chest.

"Don't lie to me, Sebastian." My voice is small. "You created an absurd lie about me and shared it with the world."

He covers my cheeks with his hands and forces me to look into his eyes. "It was a despicable thing to do, I know. I was still so fucking jealous of the limo guy. You looked so happy with him. I thought for sure you'd be married to him by now."

"You're ridiculous."

"I never claimed intelligence. But hear this. I. Never. Stopped. Loving. You. It's the absolute truth. What I did back then, the way I shunned you, it's a guilt I'll forever carry in my heart." Sebastian pauses and closes his eyes. He takes a deep breath, and when he exhales, the air is choppy, ragged.

"My parents' death was my fault." He opens his eyes, and I can see deep into his mangled soul. His hands move from my cheeks to my shoulders as his eyes glass over. "The only reason they went to LA that day was because I asked them to go. I asked them to pick up a gift I'd bought for your birthday."

The blood leaves my face as his words begin to make sense. I get off Sebastian's lap and scooch away from him, feeling light-headed. There's only one conclusion I can make from his statement, and I'm afraid to ask, but I know I have to.

"Do you blame *me* as well?"

Sebastian brings his knees up and holds them tight, as if he needs a shield. "I did for a time."

My tears return, but they're angry tears now. If only Sebastian hadn't been so stubborn, we could've sorted this mess out a long time ago.

"Say something," he begs.

I wipe my face, but it's pointless; the tears will keep on coming. "You are, without a doubt, the stupidest ass I've ever met. You are not responsible for what happened, Bas. The truck driver who fell asleep behind the wheel is the one to blame, not you, and certainly not me."

Sebastian shakes his head. "I know that! But the guilt won't leave me alone. It's so dark and twisted, I'll do anything to smother it, to make it go away. I've done awful things, Liv. Things I never thought I would, like trying every single drug I could get my hands on so I wouldn't feel the pain. I turned into a junkie."

Sebastian is shattering in front of me, and I can't stand to watch him suffer. I crawl back to where he is, and like he did to me a couple minutes before, I capture his face between my hands, forcing him to look into my eyes.

"You're more than what you've become. I can see glimpses of the boy I loved in your eyes. Of the boy I *still* love."

Sebastian sucks in a breath before he speaks again. "I don't deserve you. You're the best thing that has ever happened in my life, and I'm never letting you go again. Please tell me it's not too late. Please tell me I can have you back."

I smile through the tears. I've waited five freaking long years to hear those words from him.

"It's not too late."

CHAPTER 37
SEBASTIAN

Hearing those four little words feels like Liv has breathed life back into my soul. I stare at her, mesmerized, as my brain grapples with this new reality. Fate has been merciful for once. I kiss her again and again, and the tears I've been holding back finally fall, mingling with hers.

My body is in flames once more, and the need to bury myself deep inside her takes over everything. I'll make love to her the whole night through if she lets me.

She straddles me, and I remember she's not wearing anything under her robe. I trail my hand down her stomach until it reaches her warmth. She moans in my mouth as I begin to caress her.

"I've missed you so much," she whispers.

"I've missed you more."

Her muscles tense around my fingers. She's about to come, so I increase the pace. Then a loud knock on the door breaks the spell.

"Liv, are you there?" A male voice with an Australian accent bursts through our bubble.

I freeze and so does Liv. She looks at the door and then at me, a deep V forming between her brows.

"You gotta be kidding me," I say.

Liv stands up and fixes her robe. I'm hoping she'll tell her cheating boyfriend to fuck off, but she surprises me when she opens the door. *Fuck!* I don't want to be seen like this. I don't want to be recognized. I haven't explained my shitty dilemma to Liv yet.

"What do you want, Ryan?"

"Liv, you gotta help me. Have you heard from Lloyd?" The guy sounds desperate, and now I'm intrigued. I thought he was here to beg for forgiveness.

"An hour ago. Why?" The tension in Liv's voice shoves my concerns to the back of my mind. I stand up and move behind her, offering my support.

Ryan's eyes widen when he sees me. *Yes, I'm the guy who punched you, dickhead.* He glances at Liv again. "He saw me with Penelope."

"For God's sake, Ryan. I can't believe you let that happen. What did Lloyd do?"

"He took off, and he's not answering my calls. You know how he overacts about everything. I'm worried he's gonna do something stupid."

Why is Ryan worried about a dude named Lloyd? Unless.... Oh hell and damn. Is Ryan gay? Wouldn't that be the joke of the century?

Liv crosses her arms. "Are you concerned he's going to hurt himself, or are you concerned he's going to blow your cover?"

Ryan rakes his fingers through his hair and stares at his shoes. "Both."

"Oh, you're a piece of work." Liv starts to shut the door in his face, but he raises his hand and stops her.

I move so now I'm in front of Liv. Ryan sees my don't-mess-with-what's-mine stance and backs away. "You better leave now, pal, unless you want a broken nose this time."

He narrows his eyes at me, then looks over my shoulder at Liv. "Please, I just want to know if he's okay."

"I'll call him, Ryan. Go back to your room. Your fiancée must be wondering where you are."

"She's gone. She put two and two together and left me."

"And you want me to feel sorry for you?" Liv says.

I don't wait for him to reply, closing the door in his face with pleasure. I turn around and see Liv is already on the phone. She paces in the small space in front of her bed with an arm wrapped around her middle.

"Lloyd, it's Liv. Call me as soon as you get this message. I know about Ryan. I'm worried. Be safe."

She ends the call and stares at her phone for a few seconds. I can tell she's feeling guilty by the set of her shoulders, by how she nibbles her lower lip.

"Liv, he'll be okay."

She glances at me, and the worry in her gaze twists my insides. "I hope so. I was on my way to warn Lloyd when you came by."

"Ah, shit, Liv. You should've told me."

She shakes her head. "No, I'm glad you didn't give me the chance."

Her answer makes another piece of my heart fall back into place. "So, Ryan isn't your boyfriend?" For some reason, I have to be certain.

"No. He never was."

I take her hand and tug her to me. "Good."

A funny look crosses Liv's face and she steps back. "What about *your* girlfriend?"

Fuck, I guess we're having this conversation now. "We're on a break."

Well, not technically. Gretchen just said it would be good to spend some time apart. For all intents and purposes, we're still together, which basically makes me a cheater.

My answer obviously doesn't satisfy Liv, though. Her lips are pursed, and the deep V is back on her face.

"She's out of the country and won't be back before I go on

tour."

Oh shit. The world tour. I'll be gone in a week and won't come back until December. *No. No. No.* I just got Liv back in my life. I don't want to leave her side.

"What are you saying, Sebastian? You need to break up with her face-to-face? You can't do it over the phone? Hell, it's more than what I got."

Yup, Liv is pissed, and she totally has the right to be. If I tell her now about Hans's demands, she's going to flip. There's no reason for her to know, because I *will* break up with Gretchen as soon as we're both in London.

"Liv, are you going to hang that over my head forever? What I did to you was despicable. Do you want me to continue being an asshole? I don't want to be that guy anymore."

I feel terrible for my half-truth. I wouldn't even be with Gretchen if it weren't for Han's threats.

"I love *you*. There's never been anyone else in here." I place a hand over my chest.

My gesture and my words seem to mollify her. Her gaze softens, and she's no longer shielding her body with her arms. I pull her into a hug and kiss the top of her head.

"When are you going on tour? And how long will you be gone?" Her tiny voice makes me feel even worse.

"The tour lasts eight months, but we don't have back-to-back concerts. I'll come to London often enough."

Liv doesn't say anything, and it worries me. I push her back so I can read her face. "Hey, don't make that frown. The tour changes nothing. I have you back in my life, and I'll never let you go again. Believe me."

She lowers her gaze. "What happens now?"

I put my finger under her chin and bring her face up. "Now we get to know each other all over again."

I lean down and give her a short kiss before pulling back.

"As a couple?" she asks.

"What kind of silly question is that? Of course as a couple."

"Bas, did you forget who you are? You're not your own person anymore. You're larger than life. What's going to happen when the media gets wind of our relationship? I'm not ready to have my life dissected by the tabloids for people's entertainment. Plus, you're very much in a committed relationship with someone else. I'll be the homewrecker."

She's right. If the gossip magazines find out about us, Liv will get the worst of it, especially considering how everyone adores Gretchen. People have latched on to our relationship like we're the next David and Victoria Beckham. But I can't not see Liv until my relationship status is resolved. I just can't. I'll go nuts.

"I won't tell anyone if you won't."

She scoffs. "So, I'm going to be your dirty little secret, then?"

"Never. Think more along the lines of Romeo and Juliet."

"Bas, they died at the end."

"We'll make our own story. And right now, all I want to do is take you back to my suite and make love to you until you can't walk tomorrow."

"What's wrong with my room?" We both look at her tiny bed before she says, "Never mind."

CHAPTER 38
LIV

Lloyd finally texts me back Sunday morning saying he's in Manchester, visiting his folks. I was worried about him, but I have a feeling Ryan was exaggerating, blowing the situation out of proportion because he was looking out for himself and his secret. God, I hope Lloyd forgets him for good.

Despite their drama, I'm on cloud nine Monday morning. I spent the entire Sunday locked in Sebastian's suite. We had five years to catch up on. But one day wasn't nearly enough; all it did was make me crave him even more. There's a delicious ache between my legs, and I can hardly walk straight. I guess Sebastian got his wish after all.

I can't stop grinning like a fool, and when Mellie arrives at the office, it's the first thing she notices.

"Did you have a good weekend, Liv?"

I sigh dreamily. "The best."

She goes to the kitchen to get a cup of coffee and stops by my desk when she returns. "So, who was the lucky guy?"

I blink a couple of times as my cheeks heat up, then turn to my computer screen so she won't see my eyes when I lie to her.

I'm a terrible liar. "Some guy I met at the Halloween party Saturday."

"Oh, I like that. I wanna know all the details later. Let's go out for lunch." Mellie glances at Lloyd's empty desk. "Is Lloyd coming in today?"

"Oh, I think he's taking the day off. He was at his parents' in Manchester yesterday."

"Really? That's odd. I thought he was coming with you to the party at the pub and probably suffering from a major hangover Sunday."

I tell Mellie about Ryan and his fiancée and all the drama that followed. I even mention Ryan's visit to my room while Mystery Man was there—that's how I refer to Sebastian because I can't tell anyone else about us. It's bad enough that Ryan saw him there.

"That motherfucker," Mellie says the moment Patsy comes into the office.

She's wearing her sunglasses, and she doesn't glance at us at all, but I see her lips are curled up slightly when she says good morning to us.

"Shit." Mellie scrambles back to her desk, looking sheepish. I don't know why she's worried that Patsy heard her swearing. They do it all the time.

A minute later, a message window pops up on my screen.

MELLIE: You're not escaping so easily. I want to know everything about MM.

Ah, hell. I really don't want to create a convoluted story to protect my secret relationship with Sebastian. Why does he have to be a superstar? Even when he deals with the Gretchen issue, we won't be able to announce our relationship to the world. Technically he's a client and therefore off-limits. Patsy won't care that we have a history. I'll lose my job for sure.

I ignore Mellie's message and try to concentrate on work. I'm in this mess thanks to my inability to keep my mouth shut. She didn't have to know I hooked up with anyone, did she? *Ugh!*

Luckily, there's plenty to do in the office to keep me busy. There are several emails that I need to reply to, and I have to call a few vendors. Things are getting crazier with the holidays approaching. So far we've booked ten Christmas parties and a couple of weddings. Plus, there is the official Hollingsworth New Year's Ball, which is one of the most sought-after parties in town. Yeah, we have our plates full.

Another message pops up, but it's Saylor this time. I sent a Skype message to her last night saying I had major news, and now she's dying to know. She would never bother me during work hours otherwise.

SAYLOR: Tell me, tell me.

ME: I can't. I'm at work and can't say over message. It's top secret information. What are you doing up at this hour anyway?

SAYLOR: I haven't been to bed yet. Stop evading. Does it have anything to do with a certain dark-haired boy?

I can't help but smile at the message. Saylor is in the loop about everything involving Sebastian, including the kiss he stole from me at his birthday party. In the end, I couldn't keep it a secret from her.

ME: Totally.

SAYLOR: I told you he wanted you back. OMG, I'm doing the I-told-you-so dance right now.

ME: Shut up.

SAYLOR: Did you ask him about the fucked-up lie he told on national TV?

ME: Yes. It's a long story. I'll tell you later.

SAYLOR: Okay, okay. But answer me this at least. Did you make him grovel?

ME: Yeah.

SAYLOR: Good. I have news, too. Actually, it's not news, more like gossip. I should let Kennedy tell you herself, but hell, I can't.

ME: What is it?

SAYLOR: She got her first movie role. It's an indie production, but still. It's major and she got the lead!

ME: That's awesome! When did it happen?
SAYLOR: Yesterday.
ME: Oh, man. You're terrible. She didn't even have the chance to tell me. It's okay. I'll pretend to be surprised when she does.
SAYLOR: Ha! That's why I told you. I know you have my back, chica. Okay, I'll let you get back to work. Call me when you're home.
ME: Okay, bye.

"Message from Mystery Man?" Mellie asks.

"Uh?" I say, then realize I'm grinning again. "No. I just found out that one of my friends got cast in a movie as the lead."

"Super. Who else is in it?"

"I don't know yet. It's an independent production, so I don't think there will be any megastars in it."

"Nevertheless, that's bloody fantastic. I wish I knew someone famous. I could live vicariously through them. My life is so boring."

"I think celebrities' lives are overrated. I wouldn't want to live under the constant media scrutiny. I like my privacy."

I get a pang in my chest as I say that. There will be no privacy by Sebastian's side. Am I ready for it? The paparazzi, the lies written about us, the fans; when I think about it, it's all too much. I'm not ready by far. But I'll face the wolves, will dive right into this world of madness, because Sebastian is worth it.

Mellie and I go to the cafeteria for lunch, which suits me well. I can't really talk about my sexcapades surrounded by Hollingsworth's employees. Mellie does try to get more details out of me, but I keep it vague. When we get back to the office, there's a huge bouquet of multicolored roses on my desk. My heart does several backflips as I grab the card.

"Time goes by, so slowly. Can't wait to see you tonight. Love, S."

I smile at Sebastian's dig at Madonna's song. Only he would put a joke in a romantic card.

"Flowers from Mystery Man? That doesn't look like a one-night stand, Liv," Mellie says.

I shake my head. "Some guys are just bred better."

"Yeah, right. And the cheeseburger I ate totally didn't have a thousand calories."

CHAPTER 39

SEBASTIAN

We've been rehearsing nonstop this past week, and our days are long and tiring, but I feel energized because I get to see Liv every day after work. My mood has never been better, I can actually focus on the idiotic dance routines, and I'm staying out of trouble. Hans thinks my attitude change has everything to do with his threat. It looms in the background, though not with the same weight as before. I still love being part of the band, but it's not my whole world anymore. I can leave it behind without a glance back. It was never about the fame and money. It was about the high, and I don't need it anymore. I've got the most important thing in my life back.

The rehearsal studio is one big warehouse where we can prepare for the show on a mock-up stage with real proportions. Smaller parts of the warehouse have been sectioned off and converted into a proper music studio with state-of-the-art equipment, dressing rooms, offices, a kitchen, and an eating area. Its location is well known, and there hasn't been a single day where we haven't encountered fans and paparazzi waiting for us outside. I'm extra charming with the fans, pausing to take pictures with them and sign autographs, but not because I need to improve my image. I'm happy and I want to spread it around. I know the blogs and gossip sites have exploded with pictures of me in such encounters, and they're all wondering the same thing: What's caused my change of attitude? Of course, they all allude to Gretchen being the reason, although there's been some speculation as to why we haven't been seen together lately. If they bothered to check their facts, they would know she's out of the country. Maybe they do know and just don't care.

We're done for the day, and Hans comes to talk to me for the first time since he busted my balls. I'm in the dressing room getting ready to go back to the hotel when he comes in and shuts the door.

"What can I do for you, Hans?" I say as I pack my duffel bag.

"When is Gretchen coming back?"

I grind my jaw. There goes my good mood. "Not before I leave for the tour."

"There's been speculation about your relationship. People are wondering why there haven't been any sightings of you two lately."

"She's out of the fucking country," I say through clenched teeth, not liking one bit the direction this conversation is going.

"She mentioned her charity trip to Africa during Christmas break to me. It's a great promotional opportunity, and it would put those rumors to rest. You'll join her."

I pivot on the spot, my anger bubbling to surface. "Hell I will."

Hans's shrewd eyes narrow at me. "This is not a request, Sebastian. The reason you're still part of this band is because I sold you and Gretchen as a brand to Michael. You're the newest darling couple of Britain. We need to capitalize on that."

I take a couple menacing steps toward Hans and stop a few inches away from him. "You and Michael can go fuck yourselves. I'm not a thing, a toy you can do with as you please. I'm a person. Gretchen is a person. We won't be used for Michael's personal gain."

Hans isn't intimidated by me. He thinks he's got the upper hand. "You know what'll happen if you don't."

I laugh hard. "You want to kick me out of the band? Go ahead. I don't give a shit. Better yet, I quit!"

I turn around to get my bag.

"You can't quit, Sebastian. You've signed a contract."

"Weren't you just seconds ago threatening to fire me? Was that just a bluff, Hans?"

A devilish grin spreads over his face. "You young, stupid kids. You're all so easily seduced by the prospect of fame and fortune, you never bother to read your contracts properly. Michael can fire you for breach of contract, but that means you'll have to pay him a hefty fine for loss of income. By the time this is all over, you'll be left with nothing."

"Bullshit! That's not even legal."

"Are you sure about that?"

No I'm not. My uncle offered to read the contract before I signed, but I was too stoked about the opportunity, I brushed him off. Regardless, all the money in the world isn't worth selling my soul.

"I'm not going to Africa, Hans. It has nothing to do with the band, and therefore it's *not* breaching my contract."

Hans's face gets red as it contorts into something deformed, evil, an accurate reflection of his nature. I bask in his anger. I have him, and there's nothing he can do about it. I hoist my bag onto my shoulder and leave.

Oliver is waiting for me outside.

"You heard all that?" I ask.

His expression is solemn. "Yeah."

I'm reeling. I can't go back to Liv like that. I can't tell her about any of it. I don't want to smear her with the ugliness of this business. "I need a drink."

♡ ♡ ♡

LIV

Sebastian texted me an hour ago canceling our plans. He didn't give me any explanation. All he said was he couldn't make it tonight and not to wait up for him. My insides have been twisted since then. I don't know what it is, but I have a bad feeling about it.

I call Saylor the moment I see she's on Skype.

"What's up, Liv? Where's Romeo?"

"I don't know."

"Uh-oh, I don't like that tone. Trouble in paradise already?"

"I don't know that either."

"What do you know, chica?"

"Nothing, that's the problem. I feel so off-kilter, Saylor. I never felt like this before with him, unsure of myself, unsure of our relationship."

Saylor narrows her eyes slightly as she mulls my words over. "Do you want my honest opinion?"

"Of course."

"Your current relationship isn't balanced. Sebastian has all the power now. He can come and go as he pleases, disappear at any moment, leaving you feeling insecure as hell. You, on the other hand, are stuck in one place. You go to work, you come back. Sebastian can always find you. It doesn't help that you're his dirty little secret either."

"Don't say that."

"What? Am I lying?"

I open my mouth to argue, but Saylor raises her hand. "I understand the reasons, and I'm not judging you or criticizing Sebastian. I'm just stating the facts. You're in a very sucky position."

I rest my head in my hand. "I don't know what to do, Saylor."

"Well, for starters, stop being so available to him. You're all upset because he stood you up. It's Friday night and you're all alone, feeling miserable. Go out with your friends."

"He's leaving on Monday, Saylor."

"And he still canceled on you!" she shouts, exasperated, making me wince.

Saylor is right. I put my life on hold just so I could spend every single free moment with Sebastian. And now he's probably partying it up with his buddies. I'm an idiot.

"Sorry, I didn't mean to yell at you," Saylor says.

"It's okay. I needed that. I wish you were here. I miss you, Blue."

"I miss you, too. Six more weeks and I'll be there. Now, stop feeling sorry for yourself and call Lloyd."

That's exactly what I do. He's surprised to hear from me but says I'm more than welcome to join him and his friends. They're going out dancing. Lloyd tells me to wear something sexy, and I'm more than happy to comply. Feeling beautiful goes a long way to lifting my spirits, but the moment I remove my coat at the club, I feel uncomfortable, exposed. I hug myself as if that'll protect me somehow.

Lloyd hugs me sideways. "Stop hiding your hot bod, Liv. You look scrumptious. I would do you if I wasn't gay."

"Lloyd!"

"Come on, let's get something to drink."

The 'something to drink' turned out to be many shots of tequila. Ten minutes later, we find ourselves on one of the many dance floors the club has, ready to leave our problems behind. The music is loud and there are so many people in the club, it's almost impossible to not bump into someone.

This is not my scene, and getting drunker than a sorority girl on spring break is definitely not my MO. A small and annoying voice in my head tells me that a relationship shouldn't drive me to act reckless, but I don't listen to it. There will be plenty of time to regret my actions later.

"I'm so glad you called me, Liv," Lloyd shouts in my ear. "I don't think we've ever partied together before."

"I'm glad, too."

"You know, I would've invited you, but I knew Maurice would be here."

Oh yeah, his buddy Maurice is here somewhere. Thankfully, I only had to deal with his presence briefly, while we were in line to get in. After that, he made himself scarce.

"Fuck Maurice. Let's just keep dancing."

We move to the beat like there's no one watching, and it's the best feeling in the world. We're now on the eighties hits dance floor, and besides dancing, we sing along to the songs we know. We're joined by two of Lloyd's friends, Karine and Melissa. They're loud and obnoxious, but super fun. Or maybe it's just the alcohol making everything ten times better.

Time flies and soon I find myself inside a cab, being dropped off in front of the Hollingsworth. Lloyd laughs his ass off when I stumble out of the taxi and almost fall flat on my face. I'm carrying my shoes and my coat. I must look like a hot mess.

I should put my shoes back on, but my feet are completely destroyed after dancing for hours in heels. I peer through the glass door, checking the hotel's lobby. It's deserted, and the night shift receptionist is nowhere to be seen. Screw it, I'll make a dash for the elevator.

No one sees me. Who knew alcohol would turn me into a freaking ninja? I'm laughing to myself as I open the door to my room. I notice someone's silhouette in the darkness and let out a bloodcurdling scream. The bedside lamp turns on, and I find Sebastian sitting on the edge of my bed, leaning his elbows on his thighs with his hands crossed.

I put my hand on my chest as I try to control my breathing. "Jesus, you scared the shit out of me. How did you get in?"

Sebastian looks me up and down, and his eyes turn into slits when he sees the shoes in my hands, or it could be my outfit he doesn't approve of. It's tight and short.

"Where have you been?" His voice matches his closed-off stance.

"Out." I throw the coat and shoes into the corner and walk toward the stash of snacks I have on my desk. I'm starving.

"*Out?* That's all you have to say? I've been calling you for the past three hours."

I turn to him, the tequila working as an amplifier, making my emotions expand beyond me. The resentment from earlier becomes anger in a split second. "What for?"

Sebastian stands up and towers over me. My room never felt so small; his presence seems to take over everything. He's so close to me that a whiff of whiskey reaches my nose as he exhales.

"To wish you good night."

I snort. "Right, it sounds like you were making sure I was waiting patiently for you while you were out with your friends. My life doesn't revolve around you, Sebastian."

"Where did you go?"

"None of your business."

He invades my space completely now, forcing me to retreat until my back hits the wall.

"It *is* my business. Everything about you is my business."

"I'm not your fucking property!" I scream.

That gives him pause. His face softens and his gaze lowers to my lips. "I know, but you are mine," he says in a heated whisper before he crushes his lips to mine.

I fight him, weak punches to his chest that show how puny I am in his arms. He has no right to be angry at me, yet even so, I surrender. His tongue invades my mouth with fury and my body reacts like it always does. I kiss him back with the same ferocity, with the same urgency. He pushes me against the cold wall as he slides his hands up my legs, under my dress. He curls his fingers around my panties, and with one hard pull, the fabric tears. Then his right hand is there, taking possession, driving me to the edge of madness. But it's not enough. I need to feel all of him.

With eager fingers, I unbutton his jeans and my hand disappears inside his boxers. He groans against my mouth and lifts me off the floor with one arm. I let go of his erection to hold on to his shoulders as I wrap my legs around his waist. With one powerful thrust, he's inside me, and I bite his lower lip to keep from screaming. We stop kissing, but our lips are still connected, brushing against each other while grunts and moans of pleasure escape them.

"You're mine. You'll always be mine," he says as his movements become more intense, more primal.

My head falls backward and I close my eyes as the pressure where our bodies converge increases. Sebastian pounds away, claiming me, branding me, and I let him because I'm doing the same to him. I scream his name at the same time he screams mine. I'm shaking, but he's shaking more. He thrusts into me one final time before he stops moving. It's so very quiet in the room, yet at the same time it's not. The sound of my pulse reverberates through my ears, matching the beating of Sebastian's heart. He rests his cheek on my shoulder. He's breathing just as hard as I am.

I untangle my legs, and Sebastian pulls out of me slowly. My feet touch the floor, but it feels like I'm standing on water. My legs are made of air; they can't hold me. I feel something warm trickle down, and the reality of what we just did hits me. I gasp and look down.

"Oh, fuck," Sebastian says, and my gaze snaps back up. He's staring at my legs, too. Then he does something that makes me love him even more. He grabs the little towel hanging next to the sink, drops to his knees in front of me, and begins to clean me.

"Liv, I'm so sorry. I don't know what I was thinking."

I glide my fingers through his hair, and he tilts his head up. "It's okay, Bas. I'm on the pill."

His gaze doesn't show the relief I expected. "It wouldn't matter if you weren't. And I've been tested. I'm clean."

It's great to hear that I'm not at risk, but my brain only seems to latch on to the first part of his statement. "What do you mean, it wouldn't matter?"

"I'm saying I'm here to stay. If an accident were to happen, it wouldn't change a thing. You'll be the mother of my children one day. I knew that when I was sixteen, and I know it now."

Tears pool in my eyes, and the fight we had minutes ago is nothing, vapor. It led to the most fantastic sex of my life—I'm not going to deny it. But tender moments like these are what move me, what make an imprint in my heart and my soul. They're the most precious things Sebastian and I can ever have, and by the emotion pouring out of his eyes, he knows it, too.

♡ ♡ ♡

Sebastian leaves for the Boys Future world tour two days later on a rainy and bitter morning. My heart tightens as he kisses me goodbye.

"I love you," he says.

"I love you more."

"Impossible. Settle for a tie?" His lips curl up slightly, but there's no joy in his eyes.

I nod as I try to hold it together. He kisses me one more time before taking the stairs to the living room below. We've spent the last twenty hours holed up in his apartment in Camden, forgetting the world outside existed. But we can only pretend for so long.

I roll onto my side and watch Sebastian grab his duffel bag and open the door. He turns to look at me one more time, pausing for just a second before he disappears over the threshold.

When the door clicks shut, I bury my face in his pillow, breathing in his scent, and finally let the dam break loose.

CHAPTER 40
LIV

SIX WEEKS LATER

crane my neck, trying to see beyond the heads of all the people in front of me as I scan the international arrivals. My body is a ball of anticipation, and I shuffle from foot to foot, unable to remain still. Heathrow Airport is absolute madness less than a week before Christmas break.

I don't want Saylor to miss me, so I wiggle my way closer to the gate. A couple of minutes later, I spot her colorful mane and wave like a maniac. She sees me and the biggest smile breaks out on her face. She pushes her luggage trolley faster, almost running toward me.

We hug and squeal together as we jump up and down. Saylor pivots me so now she's the one facing the sliding doors she just came through.

"I've missed you so much, Liv!"

"I've missed you, too, Blue. I can't believe you're finally here!"

"Me neither. Pinch me."

I try to, but she's wearing a thick jacket and probably felt nothing.

Saylor takes a couple of steps back, still grinning, but there's a devilish spark in her eyes. She's up to something. I know it.

Suddenly I'm tackled from both sides, and my heart almost leaps out of my mouth.

"Surprise!" Emma and Kennedy scream in unison.

"What? Oh my God, you guys came. I can't believe it." My adrenaline is still pumping as I hug them.

"Of course we came. It's London, baby!" Emma says.

"What about your father's wedding?"

Emma gives me a toothy grin. "I convinced my newest stepmom that getting married during Christmas was tacky. They got married in Hawaii last month."

"Man, I envy your powers of persuasion," I say, then turn to Kennedy. "What about you, Ken? I thought you were spending Christmas with your mom in Italy."

"I will, but Christmas is only one day. I'm flying to Milan on the twenty-fourth, so I won't miss your birthday. I'll come back to London for New Year's Eve, and I'm bringing Max with me. It's going to be epic."

"I can't wait to meet him. And by the way, I want to hear all about your new movie."

Kennedy's eyebrows squish together, and her full lips become a flat line. I don't understand her reaction at all. "We haven't started shooting yet, but the 'get to know the cast members' weekend was intense."

Kennedy pushes her trolley forward, and I guess that's the end of the conversation. She's one year younger than Saylor, Emma, and me and only moved in with us last year. It was easy to welcome her into our tight-knit group, but from the get-go we knew there were many aspects of her life she didn't like to talk about.

We start to move away from the crowd, toward the line to buy the bus tickets, when Emma puts a hand on my arm. "I ordered a car to pick us up."

I stare at her for a couple of seconds before shaking my head. Sometimes I forget that Emma has a lot of money at her disposal. Her father is a famous celebrity lawyer in LA, and he spoils his only daughter rotten. She's down to earth most of the time, except when she does things like ordering a car to drive us to the city.

I lean closer to Saylor and whisper. "Did she upgrade your tickets to first class?"

"She sure did, and it was awesome."

During the ride, the girls can't stop firing off questions about my life in London. I answer them to the best of my ability while avoiding mentioning anything related to Sebastian. I hate that I have to keep our relationship a secret. It's such a burden, and I wonder how long we'll be able to carry on before it blows up in our faces. I'm tempted to tell Emma and Kennedy about it. It would be so much easier, but I don't know how they'll react.

Am I selfish for wanting a drama-free birthday week?

The girls are staying in one of the nicest suites the Hollingsworth has, all with the compliments of Mr. Hart, Emma's dad. When I introduce them to my bento-box room, Emma freaks out and begs me to stay with them. As much as I want to, Sebastian is coming to London in a few days, and if I accept Emma's invitation, I won't be able to see him at all. I feel wretched all over again.

SEBASTIAN

I never thought I would say this, but it's good to be back on British soil. London never felt like home to me. I always felt out of place, an alien among strangers. But today, knowing Liv is waiting for me, it's the best place in the universe. Home will always be wherever she is.

The US leg of our tour was a success, with sold-out tickets at every venue, endless interviews, and invites to the best parties. I'm not going to lie and say all that doesn't thrill me anymore. It still gets me fired up, but it's a bittersweet emotion because I can't share it with Liv yet. Things won't be right until we can be together in the open.

During the tour, reporters pestered me constantly about my relationship with Gretchen, and I came close to telling them the truth. But Oliver was always there to intervene, to divert the questions to another topic when he knew I was ready to blow. My hope is that Liv hasn't watched any of those interviews.

It'll be better that way, so when I do speak up about my relationship with Gretchen, it'll be to announce the official end of it. Saying we're on a break would only lead to more speculations, and I'm afraid the tabloids' hound dogs would eventually sniff Liv out. I can't let her take the fall for my shortcomings.

As soon as the plane touched down, I texted Liv, wishing her a happy birthday. In reality, I wanted to talk to her, hear her voice, but with Hans nearby, I couldn't take the risk. There's a burning need in me to go see her right away—these six weeks apart have been almost unbearable—and it kills me that I can't. If I was a regular guy, I could show up at her work, take her out to lunch. Sometimes fame is a bitch.

Liv's reply takes longer than I can stand, and I start to feel antsy. I'm bouncing my legs up and down as I stare at my phone.

"Yo, mate! Are you coming, or do you want to fly back to the States?" Oliver asks.

My head snaps up. "What?"

"You'd better be calling Gretchen," Hans says as he walks by my seat.

I flip him off. *Wanker.*

When Hans is out of the private plane, Oliver turns to me. "No word from her yet?"

"No. Maybe she forgot her phone in her room or something."

Oliver laughs. "You're whipped."

"Sod off."

I hear a ping from my phone, and my heartbeat kicks up a notch.

I'm *so* whipped.

LIV: Thanks. Did you have a good flight?

ME: Yeah, when can I see you?

LIV: I don't know. It might be more difficult than we thought.

My thorax caves in, pressuring my heart. At least that's what feels like.

ME: Why?

LIV: My other roommates Emma and Kennedy came to surprise me. They don't know about us.

"Shit!" I say.

"Trouble?" Oliver asks. He's waiting for me, mainly because he loves gossip and is getting a kick out of my messed-up love life.

I glance at him. "Liv's other roommates are in London and they don't know about us. But I have to see Liv today or I'll go nuts."

Oliver rolls his eyes. "You're already nuts."

There's another ping, and I look at my phone.

LIV: They want to go to The Singing Olive tonight. Apparently, the club moved Throwback Thursday to Wednesday night because of Christmas and it's a not-to-be-missed outing.

"That's perfect," Oliver says over my shoulder, and I realize he read her message.

I frown at him. "How is that perfect? You know Liv and I can't be seen in public together, not even amongst a group of people. It's too risky."

"Throwback night at The Singing Olive means we can wear a costume, go incognito."

I stare at Oliver and an idea begins to form in my head. I text Liv back.

ME: *Bummer. I guess I'll see you tomorrow, then.*

"What are you doing?" Oliver asks.

I smirk at him. "Are you up to crashing Liv's birthday party?"

Oliver's smile unfurls slowly, like he's the freaking Grinch. "I'm always up for crashing something."

CHAPTER 41
LIV

stare at my phone and cannot believe my eyes. I don't know what I expected Sebastian to do—I know he can't come to The Singing Olive with me—but his reply was so noncommittal, so blasé, it makes me feel the size of a tiny ant.

Lloyd rolls his chair toward my desk and leans closer, trying to read my message. I close it quickly before he can. "So, have you heard from him?"

"Yeah, he just landed." I avoid Lloyd's gaze and stare at my computer instead, seeing nothing.

"Hmm, you don't sound too excited about it."

"We can't see each other tonight. You know why."

Since Lloyd already knew about my history with Sebastian, I didn't see the point of hiding from him that we got back together. I'm already lying to too many people, and I need someone to have my back, to vent to when Saylor isn't around.

"You know that's BS. He can't party with a group of friends?"

I chew on my bottom lip, thinking the same. He could join me if he wanted to. *Ugh!* Here I go again, feeling insecure as hell. I force a smile to my face. "I actually prefer if he doesn't come. I'll be able to enjoy the evening much more if I don't have to constantly monitor my actions."

Lloyd smacks my leg. "That's the spirit! You don't turn twenty-one every day. So, do you already know what you're going to wear?"

I smile for real this time. "Oh, yeah. Saylor has taken care of our outfits."

"Oooh, do tell. I'm intrigued."

"Say, Lloyd, are you familiar with Jem and the Holograms?"

Lloyd scrunches up his nose. "You're not talking about that silly teen movie, are you? I swear the only good thing about that disaster is Ryan Guzman. Yum-my."

"No, I'm talking about the real deal."

♡ ♡ ♡

"Holy crap! This place is surreal," Kennedy screams as her gaze darts everywhere.

The Singing Olive is packed, and the waiting line took us almost thirty minutes. For once, Emma didn't try to use her money to bribe the bouncer to usher us inside ahead of everyone else, too caught up in the exciting energy surrounding us, too. The first thing we see as we enter the place is a huge mural depicting flying pigs playing harps, serenading the most unusual group of poker players—a goat, James Cameron's xenomorph, Queen Elizabeth, and a shark wearing a tutu.

Emma flags a waitress walking by and asks her something. I can't hear a thing because the music is too loud. From where I stand, I see a group singing "Rock the Boat" on the karaoke stage, and they're pretty good. The main area is massive, and right in front of the stage is a dance floor where people wearing the craziest ensembles are dancing like no one is around.

Emma turns to us. "Follow me, girls."

Lloyd laces his arm with mine, and we weave through the round tables that are already all taken. We stop abruptly by one with six chairs that has an ice bucket with champagne chilling inside and a "Reserved" sign on it.

"Ta-da!" Emma opens her arms in a grand gesture. "Happy birthday, Liv."

"I didn't know you could reserve a table in this place," Mellie says from behind me.

"My father taught me to never take no for an answer," Emma replies.

"This is unbelievable." My voice is all choked up and my eyes well with tears. I have the best friends in the world.

Saylor hugs me sideways. "You deserve it, chica."

"Okay, we need group pictures." Kennedy takes her phone out and then turns to a guy sitting at a neighboring table. "Do you mind taking a picture of us?"

He eyes her up and down, and a sly grin appears on his lips. "For you, luv? Anything."

We huddle together and say cheese for the camera, then make silly poses. Kennedy gets her phone back, and then Lloyd takes pictures of the four of us.

"All right, enough with the camera-palooza." Saylor sits down and grabs the bottle of champagne.

I don't sit right away, taking a minute to soak everything in. I want to commit this evening to memory, because I know how rare moments like these are. There's Saylor, my sister from another mister, wearing her Pizzazz outfit. It's so typical Saylor to suggest we dress up as Jem and the Holograms and then choose to be the lead singer of the Misfits, Jem's archenemy.

Weirdly enough, no one wanted to be Jem. Kennedy bought a hot pink wig yesterday and decided to dress up as Kimber, Jem's younger sister. Emma and I didn't want to go the wig route, so we used washable color dye on our hair. She has blue stripes in hers, and the tips of mine are purple. I just hope the color does wash off like the instructions said it would.

"How in the world do you even know what bloody *Jem and the Holograms* is? You were born a decade after it was popular," Mellie says.

Saylor, Emma, Kennedy, and I all stare at each other, but it's

Emma who answers Mellie's question in the end. "Has Liv ever told you about our school?"

"No," Mellie and Lloyd say in unison.

"Well, DuBose College specializes in creative and performing arts, so it has a pretty unique academic atmosphere. First of all, there are no fraternities or sororities. The campus is shaped like a compass, and the student body is divided in different houses—North, South, East, and West."

"Oh, like Harry Potter," Lloyd says.

"Yeah, and like in the Harry Potter books, the houses compete throughout the year. It instills a sense of belonging and motivates students to always do better. It's a pretty awesome system. But anyway, I'm going off topic here. There are games and competitions, and one year, the houses had to put up a show based on a pop icon from the eighties. We chose to do a play of one of the *Jem and the Holograms* episodes."

"That's brilliant. I hope you won," Mellie says.

Kennedy pouts. "We didn't win. We lost to the Northerners. They recreated Michael Jackson's 'Thriller' video clip. It was freaking awesome."

"So which house do you belong to?" Lloyd asks.

"South," I say.

"Southies forever!" Saylor raises her glass, and we all do the same.

"Champagne is all fine and good, but we need some shots." Kennedy flags a waiter. "Six tequila shots please, the best you have."

"Six shots? What are you, an amateur?" Emma chimes in. She turns to the guy wearing a muscle shirt and a fluorescent green bow tie. "Bring the entire bottle, mister."

"Oh boy. You do realize we all have to work tomorrow, right?" Mellie rests her head in her hand.

"But it's the day before Christmas." Kennedy sounds surprised and outraged at the same time.

"We work in events, Ken," I say.

"Blah, blah, blah. I don't wanna hear another word about work. It's your twenty-first birthday, girlfriend. We're all getting hammered. Now, how do we get a go on that stage?" Saylor points ahead, and I let my gaze travel past the dancing crowd. The stage is presently empty, and the music blasting through the speakers is being spun by the DJ tucked into a dark corner of the room.

"I'm not singing!" Mellie squeaks.

I'm about to announce the same thing when Saylor looks pointedly at me. "Don't even try bailing on us, Liv. You're singing with us."

Damn! Saylor knows me too well. I'm not the worst singer in the world, but I can't compare to her, or Emma and Kennedy for that matter. I need liquid courage.

"Not before I drink some tequila."

"What should we sing?" Emma asks.

"Oh, I know, I know!" Kennedy raises her hand. "Let's repeat our Spice Girls number. It was frigging fantastic."

"Another houses' competition performance?" Mellie asks.

"No, it was a number we put together for my sister's wedding last year," I say and then involuntarily remember what transpired after that. I shake my head because the last thing I want to think about is Derek.

I immediately get a pang in my chest that Sebastian isn't here with me. I love my girlfriends, but tonight is a milestone for me, and the disappointment that he didn't even try to come won't go away. Then guilt mixes in, making my heart feel twice as heavy. Sebastian's parents passed away almost a week before my birthday. I know this is a terrible time for him.

Saylor puts her hand on my arm. "Hey, are you okay?"

I lift my gaze to meet hers. "Yeah. Everything is great."

Saylor narrows her eyes a fraction, and I think she's about to say something else when Emma interrupts.

"Yay! Tequila is here!"

CHAPTER 42
SEBASTIAN

Oliver's idea of going incognito is for us to wear full-blown Kiss regalia, weird wigs and black-and-white makeup included. No one will recognize us for sure, but we look ridiculous. Being in disguise also means we aren't granted the perks that usually come with our fame, so we have to wait in line like everyone else to get inside The Singing Olive.

People stare at us, and I find it unnerving that those looks of curiosity aren't followed by screaming and camera flashes. When we finally reach the bouncer at the entrance, he looks us up and down, and for a second, I think he's going to send us away. But he surprises me when he says, "Nice costume."

Once inside, Oliver turns to me. "So what's the plan now, Romeo?"

A quick scan of the main room ahead tells me that we won't get a table at this hour. It also tells me that finding Liv will be difficult. I settle for finding Saylor instead, hoping her current bright blue-and-green hair won't blend in with the sea of crazy wigs here. I'm glad Liv showed me a recent picture of Saylor; otherwise, I wouldn't recognize her either.

"Let's get a drink and then walk around the room. Look for a chick with blue-and-green mermaid hair," I say.

Oliver gives me an incredulous glance. "You're joking, right?"

I don't answer him and make my way to the main bar. I haven't been in this place since our performance of "Africa" that ultimately landed us in Boys Future. I'm pleased to see that nothing has changed. I know it's odd, but I'm feeling a bit sentimental now. God, I'm such a pansy.

Five minutes later, and with drinks in hand, we begin our mission to locate Liv and her friends. I wonder if she'll recognize me. Gremlins invade my stomach, and my heart receives a jolt of adrenaline. I feel like a teenager again, standing in front of Liv's darkened window, ready to confess my love to her.

I'm scanning the tables when I feel Oliver's hand on my upper arm. "Please tell me that's the chick I'm looking for."

I follow Oliver's gaze, and sure enough, there's Saylor wearing some kind of white, black, and neon green eighties costume on the stage. My eyes immediately wander to her right and find Liv in a similar outfit but in different colors. Her hair is curly and has a purple hue to it. There's weird makeup on her face creating geometric shapes. The microskirt she's wearing stirs all my senses awake, and I'm hit with two distinct impulses —take her to a private place so I can remove that tiny piece of cloth with my teeth *or* cover her up so none of the baboons in the room can ogle her.

There are two other girls on the stage. They must be Liv's roommates. The four of them take their spots and wait while the crowd cheers and whistles. Liv and Saylor trade looks before Liv smiles. I can't stay this far away from her, so I make my way toward the stage, heedless if I'm shoving people out of my way or not. I hear Oliver apologize here and there, but the sound is muffled.

Suddenly, a familiar tune blasts through the speakers.

"Bloody hell! They're singing Spice Girls here? That's ballsy!" Oliver says behind me, and I laugh.

I manage to get to the front row and stare unabashedly at my gorgeous girlfriend as she struts, turns, and sings like a pro. My jaw is loose, and I may be drooling. The room is hot, and while the wig and the costume don't help, I'm burning up for entirely different reasons.

♡ ♡ ♡

LIV

People say once you're on a stage, it's easy to forget you're performing in front of strangers because with all the lights on you, you can't see the audience. Nonetheless, I can feel his stare bearing down on me. I try to ignore it, but something inside makes me want to search for the owner of that intense gaze.

About a minute into our routine, I find him. There's a guy wearing the most ridiculous Kiss outfit in front of the stage, looking at me in a way that makes me uneasy and warm at the same time. Quickly, I convince myself that it must be the tequila talking.

I focus on finishing our performance of "Wannabe" without making a fool of myself, but I'm completely aware of the stranger following all of my movements. The song ends, and people actually clap and cheer for us. My heart is going a thousand miles per hour, and the feeling of excitement is overpowering and amazing. I get why Saylor and Sebastian love singing so much.

We return our mics to the sound assistant and exit the stage. Lloyd and Mellie are right there when we take the stairs down. They're bouncing and screaming, gushing about how awesome we were. Emma says something about drinking, and we begin moving back to our table. The dance floor is so full, we have to walk in single file, and I'm bringing up the rear. I get a sense of unease as the tiny hairs on the back of my neck rise. Someone grabs me by the waist, and I find myself flush against Kiss man. I'm about to yell when my eyes connect with his, and I want to scream for completely different reasons. Sebastian is looking at me with a shit-eating grin plastered on his face.

"That was some show you put on there. I never knew you could sing, birthday girl."

"What are you doing here?"

He picks up a strand of my purple hair before he breaks the distance between us and kisses me, right there in the middle of the dance floor. His lips taste strange with the makeup on, but it's easy to ignore that when his expert tongue is exploring my mouth. My arms circle his back as I try to meld with him. I can feel how happy he is to see me through our clothes. Desire erupts in my belly, and I'm hit with a need so grand it verges on desperation.

Another song starts and someone bumps into us. We break apart, and our breathing is ragged, out of control.

Sebastian rests his forehead against mine.

"God, I've missed you so much," he says.

"I've missed you more."

He kisses me again, a sweet peck on the lips that's almost too brief to count.

"I can't believe you came. What if someone recognizes you?"

"Liv, if you couldn't recognize me right away, no one will."

"How did you—"

"I noticed how uncomfortable you got when you were up there and caught me staring. You thought I was a creep, didn't you?"

"That's not fair. I could hardly see with all those lights on my face."

Sebastian chuckles and the sound is so light, so warm, that I want to put it in jar and preserve it forever. He lets go of my waist and laces his fingers with mine. "Come on. Your friends must be wondering where you are."

"Did you come by yourself?" I ask.

"No, Ollie is here somewhere."

We get close to our table just in time to see Saylor standing up with her hands on her hips, screaming at another guy wearing a Kiss outfit. It must be Oliver. I don't catch the end of her rant, but I'm there to witness the grand finale. Saylor picks up a glass of something and throws its contents on Oliver's face.

"Bloody hell!" he shouts and stands up as well. "You crazy—"

"I wouldn't finish that sentence, mate," Sebastian says jokingly, but I detect a warning tone, too.

Emma's gaze connects with mine, and her eyebrows shoot to the heavens. "Liv, why do you have shit smeared all over your face?"

I touch the area around my lips, and sure enough, my fingers have gray goo on them. I turn to Sebastian and see he's missing part of his makeup.

Freaking great. Now I look like a clown.

Lloyd glances from me to Sebastian, making the connection almost immediately. His mouth makes a perfect O, and then he smiles and gives me two thumbs-up.

"What are you doing?" Sebastian shouts, and I follow his gaze.

Oliver has removed his wig and is now wiping his face with a napkin. I can see the moment my friends recognize him.

"Holy shit! It's Oliver Best!" Emma shouts, making me cringe.

In a panic, I look around us, hoping her outburst has gone unnoticed.

No such luck. It only takes one person next to our table to recognize Oliver before the news that a Boys Future member is in the house spreads like wildfire through the club. It won't take long for fans to approach our table.

"You moron! Look what you've done!" Sebastian yells at his friend.

"It wasn't my fault." Oliver points at Saylor. "If this crazy mermaid had any sense of humor—"

"Oh, so it's *my* fault you're a dickhead who can't take no for an answer?" Saylor spits back.

We're still standing glued to the spot when two girls get in between us and Oliver to ask for pictures. Sebastian grabs my arm and pulls me back with him. "Liv, we gotta go. I'm sorry."

I can see regret reflected in his eyes. Sebastian hasn't been recognized yet, but it won't take long now. I turn to my friends, but they're too preoccupied getting pictures with Oliver as well. Except Saylor. Her gaze connects with mine and she mouths, "Go."

I let Sebastian drag me from the main room, only stopping by the coat check counter to get our jackets. Outside, the air is bitter cold, and I wrap my arms around my midsection, trying to get warmer. Sebastian pulls me to his side and kisses my temple as he flags a cab driving by. Once we're inside, he gives the driver his home address.

I look out the window and feel a pang of regret and sadness to be leaving my own birthday party so abruptly. Is this what my life with Sebastian will be like? Will we ever be able to have a private moment without having to worry about fans and paparazzi?

Sebastian must've sensed my turmoil. He touches my chin with his index finger and turns my face to his. "I'm so fucking sorry we had to leave."

I sigh and look at my lap. "I know."

I'm not mad at him. I can't fault Sebastian for what happened. I'm frustrated and disappointed with this whole situation.

"Liv?"

"Yeah?"

"I've got a present for you."

Something in his tone makes me laugh. "If you say your present is between your legs, I'm gonna kick you in the nuts."

He puts a protective hand over his crotch. "Don't even joke about that. After six weeks of no action at all, I need Junior here to be intact."

"*Junior?*" I laugh even harder and can't seem to stop. I have the giggles.

"Come on, Liv. Don't laugh. I'm trying to be romantic here."

I wipe the rogue tears that have escaped the corners of my eyes and curl my legs under me, turning my body to Sebastian's. "Okay, okay. No more laughing."

Sebastian retrieves a square box from the inside pocket of his jacket, and I stop breathing for a split second. But then I take in the size of the box—it's way too big to house an engagement ring. The pressure on my chest eases. We've barely started dating again, plus I hardly think a proposal inside a cab is romantic.

He gives the box to me, and I loosen the pretty pink bow with eager fingers. When I open it, there's a white gold bracelet inside, and next to it is a key.

"It's beautiful."

"It's a promise bracelet." He takes the jewelry from the box and puts it on my wrist. Once it's fastened, he uses the key to lock it.

"It can only be unlocked with this key." He places the key on my open palm and then closes my fingers over it. I look at him, finally catching on to the significance of this moment.

"I know it's too soon to ask you to marry me," Sebastian continues, "but I want you to know I'm not going anywhere, I'll never abandon you again, no matter what. This bracelet symbolizes that promise. I hope you never have to use its key, because if you do, it'll mean I failed." His voice catches at the end, and I'm overwhelmed with emotion. I can't speak, can't think. My heart is pounding away, and there's a buzz in my ears. Air breaks free from my lungs in one powerful gale.

I drop the key inside my purse, and then I hold his face between my shaking hands. "I know you won't fail." Those are the only words I manage to say before I kiss him with my whole heart and soul, accepting his vow, believing in his promise with absolute faith.

CHAPTER 43
SEBASTIAN

spent the last ten minutes staring at Liv's sleeping form. Her hair still has some curls, and it's kind of wild. I smile, knowing I'm responsible for the tangled mess. My dick has been standing at attention even before I opened my eyes, and it's a Herculean effort to just look at her and not touch.

Her eyelids flutter before they open lazily and I'm rewarded with one of Liv's sweetest smiles.

"Morning," she says so softly it's almost a purr.

She's my little sexy kitten, and the fact that I can now be near her, hold her tight whenever I want, makes my heart expand until it feels like it's going to burst of happiness.

"Did you sleep well?" I ask.

"Marvelously." She stretches her arms at the same time her legs tangle with mine. Our chests touch, and that's my undoing.

My hand seeks her body like I have no control over my movements. I trace the curve of her hip with my fingertips, leaving a trail of goose bumps on her skin.

"Bas, what are you doing?" Her voice already sounds breathless, and my lips twitch upward.

"Nothing," I say and let the smile unfurl completely.

When we got to my apartment last night, we couldn't get out

of our clothes fast enough. The six weeks apart were torture, and in moments of insanity during the tour, I began to doubt that I had gotten Liv back into my life for real. So every kiss, every caress was a way to reassure myself that the woman next to me was not an illusion. That meant we spent the entire night between the sheets. But my desire hasn't diminished; on the contrary, I want her even more now, with her glorious morning hair and her warm and smooth skin. My hunger for Liv is insatiable.

My fingers continue their path toward her center, and I find it's already burning up and ready for me. Her legs part, granting me better access as she leans her body even closer to mine. I put more pressure against her and she kisses the hollow of my neck, making *me* break out in goose bumps this time. When I plunge a finger inside her, she sucks in a breath. Her long nails scratch my bare chest, not hard enough to hurt or break skin but enough to turn my need into an almost unbearable thing.

Her hand moves down until her apt fingers curl around me, making me grunt. We don't speak, the only sounds in the room our ragged breathing and the occasional moans of pleasure that escape our lips. Liv tilts her head backward and our heated gazes collide. We keep them locked, and it's a challenge now, a race to see who'll finish first. I insert another finger in her, increasing the pressure both inside and outside of her. I don't want to win; I want to make Liv fall apart first, because the way I envision finishing this race is buried deep inside of her.

It doesn't take long for her to come. In the short amount of time we've been together again, I've become an expert on everything Liv. I know every contour of her body, every sweet spot that makes her go crazy. She screams my name as her hold on me slackens. Once the tremors pass, I roll over her, then kiss her long and hard as I thrust inside her with one precise push. I swallow her moans, eating them up like they're candy, but I have to go deeper. There's a primal need in me to brand her, mark her as mine. I grab her leg behind the knee and pull it between our chests, holding it firmly against my shoulder.

"Oh my God, Bas, I can't...." Her whisper trails off as her head falls backward, her eyes shutting.

I pound against her, trying to keep the wave of pleasure in check, unwilling for this moment to end. But eventually it does, and I say her name over and over again until I'm all empty. I hold Liv against the mattress with my weight and hide my face in the crook of her neck. I can't hear anything besides the sound of our hearts drumming away in sync.

I pull out of her and tuck her to my side, refusing to let go. I'm a greedy man when it comes to Liv.

She rests her cheek on my chest and sighs. "It's official. I'll never be able to leave this bed. My legs are mush."

I smile and kiss the top of her head. "Fine by me. Are you hungry?"

"Famished."

"Good. I'll order some breakfast from the café next door."

Liv leans back, resting on her elbow to look at my face. "They deliver?"

"To me? Yeah."

♡ ♡ ♡

Thirty minutes later, we're both showered and Liv is presently making coffee, wearing one of my T-shirts. There's nothing sexier than seeing the girl of my dreams in my clothes. Liv wasn't planning on staying the night, so her only option was to borrow something from me or wear last night's outfit. The fact that she doesn't have any personal belongings in my apartment is a problem we need to remedy soon.

"You're coming with me tonight to my uncle's Christmas dinner party," I say.

Liv turns to me, carrying a steaming mug of coffee in her hand. Her deer-in-headlights expression is adorable.

"Bas—" she begins, but I don't let her finish that sentence.

"Liv, I haven't spent Christmas with my family since I moved out two years ago. And even so, when I was present, it felt very much like I wasn't even there. I hated every single moment of it and made no attempt to hide it. This year is the first time I'm actually excited to celebrate Christmas, and the reason is *you*."

Liv opens her mouth to speak again, but my doorbell rings.

"Breakfast is here," I say.

I take the flight of stairs down faster than Superman and open the door to the street without bothering to look through the peephole. I'm only wearing my old sweatpants and didn't bother with a T-shirt; I like to catch Liv checking me out when she doesn't think I'm aware.

I find Jimmy, the café owner's son, at my door carrying two bags of heavenly goodies. But right behind him is a group of paparazzi, waiting for the opportunity to snap shots of me. They haven't bothered me in ages at my house, and I'm taken aback by their presence.

Jimmy gives me an apologetic look as he takes my money. I don't know why he's feeling guilty; it's not his fault that today of all days, those pests decided to bother me.

The paparazzi only wait a couple of seconds before they start to ask questions as they take their godforsaken pictures.

"Bas, who's the friend staying with you?"

"Coleman, what does Gretchen think of you kissing another woman?"

"How long have you been cheating on Gretchen?"

The blood drains from my face, and Jimmy takes off quickly. I shut the door and go back to my apartment in a daze, feeling like I've just swallowed dozens of lead balls. As soon as I'm through the door, I go to the windows and shut all the curtains.

"Bas, what happened?" Liv asks, standing in the hallway.

"The paparazzi are outside."

"Why?"

I glance at her, feeling like the biggest bastard who has ever lived. "They know about us."

Liv's eyes widen, and she drops her mug of coffee to the floor. It breaks into pieces and dark liquid splatters everywhere, mainly on her naked legs. She doesn't seem to notice. Her panicked eyes are fixated on me.

"How?"

I put the food on the kitchen table and go to her, grabbing her shoulders to make sure she doesn't pull away from me.

"I'm not sure, but it'll be okay. I promise you."

Liv nods and I pull her to me, hugging her tight. I'll do anything to protect her. I won't let the media destroy the love of my life, even if I have to damn my soul beyond salvation.

She pulls away first and looks at the mess on the floor. "Shit. Let me clean this up."

"Don't worry about that," I say, but she's not listening to me any longer. I think she's in shock. She opens a few cabinet doors until she finds the cleaning supplies.

I walk to the living room and grab my phone. As usual, there are several messages there, all meaningless from people I don't care about. There's only one text from Oliver with a simple *I'm sorry*.

After the kitchen floor is clean, Liv goes in search of her own phone. I fire up my laptop, knowing I won't like what will come up when I search my name. Liv joins me on the couch, but her face is glued to the device in her hand.

"Any word from Saylor?"

"Yeah."

I don't like the sound of her voice. It's defeated and sad.

My computer is finally on, and I go straight to Google. There are several articles talking about Oliver's surprise appearance at The Singing Olive. I click on the link at the top of the page. The first pictures in the article have him and Saylor in the frame, then Oliver surrounded by fans. It's not until I scroll all the way down the page that I see the picture that makes me sick to my stomach. It's a shot of Liv and me, kissing in the middle of the dance floor.

"Oh my God," Liv says.

My mind is reeling. How did they get that picture? We're both unrecognizable, but the caption says "Sebastian Coleman caught kissing mysterious girl."

Fuck, fuck, fuck.

Liv jumps from the couch before I can say anything. She has her phone glued to her ear, and a second later, she's talking.

"Saylor? Did you see the pictures?"

Liv starts pacing in front of me, her movements skittish and tense. I did that to her, brought her to my world of lies and exploitation. She's tainted and it's my fault.

Saylor says something to her that makes Liv's shoulders slump forward.

"How did they react?" she asks. "Really?"

My phone starts to ring, and I see Oliver's name flashing on the screen.

"Mate, I'm so fucking sorry," he says as soon as I answer.

"It's not your fault," I say but not truly meaning it. Part of me does blame Oliver for the aftermath. But it's pointless to point fingers. The damage is already done.

"Are you home? Is she there?"

"Yes and yes. And the vultures are outside. They suspect I have a guest, and they won't leave my doorstep until they can have their prize picture."

Liv's head snaps in my direction, her face completely ashen. She repeats to Saylor what I just told Oliver.

"I'm on my way," Oliver says, and the line goes mute.

A moment later, Liv ends the call with Saylor.

"I need your address. Saylor is coming over."

CHAPTER 44

LIV

managed to evade the paparazzi thanks to Saylor's and Oliver's help. They somehow convinced Sebastian's rear neighbors to let me use their garden as an escape route. What I didn't succeed in doing was surviving the experience unscathed. I've never felt more humiliated in my life, sneaking out like I've committed the biggest sin, like being with Sebastian is a crime against all that's holy and good in this world. I suppose if our secret ever came out, that's how the world would see me: a homewrecker, a whore coming in between the most perfect couple in Britain.

Sebastian made me promise before I left that I would see him later at his uncle's house. Reluctantly, I said yes, knowing deep down that it would be a hard promise to keep. He clearly saw in my eyes the doubt, the hesitancy, so to sway me or make it easier, he also invited my friends. A valiant effort, but unbeknownst to him and me at the time, also fruitless. Once inside the cab heading back to the Hollingsworth, I learned from Saylor that Emma had decided to go to Milan with Kennedy at the last minute.

"Does Emma's decision have anything to do with me keeping this from them?" I ask Saylor.

She's looking out the window, distracted, but she turns to me before she answers. "I don't know, chica. I'm not going to lie and say they were thrilled you never told them about Sebastian."

I stare at my hands on my lap, feeling more wretched by the minute. "I suck."

"No, you don't suck. There's no rule saying you have to share all of your deepest secrets with your friends. It's okay to keep things to yourself."

I look up and catch a glimpse of guilt in Saylor's eyes that fades almost as fast as it appeared.

"Saylor, are you okay? You seem odd."

She faces the window again. "I'm just tired."

She doesn't even attempt to hide the lie. She's definitely off. "I never got the chance to ask what happened between you and Oliver at The Singing Olive last night."

She takes a deep breath, and her shoulders slump forward as she exhales. "He's a total bastard, and he's lucky all he got was icy water on his face."

I mull her answer over. Sebastian did mention his dark days in high school, how he was a complete asshole, caring about nothing and no one. That was the time he and Oliver became best friends. It's not difficult to conclude that Saylor is probably right about her assessment of Oliver. Even so, it's hard to imagine that this new Sebastian, the one on the path of redemption, would still consider Oliver his best friend if he didn't have any redeemable qualities. There's a bond thicker than blood between them, I can tell that much.

"Are you spending Christmas Eve with Sebastian's family?" Saylor asks.

"I don't know."

She faces me again, and then she squeezes my hand. "You should, Liv. Don't let the outside world drive a wedge between you and him. I saw the way he looks at you. He loves you deeply, even more so than before."

"Since when did you become Sebastian's champion?" I narrow my eyes at her, but my indignation is halfhearted.

"I'm not his champion. I'm on *your* team. I always will be. And your happiness is by his side. It's written in the stars." She smiles at me, a sad sort of smile that makes my chest cave in. I see darkness in my friend's eyes, a sorrow I'd thought had left her for good. But maybe I was wrong.

"I'll go, but only if you come with me."

Saylor scrunches her nose in an adorable scowl. "Will Oliver be there?"

"I think so. But since when do you let a stupid boy dictate where you go or not?"

I see Saylor's lips twitch upward and know I've won.

"Never."

♡ ♡ ♡

SEBASTIAN

After Liv left with Saylor, Oliver came over, making sure his appearance at my house wasn't missed. The paparazzi showered him with questions before I let him in, but a couple hours later, they got tired of waiting for the condemning picture of me and the mysterious girl I'd been kissing at the club, so they left.

Oliver apologized a million times for his reckless behavior, to the point where I threatened to cut his tongue off if he didn't stop talking. We searched the internet throughout the rest of the morning, and it quickly became apparent that most gossips sites only had that one blurry picture of Liv and me. My solace was that it was impossible to tell if it was really me in the low-quality frame, and Liv's identity was also obscured. The tabloids had nothing but pure speculation to go on.

Oliver left sometime after noon, claiming he needed a good nap before coming to my uncle's dinner. He asked if Saylor was coming, too, and when I told him there was a great chance of that happening, he gave me a funny look. I never got the chance to ask about his incident with Saylor last night, but if there was a girl who could unhinge my friend, it would be her.

♡ ♡ ♡

Liv and Saylor arrive at my uncle's house at precisely six o'clock. I feel the pressure leave my chest as I spy on them exiting the cab through the partially open curtains. Up until that moment, I wasn't sure if Liv would come.

My uncle and aunt were ecstatic when I told them about Liv and me and that I had invited her to Christmas dinner. A sliver of guilt embedded itself in my heart seeing them genuinely happy for me. After everything I've put them through, after all the awful things I've said to them throughout the years, their reaction was humbling. I'm not proud of the person I became, but maybe it isn't too late to make amends. Maybe with Liv by my side, I can be strong enough to change into a man my parents would be proud of.

I let Aunt Tanya answer the door, just in case there's a stray paparazzo waiting to take a picture of me. I remain in the living room as my aunt gushes over Liv and Saylor.

When Liv enters the room, my eyes widen and my heart almost leaps out of my chest. The shadow in her eyes from earlier is gone, and there's a glow about her that almost makes me weep. I don't know what's happening to me. It could be that I still can't believe fate has granted me another chance at happiness, or it could be the time of the year, when so many joyful and awful memories compete for my attention.

I finally notice her loaded hands. "What have you done?"

She shrugs. "Well, I couldn't show up at your house empty-handed. Saylor and I took a trip to Oxford Street."

"I think you may have gone overboard." I retrieve the bags from her hands and place them on the coffee table.

"Hi to you, too, Sebastian," Saylor says as she dumps her own bags next to Liv's.

I turn to her, and her glower makes me take a step back. I forgot how intimidating Saylor could be. Right now, I don't know what she's going to do. I don't think she's crazy enough to strike me at my family's home, but with her, you never know. And it's not like I don't deserve what she has in store for me. Her loyalty to Liv is the stuff of legends.

She smirks and her big doll eyes sparkle. "Good Lord. Stop looking at me like I'm about to disembowel you."

She moves closer and stops a few inches from me. The difference in height doesn't faze her one bit. She stares into my eyes, searching for the answer to an unspoken question. It takes only a few seconds, and then she smiles broadly.

"It's good to have you back, Bas." She hugs me tight, and my body stiffens in surprise.

I peer over her shoulder at Liv, and she grins at us. I recover from the shock and hug Saylor back, not wanting to question her motives. Better a hug than a kick to the balls.

Before we pull apart, Saylor whispers in my ear. "Break her heart again and I'll rip your nut sack off."

Ah, that's the Saylor I remember.

I take a step back and put a protective hand over my crotch. "Come on. Ollie is already here, hanging out with Shane in the TV room."

I can hear Oliver's loud voice even before we enter the room. "You bloody cheated!"

"One wouldn't need to cheat. Your lack of dexterity is appalling," Shane replies in his cool and detached manner. He's a fifteen-year-old boy going on fifty. I've never met anyone as awkward and socially inept as him. Oliver is the only person who Shane seems somehow comfortable with.

I clear my throat by the door. "Children, the girls are here. Behave."

Shane pauses the game and turns to look at us. His face

flushes when his gaze settles on Liv and Saylor next to me, and he quickly stares at his shoes. He's gotten taller since the last time I saw him, and his body is gangly and out of proportion. At least it seems like that. His dark hair is shaggy, and the long bangs almost cover his eyes completely.

"Ladies," Oliver says as his lips curl up. His gaze lands on Saylor, and there's a flash of mischief there.

Oh fuck no. I won't let Oliver ruin my relationship with Liv by messing with her best friend. I know Saylor can handle assholes like him, but I feel it's my duty to keep Oliver far away from her.

Saylor moves forward, ignoring Oliver completely, and stops in front of Shane, offering her hand to him. "Hi, I'm Saylor. Nice to meet you, Shane."

He glances up and, surprisingly, shakes her hand. But in true Shane fashion, he doesn't let go right away and stares at her with what I can only call puppy love eyes.

Oh boy.

Oliver smacks his head. "Stop ogling her."

Shane drops Saylor's hand and glares at Oliver. "Piss off, Best."

"That I am, the best."

"Shall we leave you two alone so you can take care of your unresolved sexual tension?" Saylor says.

"What?" Shane whips around to face her again with eyebrows raised.

"Ignore her. She might look like a fairy, but she's actually a witch." Oliver stares hard at Saylor.

She flips him off and turns on her heels, her eyes flashing. I mentally chuckle at my silly thoughts. I can't believe I considered for a second that those two might hook up.

♡ ♡ ♡

Dinner happens relatively drama free, but I can't say it's not emotional. My uncle sits at the head of the table, and as I look at him, I can see a little bit of my dad in him. My chest feels tight, and I try not to dwell on the fact that the void my parents' death has left behind is still there, and it seems to get bigger if I don't fight back, if I'm weak. A lump forms in my throat as Uncle Paul says a prayer, blessing our meal. He's serious and proper whereas my dad would've said something funny.

Liv squeezes my hand and I peer at her. Her eyes are bright and her face is full of understanding. It makes my heart push away the sadness, and my breathing becomes a little bit easier. I smile at her, trying to convey that her mere presence is a balm of peace to me.

"Thank you so much for inviting us," Liv addresses my uncle and aunt.

"Liv, it's a pleasure to have you and Saylor here. It brings us immeasurable joy," Aunt Tanya says. Her broad smile makes her eyes twinkle.

"I haven't had a meal like this in ages. Thank you so much," Saylor says as she breaks a dinner roll in two.

"Why? Are you financially handicapped?" Shane asks, and my uncle chokes on his food.

"Shane!" Aunt Tanya shouts.

I expect Saylor to offer a snarky remark, but her face turns red and she gazes at her plate. I look at Liv, trying to understand what's going on. Her face is somber and her shoulders are tense.

"My mother is an ER nurse, and I can't remember the last time she had Christmas Eve off. I usually order Chinese," Saylor says in a small voice.

Shane opens his mouth, but Oliver does something to halt my cousin's inquisitive quest. He might've kicked him under the table for all I know.

My friend's gaze settles on Saylor, who chews her food

without glancing up, lost in whatever problems plague her. Oliver's expression is unreadable.

♡ ♡ ♡

Liv didn't spend Christmas Day with me as I thought she would, as we had planned. I didn't beg her, but I came close. I would've pressed the matter, even gone as low as guilting her into it, but I knew the reason she didn't want to be with me.

Instead, I spent most of the day obsessing about my contract with Schutz Productions, trying to find a way out. I must've stared at those papers for hours, reading the clause that had me bound to Michael a thousand times. I couldn't believe I hadn't seen it before. It wasn't even written in small letters.

If I break my contract, I'll be liable for a lawsuit, depending on how much money my exit will cost. And I know if I leave the band before the tour is over, the loss to Michael's overflowing pockets will be significant.

My only alternative is to force them to fire me. Despite Hans's twisted words, if they kick me out, then I'm not liable for anything. But for that to happen, I'll have to expose Liv, literally throw her under the bus. And that's not an option. I saw what that picture splattered all over the tabloids did to her, even when she suppressed her hurt at Christmas dinner for my sake. That's the true reason she decided to go sightseeing with Saylor even knowing the rest of my week is filled with more rehearsals and interviews.

Oliver came over to my place, and thank God for him. Without him distracting me, I would've gone mad. But I have to endure this nightmare until the tour is over. It's the only way Liv and I will be able to build our lives together in peace.

CHAPTER 45
SEBASTIAN

I didn't see Liv at all after Christmas dinner; I was being followed everywhere by paparazzi and couldn't risk another exposure. I called her whenever I could, but it wasn't the same. I began to dissect everything she said, every inflection of her tone and wording of her responses, trying to assure myself that she was okay, that we were okay. I gained nothing, only a sense of foreboding that caved my chest in further and further.

I know Liv's friends are back from Italy and they have plans tonight for New Year's Eve. I wish with every fiber of my being that I could spend the evening with her, but the old adage 'you can't always get what you want' never rang truer.

Instead, I'm in my full concert regalia, waiting to hop onstage. We're performing near Big Ben in the buildup to the clock striking midnight. The show will be broadcasted live, and I'm afraid it'll be my most uninspired performance to date. Not even the clamoring of thousands of fans makes my heart kick-start or the adrenaline flow through my veins. I feel numb.

Oliver taps me on my shoulder. "Ready?"

"Let's get this shit over with," I say.

We sing for about an hour, and right before midnight, we

take a break and the TV presenter comes onto the stage. We stay put, listening to him recite a bunch of idiocies about the evening, about us. My mind wanders, and maybe tomorrow there will be a story in one of the tabloids about how bored I looked tonight. I don't give a shit.

I hear my name and snap back to the here and now. The evening's host isn't looking at me but staring at someone coming from the side of the stage. I follow his gaze, and when I realize what's happening, it feels like I've been sucker punched in the gut. Gretchen is here, looking more radiant than ever, walking toward me. I haven't heard from her all the time she's been gone, and I've deluded myself into thinking that maybe she decided to just let our relationship evaporate into thin air.

I chance a fleeting, panicked glance at Oliver, but he's just as stupefied as I am. Anger takes over. I should've suspected Hans was plotting something when he made no comment about the picture of Liv and me. How stupid was I for believing he'd let another scandal involving me go by without repercussions?

I curl my hands into fists by my side and clench my jaw. Gretchen stops in front of me with a smile that could light up the entire city of London after dark.

"Surprise!" she says, and maybe it's my imagination, but her voice is too high-pitched to be natural. She's nervous.

She kisses me on the cheek, and the crowd goes wild. I do nothing, just stand frozen on the spot. Gretchen's expression falls when she notices my stony face. I glance to the side, and even in the dark, I can see Hans's partially hidden form smirking at me. *Fucking asshole.*

The TV presenter begins the countdown, and when it's over and fireworks explode in the sky, Gretchen grabs my face and pulls me to her, kissing me with an open mouth. I don't reciprocate, but I don't push her away either. Even if my mind is reeling, even if my only desire is to storm off the stage and punch Hans in the face, I stay put. I don't want to cause a scene on live television.

Then Liv is at the forefront of my mind. *Fuck!* She's probably watching this.

I finally take a step back and glare at Gretchen. Her smile wilts immediately.

"We need to talk. Now!" I say.

I drag her backstage and whirl on her. "Why are you here?"

Her eyes are round and bright with unshed tears, her face drained of color. "I thought you would be happy to see me. Didn't you miss me at all?"

"Answer the fucking question, Gretchen. Why are you here?"

She winces and takes a step back. For once, I don't feel badly for my behavior. "Hans invited me. He said I should make an appearance to put those rumors to rest."

"Put what rumors to rest?"

"That we're no longer together. That you've moved on."

In that moment I snap. I don't care about the lawsuit, about the consequences. Michael can take all my money away and shove it up his ass.

"I *have* moved on. We are over!" I shout, not giving a fuck if anyone is listening.

Gretchen sucks in a breath as her tears fall freely down her face. I'm so angry that I can't bring myself to feel guilty right now. It'll come later, but my only concern is Liv at the moment. If she saw that spectacle, if she saw that kiss… I don't even want to think about it.

"You're breaking up with me?" Gretchen asks in a small voice.

"We've been broken up way before this and you know it."

Her eyes flash with indignation before her open palm connects with my face. The sting of her slap burns, but I deserve it.

"Goodbye, Gretchen," I say and leave her behind.

I find the exit and take the stairs down two at a time. We're supposed to sing a few more songs, but there's no way in hell

I'm going back on that stage. I need to find Liv and explain, apologize.

Two huge security monsters stop me before I can cross the gate to the street and freedom.

"Sir, your car isn't here. You can't go outside."

"Get out of my way!"

"We can't. You'll get mobbed. Let us call the chauffeur. It'll only take a couple of minutes."

He's right, I can't go out in the middle of a packed street like that. I'll be killed if people recognize me. This fame is a fucking plague. I'm beginning to hate it with a passion.

A few minutes later, one of the guards says, "Sir, the car is here."

"Where are you going?" Oliver asks behind me. "We're supposed to resume the concert."

It took him long enough to catch up with me.

"Fuck the concert. I gotta find Liv."

"What about Hans and Michael? What about the lawsuit?"

"They can sue me all they want. I don't care."

Big security guy number one opens the door, and I quickly jump inside the waiting limo. Oliver follows me.

"What do you think you're doing?" I ask him.

"I can't let you rebel by yourself. I'm taking a stand."

CHAPTER 46
LIV

Kool and the Gang is blasting through the speakers, and sweat covers my skin. The air is thick and warm, and the blend of contrasting smells is almost sensory overload. Around me, my friends dance, jump, and sing along to the lyrics of "Celebration." It's one of our favorite party songs, and even though my heart isn't committed entirely to having fun, I can't help but join them.

Kennedy and Emma have forgiven me about Sebastian. Emma even apologized for being a crazy Boys Future fangirl. I assure them everything is good now.

At least, I hope it's true.

We're a large group. As promised, Kennedy's friend from Milan, Max, has come with her to celebrate New Year's Eve in London. It was great to finally meet this iconic person from Kennedy's life. Lloyd, who told us about this party, can't stop gawking at Max. Kennedy never mentioned that her friend was an internationally famous male model.

"Man, I want to bite those full lips. And look at his biceps," Lloyd says in my ear.

I laugh. "You're terrible."

I wish Max was interested in Lloyd. I know my friend could use a little pick-me-up in the romance department after the whole fiasco with Ryan, but I'm certain Max is strictly a lady's man.

Suddenly, the club starts to play "Popular," Boys Future's first hit. I stop dancing and can't catch my breath.

Saylor notices my reaction and touches my forearm. "Liv, are you okay?"

No, I'm not okay, and I don't know why. It's the first time I've heard a Boys Future song since reconciling with Sebastian, and I'm surprised how it still affects me in the worst possible way.

"Come on. Let's find a less crowded room."

Saylor begins to drag me away, but Kennedy notices and shouts, "Where are you guys going? It's almost midnight."

"Oh, shoot. We need champagne!" Emma yells.

We all head to the nearest bar and somehow are able to get to the counter. I notice the television on the upper corner of the room, and my stomach clenches painfully when I realize that the Boys Future concert is on. It seems I've just caught the end of it.

Emma orders a couple of bottles of champagne, and a full glass of the bubbly drink appears in my hand. My gaze stays glued to the TV. I can't hear a word the presenter is saying, but I don't need to hear anything for the blood to freeze in my veins.

Gretchen, Sebastian's official girlfriend, appears on the stage, looking regal and stunning in a sparkly white gown. She stops in front of Sebastian and gazes at him in adoration. The camera focuses on their faces. My mouth tastes like ashes. Sebastian just stands frozen like a statue and lets Gretchen kiss his cheek.

Did he know she was going to be there?

The music in the club ceases, and the crowd begins to count. When the countdown ends, the whole room erupts in cheers, but it's all white noise to my ears, as that's when Gretchen kisses Sebastian fully on the mouth. I expect him to pull away, but when he doesn't, my heart folds in on itself, bleeding like it never has before.

"What the hell!" Saylor shouts next to me while all around us everyone is saying "Happy New Year."

Tears blur my vision, and I whisper to no one in particular, "I can't believe he did that."

"Was that Sebastian kissing Gretchen on TV?" Kennedy asks.

"Isn't he your boyfriend?" Max turns to me, and I can't summon an ounce of anger at Kennedy for revealing my secret. All my emotions have turned into lead.

"Hey! Snap out of it." Saylor grabs my arm. "It's fucking New Year's Eve, and you're not going to let that asshole ruin your night. I won't allow it." She orders a round of tequila shots, and numbly, I toss a couple back.

"That's my girl. Now, let's kick this party up a notch."

I let Saylor take control. I feel like a puppet, no soul or will left in me. The only thing keeping the pain at bay is the quantity of drinks I consume. I dance and dance until my feet begin to throb, but with the amount of alcohol I've ingested, the pain is easily forgotten.

I feel a pair of strong arms circle my waist from behind. I don't even tense up. "He's an asshole and he doesn't deserve you," Max whispers in my ear.

He's yanked from me. "Don't even think about it!" Kennedy shouts at him.

They begin to argue, but it doesn't matter. I keep on dancing.

We stay in the club until the party is over and they kick us out. It's very late, or very early. I can't decide, but I can feel it in my bones. Outside the stuffy club, the air is frosty; not even my warm coat can keep the cool air from seeping in.

We stand outside, not making a move to find a way back to the hotel. Securing a cab will be almost impossible, and we need two. I foresee walking, but I don't want to go home yet, because then I'll have to deal with the gnawing pain in my chest. There's a crowd milling about. I don't think anyone is ready for the evening to be over. Then a group approaches us.

"Hey, do you know where we can go? In Spain, we party

until ten in the morning," a girl as pale as the moon with blonde dreadlocks and a nose ring asks.

"I heard there's an underground club a few blocks from here," some guy to my left says.

There's a contagious feeling of euphoria in the air. Usually, I would never party with strangers, but this is London, and the night is still young. Plus, I'm not alone. We start to walk, laughing and singing, without a care in the world. Someone produces a bottle of vodka, and we all take turns sipping from it. I'm not a vodka drinker, but I'm beyond being picky, and the potent liquid helps keep me warm. No one knows which direction we're supposed to go, but it doesn't seem to matter.

In my foggy state, I notice when a limo stops ahead of us by the curb. I only rode in a limo once, with Derek, and that ended in disaster. A shudder runs down my spine. The door opens and Sebastian emerges from it.

"Liv!" he screams, and everyone turns to look at him.

"Oh my God. It's Sebastian Coleman," dreadlock girl says.

"And Oliver Best. I can't believe it," her friend continues.

Red clouds my vision. I replay the scene of Sebastian kissing Gretchen, and instead of feeling miserable, I'm livid. I break away from the group and begin walking in the opposite direction.

"Liv, please wait." He catches up and grabs my arm, spinning me around.

I try to break free from his grasp, but his hold doesn't ease. "Let go of me. Where's Gretchen?"

"I had no fucking clue she was going to be there. Hans set me up."

"Did he force you to kiss her, too?"

"I didn't kiss her, she kissed *me*."

Max appears behind Sebastian, grabs the back of his jacket, and yanks hard. "Let go of Liv."

Sebastian stumbles back, and once he recovers, he glares at Max. "Who the fuck are you?"

I can see this situation going from bad to disastrous pretty fast, so I put myself between Sebastian and Max.

"He's Kennedy's friend. Why are you here, Sebastian?"

His gaze meets mine and it's desperate, broken. "To explain, to beg for forgiveness."

I don't say anything, my brain struggling for words. My anger is dissolving like salt in water, and I'm mad at myself for being so pathetic. Sebastian places his hands on my shoulders and lowers his head. His mouth is inches from mine. "Liv, I love you. Please believe me. I had no idea she was going to be there."

He doesn't wait for my response, his lips finding mine. There's a faint flavor of whiskey on his tongue, but it doesn't matter; nothing matters when our lips meet, when our tongues dance. We kiss and kiss like there's no tomorrow, like it's the only thing that can keep us alive.

We finally break apart and stare at each other, but movement in my periphery catches my attention. I turn and realize we're surrounded by a circle of stunned spectators, most with their phones pointed at us.

"Mate, we need to get out of here," Oliver says with Saylor by his side.

We move fast toward the parked limo as the crowd just stares at us. I hear murmurs behind me, and I know we're moments away from the madness, from the stunned fans realizing Sebastian and Oliver are leaving. Kennedy, Emma, Max, and Lloyd are already next to the limo, and after a hand gesture from Oliver, they enter the vehicle. I hear a couple of people shout Sebastian's and Oliver's names, but it's too late. Sebastian ushers me inside and then follows me.

The limo isn't big enough for our large group; it can only accommodate six passengers, which means I end up sitting on Sebastian's lap. Across from me, I see Saylor in the same situation, sitting on Oliver's lap. He leans closer to her ear and whispers something, making her spine stiffen. I stop paying attention to them when Sebastian's warm hands stroke my thighs up and down, rendering my brain cells useless.

CHAPTER 47
LIV

don't spend the night with Sebastian. Once the limo stops in front of the Hollingsworth, my friends save me from that very bad decision.

The consequences of Sebastian's careless actions don't take long to catch up with me. Photos of us kissing in the middle of the street are soon in every single tabloid, plus there are videos of us on YouTube. There's no hiding my identity this time. The entire world knows who I am. They know my name and where I work. I don't know how they've managed to get that information so quickly, but they're nothing if not resourceful. What they conveniently forgot to mention was that I was Sebastian's high school sweetheart. The gossip outlets aren't interested in that. To them, it's just as I feared: I'm a slut, the homewrecker responsible for tearing Britain's favorite couple apart.

I spend the entire weekend curled up in bed, crying my eyes out. I avoid calls from my parents and Kimmy. Saylor talks to them, and by the hushed conversation, I know the news has crossed the Atlantic. Kennedy and Emma try to cheer me up, convince me the situation isn't that bad and that soon the tabloids will find someone else to exploit. But it doesn't matter. I'm tarnished. And worse, I can kiss my internship goodbye.

Sebastian calls me several times, and every time I see his name flash on the screen, I cry harder. On his umpteenth attempt, Saylor picks up the phone and threatens to cut his balls off if he so much as dares to show his face at the Hollingsworth.

"Haven't you done enough?" she asks.

He doesn't call again after that, and a part of me dies inside. It's only taken a threat from Saylor for him to give up. *Am I worth so little to him?*

I stare at the promise bracelet he gave me, and it feels heavy against my wrist. I want to tear it off, break it to pieces, but the effort is too much. I don't know where I put the key. It seemed inconsequential to remember its location, since I believed with my whole soul that he wouldn't break his promise.

How foolish of me.

On Monday morning, I report back to work looking like hell. My eyes are puffy and red, and there's no amount of makeup in the world that can conceal the evidence of my pain.

"Liv, I had no idea," Mellie says.

I sit behind my desk and stare at the black screen. I don't turn my computer on. What for? I know what's in store for me.

"It doesn't matter anyway. It's over." My voice is flat, devoid of even a hint of emotion. I have nothing left to give. All of my feelings have leaked from my bleeding heart, leaving it empty and hard as stone.

"But why? He declared his love for you in front of a bunch of strangers. Wasn't that what you wanted, to be able to love him out in the open, without fear?" Lloyd says.

I glance at my friend. He's looking at me with such hope that my mangled heart shatters a little more. "You don't understand. He wrecked my life, and he walked away."

"What do you mean, he walked away?" Lloyd is frowning at me now.

I don't get the opportunity to explain. Patsy arrives in the office, and without glancing my way, she says, "Olivia, could you step into my office please?"

Despite the polite tone, her voice is ice cold. I stand up on shaky legs, the lump in my throat threatening to choke me to death as I head to her office.

"Close the door, please," she says as she sits down behind her desk.

I take a seat and brace myself for the blow. Her gaze is hard as she stares at me, and I want to disappear.

"Weren't you told upon the start of this internship that the Hollingsworth does not tolerate employees mingling with guests?"

"Y-Yes."

"And yet you not only got involved with one, you managed to get caught with said guest and drag the Hollingsworth reputation through the mud."

"You don't understand. Just let me explain. Sebastian was my boyf—"

"Silence!" She smacks her open palms on the desk, making me jump in my seat. "I don't care how you came to get involved with him, only that you did."

Tears gather in my eyes. I have no rebuff for that.

She continues with her tirade. "And here's the result." She retrieves a stack of magazines and newspapers from her purse and dumps all of them on her desk. Then she proceeds to pick them up one by one and read the headlines.

"'Hollingsworth's employee seduces Sebastian Coleman.' 'Gretchen shocked to discover Sebastian cheated on her with Hollingsworth events coordinator.' 'Is the prestigious Hollingsworth hotel a front for a high-class escort service?' Shall I continue?"

"No." I try to fight back the tears, but they escape my eyes nonetheless.

"You, Miss Dawson, single-handedly tarnished the hundred-year reputation of this hotel."

"I'm so sorry."

"I'm surprised you had the audacity to show your face here.

Retrieve your personal belongings and leave the premises immediately. You're fired. You have one hour to vacate your room."

The implications of her words finally hit me, and my stomach drops to the floor. "One hour? Where am I supposed to go?"

"Not my concern. Goodbye, Miss Dawson."

I scramble out of her office and make a beeline for my desk. There's nothing here that I want, only my purse. I can't bring myself to look at Lloyd or Mellie, running out of there before they can shower me with questions. Although, I doubt they need to ask me anything. I'm sure they heard every single word Patsy said to me.

On my way to my room, I bump into Ryan.

"Where's the fire?" he asks.

"I can't talk right now." I try to sidestep him, but he blocks my way.

"How does it feel?"

I finally look at Ryan and find him grinning with a victorious glint in his eyes.

"Excuse me?"

"How does it feel to have your deepest secret exposed to the world?"

Things finally click.

"It was you. You told the tabloids my name, where I worked. Didn't you?"

"Payback is a bitch, isn't it? If you weren't busy screwing that asshole from Boys Future, Lloyd wouldn't have exposed me to my fiancée."

I take a step back, reeling not only because of his admission but because of the ugliness of his heart. I can't believe he would do such a thing on purpose.

I narrow my eyes at him. "I'm glad Lloyd found out the truth about you. You don't deserve him. Have a nice life, Ryan."

I step around him and don't look back.

CHAPTER 48
SEBASTIAN

'm pacing in my living room, holding a tabloid magazine in my hands as I read the same passage over and over again. I have bile in my mouth as I stare at a statement from me that I never gave.

"How can they publish such lies? I never answered any of their questions!"

Oliver glances my way from the couch. His eyes are blood-shot, and he needs a shave. He hasn't been home since the New Year's Eve disaster. It's Tuesday morning, and most of the gossip magazines are talking about the same thing. I don't know how they managed to publish my ill-timed love declaration in their weekly issue so quickly. They must've had people work nonstop over the weekend.

"Have you forgotten who pays our publicist? This is Hans's and Michael's attempts at damage control, and also their revenge."

I stop midstep and face him. The rage bubbling inside is a vicious, live thing, ready to burst. In all the articles I've read, online and in print, none of them mention my past with Liv. The hook is the same in all of them—Liv is the villain of the story. I knew this could happen, and in my act of carelessness, I failed to protect her. I broke my promise. So I'm staying far away from her until the worst of this clusterfuck passes. I don't want to bring more havoc into her life. But every second I'm not by her side feels like a knife in my gut, twisting as it goes deeper into my flesh.

"I'm going to kill them!"

Oliver raises his hands as his eyebrows shot up. "Whoa! I don't think homicide is the answer here. You need to play their game, fight fire with fire."

I begin pacing again, pulling at my hair. "Fuck!"

"I have an idea, but you have to pretend everything is fine until we're deep in the tour again."

I whirl on him. "You expect me to go back on the bloody tour like nothing happened?"

"Yes."

"You're fucking mental."

"That, too, but I'm also fucking smart. Do you want to be free of Hans and Michael forever and have your happily ever after with Liv or not?"

CHAPTER 49
LIV

Two weeks have passed since I returned from London, but instead of going back to my apartment on campus, I came to my parents' house. It's funny how when your life is in shambles, all you want is to curl up on your mom's or dad's lap and let them take the pain away. That's what I did the first day back. I cried nonstop while Mom traced her fingers through my hair, saying nothing, just letting me release all my anguish and pain. That day was the only time I let my family see my tears. I only cry now when I'm locked in my room, though not as often.

I refuse to leave the house. If I could have my wish, I would stay in my bedroom all day, but Mom won't have any of it.

The only highlight of my returning home early is that I finally met Grace, my sweet niece. She's the most precious little thing in the world, and playing with her almost makes me forget the constant pain in my chest. *Almost.* In the past week, Kimmy has brought her to the house every day, and I silently thank my sister for her kindness. Grace is my only solace in the very dark world I now live in.

Saylor comes to see me every day as well, but she never mentions his name. Instead, she tries to distract me with idle gossip about her band members. We also watch DVDs of *Seinfeld*. It's the only thing I can stomach—there's no romance whatsoever in that show, only pure, nonsensical fun.

I hear from Emma, and Kennedy too. They invite me to do stuff with them, go to a movie or dinner, but I never accept their invitations.

I didn't see Lloyd before I left the Hollingsworth, but he's called me on Skype a few times. Mellie has sent me several emails. I ignored all of their attempts to contact me. I'm not ready to talk to them. The humiliation of my dismissal is too raw, too painful.

I also avoid watching TV or checking the internet. I can't bear to read or hear any more hurtful comments about me. It isn't only the media that's being vicious about it—Boys Future's fans have also expressed their disgust with me. I'm 100 percent sure that their outrage has more to do with them being jealous that Sebastian has picked me, a regular girl. Apparently, it's only okay for superstars to date other superstars.

They don't need to worry, though. He's clearly moved on. Maybe he realized I'm not worth the headache. He never attempted to call me again after Saylor told him off. No, he went on his merry way on his tour like nothing happened, like my life hasn't crumbled completely.

His stupid promise bracelet stares at me in mockery. I feel sick to my stomach every time I look at it. The key is long gone, but going to a jewelry store and asking them to cut the thing off requires me leaving the house. So it stays on for now, I just have to keep it hidden under a long-sleeved shirt.

I'm already planning to spend another day holed up in my room, curled in my bed, reading *The Mists of Avalon* for the tenth time, when Mom walks in.

"It's a beautiful day outside, hon. Why don't you join Kimmy when she takes Grace to the park?"

"I really don't feel like going anywhere."

Mom sits at the end of my bed and looks at me. "Olivia Marie

Dawson. You disappoint me. I didn't raise any of my children to cower in their room when the world throws them a curveball."

I close the book and stare at my hands. The nail polish is chipped, almost entirely gone. It's the color I used for New Year's Eve. It feels like a lifetime ago and at the same time like it just happened.

"I'm not ready to face them."

"Face who, Liv?"

"Everyone! I can't take the staring and pointing, the judgmental whispering."

"No one will do that here. You can't let those internet trolls get to you. They're vapor."

"Then they must be some kind of acid fume, because their words hurt, Mom. So much."

Mom shuffles forward and envelopes me in a tight hug. I rest my head against her shoulder, but there are no tears in my eyes this time. I'm all cried out.

"I know, baby girl. I know." She gently pushes me back and peers at my face, holding me by the shoulders. "You're strong, Liv. This will pass."

"It's not only that. I'm still reeling from the humiliation of being fired. I needed that internship to graduate. Who will hire me now?"

"Don't despair. Things will work themselves out, you'll see. Just take one step at a time, starting with today. Now come on, let's fix your awful nails."

♡ ♡ ♡

do go with Kimmy to the park that afternoon, and to be honest, it isn't that bad. It feels good to breathe fresh air, to be out in the open. I don't realize until I sit on a bench facing the lake how much I've missed my hometown.

Little by little, I begin regaining my confidence. The next day, I venture to the drugstore by myself and even dare to glance at the magazine stand on my way out. Another scandal is plastered on their covers. The gossip mill has found other prey. The checkout girl doesn't look at me twice. Mom is right, things will get better.

But the one ache that won't go away is the one of my obliterated heart. Despite my desire to be strong, I had clung to the hope that Sebastian would contact me, even just to check if I was okay. But his complete silence is too similar to his behavior of five years ago. It creates a dark void, and I can't escape from it.

Inside the car, I peer at my reflection in the rearview mirror and am horrified by my appearance. My skin isn't pale, it's completely washed out. The dark circles under my eyes could be mistaken for bruises. I look like death. And here I thought I was doing better. I clutch the steering wheel hard until my knuckles turn white, and I take deep breaths. Who's this girl staring back at me? I don't recognize her. Loving someone shouldn't cause this.

Something erupts in my chest, a kind of fire that won't be extinguished. I look at the bracelet, so perfect and delicate, and that's when it hits me. I'll never be able to truly move on as long as I'm wearing it.

It's too early in the morning for the mall to be open yet. I peel out of the parking lot and race back home. It takes me five minutes to get there. I jump out of the car and call out to Dad as I burst through the door. There must be a tool in the house that can break the damn thing.

♡ ♡ ♡

"Come on, Dad. You're not trying hard enough. This bracelet isn't made of steel."

"I'm sorry, honey. It's too tight on your wrist. I'll end up hurting you."

"I don't care!" I scream and jump off the high stool. "I'm

going to the mall as soon as it opens. I'm sure they'll be able to cut this thing off at the jewelry store."

I notice when Mom and Dad trade worried looks. "What?"

"It's such a lovely bracelet, Liv. It'll be a pity to destroy it. How about if we search online for a replacement key? I'm sure we can find it," Mom says.

I open my mouth to argue, but the house phone rings, and Mom is only too happy with the distraction. She answers it promptly, and after a few exchanges, she turns to me. "Yeah, she's standing right here."

Mom offers me the receiver. "It's Emma."

Grumbling all the way, I take the phone from Mom's hand. "Hey, Emma."

"Liv, I won't take no for an answer," my friend fires up without preambles. "Rodrigo is in town, and we're all going to the Surf Shack for dinner. You're coming."

"Sounds good, Em. What time?"

She's silent for a moment. "Wait? Are you serious?"

Ha! She wasn't expecting my prompt compliance. "Mourning period is over."

Emma screams in my ear, and I have to pull the phone away or risk going deaf.

"Oh my God. I'm so excited. We'll have the best of times. You'll see. I'll pick you up at seven. Dress to kill, Liv."

CHAPTER 50

SEBASTIAN

Tonight is the night everything will fall into place. Tonight shit will go down. I've bided my time, followed Oliver's plan, let Hans believe he was in control so I could tell my side of the story. Earlier today, I came into possession of the ultimate proof that Hans and Michael are worthless scum. A tape of both of them scheming, talking about what they did to Liv, Gretchen, and me. I could easily use that tape to buy my way out of the band, but it's not enough. I want to expose them, let everyone know how low they'll go for money.

There's a renowned reporter in the US interested in the story, but she needs more reasons to run it, and that's exactly what she'll get tonight.

Our performance goes as planned. We play our newest songs, then sing our biggest hits. One of them is a solo, *my* solo, "Girl of My Dreams." Throughout the show, there are planned breaks where we're expected to interact with the audience, catch our breath. There isn't any such pause before "Girl of My Dreams," though. But tonight, the band knows to prolong the song's intro because I've requested it. They have no idea what I have in mind, only that I'm going to speak before I sing.

"Good evening, Sydney!" I scream, and the crowd answers back.

"Before I begin this next song, I'd like to say a few words." I pause and let the cheers die. I want their undivided attention.

"In the past couple of weeks, I witnessed the worst fame can bring. I saw my life and the lives of the ones I love exposed and dissected for financial gain."

Sudden silence expands beyond the crowd. It's deafening. "But that's the trade-off, right? I get it. I'm not here to whine and complain, because I was willing to pay that hefty price. But someone else got hurt in the process, someone who never wished to be part of the limelight." I laugh without humor and shake my head. "But the sharks, they don't care. They smell blood and come to feast."

I stop and let my words sink in. There's a rushed murmur now, and if I could see their faces, I might find them leaning forward, eager for my next words. I don't let them wait any longer.

"The girl the media called a homewrecker, a whore, is a girl I've known my entire life. It's funny how no one ever mentioned she used to be my next-door neighbor, that she used to be my best friend. No one bothered to ask *me*, Sebastian Coleman, who she was. So I'm going to tell you. Olivia Marie Dawson is the girl who was by my side when a twisted ankle kept me from playing in the hockey championship game in junior high. She's the girl who inspired me to learn to play the guitar so I could woo her with my singing. She's the girl who fought for me, who never gave up, even when I seemed to be a lost cause. She's the only girl I've ever loved, the only girl I *still* love. So tonight, I'm dedicating 'Girl of my Dreams' to her, the love of my life."

The band takes my final words as their cue and restarts the intro of the song. I sing like I've never sung before, giving my all to those lyrics. I let my emotions take over, and when the tears escape my eyes, I don't try to hide them. Let the world see how much I bleed.

When I belt out the final notes of the ballad, the crowd goes wild. It's like a collective roar, a wave of sound coming my way. I drop my chin and soak in the moment, knowing it's my last night on such a stage.

When the cheers die somewhat, I speak again. "Thank you. It's been real. Goodbye." I make the peace sign and exit the stage. It won't take long for the true meaning of my words to sink in. We're in the middle of the show, but I'm not coming back. I'm never coming back.

I walk fast, past the sound engineers, the stage assistants, going backstage. I stop when Hans gets in my way.

"That was some poetic declaration. Not my style, but I can work with it."

I make a motion to sidestep him, but he blocks my way again, using his girth to his advantage. I'm keeping my anger under control by sheer willpower. My hands curl into fists and they itch to connect with Hans's nose.

"Get out of my way, Hans," I say through clenched teeth.

"Where do you think you're going? The concert isn't over yet."

"It is for me. I quit."

"You can't quit!"

"Watch me." I shove him out of my way and keep moving. Behind me, he screams promises of retribution.

"You'll regret the day you were born!" he says.

Maybe, but I don't care. A weight's been lifted off my shoulders. I'm not sure if my act of defiance will serve a higher purpose. It doesn't matter. I'm free, and I have to prepare for my final performance, the most important one of my life.

CHAPTER 51
LIV

Thursday night at the Surf Shack means it's a full house. They have the best tacos near campus, and it's a favorite spot among students. The restaurant's parking lot is full, and we have to park across the street by the post office. There's a sign saying parking is for post office customers only and violators will have their cars towed. It's a warning we quickly learned to ignore. No car has ever been towed for parking there after business hours.

It would've been more practical for me to drive solo to the restaurant instead of having Emma drive all the way to Littleton to pick me up. I know she did it because she wanted to make sure I wouldn't bail on them.

When we enter the crowded place, we stretch our necks, trying to see beyond the sea of people. I spot Saylor's multicolored hair right away. She's hanging out by the bar with the rest of our crew: Kennedy, Mandy, and Rodrigo. Emma leads the way, carving a path for us with ease. I don't know how she does it.

Kennedy is the first to notice our arrival, and she smiles ear to ear.

"You're here!" she says.

Mandy turns to me, and I'm surprised when she pulls me into a hug. She's not the affectionate type. "You look great, Liv."

"Hey, I want a hug, too," Rodrigo, the only dude in our tight group, says. He's Emma's best friend from high school and the most down-to-earth and friendly guy I've ever met. I'm engulfed by his embrace, and I laugh out loud when my feet leave the ground.

"I've missed you, Olive Oyl," he says.

"Put me down, Mr. Harvard."

He complies, and that's when I see there's something very different about him. "You cut your hair!"

"Wow, it only took you three minutes to notice." Saylor laughs.

"But you loved your hair and swore you would never cut it. Did you cave to the Ivy League pressure?"

"For your information, not everyone at Harvard dresses like they've sprung from a Polo ad."

"I'm just teasing. So what gives? Did you lose a bet or something?"

Rodrigo looks sheepish and scratches the back of his neck. "Allana asked me to."

"Allana? Who's Allana?"

"Rodrigo's *gurlfriend*. Can you believe it? Our baby boy has finally grown up," Emma puts a hand over her chest and pretends to pat dry tears with a napkin.

"Shut up, Em," Rodrigo grumbles as crimson creeps up his neck.

"Liv, would you like something to drink? Our table won't be ready for another ten minutes," Saylor says.

"Sure, I'll have a margarita." I fish my brand-new driver's license from my mini purse. No more fake ID for me.

"You already went to the DMV? When did that happen?" Saylor takes the plastic card from my hand.

"This afternoon. My hermit days are ov—"

"Excuse me." A short brunette taps my shoulder. "Aren't you Sebastian Coleman's girl?"

My mind turns blank, and I stare at the stranger with what can only be described as a dazed face.

"It is you. Oh my God! That was the most amazing love declaration of all time. You're so lucky."

Feeling more confused than ever, I look at Saylor, hoping she can make sense of what this girl is saying. Saylor avoids my questioning gaze and chews her lower lip.

What the hell?

"Yeah, yeah. She's very lucky. Now move along." Emma puts herself between me and the girl and efficiently shoos her away.

I whirl on my friends. "What's going on?"

"Oh, Liv. We thought you knew," Kennedy says.

My heartbeat picks up its pace, and there's a weird sensation in my belly. "Knew what?"

"Sebastian dedicated a song to you during his last concert," Mandy answers.

"He did what?" It seems the only word left in my vocabulary is 'what.'

"You'll have to see it for yourself. We won't do it justice if we tell you. It was amazeballs." Kennedy sighs.

I'm beyond curious now, and I can't wait to get home to search for the aforementioned dedication. I grab my phone with eager hands, only to discover there isn't good coverage in the restaurant. I'm tempted to go outside for better reception, but our buzzer flashes. Our table is ready.

Disappointed, I put the phone away, and we all follow the hostess. Doubt spears the little bubble of excitement that I allowed to take form, and I begin to wonder what Sebastian's dedication truly means. Could it have just been his atonement, a way to make him feel better for the mess he created? I don't dare to let my heart hope that he loves me still. He would've called me by now if that were true.

The hostess stops in front of a round booth, close to the small stage at the far end of the restaurant. Surf Shack has live music every night from nine until the restaurant closes, and each time it's a different performer or band. It's early, so the stage is empty.

We order our food and another round of drinks. As the dinner progresses, my mind stops obsessing about Sebastian. I pay attention to my friends, their stories, and let myself get lost in their lives. I've been submersed in my own misery for so long that I didn't realize how much I've missed them. I don't remember the last time I laughed so hard.

"So, Liv, what are you going to do about your internship?" Emma asks.

She's a business major like me. DuBose College is famous for its arts programs, but the business school is one of the best in the country.

My shoulders slump forward. "I don't know. I have to find something quick or I won't earn the credits to graduate next year."

"Hey, there's an open internship position in the marketing department at Reinhardt's Headquarters," Rodrigo cuts in. "It's not in events, but at least you won't have to worry about not graduating."

"You can't ask your mom to give me the position just because we're friends. It won't be fair."

Rodrigo peers at me with a frown. "First of all, I won't be asking Mom anything. Do you think she cares who's interning at her company? Second, you'll be doing the marketing director a favor. His last intern quit yesterday in the middle of a very important project. He doesn't have time to interview candidates and go through all that bullshit."

"Are you sure?" It seems too good to be true.

"Stop playing hard to get and accept it already," Saylor says, exasperated.

I stick my tongue out to her, and then I turn to Rodrigo. "If you're sure, I'll accept the internship. Gladly."

Rodrigo claps his hands. "It's settled, then. I'll talk to Samuel tomorrow."

From the corner of my eye, I see movement on the little stage. A couple of guys begin to set up the sound equipment. There's a lonely chair on the stage now. I glance at my watch and realize it's almost nine o'clock. "I wonder what kind of music we'll hear tonight."

"I'm willing to bet it'll be something unforgettable," Saylor says as she fights the smirk trying to peek through. She's up to something.

I narrow my eyes at her. "How do you know?"

She shrugs and eats a tortilla chip. "Just a hunch."

There's a high-pitched noise as someone tests the mic. Suddenly, the loud conversation in the restaurant stops and is replaced by a low buzzing. I glance at the stage again, and my heart almost leaps out of my chest. Sebastian is standing there, in the flesh, with a guitar strapped across his chest.

"Good evening, everyone." His voice is loud and sure, a complete opposite of what my voice would sound like right now. "I hope you're enjoying your dinner. My name is Sebastian, and I'll be your entertainment for the night."

The buzzing becomes more animated, and flashes go off. Sebastian seems unaffected by it all, completely at ease on that stage. But then he looks my way. When our gazes collide, I see his cool manner is just a façade. There's fear in his eyes. Of what I don't know.

"A couple of days ago, I dedicated a song to someone very special to me. But unfortunately, I believe she missed that performance. So tonight, I made sure she would be in attendance. I even bribed her friends to drag her here, kicking and screaming if necessary."

I look around the table, and everyone sitting there has the word 'guilty' flashing on their foreheads.

"This is the first song I learned to play on the guitar. It was the song you picked, Liv."

My breath catches as he addresses me, his eyes never wavering from mine.

"Who knew that so many years later, that particular clichéd song would fit our story like a glove?"

My vision becomes blurry as my heart breaks free from the chains that have been squeezing it tight for the past few weeks. I mouth to him, "What's wrong with cliché?"

He smiles slowly, a smile that's meant only for me. "Olivia Marie Dawson, this song is for you."

Sebastian takes his seat and begins to strum the guitar. The familiar intro to "Wonderwall" fills the restaurant, and the tears flow freely. Saylor squeezes my hand, and I smile at her in gratitude. I know she's the mastermind behind this surprise.

I face the stage again and drink in the sight of Sebastian. I almost want to pinch myself to make sure I'm not dreaming. I can't believe he's here, mere feet away from me.

The entire place explodes in a cacophony of applause, whistles, and cheers once Sebastian finishes the song. He removes his guitar and places it on the floor, next to the chair.

"Now, if you'll excuse me, I have to attend to something first before I continue with my set."

Sebastian strides to our table and kneels in front of me. He clasps my hands in his and stares at me with his intense and soulful eyes. They're filled with tears, just like mine.

"Liv, I know I can never take back the hurt I caused you. My only hope is that you give me the chance to make it up to you for the rest of my life. Please say you will." His voice is strained, filled with longing.

There's whooshing in my ears, and all the people around us have ceased to exist. A slow grin unfurls on my lips until it becomes a full-blown smile.

Sebastian takes that as a sign. He stands up and pulls me along with him. His strong hands cup my cheeks, and then he kisses me. I hear clapping and more whistles. I know this moment will be plastered all over the internet in a few hours, but videos and words can't capture or steal the essence of it. This long-time-coming reconciliation of our souls is ours only. No media, photos, or fans can take it away from us.

CHAPTER 52
SEBASTIAN

My legs can't stop bouncing, and I fidget beneath my suit jacket. The air is cool and oddly stifling. I don't know why I'm so nervous. I receive a light elbow shove against my arm and turn to see Owen's impassive profile. I will my legs to stop and the corner of his lips twitch up.

My gaze lowers until I'm staring at the most angelic face in the world. With her mass of curly, strawberry blonde hair, rosy cheeks, and a button nose, Grace is the perfect image of a cherub, at least when she's sleeping peacefully against her dad's shoulders.

I glance around and see that every seat is taken in the grand theater of DuBose College. We arrived early to guarantee a prime spot, and our group takes up almost an entire row. Besides Liv's parents, Jeremy, Kimmy, and Owen, her friends Saylor, Kennedy, and Mandy are also here. Liv is graduating today, and despite my lack of faith, I've sent a little prayer to the heavens for allowing me to be here for this moment. I know I've missed many firsts in her life in the years we've spent apart, but I vowed to never let that happen again. And if everything goes according to plan today, I'll have my wish.

A few minutes later, the crowd settles and the graduation ceremony begins. Less than an hour into it, Liv, the girl of my dreams, takes the stage to receive her diploma. She looks absolutely breathtaking even wearing her shapeless gown. The dean hands her a rolled-up parchment, and she shakes hands with him. Then she faces the audience and shifts her cap's tassel from right to left. Her eyes search the audience, and a few seconds later she finds us. She beams even more, and when her gaze connects with mine, she winks at me. My heart swells until it feels like it's going to explode from happiness. I blow her a kiss, and Owen mumbles, "Whipped," next to me.

Moments later, Emma, Liv's roommate, goes up on the stage to accept her diploma, but my mind is no longer paying attention to what's going on. My thoughts have gone inward, and I run through the details of what's going to happen later tonight again and again.

The past six months Liv and I have been together, as a real couple out in the open, have been the best days of my life. After my performance at the Surf Shack, I only went back to London one more time to tie up loose ends. I sold my apartment, said goodbye to my family properly, and most importantly, dealt with the aftermath of my quitting Boys Future. The fans were devastated, and in the UK, where we were most popular, many of them blamed Liv for my departure. They compared her to Yoko Ono, and Liv said it was an honor.

Michael Schutz was set on suing me, but when my candid interview ran in the US coupled with his condemning video, it was game over for him. No, he's not done with show business, not by far. A shark will always be a shark. But he has no grounds to sue me anymore. My leaving the band was more than justified. Plus, he wanted the scandal of his tape to disappear from the tabloids as fast as possible, so it was in his best interest to let me go without a fight. The band still exists, and it has so many hits already, Michael will be able to milk that cow for years to come. That is, if he doesn't lose another member. I have a feeling Oliver is ready to say goodbye, too.

I moved back to California and can finally say I'm at peace. I don't know what I'll do with the rest of my life yet, but I decided attending college is a good way to start. I've enrolled at UCLA and will start next fall.

I got an apartment not a minute away from Liv's place. I almost begged her to move in with me, but she wouldn't have it. She wanted our relationship to progress naturally. And it did, for us anyway. She spends most of her time there with me, so I got my wish in the end. But today, I'm tired of waiting. Today I'm taking the giant and most decisive step of my life. My only hope is that she agrees to come with me.

The ceremony finally ends, and we all head out of the theater. The graduates are already outside, and I want to leap over everyone, fly if I could, to reach Liv faster. I still receive glances of recognition from strangers now and then, but no one approaches me asking for autographs or pictures anymore. My life is almost back to normal, and being anonymous never felt so good.

I spot her before she sees me. She's with a group of friends, talking and laughing. I increase my pace until I'm almost running. She only notices me when I'm upon her. I scoop her up in my arms and twirl her around.

"Bas, put me down," she says through giggles.

I spin a couple more times before setting her down, but my hands remain locked tight around her waist. I smile at her. "Congratulations, Liv."

She stands on her tiptoes and rewards me with one of her sweet kisses. I tuck her closer and have to refrain from devouring her mouth right here in front of her family and friends. I hear a throat clear behind us and reluctantly step back.

Mr. Dawson is staring at us with his arms crossed and the

worst impression of a pissed-off father I've ever seen. I remember what his true glare looks like, and that ain't it.

Liv goes to him and he opens his arms for her. I stand back and let her spend time with her family, let her bask in all their love. Grace is awake now, and when Liv takes her in her arms, another chip falls into place in my heart.

♡ ♡ ♡

Liv's graduation party is at her parents' house, in their backyard. It seems the entire neighborhood was invited. I see many familiar faces, people who used to be my parents' friends as well. They all say how good it is to see me, that they're beyond happy I've finally found my way back home. I peer at Liv when I hear those words, because it's the absolute truth. Liv *is* my home.

Little monsters take over my stomach as the moment of truth approaches. My guitar is tucked away in a corner, ready for when I need it. The party is in full swing now, and I know it's now or never. I search for Mr. Dawson in the crowd, and when I catch his attention, I nod to him. He nods back, and like we've planned, he turns off the background music. He knows I've prepared a special performance for his daughter tonight. He knows what I'm about to do because I've asked for his blessing first.

I pick my guitar up and move to the middle of the makeshift dance floor in the yard. My heart has fled the confines of my chest to lodge itself in my throat.

"Sorry to interrupt, folks." Mr. Dawson's voice booms through the open space, commanding everyone's attention. "Our very own in-house soprano asked me if he could sing a few songs tonight." He looks at me with mischief in his eyes. "And I said sure, as long as it was free."

People laugh but I remain as tense as a coiled spring. Liv is right in front of me, and she must be wondering what I'm up to. I haven't sung in public since the Surf Shack.

"Hey, I still have to put one more kid through college," Mr. Dawson continues, and then he turns to me. "Break a leg, son."

I take a deep breath and try to steady my heart. "When I first started learning to play the guitar, Liv asked me why there were only music sheets of angst-ridden nineties songs in my room. Why wasn't I playing something from this century?"

I hear a couple of chuckles and relax a fraction.

"I told her I would get to them eventually, but the truth is, there wasn't a single current song at the time that spoke to me. Yeah, I'm a traitor to my generation."

I pause and stare at Liv while I gather my courage. "Well, Liv, I've finally found a song from this century good enough to sing to you. Here is 'Photograph.'"

Liv gasps and puts a hand over her throat. She probably never dreamed in a million years I would choose an Ed Sheeran song. I tease her to no end when she listens to him, and I even say she must be secretly in love with him. I pretend I loathe him just to get a rise out of her, but the truth is, I like his music. And the one I'm singing right now is by far my favorite, because it talks about the perfect imperfection of love.

I don't break my gaze from hers as I sing the lyrics, trying to pour all of my feelings into the words. I hope she knows, I hope she understands that what we have is infinite. It's forever.

When the song ends, there's only stunned silence around us. I set my guitar down and walk to her. I take her hands in mine, and like I did at the Surf Shack, I go down on my knees.

"Once upon a time, the most beautiful girl in the world asked me to teach her how to kiss. She thought she was being clever, tricking me into kissing her. Little did she know that kissing her was my recurring dream. That's right. You were the girl of my dreams, Liv, and that kiss sealed my fate, sealed *our* fate. "

I trace the promise bracelet on her wrist. "When I gave you this bracelet, I made a vow to never abandon you again. I said it was just a placeholder until we were ready for the next step, but that was a lie. I was ready for the next step then. I think I've always been ready, from the moment you turned a silly Valentine's Day teddy bear into a badass."

She laughs and her eyes are bright, swimming in a pool of unshed tears. I feel the prickle behind my own, but I can't let them fall yet, not until I say everything I want to say.

"The truth is, I was terrified that you would bolt out of that cab and out of my life for good if I had given you this instead." I retrieve the simple diamond ring I had stuffed in my front jeans pocket and offer it to her. "I bought this at the same time I bought the bracelet, but I knew you weren't ready for it. So I gave you the time I thought you needed, let you take a good look at all my imperfections so you would know what you were signing up for. I'm still terrified you'll run, but I can't be bound by fear any longer. I have to know if you'll have me despite all my flaws, despite all the mistakes I've made."

"Ask her the question already!" Owen shouts from somewhere in the crowd.

And I do. "Olivia Marie Dawson, girl of my dreams, will you marry me?"

She doesn't speak for a moment, and my heart begins to shrivel. Then she nods and says the most precious words in the entire universe. "Yes, Sebastian James Coleman, I will marry you."

**** THE END ****

EXTRA SCENE

Do you want to know what happened between Oliver and Saylor when they went to help Liv escape the paparazzi? Here's the extra scene. Their story is told in an already published trilogy: **Sugar, We're Going Down, Wreck of the Day,** and **Devils Don't Fly.**

♡ ♡ ♡

OLIVER

It's too early to be dealing with this shit. My head is about to split in two, I didn't have time to eat or even grab a cup of coffee, and to make my morning even more hellish, I'm horny as fuck. The image of a siren with green and blue hair and a mouth as sinful and perverse as the goddess Venus comes to mind. My cock strains against my jeans, and I grip the steering wheel hard, turning my knuckles white. The moment I saw her singing on that stage, I felt the pull, an immediate attraction that had me craving her body like a junkie craves his next fix.

A car cuts me off and I hit the brakes, narrowly missing the moron. I slam my fist against the horn and don't let up until my annoyance subsides. I switch lanes and when I pass him, I make sure to lower my window and flip the driver off. Then I stomp on the gas pedal.

I love my car. It's an Aston Martin Vanquish, the greatest fucking car in history, and it was the first thing I bought with my own money. I'd never had a problem spending my parents' fortune before, but it wasn't until I started making my own that I realized how good it felt to not depend on them anymore, to finally be able to cut the strings. No more forced monthly dinners, no more pretending I give a shit about their high-society friends and appearances.

As I approach Sebastian's place, I grapple for an idea to help him out of the messed-up situation he's in. If the paparazzi see me, they'll never leave. More likely, they'll call their friends and we'll have a mob in front of his apartment. I know I'm the reason they're stalking my friend; I don't want to make matters worse.

I park on the street parallel to Sebastian's, in front of the town house that's directly behind his place. If I'm not mistaken, I believe there's a small garden at the back. If Liv can jump off his kitchen balcony into that yard, she'll be home free. I'm aware I'm betting on a lot of 'ifs' right now.

I stare at the house in front of me, trying to guess what kind of people live there.

A cab stops ahead, catching my attention. I squint behind my sunglasses, trying to peer inside the black car, but with the tinted windows, it's impossible. A minute later, the door opens, and I see a mane of multicolored hair emerge. I suck in my breath. *You've got to be fucking kidding me.*

Her hair is even more luscious in the daylight, and it falls in waves down her back. It's the most gorgeous thing I've ever seen, and my fingers itch to touch it, to know whether those locks are as soft as they look. I let my gaze travel down her body and I commit every single detail to memory. She's wearing dark jeans so tight, they don't leave much to my imagination. She has on some kind of flouncy, asymmetric black top that peeks out of her cropped leather jacket. But what seals my fate is the pair of over-the-knee high-heeled boots on her feet.

I forget the humiliation of last night. I must have her. I won't quit until she's under me, writhing in pleasure.

She doesn't glance at my car, even though she's now standing right in front of it. Her gaze is fixated on the house I'd been looking at myself a minute ago. She hesitates for a brief moment before she walks toward the front door. I manage to take my mind out of the gutter in time to realize what she's about to do. Apparently she's here to save her friend and somehow came up with the same plan I did. A weird feeling unfurls in the pit of my stomach, something foreign that I quickly dismiss as hunger pains.

I exit the vehicle and make my presence known. She hears the noise and turns to me, narrowing her eyes. I remove my sunglasses, and recognition finally fills her eyes.

"You! What are you doing here?"

Fuck me! Her voice is like soft, rich velvet. I didn't get to appreciate it properly last night while she was screaming at me. Smooth and raspy, it's even more lethal than her mouth.

Her tone is indignant, which means she's still mad at me for my bold proposition at the karaoke bar. I grin at her as I take a few steps closer. Her porcelain skin is flawless without any makeup. Instincts are telling me to keep walking until our chests touch and I can suck her plump lips into my mouth. But I can't indulge in my crazy fantasies right now. My impulsiveness is what created this situation.

"I'm here to help your friend out," I say.

♡ ♡ ♡

SAYLOR

I cross my arms and stare at the stupid man in front of me, unable to decide if he's serious or not. The few times I'd caught him on television giving an interview, I'd pegged him to be a snobby jackass. Last night just served to prove me right.

His striking, almost surreal blue eyes are glued to my face, searching for something I can't fathom. It's almost as if he's trying to invade my mind, peer into my thoughts. His blond hair is messy, like he's just run his fingers through it without a thought. I don't want to acknowledge it, but he is a sexy motherfucker. Tall and wiry, with a face carved to be on the cover of a magazine and that arrogant mouth, he has serious potential to be my next huge mistake.

"I think you've done enough damage," I say.

He moves closer, almost invading my space, but I don't step back, I don't want to show that his nearness bothers me. He'll never know how he's affecting me right now. I refuse to drop my stare from his electric eyes, so tilting my head back is the only way. He's so damn tall.

"You know, this is as much your fault as it is mine. If you had been more accommodating—"

My jaw drops, a reflex on my part when I hear complete and utter bullshit. Quickly, I realize Oliver likes to play games, mess with people's heads. What he doesn't know is he's met his match. I take a step forward, a movement he wasn't counting on if the flexing of his jaw is any indication.

"You're saying that if I had dropped down onto my knees and taken your dick into my mouth right then and there, no one would've recognized you?"

I'm close enough that I can see his pupils dilate and hear his sharp intake of breath. But he calls my bluff and leans down until his nose almost touches mine, until his lips are close enough that I can smell his minty toothpaste. "I can't undo the past, but the picture you just painted sounds a lot like an offering."

My heart is flittering like there's a hummingbird trapped in my chest. But I won't back down, won't step away. I've gone through more shit in my life than Oliver can possibly imagine. This standoff is nothing.

I smile. "Do you wanna hear a secret? I probably would've done more than suck you into oblivion last night if you hadn't been so crass about it. I guess you'll never know what it fee—"

Oliver crashes his lips against mine, cutting off my reply. His hand cups the back of my head, his fingers curling in my hair, keeping me in place as he devours my mouth. And I let him. Not only do I let him, but I join the feast.

This is the best fucking kiss ever.

♡ ♡ ♡

Continue Saylor and Oliver's story in *Sugar, We're Going Down.*

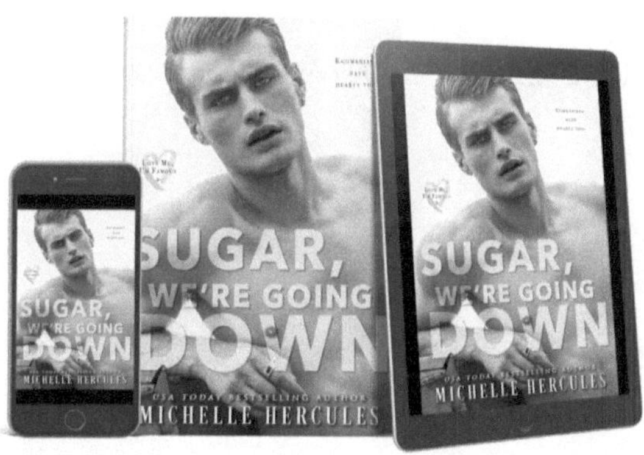

They say nothing compares to the first kiss. That sentence needs to be amended. Nothing compares to the first kiss from Oliver Best. I knew at the moment our lips touched that the cocky rockstar would be forever imprinted in my mind. I also knew that loving him would be my destruction. And yet, love him I did.

Oliver Best, former rockstar, heir to one of the largest fortunes in Great Britain, and the country's most infamous bad boy.

Saylor Blue Carter, college drop-out, lead singer of a struggling band, not a penny to her name.

When they met, it was hate at first sight. Oliver was an arrogant ass. Saylor was a cold-hearted bitch. These were the thoughts they had for each other. Until that kiss. That life-altering, earth-shattering, nuclear kiss. They knew what that kiss meant. They knew anything between them would be explosive and without hope for a happily ever after. So they vowed to forget, they tried to stay away. But now with their best friends' wedding approaching, all bets are off.

♡ ♡ ♡

ONE-CLICK *Sugar, We're Going Down* now.

FREE NOVEL

CATCH YOU

Want to read another deliciously fun contemporary romance by Michelle Hercules? Then **CLICK HERE** to get your FREE copy of *Catch You*.

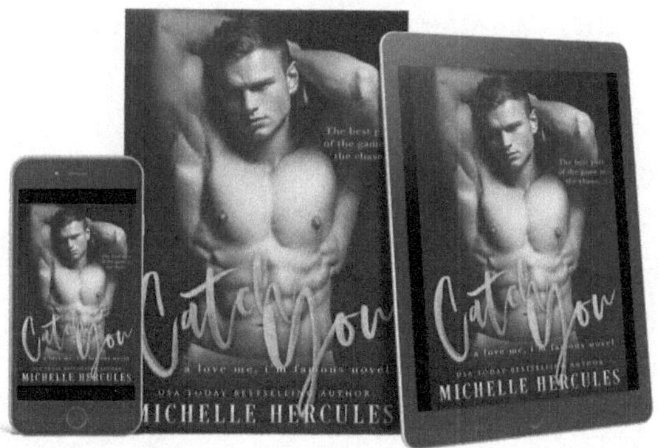

Pride and Prejudice meets Veronica Mars in this enemy-to-lovers romance.

KimberlyI had always thought Owen Whitfield fit the mold of

the brainless jock perfectly. Group of idiot friends? Check. Vapid girlfriend? Check. Ego bigger than the moon? Check. As long as he stayed out of my way, coexisting with his kind was doable. Until one day our worlds collided, changing everything. He pissed me off so badly that I had no choice but to give him a taste of his own medicine. Little did I know that my act of revenge would come back to bite me in the ass. How was I supposed to know Owen would turn out to be the best partner in crime I could hope for?

Owen never paid much attention to Kimberly Dawson, but I knew who she was. Ice Queen was what we called her. She was gorgeous, no one could deny that. But she was also a condescending bitch, which was enough reason for me to stay the hell away from her. She thought I was a dumb jock, and that was okay until she came crashing into my life. Against my better judgment, I let her embroil me in her shenanigans, forcing us to spend too much time together. It was my doom. She got under my skin. She was all I could think about. I never thought I would be the knight in shining armor to anyone, not until she came along.

CLICK HERE to get your free copy!

OR

Scan the code!

ABOUT THE AUTHOR

USA Today Bestselling Author Michelle Hercules always knew creative arts were her calling but not in a million years did she think she would become an author. With a background in fashion design she thought she would follow that path. But one day, out of the blue, she had an idea for a book. One page turned into ten pages, ten pages turned into a hundred, and before she knew, her first novel, The Prophecy of Arcadia, was born.

Michelle Hercules resides in Florida with her husband and daughter. She is currently working on the *Blueblood Vampires* series and the *Rebels of Rushmore* series.

Join Michelle Hercules' Reader Group:
https://www.facebook.com/groups/mhsoars

Sign up for Michelle Hercules' Newsletter:
https://mhsoars.activehosted.com/f/11

facebook.com/michelleherculesauthor

instagram.com/michelleherculesauthor

tiktok.com/@michelleherculesauthor

bookbub.com/authors/michelle-hercules

patreon.com/michellehercules